When Lambs Grow Fangs

Rebecca Wade

Despite significant editing, mistakes still happen.
If you find any errors in this book, please do not post them on Amazon,
as doing so can get the book removed.

Instead, please report any mistakes you find via the form at the bottom of
my website: RebeccaWade.net

Thank you!

For you, fellow weirdo.

CHAPTER 1
Spoilers

Anna woke with a jolt, surrounded by darkness.

Frigid metal pressed against her naked skin. A muffled sea of voices buzzed somewhere nearby. Not just voices. Machines beeping, wheels squeaking, pens scribbling, keyboards clacking, children screaming, alarms blaring. The overwhelming din made her head throb.

Anna tried to distract herself from the noise by focusing on her immediate surroundings. She lifted her hands. More cold metal greeted her fingertips. There wasn't room to sit up.
She was trapped.

Fear rippled down Anna's spine.
She closed her eyes, trying to remember what had happened.
Her thoughts were sluggish. They slumped unwillingly into the forefront of her mind.
Loud music. Blood on bricks. The stench of beer.
There was something else... *Something important.*

It was too quiet in here. Too still.
Anna placed her hand on her chest.
There was no rhythmic thump, thump, thump.

Anna's heart wasn't beating.

CHAPTER 2

Earlier that Year

"I wish I was dead," Anna grumbled to herself as she stepped off the bus into the searing heat.

Brisbane only had two seasons - spring and summer. Spring made for wonderful sweater weather, but only lasted for a few weeks in June. Cold breezes would rustle the leaves of the evergreen trees while the sun's gentle warmth invited colourful flowers to bloom. Summer, on the other hand, monopolised the rest of the year and insisted on transforming the city into a sauna. As it was early February, there was no escaping the blindingly bright sun or the invisible inferno masquerading as air.

Desperate for air-conditioning, Anna rushed into the nearest toy store. The Christmas, New Year and Back to School sales had ended so the shop was, thankfully, free of crowds. Anna walked up and down the aisles, aimlessly hoping the perfect gift for her newborn niece would jump off the shelves. It hadn't occurred to Anna that Clara wouldn't be old enough to play with toys for quite some time. She was basically just a pooping blob.
What do people normally buy for newborns?

"Can I help you?" The perky shop attendant enquired.
"No, thanks, I'm fine," Anna answered automatically with a polite smile. She already felt like an idiot, she didn't want to add the pity of a teenage retail worker on top of it. Leaving the store empty-handed, Anna wandered into a high-end department store. She sat on an armchair outside the men's fitting rooms. This was one of her *clever spots* in the city. No one would bother her there. The attendants knew she wasn't buying anything and the men, if they noticed her at all, would assume she was waiting for a

boyfriend or husband to emerge from the rooms beyond.

Not wanting to struggle with this task all day, Anna took out her phone and dialled.
"How'd you go?" Anna's mother sounded busy in the kitchen. Cutlery and ceramics clanged in the background.
"Bad," answered Anna, "How long until she can read? I know all the best books."
"You're overthinking it," her mother sighed, "Just get her something soft that she can snuggle."
"I looked at the stuffed toys," Anna grumbled, feeling foolish, "They were all too big. And so expensive!"
"She'll grow into them and they're not that expensive," retorted Anna's mother, then adding with a softer tone, "I take it the job hunt isn't going well?"

Despite assurances otherwise, Anna was the black sheep of her family. Her mother had been a lawyer before retiring and her father had been a landscape architect. Her older sister, Liz was a prominent plastic surgeon. She'd married a handsome psychologist named Mark and now, with their new baby, Clara, they had a perfect little family.
Anna, on the other hand, had jumped from job to job since university. She'd never been interested in pursuing a career. She'd seen the hours required for that level of work, not to mention the stress. *No thanks.* One might think that would mean Anna had chosen to focus on her social life. One would be wrong. When it came to relationships, Anna was well on her way to becoming a cliché cat lady. All she needed was an apartment that allowed pets.

"Nobody's hiring," Anna pouted, accidentally catching the eye of a man as he entered the changing room. She lowered her voice, "Don't worry, I'll find something eventually."
"If you need money, I'd be happy to-"
"I don't need money," Anna felt her face redden, "I have plenty of savings. I was just venting. I'll get Clara a nice bear or something, okay?"
"Just don't buy her a silver rattle."
Anna could practically hear her mother rolling her eyes, "Who-"
"Your grandfather, of course."
"Grandpa Rupert?" Anna didn't need to confirm. Her mother only sounded

like that when she talked about her estranged father. Other than the gifts he sent on special occasions, he never contacted anyone in the family, "How did he even know Clara was born?"

"Who knows," Anna's mother sighed.

"What are you and Dad up to today?" Anna asked, hoping to direct the subject in a happier direction.

"The neighbours are coming over for lunch," her mother answered over more clanging in the background, "Gordon's insisting on touching up the garden before they get here. As though they don't see it every day!"

Anna smiled and shook her head, "Some things never change."

"Have you read any good books lately?" Her mother enquired, "Or watched any new shows you think I'd like?"

Normally, this subject would result in an hour-long conversation where Anna ranted about the masterful intertwining of genre tropes and lovable characters in her latest fictional obsession. However, Mr Eye-contact had just emerged from the changing rooms and was looking at Anna with an air of expectation. Anna mentally crossed this location off of her *clever spots* list.

"Uh, can I call you back tonight?" Anna avoided looking at the man, hoping he'd give up and leave.

"Sure, honey," replied her mother, "Text me when you get home safely."

"Will do." Anna hung up and looked up at the man. He wore a sharp pinstripe suit and the dark stubble on his chin matched his thick eyebrows and slicked-back widow's peak.

"Sorry to interrupt," he spoke in a deep, gravelly voice, "I couldn't help but overhear you're looking for a job?"

"I, uh, yes," alarm bells blared in Anna's head. This is how women ended up locked in psychopath's basements, "I'm just looking for basic admin stuff. Typing and that sort of thing."

"Perfect," the man grinned, withdrawing a business card from his blazer, "My company's always looking to fill data entry roles. Call this number and ask for Pam. Tell her Rufus recommended you."

Anna adjusted her glasses as she took the card, "You don't even know me. I could be awful."

"Then you won't last," Rufus shrugged, walking away with frustrating nonchalance, "but I'm an excellent judge of character so I doubt that'll be the case."

Anna watched the man disappear around a corner. She could hardly believe what had just happened. People didn't just offer jobs to strangers. Not legitimate jobs. She looked at the business card. One side featured the company's name, *Kingsley & Laurant*, while the other had a generic landline number. No website or email address. If anyone asked Anna for his last name she'd have to admit she didn't know it.

Assuming she called the number.

And she probably wouldn't.

It was sure to be some sort of scam, anyway.

But what if it wasn't?

Opportunities weren't presented to Anna very often. Or ever.

The statistical probability of Rufus being a predator was minuscule. It would be silly to ignore a job offer just because she hadn't found it posted on an employment website. People often got jobs through word-of-mouth. It wasn't that unusual…Right?

With her mind sufficiently distracted, Anna quickly found the perfect gift for Clara - a small velvet koala with 'C' embroidered on its foot. She paid for the toy, along with a small gift bag and some tissue paper, before braving the food court for lunch. The clamour of scraping seats, babies crying and indistinct chatter grated on Anna's ears. She squashed through the tight crowd to order some sushi before escaping to another of her *clever spots*. The Brisbane Square Library sat at the end of the main shopping strip. It allowed food and drink but not many people ate their lunch within its quiet, air-conditioned walls. *Perfection.* Anna made a beeline to her favourite armchair, which was empty as usual, and ate while re-reading the first few chapters of *The Lion, the Witch and the Wardrobe*.

***

More people were waiting under the bus shelter than could reasonably fit, so Anna chose a shady spot nearby. As she watched random people going about their business around her, she sighed. Everyone was living the same, boring life. They worked, they came home, they did chores, they watched television for some excitement, and then, *repeat*. Some dyed their hair unnatural colours or got tattoos to feel unique. Others bought expensive clothes or fancy cars to feel important. But everyone was the same. Nothing worth experiencing ever happened in real life. There was no magic or adventure to be had in real life.

Except love.
Love was the most magical thing this tedious world had to offer. Anna's parents had found it. Her sister had found it. The people walking by on the street - holding hands, kissing and laughing - had found it.

Anna felt certain love was avoiding her. She didn't fit in anywhere. She was too quiet. Too disconnected from reality. Nobody cared about stories the way she did. To them, tales of adventure and magic were just entertainment but, to her, they were the reason she got out of bed.

As the bus pulled up and people filed in like sardines. Anna scanned the seats, ensuring she sat next to the least threatening passenger she could find. She covered her ears with noise-cancelling headphones and let her mind wander to hidden worlds, enchanted forests and epic quests.

CHAPTER 3

First Day

Kingsley & Laurant was an elite, multi-billion dollar company. However, what the company did to earn its fortune was frustratingly unclear. It was the corporate equivalent of celebrities who were *famous for being famous*. Their tower loomed over the Brisbane skyline like a middle finger made of glass.

Shivering in her stupid, scratchy blouse, Anna cursed herself for not preparing herself for the artificially freezing temperature of the office. She'd dressed in light fabrics to avoid sweating through them on the way into the city. She'd wanted to make a good impression on her first day. She'd been going for a look that suggested she was a proper adult and not a child in a thirty-year-old's body, who was just pretending to have her shit together. Unfortunately, Anna had forgotten that offices always set their thermostats to accommodate suit-wearing men, not blouse-wearing women. She wished she'd thought to bring a cardigan. And blazer. And thick trousers. And maybe a scarf. She paced back and forth in the waiting area, hoping to get her blood pumping without drawing attention to her goose-pimpled skin. Several important-looking people glided through the lobby like sharks.

Anna had to remind herself that she had nothing to fear. She didn't need to impress anyone. She'd already landed the job. The worst they could do was fire her and she'd be back where she started. Hardly a life-shattering occurrence. Still, Anna couldn't shake the feeling she was swimming out of her depth.

The haughty receptionist gave Anna a disapproving glare. Anna assumed it had something to do with the pacing. She'd been directed to wait in

this section of the foyer, which had an abundance of black leather seating available. Anna perched on the freezing cushion, jigging her leg for warmth. She took out her phone to give herself somewhere else to look.
Liz: *Good luck on your first day!*
Anna smiled. Her sister never missed an opportunity to cheer her on.
Anna: *Thanks! How've you been?*
Liz: *Tired but happy. I can't imagine leaving Clara to go back to work. Is it crazy that I'm considering cutting down to one day a week?*
Anna: *Not at all! Priorities change when you become a parent.*
Liz: *Such wisdom from one so young!*
Anna: *Sorry to tell you, but I'm not young.*
Liz: *You must be young because I'm still young.*
Anna: *And you're older than me?*
Liz: *Exactly!*

A gentle 'ding' from the elevator announced the arrival of Pam from HR.
Anna: *It's starting - Got to go.*
Liz: *Good luck!*

Though easily in her sixties, Pam looked as though a child had dressed her. She wore a startlingly pink dress with a bulky rainbow necklace and carried a bedazzled clipboard in her impractically manicured hands, "You must be Alexandra!" Pam chirped.
"It's Anastasia," Anna corrected meekly, "Or just Anna."
Anna was well-accustomed to being called the wrong name. Even if her name was literally under someone's nose, they never remembered it. She couldn't figure out why, but it seemed to be an anomaly specific to her.
"Oh yes," said Pam, double-checking her clipboard, "Welcome to Kingsley & Laurant, *Anna*. Of course, we spoke on the phone. It's a pleasure to meet you in person, follow me."

Pam led Anna through the labyrinth of offices, making all the standard stops along the way. Security, where they got Anna's ID badge. The photo was awful. Then to Pam's office where Anna signed several stacks of paperwork featuring long-winded variations of the promise *"I will robotically do the job I was hired to do and not embarrass the company by demonstrating a personality."*
After a quick stop to view the lunch room, Anna was finally taken to the office in which she would spend the majority of her life for the foreseeable

future.

It was a small room in the basement, housing only six desks. Unlike the shiny, glass offices upstairs, this room was lined with faded Victorian wallpaper and smelled like dust.

"Good morning!" Pam addressed the room. "Let me introduce our newest full-time employee." With a sickening jolt, Anna felt five pairs of eyes focus directly on her.

"This is…" Pam rechecked her clipboard, "*Anastasia Green*. She goes by *Anna*. Anna, why don't you tell us a bit about yourself?"

Fuck.
Anna wasn't a fan of public speaking.
Or public anything.
She'd specifically chosen low-level typing jobs because they offered decent pay for minimal effort and didn't require any sort of networking. Social skills were not part of the job description.

"Hey- Hi, there," Anna stammered. Her glasses slid down her nose so she took them off with a shaking hand. The room became a merciful blur of shapes. "So… I, um, grew up here in Brisbane…"
Nobody cares.
"…I like…Reading and…um…TV."
Very unique and interesting, well done.
"And…um…I'm very excited to be working here," Anna lied unconvincingly. She put her glasses back on and looked back to Pam.
"Wonderful!" gushed Pam, oblivious to Anna's humiliation. "Now, you'll be sitting here-"

The eyes returned to their screens and the pitter-patter of typing filled the room again. Pam led Anna to an empty cubicle, gesturing around the minuscule space like a realtor showing a house. "This is the stack of forms for you to digitise," Pam explained, "This is where you put the forms you've done. Your username is your payroll number. The password is *admin* but you'll be prompted to change it. Any questions?"
"No, thanks, that's great," Anna gave a weak smile.
"Fantastic! You know where to find me if you need anything," Pam turned and trotted out of the room. Anna let out a quiet sigh of relief as she dropped her handbag on the floor and, finally, began to work.

The hours passed in a blissful haze. The tedium allowed Anna's mind to fall into a soothing, meditative state. For a while, she imagined she was flying over an ancient forest, and then swimming the depths of the sea. She replayed scenes of her favourite TV shows in her mind's eye and then created stories of her own, set in worlds of myth and legend. She was having a wonderful time until a figure in her peripheral vision dragged her back to reality.

A woman in her mid-twenties perched on the edge of Anna's desk. She had soft Asian features, sparse freckles and wavy, pastel-pink hair.
"Would you like to grab some lunch with us?" The woman smiled, "I got Ace of Cups for my daily tarot so I've been keeping an eye out for a new friendship opportunity and here you are!"
Her black, rockabilly-style dress accentuated the curves of her plump figure. Anna wondered where she'd bought it since all the shops she frequented only sold clothes for skinny, shapeless girls.
"Sorry?" Anna replied.
"It's time for lunch." The woman reiterated pointing at her watch, "I'm Cassie. Do you want to grab some food?"
"Uh…Sure," Anna answered before her brain had time to process.
"Great!" Cassie replied, then turned, "She's in guys, let's go!"

Following Cassie's eyeline to the desk opposite, a man with pale skin and thick eyeliner sprang from his chair. An impish grin spread across his face as he approached. He wore a gold-embroidered blazer over a silky black shirt which, in Anna's opinion, had been unbuttoned lower than was appropriate for the workplace.
"Delightful!" The man spoke with a regal British accent, eyeing Anna, "I've been dying to sink my teeth into this tasty morsel."
"Come on, Dex," muttered a voice from the corner, "Take it down a notch, will you?"
Anna turned to see a burly, freckled man approaching in a wheelchair. His desk was littered with plants and superhero figurines. He had the slightly hunched posture of someone uncomfortable in their skin, though Anna couldn't imagine why - he was gorgeous. His strong square jawline, full lips and short sideburns reminded Anna of a hero from an Austen novel. Colour rose in his cheeks as he met Anna's gaze. His eyes had a kindness to them, though they were partially hidden by his copper hair, which hung

16

on his brow like an upturned bowl of noodles.

"S-Sorry about him," he muttered.

"Abby," Cassie wrapped her arms around both men, "Meet Dex and Finn."

"It's *Anna*," Finn and Anna corrected in unison.

Anna looked at Finn, shocked he'd remembered her name. Finn snapped his gaze to the floor. His ears had gone very pink.

"Crap!" Cassie grimaced, "Sorry, Anna! I'm usually great with names."

"It's fine." Anna shrugged.

"Let's go already!" Dex called, ducking from Cassie's arm and striding out the door with the air of someone who expected to be followed.

***

Double Bubble was a cafe famous for its vast selection of bubble tea flavours. Cassie, Dex and Finn ordered without checking the menu, which meant Anna had no time to consider her options. She made a mental note to look up the menu later so she'd be prepared next time. The dim sims she ordered didn't pair well with her peach iced tea but they were, individually, delicious.

"So," Dex grinned over his Berry Blast smoothie, "Allow me to formally induct you into our band of Merry Misfits." He gestured theatrically toward Cassie, "Cassandra Nakamura, our spiritual advisor and social butterfly, knower of literally everyone."

"Figuratively," Cassie corrected as she prodded her vegan dumplings with chopsticks.

"Lit-er-ally," Dex reaffirmed with a defiant grin.

Cassie rolled her eyes, "Nope."

"What's the name of the waitress?" Dex challenged.

"Paula," replied Cassie, "But-"

"And the temps we left in the office?" Dex winked at Anna, "The ones who'll be gone in a week?"

"Steven and Tess," Cassie shook her head affectionately, "For your information, they'll be here for *two more weeks*. Then they have exams."

While Dex and Cassie continued to bicker, Anna took in the details of the cafe. Fairy lights hung from the ceiling and the far wall was covered in plants. The other walls featured vibrant, hand-painted illustrations of various Australian animals holding boba cups. Each piece of furniture was

17

intentionally mismatched, creating a homey feel, while the staff all wore matching shirts featuring a different bubble-tea themed pun on the back.

"And if I needed someone to help me, say, build a computer...?" Dex teased.

"I know a guy." Cassie admitted with a huff, "*Girl*, actually- *woman*, to be precise. But that doesn't mean I know *literally* everyone!"

Dex took a victorious sip of his drink. Cassie sighed.

"Next up, we have Henry Finnegan," Dex inclined his head toward Finn, who'd been silent since they'd left the office, "This fine, freckly fellow is the buffest nerd you will ever meet."

"I-I'm not *that* buff," Finn blushed, absently rubbing the back of his neck, which made his biceps bulge traitorously. Anna smirked into her bubble tea. She hadn't met many men who had Finn's physique. Or *any men*, for that matter. She'd always assumed they were all gym-obsessed, testosterone fuelled airheads but Finn seemed to be the opposite.

"You could bench *me*," Dex retorted.

"You barely weigh anything," shrugged Finn.

"And how is he a *nerd*, exactly?" Cassie questioned.

"Just as you, dear Cassie, know all the people who live here in reality, Finn knows all the fine folk who exist only in our imaginations."

"It's not-" Finn muttered the smile leaving his face, "That makes me sound crazy."

"Not at all!" Dex clapped Finn on the back, "Nerd is a term of endearment! Fictional people live much more interesting lives, from what I hear. I'd much rather hear about Frodo from the Shire than Paula from the cafe."

"Paula's story is fascinating actually," Cassie interjected.

"Has she ever tossed cursed jewellery into a volcano?" Dex chided.

"Well, no," Cassie admitted begrudgingly.

"Then who cares?" Dex waved his hand dismissively.

"We're all stories in the end," Finn murmured.

"Hmm?" Dex looked at Finn with confusion.

"It's a quote from Doctor Who," Anna blurted before she could stop herself. Finn gave her a grateful smile.

"Oh no, there's two of them!" Dex lamented with a grin.

"What about you? Anna asked.

"Sorry, love" Dex replied, "I'm as unnerdy as it's possible to be."

"I figured," Anna assured, "But Finn and Cassie each got a special introduction-"

"Ah, yes!" Dex drummed on the table theatrically, "I am the one and only Dexter Duke. Dex to my friends, enemies and lovers. I'm the one to call when you're looking for good times, hot gossip, and cutting-edge fashion advice. I love your specs by the way."

Pride crackled in Anna's chest. Her gold-framed glasses were the only thing she had on that made her feel like herself. Everything else, from the too-thin blouse to her blister-inducing court shoes, felt like a costume she wore to play the role of Corporate Employee. Had Dex somehow sensed that? Or had he felt obliged to say something nice and her glasses were simply the least awful thing she was wearing?

"Thanks," replied Anna, "I wish I could wear cool clothes, like you."

Dex frowned and cocked his head appraisingly. "Why can't you?"

Anna didn't know how to explain that wearing eye-catching clothes felt like taking an unnecessary risk. Her mind replayed the Greatest Hits of the passively threatening warnings she'd received throughout her life.

"Careful not to show too much skin."

"You need to dress appropriately if you want to be taken seriously."

"Don't draw attention to yourself unless you're prepared for the consequences."

The consequences were never specified but it was clear what they were. Anna felt the shadow of potential consequences looming over every choice she'd ever made.

But that was normal, wasn't it?

Surely everyone planned their day, and wardrobe, with public perception and potential risks in mind?

"Don't get caught out."

"Don't make yourself an easy target."

"Just be smart and you'll be fine."

"I'm not the kind of person who..." Anna stammered, not wanting to offend anyone, "I don't want people to think...I don't want to stand out."

"Why not?" Dex seemed genuinely bamboozled. "You're a good-looking woman. Why not flaunt it?"

Anna hated when people, especially men, complemented her in a way that implied she didn't own a mirror. She knew she was reasonably attractive.

Not model material, perhaps, but she'd never felt ugly. Invisible, yes. Easily forgettable, usually. But never ugly.

"Not everyone wants to be the centre of attention, Dex," Cassie intervened, giving Anna a knowing glance.

"Yes, they do," Dex asserted, "They've just been brainwashed into thinking it's selfish and evil."

"Evil might be a stretch," Cassie raised her eyebrows, "But society does punish people for standing out or being different, especially women."

"Society can eat a big bag of dicks!" Dex exclaimed, "The more people let their freak flag fly, the less space there'll be for judgey assholes to ruin things. Do you like this blazer, love?"

He was looking at Anna, so she nodded.

"Then here," He removed the silk-lined suit jacket and handed it to Anna. "See how you feel with this fine piece wrapped around you."

Anna slid the blazer over her shoulders. It fit surprisingly well. Its smooth lining caressed her skin and the collar carried the subtle scents of citrus and rose.

"Stunning!" Dex beamed, clapping his hands, "See what happens when you try new things? Do you love it or do you adore it?"

"It does feel nice on my skin," Anna admitted, blushing.

"Keep it!"

"What?"

"I have more clothes than places to keep them," Dex beamed, "Besides, it looks better on you. Do you know what this means?"

"Er…no?"

"We need to go shopping together, A-S-A-P!"

"You'll make any excuse to go shopping," Cassie laughed.

"Correct," Dex smirked.

Anna agreed to join Dex on his next shopping excursion but she wasn't holding her breath. He seemed the sort of person who was easily excitable, which meant he was also easily distractable. Anna figured he'd quickly lose interest in her and forget his offer.

***

"They sound great," Liz yelled over the roar of an engine.

Anna hated when her sister called from the car, "Yeah, they're okay. Are you sure you don't want to talk about this later?"

"No, no," Liz assured, "I won't have time once I'm home, I've got a million things to do. Tell me more about the cute one, Brynn?"

"*Finn*," corrected Anna, "And I didn't say he was cute. I said he seemed nice."

"I know your tells," Liz laughed, "You're into him. Ask him out."

"No!"

"Why not?"

"Because he's…" Anna didn't want to have this conversation, "I don't even know him."

"The whole point of dating is to *get to know* him."

"It's too risky."

"How?"

"Last year there were 1,223 sexual offences reported in Brisbane," Anna recited the latest statistics she'd read online, "I don't want to add to this year's count."

Liz sighed, "Mum brought her work home too much when we were growing up. Don't let crime stats and sensationalised news reports put you off living your life. There are good men out there too."

"But-"

"No, Anna, seriously. If you're going to quote statistics you need to put them in context. Brisbane is a safe city. Over two million people live here. Based on *your numbers*, there's a less than one per cent chance of anything happening to you. What's the point of being careful if you never get to be happy?"

"I'm happy," Anna pouted. She hadn't signed up for one of Liz's lectures.

"No, you're *existing*," Liz retorted, "You hide in your books to avoid putting yourself out there. It's not healthy. Promise me you'll make an effort with these new people. You don't have to ask that guy out. Just stop spending all your free time alone in your bedroom, okay?"

"Fine," Anna knew there was no fighting Liz on this, "I'll make an effort."

CHAPTER 4

Introverts

In the following weeks, Anna resisted her instinct to avoid her new co-workers and instead spent every lunch break with them. Though she didn't talk much, they seemed happy to have her there. She even began to tentatively think of them as friends.

Cassie told numerous stories about people she'd met at the supermarket, on a walk, or during some activity where Anna would never acknowledge the strangers surrounding her, let alone talk to them.

Dex often recounted wild weekends of partying and debauchery. It seemed he found lovers as easily as Cassie made friends. Anna couldn't fathom the social mechanics of how a person could go from meeting a stranger to making out with them in a single evening but, evidently, this was a common occurrence for Dex.

And then there was Finn.

Though they'd barely spoken since their first meeting, Anna felt a strange kinship with him. Despite what she'd told Liz, she couldn't imagine him hurting anyone, least of all her. Sometimes, while Cassie and Dex were regaling them with exciting tales of romance and whimsy, Finn would catch her eye and smile. It was subtle, like a secret, and it made Anna feel a fluttering lightness in her chest.

On one such occasion, Dex was critiquing Cassie's latest wig. Anna had been shocked to discover the parade of glamorous hairstyles Cassie sported were the result of online shopping and not hours in a salon. Since this revelation, however, Anna was embarrassed she hadn't realised sooner. The stark difference in length from one day to the next should have been a dead giveaway.

"I'm not saying it looks cheap-" Dex defended.

"You said it looked fake!" Cassie huffed, "Fake equals cheap!"

"It just sits weirdly around your ears," he explained, "It needs a trim-"

"My date is tonight! I don't have time to go home and change it! Damn it, Dex, why'd you have to say anything?"

"Because real friends don't let their friends go on dates with wonky wigs!"

"What am I supposed to do?"

"Just don't wear it."

"Not an option."

"You're plenty cute without it, love. She won't care."

"I don't *feel* plenty cute without it!"

Anna had never seen Cassie without a wig on and wondered what her scalp looked like underneath. Did she have patchy bald spots from alopecia? A receding hairline? Or were the wigs just a time-saver?

"Let's pop down the road to see that hairdressing instructor. What's-her-name?" Dex jumped up from the table, "We've got time left in our break."

"Kelly?" Cassie seemed apprehensive, "She's probably busy."

"Let's go find out."

Cassie gingerly touched the artificial shoulder-length bob.

"Okay," she agreed, "But if she charges anything, you're paying."

"Fine," Dex pulled Cassie up just as the waitress placed Finn's order on the table. Anna had barely started on her bowl of noodles.

"You guys don't mind if we pop out, right?" Cassie asked, rhetorically.

Finn stared at Cassie with the wide-eyed panic of an actor who'd forgotten his lines.

"It's okay with me," Anna forced a smile. She wasn't about to let them know she'd noticed how badly Finn didn't want to be left alone with her. Or how much it hurt.

"Great!" Dex waved as the pair rushed from the cafe, leaving Anna and Finn in awkward silence.

Finn picked at the sesame seeds on his burger, avoiding Anna's eye. Anna twisted a clump of noodles between her chopsticks, blowing the steam from them before shoving them into her mouth. Hot broth flicked onto her chin. She quickly grabbed a napkin and patted it dry, hoping Finn hadn't seen her making a mess of herself.

"So," Finn mumbled into his burger, "H- How are you liking the, uh, job so far?"

"It's good," Anna answered, "I like to get lost in the mindlessness of it, you know? It's relaxing."

"Yeah," Finn nodded, "I like that about it too."

She wished she had something interesting to say. She realised Liz was right. All Anna did was sit in her room alone. She had nothing to talk about. No wonder Finn didn't want to be left alone with her. He took a bite of his burger as his eyes darted around the cafe.

"You live with Cassie, right?" Anna asked. She knew that he did but the silence was painful.

"Yeah," Finn answered, squeezing his burger a little too tightly,"B- But not, like, *together* as a couple. We're just roommates. I mean, we're also friends. But that's all."

"Well, yeah, I'd hope so," replied Anna.

"What?" Finn coughed on his drink, spluttering strawberry milkshake into his napkin.

"Cassie's going on a date tonight," Anna frowned, "Which would be weird if you two were together."

"Right!" Finn's ears turned pink. He ran his fingers through his hair before realising he had sauce on them. Turning a deeper shade of red, he wiped his curls with a napkin, "Obviously. Yeah."

It occurred to Anna that Finn might not have been okay with Cassie's date. Maybe he was harbouring a secret crush that Cassie didn't know about. She was beautiful, charismatic and confident. Cassie was a woman who lived her life and had the stories to prove it. Anna could never compete.

She refocused on eating her noodles, trying avoid making a worse mess.

"So," Finn broke the silence, "You like books and TV…?"

Anna winced.

"What?" Finn drew his eyebrows together, "You don't?"

"I do," Anna sighed, "I just- I wish I'd said something more interesting on my first day."

"Like what?" Finn's eyes were fixed on her. He seemed genuinely interested.

"That's the thing," Anna focused on her chopsticks, "I don't have anything better to say. I'm boring."

"I don't think you're boring."

"You don't know me."

"I'd like to."

Anna looked up to see Finn smiling at her. It wasn't forced or awkward this time. His dimples made her heart flutter. *Get over yourself. He's just being polite.*

"Like I said," shrugged Anna, "I like books, shows, movies, and even podcasts if they tell a good story because that's what I really love...stories."

"Me too," Finn leaned forward, "What's your favourite genre?"

"Fantasy," Anna grinned, despite herself. No one in her family read fantasy. They'd never said it in so many words but Anna had gotten the impression they saw it as a childish genre. Her father favoured biographies and non-fiction tales of war. Her mother loved literary classics like Ray Bradbury's *Fahrenheit 451* and Vladimir Nabokov's *Lolita*. Her sister rarely had time to read anything other than medical journals but, when she did, it was always some high-brow novel where the characters were all miserable and usually died at the end.

"I know it's a bit juvenile," Anna blushed, "but I love how writers can build entire words from nothing and make you feel like you've lived there. It doesn't have to be fantasy though. Anything with compelling characters will draw me in."

Finn nodded, "I love reading about people who feel so real you forget you'll never meet them."

"Exactly!" Anna beamed, "Stories make living in reality bearable."

Finn paused.

Anna suddenly felt exposed.

She'd never phrased her passion for stories like that before. It had spilled out by accident. She waited for Finn's reaction, expecting either a judgemental sneer or pity masked as concern.

"That's quite beautiful," Finn smiled at her pensively, "But reality isn't *that* bad, is it?"

"It's not that it's bad, per se," Anna shrugged, "It's just...empty. Don't you ever feel like something's missing?"

A strange expression crossed Finn's face. "What do you mean?"

"Everyone else seems content living their lives but I'm just...not," Anna hadn't admitted this feeling to anyone else before. She'd never felt like anyone would understand but there was something about Finn that made her suspect he might, "I want *more* than a nine-to-five job, a boring routine and the occasional holiday. I want magic and adventures. Stories fill the gap in my soul but I wish they didn't have to."

"I know what you mean," Finn nodded thoughtfully, "but I've been through enough exciting stuff that I'm grateful for my quiet life."

"Oh, shit," Anna glanced at Finn's wheelchair, "I didn't mean to-"

"No, it's okay," Finn self-consciously ran his hand over his left leg, "If you could write your own story, what would happen?"

Anna blinked, "That's a big question!"

"I don't mean the full plot," Finn smiled assuringly, "Just the general themes. What genre would you want your book to be?"

Anna took a moment to think. She'd pictured herself as a new character in every book she'd ever read but it was always a more impressive version of herself. One who kicked ass and had magic powers. One who thrived in a world of magic, monsters and sword fights. The sad fact was *real-world Anna* wouldn't last five minutes in any of her favourite stories. She wasn't the dive-into-battle type, she was the avoid-the-weirdo-on-the-bus type.

"I guess I'd want to be the lead in a trashy romance novel," she admitted with a crinkled nose, "One set in a small town where I ride into the sunset with a charming man at the end."

"I see," Finn touched his fingertips together and spoke in the voice of an elderly wizard, "So you seek an adventure of the heart, rather than one of the body?"

"As much as I wish I had the skills for an epic quest, I don't think I'd do well," Anna chuckled awkwardly, "I'm sure you've never read a romance novel but they usually have some *adventures of the body* too."

"Actually," Finn leant back in his chair with a grin, "Romance novels were my introduction to the wonderful world of reading."

"What?" Anna laughed.

"It all started with my sister's collection of Mills and Boon," he began with a sheepish grin, "The other kids were reading Goosebumps and The Famous Five, but not me... I was obsessed."

Anna grinned at the thought of a young Finn blushing over a book with a windswept couple embracing on the cover.

"Go ahead, judge me!" He laughed, "I can take it."

"I'm not judging!" Anna exclaimed, "Though, you may have been a little young for some of the, um, *intimate scenes* that usually appear in those books."

26

"I skipped past those bits...at first," Finn confessed, the pink in his ears spread quickly across his face, "But later on, I found them highly informative. On a scientific level, of course."

"Of course," Anna laughed.

Anna had grown used to people's eyes glazing over when she talked about her favourite stories. They didn't care about the characters on a deep, emotional level, or lose sleep over ingenious plot twists. Her family had always *tried* to support her. They used to feign interest when she'd rant about characters making stupid life choices but it was clear they couldn't relate to her frustration. Over time, she'd adapted literary discussions into clinical reviews of the concepts and themes in a book, rather than her feelings for the world and its characters. She'd learned to keep the passionate part of herself locked away.

Until now.

Finn had opened a floodgate for her and it seemed she'd done the same for him. They became so enthralled in conversation that they nearly forgot to return to work. It took several text messages from Cassie to draw them back to the office.

***

The following day, Anna arrived at her desk to find a book with a green post-it stuck to the cover.

Thought you might like this
- Finn

The blurb on the book described a modern fantasy romance where the female protagonist discovered magic, fell in love and saved the world.

Anna looked over to Finn's desk. His head was hidden behind the screen but there was a collection of green scrunched-up post-its in his rubbish bin. Smiling to herself, Anna slipped the book into her handbag. Instead of letting her mind wander into realms of fantasy while she typed, she spent most of her morning compiling a mental list of books that Finn might like so she could return the favour.

27

CHAPTER 5

The Almost Date

Anna and Finn developed a habit of hanging back after work so they could talk more about their passion for all things fiction. It started with Anna thanking Finn for the book. He'd grinned and spent ten minutes explaining why he thought she'd like it. The next day they'd stayed for half an hour to discuss the first few chapters. By the middle of the following week, their *Book Club* meetings lasted over an hour. The only problem with this arrangement was Cassie. She and Finn carpooled into the city and, though she'd happily disappeared to *run errands* during their meetings thus far, Anna was conscious that Cassie's patience could only stretch so far.

"Why don't you two go somewhere nicer to nerd out?" Dex asked on his way out the door one evening.

"Just let them do their thing," Cassie chastised.

"I'm just saying," Dex continued leaning into the hand on his hip as he gestured to the peeling wallpaper of the basement office, "This place has the ambience of a psycho's basement. Grab a drink somewhere. Make an evening of it. "

"We won't be too long this time," Anna assured, glancing at Cassie.

"I'm happy to wait," Cassie replied, then hastily backtracked, "I mean, I have a few things I need to do in the city anyway...So, I'm not *waiting*. Take your time."

"We all know you don't have things to do," Dex scoffed.

"Dex is right," Finn spoke up, "Tomorrow Cassie and I can come in separately."

"I really don't mind!" Cassie insisted.

"And...?" Dex prompted.

"*And* we'll go to Starbucks or something," Finn turned to Anna, "If you're okay with that?"

"I-" Anna dug her nails into her palm to distract herself from the vexatious butterflies playing with her ribcage, "Yeah, that sounds fine."

Dex smirked before strutting from the room.

Anna hoped the heat rising in her cheeks wasn't as obvious as it felt. On one hand, Finn had just invited her to have coffee. Some might consider that a date. On the other hand, he'd only asked because Dex had essentially forced him. This was just a change of location for their regular book club meetings. It wasn't going to be any different than what they'd been doing thus far. Unless...no.

He's just being friendly. He's your friend. Don't make it weird.

***

Anna took a long time picking an outfit for work the next day. She wished Dex had taken her on that shopping trip. He would have dressed her in something sexy or cool. All she owned were ill-fitting corporate ensembles. Winter had finally shuffled into Brisbane. The skies were clear and the forecast predicted a blissful 21°C, so Anna decided to wear a plain black dress with Dex's gold-embroidered blazer, dark stockings and ankle boots. The blazer covered the worst parts of the dress - large armholes displayed the sides of Anna's bra, the fabric pulled too tightly over her breasts, and there was a scrunch of fabric around her waist where it was too loose. Anna sighed. She constantly saw women on the street with fuller figures. *Where do they buy their clothes?*

Liz insisted it was just a matter of buying a size bigger and then getting the pieces tailored to fit but Anna didn't have a surgeon's salary. She didn't want to waste her savings by paying to buy an outfit and then paying again to make it fit. She used to hate her body for this very reason. Every time she tried on an article of clothing the attendant had commented that her hips and breasts were *too big*, or her waist and shoulders were *too narrow*. It wasn't until she was in her mid-twenties that Anna realised everything was backwards. Customers shouldn't be changing themselves to fit the clothing on offer in stores. Clothing should be designed to fit the customer. Her hips weren't too big. Her waist wasn't too narrow. There was nothing wrong with her body's shape. The proportions of the clothes simply weren't made to fit her. However, while this revelation had helped her self-esteem immensely, it did nothing to fill her wardrobe.

Anna pushed her gold-framed glasses up her nose as she looked in the mirror. *That'll have to do.*

***

"You look nice today," Cassie smiled as Anna walked into the office.

"Thanks," Anna blushed as she took her seat, tugging her dress. She hoped the extra effort she'd put into her appearance would be less obvious to the others. She didn't want Finn to think she had any expectations. This was, after all, just a change of location. Not a date.

"Hey, hot stuff!" Dex strutted through the door, "You're looking glam today. New lipstick?"

Shit. Shit. Shit.

"No," Anna flushed, trying to sound casual. "Old lipstick. Nothing special."

"My mistake," Dex shrugged as he dropped into his chair.

Cassie's handbag buzzed. She extracted her phone, frowning at the screen before pacing out of the room to answer the call.

"Have I offended you?" Dex whispered. His smirk was gone as he looked at Anna with an appraising eye. Anna hadn't seen him be serious before. It was a shock to realise he might actually care about her.

"No," Anna muttered, "I just don't need you telling me I look hot whenever I try something new."

"I thought you weren't doing anything new," Dex chided gently.

Anna glanced at the door, checking there was no sign of Finn before replying.

"The lipstick is old but wearing it is new," confessed Anna, "Okay?"

"Understood." Dex smiled, "I'm sorry. I didn't mean to embarrass you for branching out. I've been there. It sucks when people make a thing out of it."

"*You've* been there?" Anna frowned in disbelief.

"Believe it or not," Dex leaned forward in his chair, "It took me a while to *find myself.* I promise, moving forward, I won't tell you how devastatingly sexy you are unless you specifically ask for my opinion. Scout's honour."

"I don't think that's the kind of promise a scout would make," Anna smiled, "but apology accepted."

Cassie returned biting her lip, "So, um, Finn's not feeling well. He's not coming in."

Anna's heart dropped.

"Damn," Dex replied, "Nothing serious, right?"

"No, he'll be fine," Cassie gave Anna a reassuring grimace, "He just couldn't make it in today."

***

Anna collapsed on her bed. The sunflower sheets mocked her with their cheeriness. She felt like such a fool. She'd been stood up. For a non-date. That had to be some sort of record.

Her phone buzzed. She ignored it. She didn't want to talk to Liz right now. It buzzed again. With a sigh, Anna looked at the messages on her screen. They weren't from Liz.

Finn: *Hey, sorry about today.*
Finn: *Are you free to talk?*

Anna stared at the messages. What could he possibly have to say that he couldn't send via message? She briefly was tempted to ignore the messages but curiosity got the better of her.

Anna: *Are you feeling better?*
Finn: *Yeah, I'm sorry I ruined our plans.*
Anna: *It's okay. We can talk about Chapter 23 tomorrow.*
Finn: *Or right now. Would you be okay with doing a video call?*

Anna generally hated video calls. No one looked good in them and you were stuck focusing on one thing - usually your own horrid thumbnail image on the screen - until the call ended. However, this felt like an invitation to see Finn in a different setting. It was a step in their relationship, albeit a small one.

Anna: *Sure.*

Anna's fingertips tingled with a sudden burst of nerves as her phone rang. She checked her hair and lipstick before answering.

"Hi," she waved nervously at the camera, moving the phone so it didn't cut off her chin.

"Hey, Anna," Finn gave a sheepish smile, "I have a confession to make."
Anna raised her eyebrows, "You weren't sick?"
"I was but not until just after Cassie left," Finn looked off camera, "I think
it was a stress headache. It came on suddenly and...yeah."
"Why were you stressed?" Anna had a sinking feeling she knew the answer.
"I got in my head about...some stuff," he replied, "I don't want to get into
it but I was hoping we could keep our book club the same as before?"

Anna was careful to keep her expression neutral. Not only had Finn taken
the day off work to avoid going out with Anna but the very thought of it
has made him sick.
"Maybe we shouldn't do them at all," she replied in what she hoped was
a supportive tone.
"What?" Finn's room shook as he bumped the camera, "No! I don't want
to stop."
Behind him, Anna could see a wall of books and small pot plants, a wooden
bed frame and the tips of two green pillows. There was a peculiarity in
being invited into Finn's bedroom without actually being there. Did he
want to maintain professional boundaries or not?
"I don't want to be a source of stress for you," Anna frowned.
"You're not!" Finn looked dejected, "This was all me."
It's not you, it's me. Great.

"So what's the problem?" Anna hadn't meant to be so blunt but it had been
a long day of worrying. Finn leaned back onto his bed frame and sighed.
"I like hanging out with you and I want to get to know you better," he said,
"But there's stuff I can't tell you about myself, or my life. I don't want
things to be unbalanced between us. It wouldn't be fair."
The anguish in Finn's eyes told Anna he wasn't just fobbing her off but
she couldn't imagine what secret could be so bad that it stopped Finn from
making new friends. Dex and Cassie must already know. Anna couldn't
help but feel a bit resentful toward them. If they were fine with it, whatever
it was, then surely Anna would be too.

"Let's play a game," suggested Anna, "You tell me something about
yourself, something you're comfortable sharing, and I'll tell you something
similar about me."
"Like what?"
"You said you got into romance books because of your sister," Anna

prompted, "What's her name? Is she your only sibling?"

"Oh," Finn smiled sheepishly, "No, I'm the youngest of seven. The books were Quinn's, but there's also Jed, Jen, Grant, Wallace and Fern. "

"Wow," Anna laughed, "Sounds like your parents had their hands full."

"They had a lot of help," Finn blushed, "What about you?"

"I have a sister. Her name's Liz," Anna replied, "And a brother-in-law. They just had a baby."

"That's great!" Finn smiled, "Are you close?"

Anna explained how she and Liz kept in touch but, with Liz's career and new family, there wasn't time for them to see each other anymore. Her venting led into an overview of her super-successful family and how she felt like the black sheep.

"I always feel a bit left out with my brothers or sisters," Finn confided, "Don't get me wrong, they're great, but they all have big personalities. I was never like that. I had a stutter until I was ten, so I've never been much of a talker. It didn't help that I was a *late bloomer*, either. While all my siblings were dating and obsessed with sex, I was hiding in books."

Anna had been an early bloomer but she'd never been obsessed with sex. Romance, yes, but not sex. She explained how her mother's career, representing abused women in court, had opened her eyes to the dangers of the world. Her constant fear of becoming a crime statistic had stopped Anna from living her life. To her surprise, Finn didn't jump to defend the reputation of men, as she'd expected him to.

"I agree with your sister about needing to live your life," Finn nodded with a frown, "But I also can't fault you for doing whatever makes you feel safe. It's a hard balance and I don't envy you for it. The worst I get is people treating me like I'm helpless. They mean well but it's not fun being a burden to your friends and family."

"You're not a burden on anyone," Anna frowned.

"Feels like it sometimes," Finn sighed, "Even before the, uh, *accident*...I always felt like I needed other people more than they needed me. I guess it's because nobody needs me at all."

"That's not true," Anna wanted to reach through the screen and hug him. She'd never felt needed either but it had been a relief. Having someone rely on you is a lot of pressure.

"If nobody needs you," Anna continued, "it's because nobody *needs* anyone. We're all fine on our own but we like company."

"I guess," Finn sighed.

"I may not *need* you but I like having you around," Anna smiled, hoping she wasn't making a fool of herself.

Finn smiled back with warmth in his eyes, "I like having you around too."

They talked until the early hours of the morning. It wasn't until after they'd hung up that Anna realised they hadn't mentioned a single book.

CHAPTER 6

Happy Birthday

The wonderfully chilly days were shoved aside by an unseasonably sweltering August. For once, Anna didn't mind the rising temperature. The two-person Book Club had been replaced by nightly video calls and the hot weather meant Finn often wore tight-fitting singlets. She would have felt guilty about ogling his chest had she not noticed his eyes drifting to a lower part of his screen whenever she wore a low-cut top. It was fun to be a little flirty without worrying about where things were going. Finn had yet to divulge his mysterious secret, so it seemed dating was off the table, but he was an amazing friend. She couldn't imagine life without him. Along with Dex and Cassie, Finn made Anna feel as though she finally belonged somewhere. She didn't have to try to fit in. She could just be herself.

***

One Friday morning, something felt off when Anna entered the office. Cassie and Finn had yet to arrive but Dex was already working at his desk. His fingers hammered the keyboard with savage intensity. Every muscle in his body looked tense. His eyes were red and puffy. Anna considered leaving him in peace - she hated when people saw her cry - but curiosity got the better of her, "Are you okay?"

Dex jumped up from his chair. He blinked at Anna in surprise before dropping his gaze to the floor. "It's nothing," he said flatly, "Family stuff. I don't want to talk about it."

"Okay," Anna turned to her desk and put down her bag but then turned back to find him standing right behind her. She'd never seen Dex like this before. His spark was gone. Anna slowly closed the space between them, gauging whether it was okay to approach. She wrapping her arms gently around his shoulders. Neither spoke. The tightness in Dex's muscles slowly softened. He wound his shaking arms around her and buried his face against her shoulder, sobbing quietly.

Dex was usually a powerhouse of confidence. It was bewildering to see him vulnerable. Anna patted his hair while he wept, unsure what else to do. Eventually, he pulled his head back from her shoulder and sniffed.

"I'm getting snot all over your blazer," he whispered.

"Technically it's *your* blazer," Anna replied with a benign chuckle, "Besides, you matter more than clothes."

"Woah now, let's not go mad." Dex chuckled.

"I mean it."

He wiped his face, finally meeting Anna's eyes with an apologetic smile, "Thank you."

"HAPPY BIRTHDAY!" Cassie's voice exploded from the doorway. Anna jumped back as though she and Dex had been doing something illicit, then scolded herself for it. Cassie didn't seem to notice. She held up four coffees in a cardboard to-go tray. Finn was at her side carrying a sponge cake topped with raspberries. His brow furrowed as they approached Dex and Anna. "What's going on?"

"I got an email from my *dear brother*," Dex sighed, "Unrelated to my birthday, of course."

"Oh, Dex!" Cassie groaned, putting down the coffee and giving him a firm hug, "*We're* your family now. You know that, right?"

"Yeah," agreed Finn, "We're here for you."

Anna couldn't help but feel excluded from the conversation. She'd had no idea it was Dex's birthday, let alone what was going on with his family. She wished she could do something to let Dex know how much she cared. But, without context, she couldn't guess what might help.

"Do you want to go out tonight?" Cassie suggested, "It's not too often your B-Day falls on a Friday."

"Or a full moon," Dex added quietly.

A pregnant pause filled the office.

"Why would the full moon make a difference?" Anna asked, certain she was missing something.

"Finn's got a- a *thing*," Cassie stammered, "It's, um-"

"It's a sleep study," Dex finished, "He signed up for a bit of extra dosh. Right, mate?"

Finn cleared his throat awkwardly.

"Y- Yeah, yup," he looked at Dex, "You guys should still go out though. Have a blast."

"Thanks, my man," Dex replied, sitting on Anna's desk, "How about it, love?"

Anna wasn't one for clubbing but a night out with Dex and Cassie sounded fun. Plus, Dex's mood had brightened at the idea of going out. This was something she could do to help him feel better. She had an idea to raise his spirits even higher, "I would but…" Anna mocked an exaggerated pout, "I don't have anything to wear…"

Dex's face lit up.

"Perhaps," Anna continued playing the damsel, "*someone* would be willing to help me buy a few things in our lunch break?"

"Shit, yeah!" he exclaimed, "Clubbing *and* makeovers? I love you guys! Plus that cake looks fucking incredible. Can we have some now?"

With a sheepish smile, Finn placed a homemade cake on the nearest desk before adding several small candles and lighting them. They sang and then cheered as Dex made his birthday wish, blowing out the candles. It was a shame to pause their celebrations for work, they even tried to include the new temps in their celebrations to prolong the party, but once the cake and coffee were gone they couldn't delay their duties any longer.

By the time midday rolled around, Anna had fallen into her normal typing stupor.

"Shop-ing! Rah rah rah! Shop-ing!" Dex chanted as he strutted between their desks.

"Maybe I shouldn't come," Finn looked hesitant, "I'm not a great judge of fashion."

"What are you talking about?" Dex replied, "You're a poster boy for the *Cottagecore* trend."

"I just wear jeans and t-shirts," Finn shrugged dismissively.

"You know your vibe and you make it work," Cassie insisted.

"Please?" Anna implored.

"Okay," Finn agreed, the corners of his mouth twitching.

"Oh, this will be so much fun!" Dex skipped out the door.

***

To Anna's surprise, none of Dex's favourite clothing stores were expensive high-end boutiques. Most were independently owned, affordable, and hidden from the main foot traffic of the mall. But, as Anna had predicted, none stocked clothes that catered to her body. They were designed for tall, skinny models with no hips or breasts to speak of. Finding an outfit that fit, let alone one Anna looked good in, seemed a hopeless mission.

"Not to worry" Dex chirped happily, "I know the perfect place."
He led the group down an alleyway between two old sandstone buildings. As they approached the entrance, Finn let out a quiet groan.
"Do we have to go to this one?" Cassie protested, "It's, like, three flights of stairs up."
"It'll be worth it!" Dex affirmed.
Anna was surprised that Dex would be so inconsiderate of Finn's physical limitations.
"I'm not going without Finn," Anna said in confusion.
"What are you talking- " Dex began.
"Oh, I-" Finn interjected with a flushed glance at Anna, "I can get up the stairs."
He removed a collapsible walking cane from the back of his chair and stood with a wobble. He leaned heavily on the cane for a few steps but, once he'd found his balance on the uneven pavement, he walked quite gracefully. If Anna hadn't been focusing on his gait, his subtle limp wouldn't have been noticeable at all.
"I- I just," stammered Finn, "It can take a lot out of me sometimes. That's all."
He used a bike lock to secure his wheelchair to a nearby pole and then disappeared into the building.

Anna couldn't believe what she was seeing. Her face flushed with humiliation. This was the guy she thought of as her best friend. She knew his first word was "crap" because his older brothers thought it'd be funny. She knew he hated coriander, mint and capsicum. She knew he'd broken a plate when he was nine and blamed it on the dog. But she didn't know he could walk! When they'd met, Anna had made a conscious decision not to ask why Finn needed a wheelchair. It seemed such a personal, painful subject and yet one she was certain most people asked before they bothered to learn his name. Then, as she'd gotten to know him, Anna had stopped noticing the wheelchair altogether. It was like Dex's eyeliner or Cassie's wigs - a minor detail in a sea of more important traits. Still, she felt like a jerk for making assumptions.

"His left leg's prosthetic from below the knee," murmured Cassie as they climbed the stairs. "He uses the chair at work because we're always sitting at our desks anyway. But normally he tries not to use aids if he can. It depends on what he's doing and how much energy he's got. Sometimes he uses a cane or crutches. Sometimes he's fine with nothing."

"I'm such an idiot," Anna whispered back, "I hope I didn't embarrass him back there."

"Don't worry about it," Cassie patted Anna's arm, "He's just sensitive when he thinks he's holding us back. Even though it's buildings with crap accessibility like this that are the problem."

When they reached the third floor, sweaty and puffing, they found Finn holding the door open for them. He looked a little out of breath but smiled as Cassie and Dex ducked past him into the shop. The musky smell of perfume wafted from inside. Curly gold lettering above the door announced the name to be *Gracious Lace*.

"I didn't realise you've only ever seen me in the chair," Finn said quietly, "Sorry."

"No, *I'm* sorry," Anna took a step toward him, keeping her voice equally low, "I didn't mean to make it a whole thing."

He was taller than Anna but not by much. His mouth was at the same height as her eyes, drawing Anna's attention to the gentle curve of his lips and light stubble on his chin.

"Thanks for sticking up for me," he whispered into her ear. The feeling of his breath on her neck sent a pleasant tingle down Anna's spine.

"Any time," she replied, pulling back just enough to look into his eyes.

"We should go in," he said quietly.

"We should," she agreed.

Neither moved. Anna had never been this close to Finn before. His light green eyes had flecks of gold in them, like dappled sunlight hitting leaves in a forest.

"I need your body, love!" Dex called from the depths of the shop.
Anna took a step back. Finn blinked and then looked away.
"After you," said Finn, suddenly cold. His expression was unreadable.
Anna took a deep breath and walked into the shop.

It had the atmosphere of a 1920s speakeasy but, instead of tables, round clothing racks were scattered around a low stage. Jazz music played from unseen speakers and an ancient bronze sewing machine sat on the bar. Hundreds of giant spools of thread were displayed on the wall along with several jars of buttons and ribbon. The clothes didn't seem to be organised in any way Anna could decipher. She ran her fingers over the textures of various fabrics on the nearest rack. No two pieces were the same. Each looked to have been carefully handmade. Some seemed vintage while others were modern.

"Welcome, my darlings!" called a voice with a thick Slavic accent.
Dex, who'd been leaning on the bar, made a beeline to the origin of the voice while Anna craned her neck to see where it had come from.
"Dexter Duke!" A small elderly woman, barely reaching Dex's thigh, stepped out from behind a rack, "My dear *ulyublena lyal'ka!*"
The woman's thick glasses magnified her beetle-like eyes. She sparkled from head to toe with sequinned garments and gem-covered jewellery. Curled slips of white hair fell gracefully from her bejewelled headscarf and her thin lips were smeared with bright red lipstick.

"Madame Oksana!" Dex answered, kneeling to hug the woman, "It's been too long! But I'm afraid we're not here for me, I've brought a new friend and I was hoping you could work your magic on her."
"Of course, my darling Dexy!" Madame Oksana crooned.
Dex gestured for Anna to come forward.
"This is Anna," he said, presenting Anna like a prize.
Madame Oksana circled her, adjusting her glasses as she studied her subject carefully.
"It's lovely to meet you" stammered Anna. "Did you make all these yourse-"
"LADA!" Madame Oksana squealed with glee.
"Sorry?"
"You, my dear, have the divine hourglass figure of the goddess Lada!" She turned to Dex, "Oh yes, yes, I can certainly work with this…"

Oksana began zooming around the room with incredible speed. She returned with a tall stack of clothes but, instead of handing them to Anna, she trotted past the group and disappeared behind heavy curtains at the back of the stage. Her muffled voice called "This way, Miss Anna-Lada!"

Anna did as she was told, following Madame Oksana into a spacious changing room behind the curtain. Oksana piled the clothes onto a footstool and then disappeared back through the curtain.

"The mirror is out here," she called, though her voice was dampened by the thick velvet. "Come show us which of those makes you feel *mahiya*!"

Anna looked at the pile of clothes. She doubted anything would even make it over her hips, but as she tried on the first piece - a tight black dress - she found that Madame Oksana had guessed her measurements perfectly. Not believing her luck, Anna quickly changed into the next two pieces on the pile, a satin blouse and cotton pants. They fit perfectly too! She pushed back tears of joy as she made her way through the entire pile.

"Knock, knock," Cassie's voice was soft from behind the curtain. "Are you okay? Can I come in?"

Anna opened the curtain just enough to let Cassie come through, wiping her eyes.

"Oh no! What's wrong?" Cassie asked, "If you don't like any of it, we can just leave. I'll make an excuse."

"It's not that," Anna laughed as she sniffled, "They all fit! That's never happened to me before...I don't know why I'm crying. It's stupid."

"Not a all!" Cassie smiled, "I get it."

"I don't know what to pick." Anna sighed.

"That's a fixable problem." Cassie laughed. She stuck her head out of the curtain, "We're a bit overwhelmed by all the lovely choices! Standby!"

Analysing the clothes with hawk-like concentration, Cassie created three piles. Pointing at the largest pile, she said, "These are too formal for the club we're going to tonight." Then pointing at a smaller pile, "These are good for the nightclub look, but I think you'd be uncomfortable in them, especially when we're dancing. I recommend these-" She handed Anna the smallest pile. "Pick your favourite or buy them all!" Cassie smiled, "Either way, show us. Dex is about to explode with anticipation and Finn didn't climb all those stairs for nothing."

Cassie ducked back through the curtain with a wink. Filled with excitement, Anna put on her first option. It was a halter-neck A-line dress made of smooth, emerald silk. Delicate floral patterns were embroidered into the upper half. She felt like a modern-day fairy princess. Taking a deep breath, Anna stepped out onto the stage.

Dex and Finn were sitting on an ornate chaise lounge to the side of the stage, nibbling tiny sandwiches from a silver tray while Cassie was deep in conversation with Madame Oksana. Finn choked on his sandwich and stared at Anna with wide eyes. "Wow," he coughed, "You look... That dress is..."

"You look AMAZING!" Dex exclaimed, "That dress is *stunning*. It brings out your gorgeous eyes! Damn, girl!"

Anna blushed and curtseyed. She caught her reflection in a large, gold-rimmed mirror nearby. The elegant young woman looking back at her was barely recognisable.

"Pace yourselves," Cassie warned, "We narrowed it down to three options, and they're all amazing. NEXT!"

Anna laughed and returned to the changing room to try on the next ensemble.

She emerged wearing a lace camisole in burgundy with a black leather skirt. She wasn't so sure about this one. Leather wasn't usually her style but she felt powerful wearing it.

"Ooh, that would look so ho- I mean, it would look *lovely* with your blazer!" Dex gushed. Anna remembered Dex's promise to stop calling her hot unless she asked him to.

"You mean *your* blazer?" Anna chuckled, feeling giddy, "Besides, it's the middle of summer. I don't want to be hot at the club tonight."

"Oh come on," Dex winked, "Now you're just teasing me."

Anna hurried back to the changing room before anyone could see her blush. As she picked up the final outfit, Anna smiled. She suspected Cassie had ensured this one would come out last for dramatic effect. The high-waisted capri pants featured a bold geometric pattern and stretched comfortably with her movement. The black parts of the pattern were accented by the black singlet paired with them. It had a sweetheart neckline and form-fitting bodice that flattered her curves.

She emerged from the changing room grinning.

"Yes, yes!" Cassie grinned, "Do you love it?"

"I do!" Anna twirled on the spot. Then turned her attention to Dex and Finn, "What do you guys think?"

"Uh, yeah," Finn nodded.

"This," Dex jumped onto the stage and framed Anna's beaming face with his hands, "Is the best birthday present ever!" He spun her in a twirl then dipped her. Anna wasn't usually the giggling type but she couldn't help herself. Dex's excitement was catching.

"We should get back to the office," mumbled Finn, "We're already late."

Anna changed back into her boring work clothes wishing they had more time. She decided to buy the capri outfit and the green dress. She didn't know when she'd wear the latter but simply couldn't leave without it.

"That is the feeling of destiny, my dear," Madame Oksana said with a knowing smile, "The dress was made for you."

***

Back at the office, Anna struggled to concentrate on work. Every minute stretched on for hours and she could have sworn the clock went backwards at one point. By the time five o'clock finally rolled around, she was buzzing with anticipation.

"Have fun tonight," Finn smiled weakly.

"I wish you could come with us," Anna replied, sincerely remorseful he wouldn't be sharing in tonight's good times.

"Next time," he promised, moving to the door.

"I'll drop Finn at home and then I can be at yours by dinner time, sound good?" Cassie spoke over her shoulder as she followed Finn into the hallway.

"I'll have a cocktail waiting for you," Dex called back.

"So we're meeting at your place?" Anna asked.

"Yup," he replied, looking at his phone, "Texting you my address now."

"Thanks," Anna's phone buzzed as she gathered her things, "What time should I aim for?"

"As soon as you like," he shrugged, then arched his right brow, "Actually, how far away do you live?"

"About 40 minutes," Anna groaned. Peak hour was a nightmare, especially on the bus.

"You've got your clothes with you," Dex tilted his head, "Do you want to come with me now? We can get ready together at my place."

"I'd love to," grinned Anna, "Could you show me how you do that *smoky eye* thing?"

He laughed, "I certainly can."

CHAPTER 7

Rock Bottom

The elevator of Dex's building smelled like Thai food, making Anna's stomach rumble. She'd forgotten to eat lunch. Finn had saved some of Madame Oksana's tiny sandwiches for her but she had shoved them into her handbag and promptly forgotten all about them. Fishing out the squashed, napkin-wrapped parcels, Anna opened one apprehensively.

"Oh no, no, no," Dex gagged as the elevator doors opened. He snatched the sandwiches from her and tossed them down the garbage shoot, "Those'll be horrid by now. I'll fix you something."

"Thanks," Anna exhaled with relief.

Dex lived in a studio apartment with thick, purple curtains lining two of the walls. It blocked out any hint of the setting sun and, once he'd turned on the fairy lights which hung from the ceiling, Anna felt like she'd stepped inside a fortune teller's tent.

"Welcome to my *extremely* humble abode," Dex sighed.

He began taking ingredients from his fridge, gesturing to a closed door behind him, "That's the bathroom. I'm in the kitchen. You're in the *bedroom-slash-dining* area, slash lounge. That concludes our grand tour."

"It's awesome," smiled Anna.

"It's crap," he laughed, "but it's all I can afford since I don't want roommates."

Anna had two roommates whom she barely saw. One was a nurse who worked nights and slept all day. The other was a model who would vanish for weeks at a time. Despite this, Anna confined herself to her bedroom most of the time. The communal areas felt too exposed so she only visited the kitchen and laundry room as needed. She'd never even sat on the sofa in the lounge room.

"How do you feel about gourmet toasties?" Dex asked, twirling a frying pan in his hands.
"I feel very, very good about it," Anna replied.
Dex winked and turned back to the stove. The divine smell of melted butter filled the apartment and, before she knew it, Anna was biting into crunchy, gooey bliss. Prosciutto, spinach, melted brie and thinly sliced apple danced on her tongue. She devoured it quickly, wishing she had room for more.

"Do you want to shower?" Dex offered, "Or were you planning just to change clothes?"
"I hadn't thought about it," Anna flushed.
"I'm not saying you *need* to shower," Dex continued, "You smell lovely, as always. But if you *want* to, then you should go first while I clean up."

Anna took her bags into the bathroom. It felt strange to get naked in an unfamiliar place. She felt exposed even though the door was locked and Dex was banging around the kitchen. The products in Dex's shower were intriguingly foreign. She found a gentle pleasure in sampling each of the subtly-scented gels and lotions.
When she was clean and dry, she reluctantly pulled on the same underwear and bra she'd been wearing all day. At least she hadn't gotten too sweaty from the heat.

Music filled the apartment as she stepped out of the bathroom in her gorgeous new outfit. Dex was dancing with his back to her. The curtain behind his bed had been pulled back to reveal a wall full of clothes. Anna smiled to herself as he moved gracefully to the beat. He was in his element. She could see why he found it so easy to attract strangers in clubs.

"All done!" Anna shouted over the music.
Dex turned and grinned, grabbing her hand and twirling her around.
"Perfection!" he said, then released her hand and bowed. "If you'll excuse me, dear lady."
Dex pranced into the bathroom, leaving Anna standing in the middle of the room. She was tempted to look through Dex's wall of clothes but felt it might be a violation so, instead, she sat on the edge of the bed and scrolled through her phone. Finn was online.

Anna: *Hey! I hope that sleep study thing goes okay tonight. :)*
Finn: *Thanks, I hope you have fun too.*
Anna: *Dex has assured me that fun is guaranteed.*
Finn: *You know you can pull out if you're not up for it. He won't mind.*
Anna: *I want to try having Dex's kind of fun. With the dancing and cocktails. Probably not the making-out with strangers part. :P*
Finn: *Haha, you never know!*

Something deflated in Anna's chest.

Anna: *Strangers are gross! Besides I'm in this for the dancing. I'll be happy if the club's empty apart from us...*
Finn: *Don't forget Cassie's coming too.*

Anna frowned. Something was definitely up.

Anna: *Yeah, that's what I meant by 'us'.*
Finn: *Of course, sorry, I read your message wrong.*
Anna: *Are you okay?*
Finn: ...
Finn:
Finn: ...
Finn:
Finn: ...
Anna: *You know I can see when you're typing, right?*
Finn: *Sorry!*
Finn: *I just wish things were different.*
Anna: *Me too. I wish you were coming tonight.*
Finn: *When are you getting to Dex's?*
Anna: *I'm already here. We left work together.*

Finn: *Oh, cool.*
Finn: *Tell him 'hi'?*
Anna: *Will do. He's in the shower right now.*
Finn: ...
Finn:
Finn: ...
Anna: *?*

Finn: *Dex is a great guy. You should stick with him.*

Anna's chest tightened into a knot.

Anna: *What do you mean?*
Finn: *Nothing. Just have a good time tonight.*
Finn: *I've got to go. Bye.*

Finn logged off before Anna could respond. The tightness in her chest exploded into rage. Who the hell was Finn to tell her who she should stick with? Was he preemptively dumping her by fobbing her off onto someone else? They weren't even together! Sure, they'd gotten close over the past few months. And *maybe* they'd shared a moment on the stairs…but nothing had actually happened! How presumptuous can you be?!
Dex is fun, though. And supportive. And hot.
Dex never made her feel like throwing her phone at the wall. He never skirted around saying what he was thinking. His intentions were always perfectly, refreshingly clear. Maybe Finn had a point. Maybe she should stick with Dex.

As if conjured by her thoughts, Dex emerged from the bathroom in a billow of steam, wearing only a towel. Anna swallowed a gasp. His glistening naked torso was slender but muscular, like an Olympian swimmer. His hairless chest displayed an Egyptian ankh tattoo with pointed beams radiating from its head. Heat rose in Anna's cheeks. She couldn't help but notice his towel wasn't looking particularly secure. It had been a long time since she'd been alone with a naked man. And this one thought she was *devastatingly sexy*. Not to mention, if his weekend exploits were to be believed, he never left a sexual partner unsatisfied. It sounded as though he gave them all mind-blowing orgasms before sending them on their way. Anna wasn't sure she'd ever even had an orgasm. The idea of a one night stand had always repulsed her but something about Dex intrigued her. He felt safe. He could give her what she wanted. No pressure. No awkward dates, or *non-dates*. Just passion and satisfaction.

Screw it.
Anna closed the space between them.
She could feel the post-shower heat radiating from Dex's skin.
A subtle smirk played on his lips, "Well, hello there," he murmured,

leaning toward her.

"Hi," she said quietly.

He raised an eyebrow.

She'd never been assertive like this before. It was thrilling. His eyes delved into hers, daring her to act. Her heart was pounding. She took the plunge, pressing her lips against his.

Dex's lips parted under hers, sliding his tongue gently into her mouth. He pressed his hands along her waist, feeling his way into the back pockets of her pants. She ran her fingers through his damp hair.

"God, you're delicious," he murmured as they fell onto the bed in a tangle of limbs.

The towel lay forgotten on the floor. Anna moved her hands slowly down his chest and past his navel. Finding her target, she gripped him firmly. He gave a guttural moan as she massaged him.

She hoped she was doing it right. She had almost no experience with handjobs and it had been years since she'd had any practice. Dex seemed to be enjoying himself as he slid his hands into her bra. He stroked her breasts, playing gently with her nipples. It was her turn to moan. His brazen touch was thrilling, she had no idea what he planned to do next but she couldn't wait to find out. He was the master and she was his eager student. As she straddled him in her skin-tight capri pants, she could feel that he was hard beneath her. Her clothing suddenly felt cumbersome but there didn't seem to be time to remove it. That would mean stepping back. She couldn't bear the thought of unbinding herself from him. He kissed along her jawline and then nibbled softly at her neck. She gasped, dizzy with pleasure.

Dex froze.

He pushed away from her.

"I'm sorry," he gasped, "I think we should stop."

"Oh..." she blinked, climbing numbly off him, "Did I do something wrong?"

"No!" he exclaimed, wrapping the towel back around himself, "but, we can't do this. *I* can't. Not with you."

He let out a deep sigh, dropping his head into his hands.

Anna didn't know whether the heat in her face was from lust or embarrassment. *Not with you.*

"I get it," she lied, "All good."

"I'm not a monogamous person," Dex spoke slowly, choosing his words with deliberation, "My friends are *everything* to me. More important than family. I live and die for my friends. My lovers, on the other hand, are never more than a bit of fun. Sometimes there's a bit of crossover, I'll have a casual romp with a friend or two, but only if I know we're all on the same page. I don't want to hurt anyone, especially not you, and…Well, I'd rather have you in my life forever than in my bed tonight. Does that make sense?" Anna hated that it did.

"We want different things," Anna nodded, willing herself not to cry from the humiliation.

They sat in silence.

Anna didn't know what else to say. What was she meant to do now? Should she leave? Had she just ruined Dex's birthday? This was all Finn's fault. He'd basically told her to throw herself at Dex and now everything was horrible and awkward. Did Finn think Anna wanted a friend-with-benefits arrangement? Or a one-night stand? She thought he knew her better than that. She'd told him she wanted something magical. She wanted real love. She wanted romance.

She wanted a happy ending.

Speaking of happy endings, that towel hadn't done much to hide Dex's boner.

"So…" Dex offered his hand in a business-like gesture, "Friends?"

Anna choked out a laugh and shook his hand, "Friends."

Dex jumped off the bed and grabbed some clothes, changing in the bathroom for modesty's sake. Anna took some deep breaths.

Pull it together. Things can only get better from here.

She splashed her burning face with water from the kitchen sink. She refused to let this ruin things. She wasn't going to sulk over being rejected. She'd never thought about Dex sexually before tonight. This had been a silly, spur-of-the-moment whim. Why should she dwell on his disinterest? She didn't want to be with him either. Not really. She'd just wanted to know what it was like to be spontaneous and sexual. Could it have gone better? Yes, obviously. Was she grateful Dex had stopped things before they'd gone all the way? Her bruised ego said no. It wished Dex had found her so irresistible that he couldn't bring himself to stop. Her conscience, however, knew he'd done the right thing. Dex was her friend. He was more like a brother than anything else. She'd only thrown herself at him because it was easy. That wasn't fair to anyone. It had been a recipe for disaster from the start.

When Dex reemerged, Anna felt more composed. She had no idea what had come over her earlier but resolved to move on as if nothing had happened. By the time Cassie arrived with two hot pizzas, the tension between Anna and Dex had dissolved back into normal friendly banter. Dex even fulfilled his promise to help Anna with her makeup.

"You guys look amazing!" Cassie gushed.
"So do you!" Anna replied, glad the night was back on track.
Cassie was wearing an A-line dress made from rich red satin. Her burgundy lips perfectly matched the fabric and her dark wig was styled in long, loose curls.
Dex whipped up some mysterious purple cocktails.
Cassie took a trusting gulp, "Woah!" She coughed, "What's in this?"
"Many booze!" Dex winked.
Cassie just laughed. Anna took a tentative sip. To her surprise, it tasted like strawberry sherbert. She gulped down the rest and felt a warm buzzing sensation all over her body. Once everyone was feeling pleasantly tipsy, Anna, Cassie and Dex ventured into the night.

The Valley, as locals called it, offered everything from dive bars to rooftop cocktail lounges. Dex led them past several prominent clubs to an artfully graffitied side street covered in fairy lights.
"Where are you taking us?" Cassie complained, "These shoes were *not* made for walking!"
"We're here," Dex gestured at the graffitied wall, "One of the temps said drinks are half-price tonight."
"Wait," Cassie grinned, "This is where Jedda works!"
"So you approve?"
Cassie clapped excitedly but Anna was confused. She couldn't see any sign of a club. It was just a wall of graffiti. However, Dex pushed on a cartoonised painting of a door among the murals and spray-painted tags to reveal a secret entrance. Music pulsed through the opening. They were greeted by a sign that said *"Welcome to Rock Bottom"* with a neon arrow pointing down some stairs.

The graffiti theme continued throughout the club. It glowed under blacklights and made dizzying pathways on the walls, floor and ceiling. Punk-rock music blared as they stepped into the artificial fog on the dancefloor.

"Is it safe to breathe this stuff?" Anna yelled over the music.

"It's just water and glycerin," Dex called back, "It's amazing for your skin!"

Cassie was already fist-pumping to the music. Anna began to dance. At first, she just copied Cassie's moves, hoping she didn't look too silly. But soon she didn't care what she looked like. No one was looking at her and the music was so loud it seemed to vibrate her limbs into moving of their own volition. She lost track of time. One song faded into the next. She didn't realise how exhausted she'd become until Cassie dragged her and Dex to the bar. Her body was shining with sweat.

Cassie waved energetically at the bartender, leaning further over the bar than was generally allowed. The pretty aboriginal woman wiped her hands on her apron, grinned and kissed Cassie on the cheek.

"This is Jedda," Cassie bellowed against the thumping music.

"We've got a rowdy bunch in tonight," warned Jedda. She nodded toward a group of gargantuan men in rugby shirts, guzzling beers around a long table in the opposite corner.

A small group of women hurried past them, avoiding eye contact. The men's leering barks were audible over the club's thumping music. The women made a beeline to the safety of the bathroom.

"Why can't they just stay in their goddamn caves?" Cassie scowled.

"Agreed!" Dex rolled his eyes.

Anna remained silent. Men like that were the reason she'd never gone clubbing on her own. One of them looked over and sneered as he caught her eye. She quickly turned away.

"You're Dex, right?" Jedda enquired as she poured them each a glass of water.

"The one and only!" Dex winked.

Jedda pulled a note from her apron and handed it to him, "The guy at that booth asked me to give you this," She nodded to a diner-style booth in a dark corner. A raven-haired man sat with his back to them.

"One of my many fans, no doubt," Dex grinned as he unfolded the note.

His face dropped. He scrunched up the paper in a tight fist.

"I don't suppose you have a pen I could borrow?" he asked with a forced smile. Jedda pulled a biro from her apron and waited as Dex scrawled a message on the back of the paper. "Not to be childish," he said, "but would you mind?"

Dex handed Jedda the paper, along with a ten-dollar note. Jedda rolled her eyes, pocketing the money as she strode over to the booth. Dex made a point of not watching the exchange.

"Who is that?" Cassie asked, openly staring as the man followed Jedda back toward the bar.

"My bloody brother," replied Dex.

"Arik?" Cassie gasped.

The family resemblance was striking. Arik had the same blue eyes, black hair and pointed features as Dex. And, currently, the same furrowed brow. Despite their similarities, their personalities couldn't have been more different. Though Arik moved gracefully through the crowd, his posture was rigid. He was taller and more muscular than Dex. His three-piece suit clashed horribly with the cyberpunk aesthetic of the club.

"Come to wish me a happy birthday?" Dex glowered.

"Could we speak privately?" responded Arik, his face unreadable.

"Nope."

Arik flattened his tie, his jaw clenched as he eyed Anna and Cassie apprehensively.

"Very well," he continued, businesslike, "I've come to ask you to reconsider the opportunity-"

"Also, no," Dex answered flatly.

Arik leaned toward Dex with an imploring expression, "Please. Hear me out."

"I'm finally living a life that isn't poisoned by *Mother*," spat Dex, "I have a job, freedom, and friends who *accept me as I am*. I'm happy. And you think I'll take your stupid bloody job offer so I can, what? Enjoy the *privilege* of going home? Rejoin the family? News flash, this is my home and these guys are my family now."

Arik looked stung. "I'd wager the Lax doesn't accept you as you are," he glanced at Anna, "She'd have to know *what* you are first."

Dex glared at Arik, "Fuck you."

Anna was fairly sure she'd just been insulted but, because she didn't know what they were talking about, stayed silent.

"It's clear we're not going to resolve this right now," Arik regained his formal manner.

"Seems pretty resolved to me," countered Dex.

"I'll be in touch," Arik turned and left.

"So…Shots?" Jedda suggested awkwardly, "On the house!"

Accepting the distraction, Anna nodded enthusiastically while Cassie whispered something in Dex's ear and squeezed his hand. He nodded and plastered on a manic smile, "Let's do this!"

Jedda mixed a different shot for each of them. Cassie's was bright green and had a mint leaf floating on top. She removed the leaf, drank the liquid then rubbed the leaf on her lips before popping it into her mouth. Dex's was dark burgundy, almost black, and had a syrup-like texture. He gulped it hungrily before licking the remnants from the inside of the glass.

Anna's shot was amber at the top and transitioned into a deep red. It had fresh, floral notes with a citric, bitter after taste. As she slammed the empty shot glass onto the bar, elation washed over her. Her body tingled with energy. She pulled Cassie and Dex back to the dance floor. The thumping beat pulsed through her as she jumped and shimmied under the strobe lights. She had never felt so free. She was floating on a cloud of joy. Nothing could bring her down.

Nothing, that is, except looking up to see Dex shoving his tongue down some random guy's throat. Anna's stomach dropped. Just because she didn't want him anymore didn't mean she wanted to see *that*. He was rubbing his hands all over the stranger's body only hours after he'd been touching hers. Didn't he care about her feelings at all? Hadn't he said he cared about her *more than some random hook-up*?

She turned to Cassie but found only a wall of strangers. Anna was alone, surrounded by sweaty, jumping flesh. She couldn't breathe. She pushed her way through the maze of pulsating limbs until she finally found fresh air. She focused on the stillness of the glowing moon, wiping away her tears. *Get it together.*

Pacing back and forth, she willed her heart to return to a normal rhythm.

"Hey, Hot Stuff," A deep, slurring voice growled from behind her, followed by moronic laughter.

The gang of rugby fans had followed her outside. Reeking of beer and sweat, they now stood between her and the entrance to the club. Anna looked away, trying to ignore their jeering. She realised they were alone in the alleyway. No one could see her from the street.

"Oh, can't ya' hear me, bitch?" the voice bellowed, "You deaf?"

Knowing any response would only encourage their cruel game, Anna kept walking away. If she could just reach the main street, there would be safety in the crowd. She'd barely taken two steps when a massive, sweaty hand grabbed her by the shoulder and pushed her against the wall. The impact knocked the breath from her lungs.

"Get away from me!" she choked, trying to push past the man.

He forced her back against the wall, pinning her by the neck with one hand while the other savagely groped her. She clawed desperately at his arms, face, chest - anything within reach. It was like fighting cement. He hit her across the face. Her vision blurred. Tasting blood, Anna realised she could no longer move her jaw. She tried to scream but only a wet whining sound escaped her.

She pushed with all her strength. But he was too strong. The rest of the men formed a tight barrier around them, their hulking figures blocking out the world as they laughed. The man thrust her, face down, against the filthy asphalt. The graffitied bricks grated her skin as she fell. He pressed his monstrous body on top of her. She could feel his erection against her back. His hot, stinking breath heated her face as he tore her clothes, "Stop moving, bitch."

All she could do was cry. He turned her over, shredding her skin even more against the rough ground. She tried to kick him off. One of the other men kicked her. Hard. There was a loud, wet crack followed by sharp pain. Then nothing.

She couldn't feel her legs.

She couldn't feel anything.

She couldn't move. Or scream. Or breathe.

The men were still laughing. Still having their fun.

All she could do was stare at the moon and wait for it to be over.

After what felt like an eternity, the world faded into merciful darkness.

CHAPTER 8

Rise and Shine

Anna woke with a jolt, frigid metal pressed against her naked skin. She couldn't see anything. She felt drunk, or hungover. Maybe both. She couldn't remember how she'd gotten here. Wherever *here* was. She lifted her hands. More cold metal greeted her fingertips. There wasn't room to sit up. She was trapped. Worst of all, she couldn't find a heartbeat in her chest.

She must not be checking properly. Surely that was it. The alternative was...impossible. Trying not to panic, she focused on coaxing memories to the forefront of her mind. It was a familiar frustration, like when your keys aren't where you left them. Only much worse. Her memory had never failed her before.

Visions of shopping slumped begrudgingly into her mind. She remembered meeting Madam Oksana. Finn had saved her some tiny sandwiches but they'd gone bad. Dex had cooked her something...And they'd kissed. They'd done a little more than kiss but he'd shut things down. It had seemed important at the time but now, she didn't know why. She dredged more faded memories into view. Cassie arrived with pizza. There was drinking. And dancing. Then more drinking. More dancing. Blood on bricks. Fog shrouding the dance floor. The stench of beer. Strobe lights. Sweaty limbs. Then...nothing.
The more Anna tried to picture what happened, the thicker the swirling fog became.

"Help!" she yelled frantically, slamming her hands against the metal walls of her coffin-like prison.
"Coming," a muffled voice replied.

A loud click sounded and blinding light engulfed her.

"Morning, Sunshine!" A chipper voice reverberated in Anna's ears as the platform she was on slid out of the wall, "I'm Dr Singh but you can call me Ravi."

"Where am I?" rasped Anna. Her throat was like sandpaper.

"You're in hospital."

Anna pushed herself into a sitting position. Everything felt slow and forced, like moving underwater.

A dark-bearded man, wearing a lab coat and sneakers, leaned against a nearby autopsy table. He seemed disturbingly calm for someone who'd just discovered one of the bodies in his morgue was alive. *Am I alive?*

"What's going on?" Anna blinked as her eyes adjusted to the bright room.

"Like I said," answered Ravi, "You're in hospital."

"The morgue?"

"Yes."

"Why?"

Ravi's light expression faded, "What do you remember?"

Anna strained her mind again. She could remember eating pizza with Dex and Cassie, Dex's brother showing up at the club, Jedda making them shots, and then…"Nothing," replied Anna.

"Well," Ravi sighed, "I have good news, bad news, and depends-on-your-point-of-view news."

Anna stared blankly.

"The bad news," he began, "is that you died last night. I'm sorry."

Hearing the words spoken aloud sucked the air from Anna's lungs. How could she be dead? She was sitting up. She was talking and thinking. Just because she couldn't find her heartbeat didn't meant she didn't have one. She couldn't possibly be dead.

"The good news," Ravi continued, "is that you obviously didn't stay dead. It looks like a vampire has chosen to sire you, so you're in a transitional stage now."

Ravi paused as though he expected Anna to show some recognition. She was still wrapping her head around the whole *you're dead* thing. She was vaguely aware she should be freaking out. Her heart should be pummelling her ribcage but, of course, it wasn't beating so it couldn't pummel. She waited to feel paralysing anxiety shoot up her spine but it seemed her body was on strike. Realising she hadn't taken a breath for quite a while, Anna coughed and forced air into her disinterested lungs.

"I assume you've been spending time with vampires?" Ravi prompted.
"I…No?" Anna sputtered, "Are vampires even real?"
Ravi furrowed his brow. "Oh, I see."
He sat next to Anna on the mortuary tray, "Vampires are very real," he explained, "As is magic. You're talking to me right now with no heartbeat and no electrical activity in your brain. If there's a scientific explanation for your current state, no one's figured it out yet. So, yeah, *magic*. You must have ingested vampire blood before you died. It's healed your body and revived you. But the effects are temporary, which leads me to the *depends-on-your-point-of-view* news."
Ravi extended his hand for Anna to take. There was sad kindness in his eyes that told her to brace for another shock. She took his hand gingerly.

"As I mentioned, you're in a transitional stage right now," Ravi spoke in a well-practised bedside manner, "Your body is animated by magic, but it won't last. In a few hours, the magic will fade and your consciousness, or *soul* if you like, will leave your body for good. You'll be completely, and permanently, dead. If you don't want that to happen you'll need to drink human blood to complete the transformation. You'd be a vampire."
He paused for a few seconds, letting Anna absorb his words.

"I can't tell you what to do," he continued, "It depends on your beliefs and morals. But, you should know that you'll need to drink human blood regularly to stay *alive*. And I do mean alive because, contrary to popular belief, real vampires have hearts that beat, lungs that breathe, brains that fire neurons - the whole shebang."
He waited for Anna to show some form of comprehension. She nodded numbly.
"If you want to complete your transition," he continued, "I can supply you with some of the hospital's blood. If not, I'll help you prepare for the end. I'll give you some time to think about - "
"I want to be a vampire," whispered Anna.
Ravi raised his eyebrows.
"Are you sure?" he asked.

"Yes."

"Okay," he gave her hand a quick squeeze before releasing it, "I'll be back in a second."

Ravi left Anna to wade through her thoughts. She didn't know if she wanted to be a vampire, but she sure as hell wasn't ready to be dead. She closed her eyes. How did she get a vampire's blood in her system? How could vampires be real? How could magic be real?

Questions swamped Anna's mind but each new thought was weighed down by an overwhelming urge to sleep. The answers didn't matter. Anna was tired. The room was blurring around the edges. Everything was heavy. Little details from Anna's life were fading from her mind. Things she was sure she used to know...Did she have a cat when she was little or had she just wanted one? Were her mother's eyes green or blue? Was it *Buffy the Vampire Sire*? No. A sire meant something different. It meant...She used to know. Everything was sinking into murky depths.

Ravi returned with a blood bag, a small box and a clipboard of forms. "You'll need to sign these so the VA can sort things out with the cops and update your death certificate," Ravi explained, handing her the forms.

"VA?" Anna questioned, trying to control her brick-like hand enough to scrawl her name.

"The Vampiric Alliance," Ravi elaborated, "They're sort of a separate government for certain types of magical folk in the community."

"Right," Anna knew she should be paying attention, but it was impossible to focus.

"Looks like you're already starting to fade," Ravi said, pouring the blood into a beaker, "I'd recommend completing your transition sooner rather than later, if you're still sure."

Anna took the beaker and sniffed the murky crimson liquid. It smelt like rust. She closed her eyes and prepared to choke it down.

It's just medicine.

At first, the blood was completely tasteless.

But, by the second gulp, her tastebuds exploded back to life. The blood was rich and refreshing with a sweet, spicy kick. Her chest vibrated with rhythmic beats. A deafening rush pounded through Anna's ears. Her body was consumed by the tingling pinpricks of several trillion nerves waking up with renewed vitality. She gasped with delight. Fresh air flooded her lungs. She was alive. More alive than she'd ever felt before.

The ambient sounds of the hospital had changed. Among the sea of voices, Anna could now focus on distinct conversations, whispers and even heartbeats. Her vision had also improved. It was like a camera changing focus as it zoomed in. Even from across the room, she could differentiate the individual strands of thread in Ravi's lab coat. She could smell remnants of soap on his hands and traces of citrus on his breath.

"Did you eat an orange recently?" She asked.

Ravi laughed.

"Mandarin, actually," he replied, "About an hour ago. Glad to see you're feeling better. I wish normal medicine worked that fast."

Anna grinned, giddy with energy.

"What's next?" she asked, jumping off the stretcher. She'd meant to skip over to him but instead flew with such speed that, when she stopped, the inertia created a strong gust of wind that blew his hair back.

"Woah," he gasped, "Calm down!"

"Sorry!" she chuckled.

"You've got some new skills to get a handle on," he said, handing her the box, "There's some reading material in here that should cover most of it."

Anna pulled the lid off the box to find a set of medical scrubs sitting on top. She held them up in confusion. "Sorry," Ravi wrinkled his nose, "The clothes you came in with weren't, uh, salvageable."

"What do you mean?" Anna wasn't sure she wanted to know.

"I don't know if I'm the best person to tell you this," he said, "but your death was...violent."

Anna looked down. There were no cuts or bruises on her exposed limbs. A thin hospital gown covered the rest of her pale body.

"You won't find any damage now," Ravi reminded her, "The vampire blood took care of that. If your injuries hadn't been so bad you might have survived -"

"How bad?" Anna interrupted.

Ravi hesitated. That wasn't a good sign.

"Tell me," demanded Anna.

"Broken jaw," Ravi read from the clipboard in his hand, "Broken hip, severed spinal cord, severe bruising, abrasions to the skin, internal bleeding, and - I'm so sorry - the rape kit showed evidence of sexual assault from multiple men."

"I was raped?" Anna gasped, suddenly feeling repulsed by her own body.

"There's more," Ravi looked Anna in the eye now, "The men who attacked you...They were found... in bits."

"Bits?" Anna didn't know how much more weird news she could handle.

"It was like they'd been eviscerated on the spot," Ravi explained, "The cops were obviously baffled. I don't suppose you have any idea what happened there?"

Anna shook her head. Her ears were ringing. She knew she *should* care about the mysterious deaths of her attackers but it was just white noise in a blizzard of shocking news.

Besides, they attacked her. They killed her. *They raped her.*

She still couldn't remember anything but the list of injuries told a sickeningly clear story. Rage swelled in Anna's chest. Despite her caution, she'd never really thought she'd be attacked. That sort of things only happened to *other* women. Strangers on the news. Not careful women like Anna. Not the ones who followed all the rules.

"Would you like me to give you a few minutes to get changed?" Ravi's voice brought Anna back to reality.

"Uh, yeah. Thanks."

"Can I call anyone to come and get you?" he offered, "Normally your sire would be waiting for you but..."

"What's a sire?" questioned Anna. The meaning was on the tip of her tongue but she was still having trouble remembering things. Old information was taking its time to resurface from the depths of her mind.

"Whoever fed you their blood is, technically, your sire," Ravi explained, "Apparently, it creates a special connection, so sires are usually extremely selective about who they turn."

"Not for me, I guess," Anna sighed.

"In your case," Ravi mused, "I'd wager whoever gave you their blood was just trying to heal you but you were too far gone."

"Surely they'd know I died though," Anna reasoned, "That I'd turn."

"Maybe they weren't ready to be a sire," Ravi offered, "Or, maybe they didn't want to get involved after they saw what happened to your attackers."

"Could they have done it?" Anna asked, "The…eviscerating?"

"I've never heard of a vampire with that ability," Ravi shrugged, "It's a massive waste of blood, for one thing. It seems more like something a coven of unusually powerful witches might do."

So, witches were real too. Noted. Anna sighed and looked back into the box. It contained brochures and booklets as well as a plastic bag containing her glasses, phone, and wallet. In a small victory, she also spotted her shoes under the piles of paper.

"Do these explain magic?" Anna asked, holding up the brochures "Like, how it works and why it's a secret?"

"Oh, it's not a secret," corrected Ravi, "More like a very popular oversight."

Anna frowned. She'd spent a good deal of her life wishing magic was real. She would have noticed if it was being used openly.

"Are you familiar with the placebo effect?" Ravi asked, "It's a phenomenon in which the body starts to heal even if a person only *thinks* they are receiving treatment."

"Um, I guess?"

"Magic works a bit like that," he said, "Most people can't see magic because they're *certain* it isn't real. For example, you didn't think vampires were real before now, so I'm guessing you *couldn't* see the tell-tale fangs. Now, you'll be able to spot one a mile away."

He held an instrument tray up to Anna's face like a mirror. The tips of her canines protruded slightly past her upper lip. She touched them gently with her tongue.

"If this was made of silver you wouldn't see your reflection at all," Ravi said, "but it's aluminium so, tada!"

"Can you do magic?" Anna asked, hoping he'd give her a demonstration.

"No," Ravi shrugged, "I find it fascinating though."

Anna stared at the scrubs on the table. She needed time to process everything but she couldn't do that here. It was far too public, "I think I might get changed now."

"Of course," Ravi headed toward the door, "Come out when you're ready."

Anna changed into the scrubs. They were too big but at least the pants had a drawstring she could pull tight. She stepped into her flat leather shoes. Though they had been cleaned thoroughly, her newly heightened vampire senses could smell the remnants of blood in them. She opened the plastic bag and moved her phone and wallet into the pockets of the baggy scrubs. They sagged under the weight. She didn't know what to do with her glasses. Her vision was perfect now but the gold frames were part of who she was. A part she wasn't willing to lose just yet. She popped the lenses out and put them on, feeling slightly pathetic. The blurred rings in her peripheral vision were reassuringly familiar, like a fuzzy blanket.

She moved the reading materials into the plastic bag, wishing she had something bigger to carry them in. With a jolt, Anna realised she'd left her handbag, including keys to her apartment, at Dex's place.
Oh, shit! Dex and Cassie think I'm dead!
Anna whipped out her phone. She had to call them to let them know she was okay. Was she okay? *No. Not really.*
The phone wouldn't turn on. The screen was cracked and it, too, smelt of dried blood. *Fantastic.*

A small, pull-string satchel remained in the box. Anna hadn't noticed it earlier but, now that she held it in her hand, it felt important. As Ravi had said, she could see magic now. She relaxed her eyes, allowing them to change focus. Translucent waves of light rippled from the bag. She untied the satchel. A necklace fell onto her hand. The pendant felt warm despite the chill of the morgue. It featured an unnervingly familiar symbol - an ankh with rays emanating from the top. Putting on the necklace, a wave of cool air enveloped her. She felt safe. Protected.

"It's a sunlight sigil," Ravi explained when Anna joined him in the corridor. Doctors and nurses hurried past them, barely glancing in their direction.
"So I can't go outside without it?" Anna guessed. All the stories featuring vampiric lore had started to trickle back into her mind.
"Not unless you want to burn to death," Ravi shrugged.
"Would it work as a tattoo?" Anna asked.
"If a witch did it for you," nodded Ravi, "A lot of vampires prefer that option."
"Right," Anna nodded, distracted as she made alarming connection she'd just made, "Do I need to sign anything else before I go, or…?"
"Oh, no, you can go," Ravi gave a concerned smile, "But you can stay as

long as you want. You've been through a lot. There are councillors here if you'd like to talk to someone. Are you sure I can't call anyone for you? A friend or family member?"

"No, I'm fine," Anna forced a smile before remembering her phone was destroyed, "Actually, could you call me a taxi?"

CHAPTER 9

The Real World

Even with the protective charm around her neck, the sun was brutal. Anna could see raw energy crashing all around her in glowing waves. The barrier of the charm rippled like a weak forcefield. Keeping her safe. For now.
She drew her focus back to reality, ignoring the magic until it was nothing but a shimmer in her peripheral vision. She waved down her taxi as it pulled up to the hospital. The ride was short and mercifully quiet. *Thank god for non-chatty drivers.*

They pulled up to Dex's building, parking behind a large moving van. The main door was propped open. Glad she didn't have to buzz the intercom while standing in direct sunlight, Anna rushed into the elevator only to be met by a young couple standing over a pile of large boxes. The man asked how Anna's day was going as he hit the button to level five for her.
"Fine, thanks," she answered, following the script of social convention.
"Great! Have a good one," he replied, helping his partner lug the boxes onto the third floor. Anna almost laughed at how absurdly normal they were. They'd never know they'd just shared a lift with a vampire. They'd go about their day, their lives, in ignorant bliss of how horrible people in the world could be.

Muffled yelling washed through the corridor on Dex's floor. It grew louder as Anna approached the door to his apartment. She stopped short of knocking, closing her eyes to focus her heightened senses on the voices through the thick wood.
"ONE NIGHT!" Finn's voice boomed, "YOU COULDN'T KEEP HER SAFE FOR ONE NIGHT!?"
Anna had never considered how intimidating Finn could be.

"I THOUGHT SHE *WAS* SAFE!" Dex cried, "I DIDN'T KNOW SHE LEFT- "

"WHY NOT?" Finn interjected.

"I - what?" Dex stammered.

"WHEN SHE LEFT, *WHEN SHE DIED*," Finn's voice cracked, "Where were you?"

"I..." Dex stammered softly.

"What does it matter?" Cassie gave a whimpering sniff, "It won't change anything."

"If I'd been there," Finn muttered, "She'd be fine. She'd have been safe with me."

"You don't know that," Cassie's voice wavered.

"I fucked up." Dex's voice was hollow, "If I could go back, I'd have killed those fucking douchebags the second we set eyes on them. I'd never have let Anna out of my sight. It's all my fault."

"Yeah, it is," Finn growled.

"No, it's not!" Cassie interjected with a sniff, "Placing blame won't bring her back."

"So, what?" Finn barked, "Am I supposed to just forget about her then?"

"Of course not!"

"Then what..." Finn's voice cracked again, followed by low sobs, "what am I supposed to do?"

Anna had heard enough. She knocked on the door.

"Go away!" Dex shouted at the door.

"I need my bag," Anna shouted back.

Silence.

A pair of light footsteps ran toward the door. Dex opened it a crack, peaking cautiously through the gap. He looked different. His ears were longer and tapered into elegant points. He had two sharp fangs protruding from his mouth and his piercing blue eyes caught the light like a cat. Shock spread over his tear-streaked cheeks as he gazed at her. He pushed through the door and embraced her in a tight hug.

"How-?" He stammered, "Oh, who cares? Thank fuck!"

Though her suspicions that Dex was a vampire had been confirmed, Anna was disappointed. He was surprised to see her. He couldn't be the one who turned her.

The door swayed open. Finn stood in the middle of the room. Cassie was curled in a ball next to the bed. They gaped at Anna in a wide-eyed stupor. "Come inside," Dex held her arm like a child's security blanket, pulling her along.

"Anna?" Finn whispered. He looked like he was fighting a fever. His red, puffy eyes were from crying but his skin was also sallow and his balance wavered. He leaned too heavily on his crutches. Anna focused her hearing on his chest. His heart was hammering.

His breathing was shallow.

His eyes glazed over.

He fell forward.

With lightning speed, Anna caught him before he hit the ground. Finn's bulking, muscular form would normally have crushed her but, fortunately, her strength had significantly improved too.

"Finn?!" Anna gasped, lowering him softly to the carpet. She rested his head on her lap.

Finn's eyes fluttered, unable to focus, "I'm fine," he answered meekly.

"He's a werewolf." Cassie blurted, "Last night was the full moon so -"

"He's not meant to be up and about right now," finished Dex, "He needs to sleep it off."

Anna stroked Finn's hair as his eyes slowly closed, "Someone hurt you…" he mumbled, frowning, "Couldn't help…I lost you."

"I'm here" shushed Anna, "I'm not going anywhere.

His heartbeat calmed to a gentle rhythm.

"So," Dex spoke softly as he joined Anna on the floor, "What happened?"

Anna explained her recollection of the night before, skipping over the details of the attack itself. She couldn't remember that part anyway. It was just an imagined scenario she'd put together from Dr Ravi's report. Plus, if she started to break down, she'd never get the words out. Cassie and Dex seemed to know most of it already. They'd been there when the police arrived. They'd watched her body get taken away.

It helped to look at Finn's sleeping face as they recounted the parts she wasn't ready to process. His restful features gave her a sense of peace.

"How are you feeling now?" Cassie's voice was gentle.

"I don't know," Anna shrugged, "I'm trying not to think about it."

Dex was uncharacteristically quiet.

"Can I do anything to help?" Cassie offered.

"Tell me about magic?"

"What do you want to know?" Cassie ran a hand over her dark buzz-cut. Anna hadn't seen Cassie without a wig before. The pixie cut accentuated her strong cheekbones and deep, brown eyes. Dex was right, Cassie didn't need the wigs to look good.

"Dex is a vampire, Finn's a werewolf, what are you?"

"I'm a witch."

"Was I a witch too?" Anna felt silly even asking, "The doctor said I did magic that stops me from seeing it, which I don't understand, but that means I did a sort of spell...right?"

"Witches are always in control of their magic," Cassie smiled sadly, "You had something called the *Veil of Unseeing*. It happens to people when they're convinced, by a person or just society in general, that magic isn't real. Even though it's everywhere. You were probably brainwashed to believe every fantastical thing you saw was a lie or that it had a mundane explanation."

"And that made me stop seeing it?"

"Yes," Cassie replied, "It's a bit complicated but it doesn't make you a witch, sorry."

"Why didn't you guys tell me anything about all this?"

"We wanted to," Cassie put her hand on Anna's shoulder, "but we didn't think you'd believe us. I could have levitated your desk but you'd just have seen strings attached or something. If we'd told you that you were working with a vampire, a werewolf and a witch, *without being able to prove it...* Would you have believed us?"

"I guess not," Anna sighed.

"At least you know now," Cassie assured.

"So how did you become a witch?" Anna tried to hide her jealousy.

"My Dad was a witch," Cassie picked at the carpet, "he died when I was a baby but Mum made sure I knew about all his abilities. Mum's side of the family is mostly *Unseeing*, so I didn't have anyone to learn from when I was growing up."

"What about your Dad's side of the family?"

"They're all back in Japan," Cassie shrugged, "I don't even speak Japanese, so..."

"Was your mum, um, *Unseeing* too?" Anna hoped she was using the word properly.

"At first," Cassie nodded, "She wanted to believe, but only started seeing magic when she was pregnant with me."

"Does that mean there's a genetic component to magic?" Anna speculated.

"It seems that way," Cassie mused, "People who identify as *fae* definitely get their magic from genetics. Human magic is a little harder to track that way."

"Fae? As in fairies?" Anna looked from Cassie to Dex, waiting for him to laugh and tell her Cassie was joking. He wasn't even listening. He stared into the middle distance with a grim look on his face.

"Not exactly *fairies*," Cassie replied, "More like creatures from fairytales, myths and legends. The fantasy stories you and Finn love to read are all very loosely based in fact."

"How loosely?" Anna frowned.

"Fae folk look mostly human these days," Cassie explained, "No one's seen a real faerie in centuries but some people make a special effort to keep their bloodline strong. It's more obvious in races with distinct physical features too, like fauns and merrow. Though, you'd probably know them better as mermaids."

"Are those common?" Anna resisted the urge to run out to Dex's balcony and try to spot one in the river.

"Not in the city," Cassie replied, "You'll see plenty of tails and horns but merrow prefer coastal towns where there's easy ocean access."

"Are all Unseeing people human?"

"Officially, yes," Cassie sighed, "But you can often pick faerie traits in Unseeing people's ancestry. Like, those guys who attacked you would have been classified as *Unseeing Humans*, but it was obvious they had some troll in them."

"How do you know?" asked Anna.

"They were big and strong but cruel and dumb," answered Cassie. "So troll fits."

Anna tried to picture them but all she could see were fuzzy hulking blobs. "However" continued Cassie, "if they'd been massive but gentle and really into philosophy, they would probably have had some *giant* in their ancestry."

"What?" Anna laughed at the idea of a giant quoting Socrates, "You're messing with me, right?"

"Nope," Cassie shrugged, "Giants are chill."

"What about me?" Anna asked.

"You're pretty chill too," Cassie smirked.

"No-", Anna sighed affectionately, "Did I have any *fae-ish* traits?"

Cassie tilted her head, "I've noticed people forget your name a lot," she mused, "So you might have a touch of imp in you. They have magic that makes people forget them. Rumpelstiltskin was an imp. People say they're tricksters and like to be sneaky, but the whole *forget-me* thing could just be a defence mechanism against being hunted by predatory fae."

Anna crinkled her nose. She didn't want to be part imp. She'd been hoping Cassie would say she had the blood of something more flattering like a pixie.

"Or the forgetting-your-name stuff could just be bad luck," Cassie amended with a shrug.

"What about Finn?" Anna watched his broad chest rise and fall, "Is he part giant?"

"I can see how you'd think so," Cassie smiled, "but no. He's a druid. Technically he's a half-druid, half-dryad. But dryads are always female, so...druid. His family kept up with the *Old Ways*, so he's always known about magic."

"So his, uh, *classification* would be druid?"

"*Werebeast* druid, of the Tree Folk" Cassie corrected, "Werewolf is a subcategory of werebeast. It depends which animal you turn into."

"Oh, right," Anna looked down at Finn. He twitched in his sleep. Of all the times they had discussed the mechanics of magic in various fantasy worlds, he'd never mentioned magic was real in *their* world. Was that his big secret? If he'd been the one to tell Anna magic was real she probably would have believed him. Or would she? Maybe she would have thought he was unhinged or messing with her. Anna supposed it didn't matter now. She'd never have the opportunity to find out.

"Be right back," Dex muttered as he moved toward the door.

"Where are you going?" Cassie asked.

"Just...out," he answered, without looking back.

Anna and Cassie shared a look of confusion. Cassie shook her head and shrugged.

"Dex wasn't human before he turned, was he?" Anna touched her non-pointy ears.

"He was an elf," Cassie confirmed, "Tolkien's version of elves is fairly accurate. Tall, beautiful, graceful, clever and sometimes a touch pretentious."

Anna laughed.

"Unseeing humans with elven blood normally go into modelling or become dancers," Cassie explained, "But Dex comes from the Elven Empire, so he's pure-blood - or...he *was*."

"There's an Elven Empire?" Anna gaped.

"Most elves prefer to live separately from humans and other fae," Cassie replied, "Especially Underfae."

"Underfae?"

Cassie took a deep breath and looked at the ceiling.

"The fae community are split into High Fae and Underfae," she began, "Each side has its own government. As a vampire, you're Underfae. Finn's technically Underfae too because he's a werebeast. But, he's also part of the Tree Folk, which is a faction of High Fae. Unlike the elves, the Tree Folk don't care about purity of blood or whatever, so he's allowed to be both."

"Like a dual citizenship?"

"Basically, yeah," Cassie laughed.

"This is a lot," Anna's brain was buzzing.

"I know," Cassie gave Anna's hand a squeeze, "But it won't affect your day-to-day. Plus, I'm here whenever you need me. We all are."

Anna nodded and looked across the room to where her work clothes sat piled in a crinkled heap. It seemed a lifetime ago that she'd been in the office, living her normal life at her normal job with her normal friends.

"Why did you guys hang out with me?" asked Anna, avoiding Cassie's eyes.

"Hm?" Cassie yawned as she pulled herself onto Dex's bed.

"When I started working in the office," Anna clarified, "Why did you want to be my friend?"

Cassie gave Anna a weary smile.

"Because you seemed like a nice person," answered Cassie simply.

"But I was just a dumb Unseeing nobody," Anna frowned, "Wasn't it annoying to have me around? Having to hide things and talk in code?"

"We didn't," Cassie assured, "Not really. Magic doesn't define our personalities. Most of what we talked about had nothing to do with magic. And you could totally tell when we didn't share the whole truth. We're all terrible liars."

"The sleep study?" Anna smirked.

"Exactly," Cassie laughed as she sunk into one of Dex's pillows.

Dex shuffled back through the door looking exhausted. His eyes were pink and his cheeks were blotchy. Anna could smell the salt of tears on his clothes. He slumped to the floor next to Anna, resting his head on her shoulder.

"I'm sorry," he murmured.

"What for?"

"I wasn't there," he sniffed.

"It's not your fault," replied Anna.

"It feels like it is," he said, "I let my bullshit distract me. I abandoned you."

"Did you tell those guys to attack me?" Anna asked.

"Of course not," Dex lifted his head, "but -"

"Did you secretly feed me your blood?"

"No! But-"

"Then you had nothing to do with this," she said simply, "Stop apologising."

"Told you so," Cassie murmured, half asleep.

"I promised Finn I would keep you safe," Dex persisted, "He didn't like that I was dragging you out of your comfort zone to go clubbing. He said all the crazies come out on the full moon but I didn't listen. I figured just being with us, with me, was enough. But then, Cassie came back from the bathroom asking where you'd gone and I had no idea because I was so wrapped up in my stupid shit. I told myself you were fine, that you'd probably hooked up with some guy or something. Then suddenly there's an ambulance outside and police everywhere… I wasn't there. I wasn't there for you when you needed me and I'll never forgive myself."

"You're here for me now," she said softly, letting her eyelids droop, "that's what matters."

***

Anna woke to the smell of sizzling onions. She sat up on Dex's bed. Cassie and Finn were sleeping next to her. She wondered how Dex had managed to move her and Finn, particularly Finn, to the bed without waking anyone. "How long was I asleep?" whispered Anna. Dex turned from the stove.

"A few hours," he replied cheerfully, giving her his signature wink, "It's almost sunset."

Anna carefully extracted herself from the huddle.

"What are you cooking?" Anna looked at the mess of ingredients strewn across the benchtop.

"Breakfast scramble," he replied, throwing some minced beef into the saucepan.

"So vampires can eat normal food?" Anna asked.

Dex looked up from the pan, "We can but we don't need to. It's purely for the enjoyment."

"So you cook because…"

"It feels good in my mouth," he grinned at the innuendo.

"I should go home," said Anna, "I need a shower."

"Maybe don't go home just yet," replied Dex with a slight frown, "You said you have roommates, right?"

"Yeah."

"I have some things to show you first," Dex glanced at the bed then lowered his voice, "Like how to avoid eating your friends and roommates."

"I was fine with Cassie before," Anna argued. She hadn't been tempted to bite anyone. Surely movies had exaggerated a vampire's lust for blood.

"You weren't hungry before," Dex replied darkly, "Let me show you a couple of things before you go home. Please?"

"Fine," Anna could smell her sweat under her armpits, her face felt oily and the hospital's scrubs were rough against her skin, "Is it okay if I have a quick shower?"

"Of course!"

She grabbed her bags from the neat pile in the corner.

"Crap!" she thought aloud, "I don't have any underwear."

"Aren't you wearing any?" Dex chuckled, wiggling his eyebrows impishly.

"No, just the scrubs," Anna replied, distracted, "Apparently everything else was *unsalvageable*."

Dex's face dropped, "Shit," he said with a cringe, "I'm sorry."

Anna sighed. She was sick of hearing that word.

"Don't worry about it," she said, "I just…primarily I need a bra. My boobs are heavy and it's uncomfortable to walk around without support. The actual underwear I can live without, but I feel gross going commando."

Dex scanned his apartment for solutions. His eyes widened with an air of inspiration before settling on Anna an apologetic grimace.

"I have a solution," he said slowly, "I have a Bang Box-"

"A *what* box?"

"A box of things people have left behind after we…"

"Oh, no," Anna cringed.

"Beggars can't be choosers!"

"I don't want to wear someone else's underwear!"

"I washed them! They're clean! It's this or nothing."

"… Show me the box."

Dex presented her with a cardboard box filled with an interesting assortment of items including peacock feather earrings, frilly socks, stud belts, a pair of rhinestone-covered shorts and a single, pink cowboy boot. Anna shovelled through the selection, eventually finding a lace bra that was a cup size smaller than she needed.

Close enough.

She also found some grey boxer briefs that were two sizes too small and a black G-string that was, frustratingly, her size. She sighed and took the G-string and bra with the rest of her things into the bathroom.

The warm water felt incredible on Anna's skin. The fresh, fruity scent of Dex's body wash exploded in her nostrils as she applied a thick lather all over her body. Once all traces of the morgue had been scrubbed away, Anna towelled off and put on the Bang Box underwear.

Her breasts stretched the bra's fabric past its limits and some of her flesh pouted over the cups. The G-string made her feel as though she had a permanent wedgie, but it was better than going commando.

She unpacked her clothes from the Gracious Lace bag. Her work clothes smelled of sweat and were now unbearably stiff and scratchy. The dress, on the other hand, still carried hints of patchouli from the musky perfume of the shop. The smooth, emerald satin felt like liquid on her skin.

When she left the bathroom, Cassie and Finn were shovelling food hungrily into their faces. Finn still looked exhausted, but less pale than before. When he saw Anna, he dropped his fork and then, as he hastened to pick it up, spilled some of his food onto the floor.

"Crap, crap, crap! Sorry, Dex." Finn spluttered, his ears turning pink.

"No worries" replied Dex. He scooped a mixture of meat, onions, egg, cheese and potato into a bowl, then handed it to Anna with a spoon. She thanked him and began to eat.

"Wait, wait!" Dex exclaimed, snatching it back, "I nearly forgot!"

He pulled out a thermos and cracked open the lid. The spicy scent of fresh blood shot through the air. Anna's tastebuds cried out. Dex poured the thick liquid over Anna's food like gravy.

"Cheers!" Dex grinned, drinking the remaining blood.

Anna scoffed down her meal, then licked the bowl for good measure.

"Was that...human blood?" Anna whispered to Dex while the others finished their food.

"Yeah," Dex answered, "Animal blood isn't an option."

"How come?"

"It tastes awful and doesn't do anything to sustain us," Dex shrugged.

"How did you get that?" Anna pointed at the thermos in Dex's hand. She wasn't sure she wanted to know.

"I'll show you later," he smiled consiprationally.

Anna didn't know how to react. She didn't want to go around killing people for their blood but she had to survive. The practicalities of being a vampire were simpler in movies. The killing didn't matter because the characters weren't real. This was real.

"We should get going," Cassie announced, rinsing out her empty bowl, "You two have a busy night and Finn needs to recover properly."

"I'm fine," Finn mumbled.

"How long do you normally need to sleep after a full moon?" Anna asked.

"It doesn't matt-" Finn began.

"Usually it's *at least* 24 hours," Cassie interrupted, "and that doesn't take into account the additional stress his system's been processing."

"Okay, fine," conceded Finn in a huff, "Where's my leg?"

Dex snorted into his coffee. Anna hadn't noticed, but Finn's prosthetic leg had indeed been removed. His pants were long and loose, so it was easy to miss the fact that he had only one foot on the ground.

"It's here, mate," Dex grabbed the prosthetic from the nightstand and handed it to him.

Finn rolled up his pants to reveal a grizzled stump below his left knee. Anna muffled a gasp. She wasn't the only one who'd been transformed by a vicious attack. A terrifying vision of a snarling fanged beast pouncing on Finn forced its way into Anna's mind. Judging by his scars, it must have bitten his leg clean off while clawing to devour the rest of him whole.

Blinking back tears, Anna tried to clear the vision from her mind.

Finn finished securing the prosthetic to his leg, "Okay," he stood slowly, "I'm ready when you- Oh! Anna, are you okay?"
Everyone turned to stare at the hot tears streaming down Anna's face.
"Is it all just hitting you?" asked Cassie gently, "We can stay as long as you need."
"No, it's fine," Anna waved her hands dismissively, "Don't worry about it."
Anna wrapped her arms firmly around Finn, "Bye," she whispered, inhaling his sweet, earthy scent. He returned her hug with the gentle warmth of a fuzzy blanket. Of all the times she'd imagined Finn's embrace, none had been this tragic.
"Bye," Finn whispered back. Anna buried her face in his neck.
She could feel his heart beating against hers. She didn't want to let go.
He stroked her hair.

"Seriously, we can stay if you want," Cassie offered.
"No, no, I'm okay," Anna pulled back.
She gave Cassie a quick, tight hug and then retreated to Dex's bed.

Once Cassie and Finn were gone, Dex turned to Anna, "I may not be your sire but I'm going to make sure you've got a handle on the basics before you go home. Consider me your fairy godmother! *Vampy demon-father*? Whatever, you get it. Are you up for some Vamp 101?"
"We're not going to hurt anyone, are we?" Anna felt queasy at the thought.
"Not unless someone starts some shit," he punched his palm, "It'll be fun, I promise."
Anna forced a smile, grabbing her handbag. She instinctively checked her phone. The dark, cracked screen stared back. She threw it aside with a huff. Dex optimistically plugged it into his charger, but after several minutes it remained unresponsive.
"I think it's a goner," he sighed, "Sorry."
"Oh well," she sighed, adjusting her lens-free glasses.
Just another thing I've lost.

CHAPTER 10

Intro to Vampirism

The first stop on Dex's list was only a block from his apartment. It was a small shop with a blacked-out gallery window featuring large, gold lettering that said *The Black Quill*.

A bell on the door chimed gently as they entered. Incense wafted through the air and antique wooden shelves filled with strange trinkets lined the walls. Anna briefly wondered if she was about to have her future read by a psychic. *It's a bit late for that.*

A man appeared from behind one of the shelves. He wore skinny jeans with suspenders. His shirt was embroidered with the name "Trent".

He greeted them with an earthy voice, "What can I do for you?"

"We've got an appointment," Dex replied.

"Right," Trent smiled, "Cassie's friends. Follow me."

He led them through thick velvet curtains into a tattoo studio. It was brightly lit, but the black wallpaper and dark flooring made the space feel intimate. Portraits of silhouettes hung along the walls in round golden frames. Three padded tables were arranged evenly across the room, each with an accompanying ink station.

"We've got the place to ourselves tonight," announced Trent, gesturing dismissively at the other stations, "Which of you is getting the Sunshield Sigil?"

Dex looked at Anna expectantly. She felt a surge of annoyance that neither he nor Cassie had thought to ask if she wanted a tattoo. Tattoos were a big deal. They were permanent. But, then again, so was burning to death. There was no guarantee the amulet around her neck wouldn't break at an inopportune moment.

"Me," answered Anna, fiddling with her pendant. "I've got this amulet, but..."

"You need something more reliable." Trent finished knowingly, "Sigils are my specialty, so you're in very capable hands. Any idea where you'd like it?"

Anna looked to Dex, who raised his eyebrows and shrugged. She'd never planned on getting a tattoo. This was the sort of thing she would normally spend a good deal of time researching. She'd look at samples of where other people had gotten tattoos and read reviews of the pros and cons for each spot. This was all happening too quickly. She wished she could hit pause and come back later. But this had to be done now.

She had to make a decision.

She didn't want it to be anywhere too obvious.

She didn't want to see it every time she looked in the mirror.

She decided the back of her neck was a logical spot. She could cover it with her hair if she needed to, and the sigil would literally sit between her and the sun's rays as she ducked away from them.

The process wasn't as painful as Anna had anticipated. It was less of a stabbing pain and more of a prickling sensation. It was nothing compared to a leg-waxing session. Trent murmured quiet incantations as he worked. Images floated into Anna's mind of the sigil doing its job. She was walking in the sunlight, relaxed and comfortable. Safe. She could tell the thoughts came from Trent's mind, rather than her own. It was unnerving at first but she quickly got used to the sensation.

"Are you okay here if I dip out for a bit?" Dex grimaced at his phone, "Arik keeps texting me. He's still in town. It'll be faster if I just go see him."

"Sure," Anna had forgotten he was there.

Curtains rustled, followed by a gentle chime announcing Dex's departure from the shop. Trent's incantations stopped shortly afterwards, "I'm just finishing the artwork now."

A few minutes passed with only the gentle buzzing of the tattoo pen to break the silence.

"So," said Trent softly, "What made you decide to turn? Cassie didn't tell me much on the phone."

"I didn't." Anna replied, "Decide, that is. I mean, obviously I *am* a vampire... I got attacked and I guess I had vampire blood in my system. So I came back."

"Intense," Trent replied with a low whistle.

"Yeah," Anna didn't know what else to say.

"So, that guy you came in with," Trent said in a low voice, "He didn't force you into this? I know he's Cassie's friend, but she can be overly trusting sometimes and a lot of seemingly charming vampires turn out to be predators."

"Dex isn't like that," assured Anna, "He's just as upset about all this as anyone."

"That's good," said Trent, "Not good he's upset, but...you know."

"Yeah, thanks."

"We're all done here, take a look."

As Anna sat up, Trent took a large mirror and angled it against the one attached to his ink station so she could see the back of her neck. She was surprised at how much she liked it. The tattoo was less obtrusive than she'd expected it to be. It was much smaller than Dex's, only about five centimetres in height, but it was beautifully intricate. It reminded Anna of a Celtic knot.

"It's lovely," she smiled, "Thank you."

"You're welcome." Trent beamed, "And it's already healed so you don't need any special products to care for it. That's one good thing about being a vampire, at least."

Anna hopped off the table and reached for her bag.

"What do I owe you?"

"Nothing, Cassie paid in advance." Trent replied, handing Anna his business card, "But if you want any other ink, enchanted or otherwise, hit me up."

She made a mental note to check Trent's portfolio. She still didn't see herself as a *Tattoo Person* but the idea of what other magical tattoos might do intrigued her.

***

Inhaling the fresh night air, Anna felt rejuvenated. The night seemed cooler than it had before. Perhaps the sigil was already doing its job. After all, the

moon was bouncing the sun's light back to Earth. Logically, the moonlight should warm her skin more than usual. Intending to check the weather app on her phone, she reflexively reached into her bag. *Damn.*
With no way to contact Dex, she lingered awkwardly on the pavement.

The street was quiet. The other shop fronts were dark and lifeless. Thumping music and the rumble of crowds echoed softly from the distant party strip. It was unnerving to think that less than twenty-four hours ago she'd been heading into that ruckus. Happy and ignorant. Human. Alive.

"Sorry," Dex appeared next to her, "Were you waiting long?"
"We just finished." Anna showed Dex the completed tattoo.
"Perfection!" Dex exclaimed, running a finger over the design "Do you like it?"
"I love it," she smiled.
Dex grinned. His fangs seemed to shine brighter under moonlight.

"Oh, come on!" he sighed, taking out his buzzing phone, "If that's Arik again I'm going to- Oh, wait. It's just a message from Finn…Wants to know how things are going."
"Tell him to go back to bed!" Anna didn't want him to suffer because of her.
Dex chuckled, shaking his head as he typed.
"Can you also tell Cassie I'll pay her back for the tattoo?" Anna asked, feeling like a child, "I *really* need a new phone."
"But I love being your messenger boy!" Dex laughed, hitting send, "Are you ready for Stage Two of your vampire orientation?"
"Maybe?" Anna narrowed her eyes apprehensively.
"It might solve some of your phone withdrawal," teased Dex.
"How?"
"You'll see," he winked, "But first, we need a change of scenery. Fancy a jog?"

He extended his arm to Anna with a regal bow. Though Anna had never been one for physical activity, she had a feeling this was going to be fun. She took Dex's arm and he pulled her forward gently, building speed until the world around them blurred and air rushed past Anna's face. In less than a minute they had travelled over a bridge and through the city, coming to a stop at the Botanic Gardens.

A popular picnic spot during the day, the gardens were now dark and quiet.

"Can we do that again?" Anna laughed.

"All in good time," Dex chuckled, "Can I do my lesson plan first?"

"Fine, fine." Anna conceded.

"Each vampire is different," Dex began, his accent making him sound like a fancy professor, "Depending on your bloodline, also known as a *clan*, you can develop some pretty impressive skills over time. None of us can do what is considered *real magic*, like rituals and spellwork. But we have super-senses, superior strength and speed. Plus, we can do cool stuff like crawling up walls, hypnotising people and using animals as messengers."

"How is that not *real magic*?" Anna frowned.

"In the community of spellcasters, we're thought of as the *subjects* of a spell. So, our talents are seen as *side-effects* rather than talent."

"Who did the spell that created vampires?"

"Each clan's line is named after an ancient faerie," Dex scrunched his nose, pondering his answer, "I assume that means they each did some mad necromancy to create the first vampires...but who knows."

"And...hypnotising people?" Anna raised an eyebrow, "Did you ever do that to me?"

"No." Dex said seriously, "I don't hypnotise people. Consent is important and mucking with people's minds can lead you down a nasty path. I thought we could start with the animal one. It's great because it only works on *willing* creatures."

"How do we start?" Anna asked, keen to do some magic. Even if it wasn't considered real magic.

"First we need a willing creature to *come hither*," he winked, "There are plenty of animals around so it's just a matter of reaching out with your mind and asking for help. Give it a try."

Anna closed her eyes and thought about all the nocturnal animals that might live in these gardens. Ringtail possums, fruit bats, barn owls, green tree frogs, mice and rats. She imagined all of them listening to her from their various burrows and branches and, as politely as she could, asked for their help.

"Woah!" Dex gasped.

Anna opened her eyes to see a crowd of nocturnal animals gathering in front of her.

"What do I do now?" she whispered.

"I've never seen so many volunteers," he chuckled, "You're a natural!"

"Dex!" All the tiny eyes were staring at Anna expectantly.

"Okay!" Dex laughed, "If you needed an animal hoard, you'd ask all these little guys for help. But, as we're just sending one simple message, focus on the one you want to use and dismiss the rest."

Anna spotted a fruit bat whose red fur reminded her of Finn's hair. She asked it to stay and help her. It nodded. Anna smiled at the remaining group of animals, mentally thanking them for coming. The creatures scampered back into the darkness as the bat approached.

"Now," said Dex, "I'm going the other side of the park. I want you to think of a message to send me, then ask the bat to send me that message. You might have to picture me so it knows who to look for."

Dex disappeared in a burst of air. Anna looked at the bat. The bat looked at Anna expectantly.

"Do you have a name?" She asked the bat.

The bat tilted its head looking confused.

"Would you like one?"

It nodded.

"What's your favourite food?" she asked.

The bat blinked as an image of a large, juicy mango appeared in Anna's mind.

"I see," she smiled, "How about we name you after my favourite type of mango, Calypso?"

The bat nodded enthusiastically and began to fly happily around her head. Anna laughed.

"Can you tell Dex your name is Calypso?" She pictured Dex in her mind and the bat flew out of sight. About a minute later, Calypso reappeared.

Anna saw Dex in her mind's eye, he laughed and bowed to the bat.

"Delighted to make your acquaintance, Calypso," he said, "Could you please tell Anna she's a natural at this?"

The bat landed on the grass and chirped happily. Dex reappeared by Anna's side.

"How about a bigger challenge?" he suggested, "Try sending something to Cassie."

Anna pictured Cassie and asked Calypso to send a message of thanks to her for organising her tattoo. Calypso circled Anna to get a visual of the tattoo before disappearing into the night sky.

"See?" said Dex, sitting on the ground, "There's good stuff about being a vampire."

"Yeah," Anna replied, joining him on the soft grass. "But what about the bad stuff?"

"Like being dead?" Dex sighed, "Only being able to tan from a bottle?"

"And…drinking blood."

"Oh, that's not so bad."

"It's not?"

"I'll show you." Dex sprang to his feet and offered his hand once more.

Anna didn't reach for it this time.

"You said we weren't going to hurt anyone," she said.

Dex's smile faded. He knelt next to her.

"I have never hurt someone for their blood, Anna," he said solemnly.

"Then how-"

"Let me show you."

"…Okay," Anna took Dex's hand, allowing him to help her to her feet.

"Race you to City Hall!" he winked, then disappeared in a blur.

Anna kicked off the ground with a little more gusto than she'd intended and found herself flying over the treetops. She landed, cat-like, near the garden's entry gate just in time to spot Dex rushing past. She bolted toward the centre of the city, fast as the wind, laughing as she dodged the slow-motion people on the streets. None of them seemed to notice two vampires weaving through them. In seconds, Anna stood between the bronze lions outside City Hall.

"Guess it's a tie," Dex mock-pouted, "Follow me."

He led Anna around the block and then through automatic doors under a sign that read *Lifeblood - Donor Centre.*

"A blood bank?" Anna frowned, "Don't hospitals need that blood to save lives?"

"Giving some of it to the vampire population *does* save lives," Dex shrugged, making his way to the reception counter, "Besides, the VA - that's the *Vampire Alliance* - has a deal with them."

"Do they give vampire blood to hospitals in exchange for human blood?" Anna recalled Dr Ravi telling her vampire blood could heal injuries.

"I don't think so," Dex mused, "Most vampires think of their blood as too *sacred* to share around willy-nilly. If a patient dies after being given vampire blood, the donor would become a sire. They'd feel a connection to the patient for the rest of their lives. That's a big commitment."

"Do you think my sire can feel me?" Anna wondered aloud.

"They'd have to," Dex put his arm around Anna's shoulder, "We'll find them. Don't worry."

A clean-shaven man smiled placidly at them from behind the reception counter, "How can I help you?"

"We need a red envelope, please," said Dex authoritatively.

The man raised his eyebrows. He seemed intrigued by the request but didn't question them further. He simply opened a drawer to his left and withdrew a large, sealed envelope.

It was rich scarlet with a metallic sheen and had a wax seal with a letters VA imprinted on it. Dex took the envelope, ushering Anna to sit in the chairs furthest from the counter. He opened it, extracting a brochure and form. The brochure was advertising an app, which would allow Anna to have blood delivered *"any time anywhere"*.

Without a phone, however, she had to fill out the form and elect when and where she wanted her deliveries to go.

"Did you notice anything about him?" Dex asked quietly.

"Hmm?" Anna scribbled her address on the form.

"The receptionist? Notice anything?"

"No?"

"Take another look."

Anna scanned the man for abnormalities. He had short brown hair and several pimples on his chin. His shirt had a few creases in it but seemed clean enough. He seemed completely normal.

But then she saw it. A hazy mirage hovered around the man's head. She relaxed her eyes, allowing the magic to appear more distinctly. The barely perceptible cloud covered his eyes and ears like a helmet.

"What's wrong with him?" she asked.

"You used to look like that," Dex whispered, "It's the *Veil of Unseeing*. His is thicker than yours was. I guess he's not as open-minded as you were."

"That's so weird." Anna stared. The translucent fog swirled like oil in water. When the man glanced up, she quickly returned her focus to the form in her hands.

"So he has no idea what we are?" Anna muttered from the side of her mouth.

"None," replied Dex, "I bet he's desperate to know what these red envelopes are for."

"Maybe he doesn't care."

"You think?" Dex smirked quizzically.

Anna shrugged, filling out payment details and then signing the form before resealing it in the envelope, as per the instructions, "We process heaps of forms in our office, but I wouldn't have a clue what any of those are for."

"Fair point."

Anna handed the red envelope to the man, who took it from the room and returned a few seconds later with a tall box wrapped in black paper with gold ribbon.

"For you," the receptionist gave a well-practised smile, handing the box to Anna.

"Thanks," she smiled back. The box was cold to the touch.

She waited until they'd left the building to open it.

Presumably a vampire starter pack, the box contained another Sun Sigil amulet, a guidebook of VA-affiliated venues across the city, and a heavy red thermos. She unscrewed her first order of blood hungrily, taking several massive gulps. The flavours danced on her tongue in a giddy frenzy. Sweet then salty, bitter with hints of butter, sour then sweet again.

"Mmm," Anna licked her lips, "Do you want some?"

"I'm alright, thanks," smiled Dex, absently looking at his phone.

"So, you've never taken blood directly from a person?" Anna reaffirmed.

"I didn't say that," Dex replied. He walked slowly down the street.

"You said you've never hurt anyone- "

"When we bite people," he explained, "it puts them in a euphoric state. They're immobilised with bliss. Some people get addicted to it."

"So, you...?" Anna frowned.

"I occasionally drink blood straight from the vein," Dex shrugged, "but it's always consensual and everyone involved enjoys themselves. Plus, rubbing a dab of my blood on their bite marks heals them like nothing happened. Our blood can give people a little high but it's nothing like our bite."

"Is fresh blood better than this?" Anna sloshed the remaining blood back and forth in the insulated bottle.

"Oh, yeah."

"Why don't you always feed on people then?"

"It turns a simple meal into a whole social endeavour," Dex sighed, "It would be like needing to have sex before you can fall asleep. Sounds fun until you've had a long day and just want to pass out."

Before she could respond, a tingling sensation tickled the back of Anna's hand. A thin line of blue ink traced words across her skin as though written by an invisible hand.

Love the tatt & the bat!
No payback required.
Xoxo, C

"Show-off," Dex rolled his eyes affectionately.

"I can't do that sort of magic, can I?" Anna surmised.

"I'm afraid not," Dex replied, "I'll show you some of the other cool stuff we can do. But not tonight. I'm beat. How are you feeling?"

"Okay," Anna wasn't sure if she was being honest or not, "Is there any other major stuff I should know?"

Dex looked pensively toward the sky, "Even though our hearts are beating and we breathe and stuff. We don't *have* to."

"What?" Anna coughed.

"Like, if you're underwater or something," Dex elaborated, "You can stop breathing and you'll be fine. Or if you need to play dead, you can make your heart stop by, like, focusing."

"Doesn't that stop your brain from working?"

"If you do it for too long," Dex nodded, "But then you lose consciousness and everything starts up again automatically, so it's fine."

"Good to know," Anna couldn't imagine how that could ever be useful.

"Do you have any questions for me?" Dex asked, "Stuff I've missed? I know you're into those stories with fake vampires in them. I can help separate fact from myth."

"Do we sparkle in the sun?" Anna joked.

"Only when body glitter is involved," laughed Dex.

"Do crosses and holy water hurt us?"

"Depends on your faith," Dex answered more seriously, "If you believe in a particular god and that *He, She, or They* would smite a vampire, then any symbol of your faith will have some negative effect. I'm an Atheist so I can swim in holy water and be fine."

Anna nodded.

"What about garlic?"

"Very tasty."

Anna's strained her memory for any storybook lore she'd missed, "Does running water negate our powers?"

"Nope." Dex sneered, "That one comes from a self-righteous delusional myth. In the old days, vampires were seen as *wretched, disease-ridden abominations*. Running water is less likely to carry diseases than stagnant water, so people thought the *purity* of rushing rivers made us weak. It didn't help that most people at the time, vampire or not, couldn't swim and were therefore cautious around rivers. The idiots applied the same logic to witches and anyone else they didn't like."

"So, when they tortured women during the witch trials?" Anna asked, "*If she drowns, she's innocent-*"

"*And if she floats, she's a witch,*" Dex affirmed, "Yeah, those pathetic dickheads killed a bunch of innocent people, mostly women, just to feel superior."

"What's new?" Anna grimaced.

"Good point," he swallowed, "So...you really can't remember what they did to you?"

"Nope," Anna knew she should be grateful but none of this felt real without the memories of how it all began. What if she'd seen her sire during those last vital moments?

"Are you okay?" Dex looked at her critically.

"I- yeah, it's a lot," Anna sighed, "I just need to process everything."

"I wish-" Dex sighed, "I wish I was better at this. At helping."

"You've been a huge help!" Anna insisted.

"Not really," he grimaced, "You could have figured this stuff out on your own. Your sire is supposed to connect with how you're feeling and help balance it out. They can keep you calm and stuff. I can't do that."

"I don't need you to," Anna took his hand, "I'm okay. I just need time to wrap my head around everything."

"Let's call it a night, then," Dex put his arm around Anna, "How about I walk you home?"

They took a scenic route along the river, talking about fashion, makeup, and anything that wasn't related to magic or death.

"Thanks for tonight," she hugged Dex, "I don't know what I'd do without you."

"You might be better off," he joked wearily, "G'night, Anna."

CHAPTER 11

New Me

As Anna slid the key into the lock of her apartment, a sobering thought occurred to her.

What if I can't enter without being invited?

She'd forgotten to ask Dex about one of the most common pieces of vampiric lore! She couldn't remember if he had invited her into his place. Even if he hadn't, as a vampire who lived alone, the rule might not apply. Why hadn't she asked him about it? She'd remembered to ask about *running water* but not this?!

She opened the door and, holding her breath, stepped over the threshold. Nothing happened. With a sigh of relief, she rushed to her bedroom, closed the door, and collapsed on her bed. Finally alone.

No one was giving her concerned looks and well-meaning pity.

No one was waiting for her to fall apart.

There was no one to hold herself together for.

She began to sob uncontrollably.

She'd died. *DIED!*

And not in a romantic, vampire movie way. She'd died in a dirty alleyway, broken and violated. The very thought of it made Anna gag. Had they killed her first? Or did she die from the pain? Would the memory of it help her accept what happened or make everything a million times worse? She imagined every possible scenario of how things might have gone down, wishing none of it was true. But one of the scenarios had to be right. The report was clear. She cried until she was gasping for air, then laughed savagely, remembering she *didn't need to breathe.*

Feeling numb, she dragged herself into the shower, sitting on the tiles while the cool water rained down. She lost track of how long she stayed there, staring into the void. Event after she'd turned off the water, she couldn't bring herself to stand. Her skin was dry by the time she dragged herself out of the glass cubicle. A gaunt reflection grimaced at her from the mirror. Realistically, she was just as pale as always but knowing she'd died emphasised the corpse-like pallor. *Weren't vampires meant to be beautiful?* Anna didn't feel beautiful. She felt like a filthy broken doll, ready for the trash.

She lay on her bed, willing herself to get some rest. She managed to drift off for a few minutes at a time, only to jolt awake with terrifying visions assaulting her vision. Trolls chased her through a maze of infinite graffitied alleyways. Laughing men exploded into blood and viscera. Fog swallowing everything and everyone. She was lost. Alone.

***

Morning light barged into her room like an entitled teen. Too exhausted to return to her nightmares, and sick of watching her ceiling fan spin, Anna got dressed. Her jeans were stiff and uncomfortable. Her whole wardrobe sucked. Why had she tolerated these ugly, uncomfortable clothes for so long? She squashed everything except her green dress into garbage bags and threw them in the basement dumpster.

She emerged from the building into blistering heat. For a terrifying moment, Anna feared her tattoo wasn't working. She relaxed her vision to see the magic glimmering around her. The sigil was protecting her, just as it was meant to. Its shield cast a translucent blue layer across her skin. Rays of light crackled and dispersed as they made contact with it.
She closed her eyes and refocused her hearing. A radio in someone's car announced *"Today's going to be a real scorcher with the Brisbane area reaching highs of 40°C! Can you believe it's still winter? Make sure to bring your brolly, though, because storms are on their way..."*

Anna groaned. She'd intended to run to the city. The rush of wind in her face would have been a welcome refresher but the sun was burning away what little energy she had left. Keeping to the shadows, Anna dragged herself to the bus stop. It was only a few blocks but the journey was more draining with every step. Collapsing onto the sheltered bench, Anna focused on her breathing until the bus finally pulled up. She had never been more grateful for the invention of air conditioning. She rushed to the back where she could sit directly under a vent, drinking in the cool air. It reeked of dust and petrol but she didn't care. Anything was better than the inferno outside.

Her stomach rumbled threateningly. She'd left her thermos in the fridge and now she was surrounded by humans. Panic tightened her chest. The craving for blood forced Anna's focus onto the necks of her fellow passengers. Miraculously, however, the thought of biting into any of them disgusted her. From the man who had sweat and dirt stuck to his gritty beard stubble to the woman whose perfume reeked of poisonous chemicals, Anna gagged at the thought of pressing her mouth against any of them.

Closing her eyes, Anna distracted herself with the memory of a conversation she'd had with Finn months ago.
"Being a vampire would be cool," she'd asserted, "You'd get to be beautiful and mysterious and live in a beautiful gothic castle, surrounded by a haunted forest..." Why did reality have to ruin everything?

Once in the city, Anna scurried to the sanctuary of the shops. Throngs of people were taking advantage of the latest sales. About a quarter of them had obvious faerie features. Wings, tales, horns, and even hooves. Whatever these creatures were, they went about their day with the same casual disinterest in each other as everyone else. Anna wondered what each of them would have looked like if she'd seen them a week ago. The wings had probably looked like backpacks. The horns had probably looked like hats. The hooves were probably stilettos.

Choosing a new phone took no time at all. They were all the same except for the logos on the back. She bought an updated model of the one she'd had before. The cases, on the other hand, ranged from purely decorative to army-grade. Anna took over an hour to decide which one would suit her new lifestyle best. In the end she went with a heavily discounted "indestructible" case. She assumed it had been marked down because it was pastel pink - too chunky for the girly customers, too girly for rugged customers. Feminine yet indestructible. *Life Goals.*

When Anna left the store, the sticky, suffocating heat had intensified under

91

a suddenly overcast sky. The city had pulled a blanket over itself and only the imminent downpour would break the fever.

Huge drops plummeted from the sky as Anna scurried down an empty side street. The cool water exploded on the cement like liquid grenades. Anna had a sudden urge to open her arms and let it drench her, but she ducked under an alcove in the bricks to keep her new purchases dry.

The entry to Gracious Lace was just across the road. The raindrops were getting smaller but more frequent, indicating the deluge would not be over soon. Taking this as a sign, Anna dashed into the building, climbing the stairs with unexpected ease before entering the shop.

Madame Oksana greeted her with the warmth of a doting grandmother.

"Welcome back, my dear!" She exclaimed. Her Ukranian accent seemed stronger now, "Oh, but you've changed!"

"Yes, I-, " Anna was startled to see the shopkeeper had changed too. Her eyes were three times their previous size and had narrow frog-like pupils. Unlike Dex's ears, which pointed subtly upward, Madame Oksana's stretched outwards with exaggerated length and sagged down at the tips.

"I've had a big weekend." Anna finished.

"Your *Veil* has lifted!" Oksana gushed.

"Yes," confirmed Anna, "This is the new me, I guess."

"Not yet!" Oksana held up a finger, "But that is why you are here, yes? Come, come…"

Anna spent a good chunk of her savings on new clothes. There was a strange exhilaration in it. She wasn't buying things she was *supposed* to wear, she was buying things she *wanted*. She no longer cared if her clothes attracted the wrong sort of attention or invited critical judgement. She'd played it safe her whole life and she'd still ended up dead in an alley. She wasn't about to waste her second chance at living.

"I've put everything in a *special* bag," beamed Oksana with a wink, "Now you are the vampire, I do not need to hide such wonders! But the magic only works once, so don't unpack until you're home, yes?"

"Right," smiled Anna, taking the small boutique bag which somehow contained a full wardrobe of clothes. "So…you don't mind being around me? Or Dex? You're not worried we're dangerous?"

"I am getting all kinds here," Oksana waved her hands dismissively, "It is the *who* that makes the danger, not the *what*."

"What kind are you?" Anna asked, "If that's not a rude question."

"Not at all!" Oksana beamed, "I am a gnome. We are quite good at making things."

"That's an understatement," grinned Anna. She glanced over the remaining racks of handmade clothes, "Your work is incredible!"

"Thank you, my dear, you are too kind," blushed the gnome, "If you need more shoes, I have a cousin..."

***

Anna's wardrobe wasn't as full as it had been but each new piece was exquisite. She smiled, running her hand over the collection of soft fabrics. Then, returning to more practical matters, Anna unpacked her new phone. She'd salvaged the SIM card from the broken one and, hoping her blood hadn't reached damaged the chip, held her breath to see if it still worked.

The phone buzzed as several notifications arrived at once. Starting with the oldest, Anna read through her messages:

Cassie: *Where'd you go? I can't see you*
Cassie: *??*

Dex: *Hey gurrl, did you meet a special someone? ;)*
Dex: *Cassie's freaking out, holla back!*

Cassie: *Seriously, where are you?! We're worried!*
Dex: *Okay not funny, plz let us know ur safe*

Finn: *Cassie left a message saying something's happened but she won't say what. I could hear sirens. Are you okay?*
Finn: *????*
Finn: *Are you okay?*

Finn: *I'm on my way.*

Finn: *Please be okay.*

{UNKNOWN}: *Thank you for registering with 'BloodBank' by the Vampire Alliance (VA). To ensure your delivery preferences are up to date,*

please download the app via https:bit.ly/3Ceo0aG
Reply STOP to opt out.

Mum: *Hi honey, sorry I missed you. Just calling for a chat. How's work going? Let me know when you're free. Love you! Stay safe xoxo*

It had been a couple of weeks since Anna had talked her mother. They usually talked every month or so just to check in. What was Anna meant to say this time? *Hey, Mum, guess what? I died.*

She wasn't ready to have that conversation with her mother. She didn't even want to admit she'd been attacked. Her mother had always been protective. She'd made sure they knew all the risks of going out and how to avoid putting themselves in danger.

How could she admit that she'd wandered, alone, into an empty alleyway? She'd been attacked, *killed*, in one of the safest cities in the world. The statistical probability of what happened was *astronomically low,* yet she'd somehow managed it.

Anna knew, rationally, that none of this was her fault but she couldn't silence the tiny voice in her head that told her otherwise.

You were dressed like a slut.

You went into that alley alone.

What did you expect?

Imagining the conversation made her stomach knot. Anna couldn't bring herself to burden her mother with such devastating news. Not yet, at least. Not while Anna was still reeling from it herself. She briefly considered talking to Liz first, or her Dad, but didn't want to force either of them into keeping secrets. Not to mention, if she wanted to tell the whole story, Anna would have to convince them that magic was real without being able to prove it.

Anna gritted her teeth and hit the call button. It rang twice before her mother picked up.

"Hi, honey! How's it going?" her mother's voice echoed through the speaker. The news was playing loudly in the background.

"Yeah good," Anna answered automatically, "How are things there?"

"Oh, you know,'" her mother sighed. "Gordon's started another project in the shed. He's so busy, you'd hardly know he's retired. Meanwhile, I've

just been catching up on my shows and reading."
"Any recommendations?"

Anna hadn't realised how scripted these catch-ups had become until now. They talked about the latest in literature, current events, upcoming holiday plans and the weather. It shouldn't have been surprising that, after years of having nothing interesting to say, her mother didn't notice when Anna lied about being fine. But she wasn't fine. A childish part of Anna wished her mother could somehow feel it.

After the call ended, Anna sought distraction by scrolling through social media. The videos of puppies helped a bit. There was one of a panda rolling down a hill that made her smile. Anna wondered if there were any magical creatures she could see now that'd been invisible, or appeared as different animals, before.

Finn: *Hey! You're online!*
Anna: *Yup! New phone who dis? ;P*
Finn: *Haha :D*
Finn: *Do you have the same number?*
Anna: *I do! I just saw your last messages. I'm so sorry to scare you like that.*
Finn: *Don't be! I'm sorry you had to read my stupid messages.*
Anna: *They're not stupid.*

Anna reread Finn's text messages. He sounded so worried.
Finn: *Feels like a dumb question but how are you dealing with everything?*
Anna: *Fine.*
Finn: *No, but...really?*

Anna stared at the screen. If it had been anyone else asking, she would have lied and reassured them that everything was, in fact, fine. But this was Finn. He might not have told her everything but she knew he would have if he felt he could. Silly romantic feelings aside, he was her best friend. She didn't need him to be in love with her to know that he cared.
Anna: *Everything sucks right now.*
Finn: *Do you want to talk about it?*
Anna: *I don't know how to put things into words.*
Finn: *I know what you mean.*

With a shock of sudden noise and vibration, Anna's phone nearly jumped out of her hand. The caller's number was withheld. Anna briefly thought it might be Finn but he would have mentioned calling in his messages. Against her better judgement, she answered.

"Hello?" Anna waited for the robotic voice of a telemarketer to greet her.

"Hello, Anastasia," replied a formal, yet distinctly human, voice, "This is Rupert Bolt, your grandfather."

Anna stared blankly her phone. Compared to recent events, a call from an estranged relative shouldn't have registered as strange but it rattled her nonetheless.

"I'm hoping you might be free to meet me tomorrow for lunch?" Rupert continued.

"I- uh- I have work tomorrow," Anna answered automatically. It occurred to her that taking some time off work might be a good idea, all things considered. Surely Dr Ravi would give her a medical certificate for some sick leave. Or should she take Bereavement Leave instead?

"Would you be willing to spend your lunch break with me?" he prompted, "I have some matters to discuss that are quite urgent."

"Sure?" Anna agreed, wondering what he could possibly want to talk about.

"Perfect," Rupert replied, I'll book us a table and send you a text message with the details. See you tomorrow."

"Oka-" Anna realised he'd hung up before she finished speaking.

Anna could hear someone moving around the kitchen. The smell of aromatic spices, coupled with Ghanaian music meant it was probably Abina, back from a long shift at the hospital. Anna liked Abina but she wasn't in the mood for another polite conversation right now. She waited until the apartment was silent before sneaking out to finish the blood in her thermos.

The next delivery arrived by courier around dinner time that evening. Glad she didn't have to worry about being tempted to feed on her roommates, Anna settled in for another sleepless night, disrupted by more panicked visions of monsters and blood.

CHAPTER 12

Lunch

By the time her alarm sounded the next morning, Anna couldn't stand being in her bedroom any longer. It had once been her sanctuary from the world but now it felt claustrophobic. She couldn't sleep, she hated staring at her ceiling. Even the books and shows she'd once loved were now ruined. They all emphasised the wonders of magic. The hardships were always centred around noble sacrifices and love triangles. They never addressed the pain, or helplessness, of death. They never explored the idea that the discovery of magic could make a person feel more alone than when they lived in ignorance.

"Good morning!" Cassie's enthusiasm was manic as Anna entered the office, "We didn't know if you were going to come in today. What with... um...how is everything?"
"Fine," Anna replied, failing to hide her exhaustion.
"You look great," Cassie assured her, unconvincingly, "is that a new outfit?"
"Yeah."
"No more glasses?" Finn asked.
Anna lifted a hand to her face. She'd forgotten to wear them.
"Um, yeah," Anna confirmed, numb to the loss, "No more glasses."

"Mornin'," Dex's voice drawled from the doorway. He carried an enormous coffee cup and large, reflective sunglasses masked his eyes. His shirt was creased and his hair was matted. He dropped into his desk chair, leaning it as far back as it would go.
"Rough night?" Finn enquired. His eyes darted from Dex to Anna.
The colour had returned to Finn's cheeks but his eyes were still sunken

and pink.

"Only in the carnal sense, m'dear," Dex winked with a weary grin.

Finn tensed his jaw but said nothing, dragging his gaze to his monitor. Anna caught Cassie's eye. She seemed just as confused as Anna. Were Finn and Dex arguing? If so, Dex didn't seem particularly bothered. Anna shrugged it off. She had enough on her plate without butting into other people's private business.

The rest of the morning passed quickly. Pam made an appearance, dropping off two new temps. At a quarter to twelve, Anna slouched into the blistering heat. The Corinthian columns and grand marble staircases of City Hall radiated an atmosphere of grandeur. She walked across the mosaic floors feeling a nostalgic sense of insignificance. Hundreds of people had walked these halls before her, and hundreds would come after. She found the thought comforting until she remembered she was no longer human.

She could return to this spot in a thousand years and everyone she knew, apart from Dex, would be long dead. She'd watch them live their lives, growing and changing, while she stayed the same.

She wondered if it would be better to separate herself from everyone now to make it easier in the long run.

No. Just because she wasn't aging didn't mean she couldn't die. There was no guarantee she'd outlive her friends and family. She could die tomorrow, for all she knew. And, even if she did outlive them, what was the point of avoiding them? Knowing something's going to end doesn't mean you can't enjoy it while it lasts. Time was precious. Moving forward, Anna resolved to not waste a single moment.

She turned toward the cafe. A collection of squashy, red armchairs sat outside the entrance. Dark wooden booths filled the small room inside, leaving little space for the servers and patrons to move around. A tall, rotating cake stand gleamed in the middle of the tables, displaying an assortment of gourmet creations.

Despite arriving early, Anna found her grandfather had already been seated in one of the booths along the back wall. He wore a brown suit, complete with a vest, pocket watch and bowtie. His silver hair matched the frames of his spectacles. Though Anna was sure they'd never met, his presence felt familiar. As she approached the table, he stood and offered his hand, "Anastasia," he greeted her with unexpected warmth. "Thank you for coming."

Anna shook his hand. "Thanks for inviting me," she replied politely.

"I understand your time is limited," he said, switching to a business-like tone, "so I shall try to keep things brief."

"Er, thanks?" Anna slid into the seat opposite her grandfather.

"You seem confused," he frowned, "Have you not surmised why I asked you here?"

"Sorry," Anna shook her head.

"None?" Rupert arched an eyebrow.

Anna shrugged apologetically. She felt like she'd come to class without her schoolbooks.

"My timing should be an obvious clue," he prompted, "Perhaps you need a moment to *see things more clearly*?

Rupert perused the menu while Anna pondered. Looking around the cafe, she could see a mixture of people. Some had tell-tale signs of faerie heritage. A man with small horns sat in the opposite corner, working on a crossword puzzle. An elderly pair of gnomes shared a large slice of cheesecake, giggling like children. A blonde elf pouted at a man in a sharp, blue blazer. He carried the translucent haze of the Unseeing around his head and grinned widely as he handed the elf a long, velvet-covered box. Her perfect pout transformed into squeals of delight as she extracted a sparkling diamond bracelet. Returning her gaze to Rupert, Anna realised he had no mystical fog around to cloud his senses.

"Are we ready to order?" A waiter appeared at the table.

"Yes, thank you," Rupert replied smoothly, "May I please have the pumpkin soup?"

"Oh, um, the same please." Anna floundered.

"Excellent," said the waiter, taking their menus, "Those will be right out."

Anna was reeling. Was her grandfather a witch like Cassie? He didn't have fangs, so he couldn't be a vampire. *What's going on?*

"You seem perturbed," Rupert observed, "Can I assume, then, that you've deduced I can see the truth of the world? And that I'm aware you were killed two nights ago and have since been transformed into a vampire."

"How-" Anna stammered. It seemed ridiculous that her estranged grandfather would have a better handle on Anna's situation than the rest of her family combined.

"I've made great efforts to keep my family, to keep *you*, safe from the magical community," he grimaced, "Obviously, it was not enough. For that, I apologise."

Anna stared at him in confusion, "We never see you."

Rupert looked at her with a weary smile.

"That is by design, I'm afraid," he sighed, "My reputation in the magical community has forced me to choose between enjoying the company of my family or keeping you safe."

"What does that mean?"

"It means there are those among the Fae who would put you in danger as a means to control me," his voice lowered, "My abilities make me a target and those I'm close to are always at risk."

"Why?" Anna leaned in, "What can you do?"

"I'd rather not go into detail right now," he said, as the waiter placed their meals in front of them, "We are short on time and there are more pressing matters we need to discuss."

"Like what?"

"The circumstances of your death, for one," Rupert replied, "I will never forgive myself for arriving too late to save you-"

"You were there?" Anna choked on a mouthful of hot soup.

"I was," he admitted, "Not quickly enough to change your fate but I was, at least, able to ensure justice was dealt swiftly to your attackers."

"That was you?" Anna felt pale. She understood why people wanted to control his power. The doctor had said it looked like the work of a full coven of witches.

"It was me, yes," there was no remorse in Rupert's eyes, "Would you fault me for it?"

Anna didn't know what to say. Those so-called *men* didn't deserve to be free. Even if they'd been arrested and found guilty, the average prison sentence for manslaughter in this state was only eight years, while the average for rape was only six and a half. Was Anna's heart hammering because she was terrified to be sitting across from a killer or was it because she was furious she'd never get the chance to kill the bastards herself?

"Did they suffer?" Anna whispered.

"No," Rupert regarded her, "Their deaths were instantaneous."

"Then, yes," Anna answered with a savageness she hadn't expected, "They deserved worse."

"Understandable," Rupert nodded with a strange glimmer in his eye, "I apologise for depriving you the solace of their pain. At the time, I believed you wouldn't have the opportunity to pursue such things."

"At least they're not around to hurt anyone else," Anna grumbled.

"Indeed" he nodded, "But I digress. I brought up your death, not to confess my involvement in the events of that night but to discover who had a hand in your transformation. Whose blood did you drink that night?"

"I don't know," she said.

"*You don't know?*" Rupert asked incredulously.

Anna shrugged, feeling childish.

"Anastasia-,"

"Anna."

"Anna, this is important," his tone was urgent, "Whoever sired you has power over you. If they choose to, they can control your mind. They can force you to act against your own interests. *Kingsley & Laurant* is a company owned by vampires. Ambrosia Laurant is on the tribunal for the Vampiric Alliance and Rufus Kingsley is one of the oldest vampires on record. Hundreds of vampires work in your building. Have you formed a relationship with any of them?"

"Dex is the only vampire I know," Anna frowned, "but it definitely wasn't him."

"Dex?" Rupert repeated the name, taking out a notebook filled with indecipherable markings. "Dexter Duke?" he read from his notes, "You were with him the night you died, correct?"

"Yes," answered Anna, "How did you-"

"Witnesses statements," Rupert waved impatiently, "Are you aware that Dexter Duke's mother is the Elven Empress. She oversees the Council of High Fae."

"What?" Anna was sure there'd been a mistake, "No. Dex is just an office grunt like me. He does data entry. He's not a...*prince* or whatever."

"Not anymore," Rupert agreed, "but he was once heir to the throne of the Elven Empire. He could be using you as a pawn to regain his status."

"Tha- That's crazy," Anna stammered. "Dex is my friend. He'd never do anything to hurt me. He was shocked when I showed up at his apartment as a vampire. It wasn't him."

"Perhaps not intentionally." Rupert mused, "My investigations indicated his brother was present on the night you were killed. Could he have manipulated Dex?"

Anna had forgotten all about Arik.

"He," she began, trying to remember, "He wanted Dex to talk to their mother. Something about a job offer."

Rupert's eyebrow arched upward.

"But Dex turned him down," Anna defended. "He didn't want anything to do with his mother. He said he doesn't want to go back."

She decided not to mention Dex had gone to meet Arik last night.

"Fair enough" Rupert made some notes before continuing, "What can you tell me about Cassandra Nakamura? I understand she's a witch, connected with several local covens, but otherwise unaligned in the magical community?"

"That sounds about right, I suppose," replied Anna, "She's a good person."

Seeming satisfied with her answer, Rupert nodded, "Have you formed any other significant relationships recently?"

"I mean, there's Finn," Anna's stomach tensed, "He wasn't even there, though."

"What can you tell me about him?" Rupert scribbled notes.

"He's-" Anna stopped herself. She didn't know if Finn was open about being a werewolf. Was it something people shared freely? He'd seemed relieved that she hadn't minded. Maybe there was a stigma attached to it. "He's a druid," she finished.

"Would Finn be short for Finnegan, by any chance?" Rupert narrowed his eyes inquisitively.

"I- yes," Anna stammered. "Henry Finnegan."

Rupert flipped rapidly through his notebook. The pages changed their content based on the way he touched them. Finally, he found a spread featuring an intricately drawn tree with dozens of names on each of the branches.

"Henry Finnegan," he said, "Is the youngest son of the Tree Folk's matriarch, Elowen Finnegan. He is royalty in his own right, after a fashion."

"After a fashion?" Anna asked. She felt disconnected from her body. How could both Dex and Finn be royalty? Why hadn't they said anything? Did she know them at all?

"Though Elowen sits among kings and queens on the Council of High Fae," Rupert explained, "she considers herself to be a protector of her people, rather than their ruler. Titles like 'Queen' or 'Prince' mean nothing to the Tree Folk. They're a collective of equals who follow Elowen for her wisdom."

"Right," Anna replied blankly. She couldn't believe how much she didn't know about her best friends.

"I find it interesting," Rupert said quietly, "that the sons of two members of the High Fae Council are entangled in your life. And Mr Finnegan now finds himself in the close company of two vampires."

"What difference does that make?" Anna felt a headache coming on. All this speculation was exhausting.

"The Finnegans are an extremely well-respected magical family," Rupert seemed to be forming a hypothesis as he spoke, "So much so that many would stand with Elowen in circumstances of war. To those of us paying attention, the Finnegans have a vastly more powerful army than the other factions combined."

"It sounds like they only have it because they'd never use it," Anna countered.

"Unless," Rupert replied, deep in thought, "Someone wishes to manipulate their power using you, or Mr Finnegan, as pawns."

Anna stared. That felt rather dramatic.

"Do you really think there's some grand conspiracy behind my death?"

"I would be foolish not to consider the possibility," Rupert responded wearily, "Though, I'll admit it seems unlikely."

"Does that mean you're going to disappear again?" Anna had only known Rupert for half an hour, but the thought of never seeing him again gave her a sinking feeling.

He blinked and removed his glasses, cleaning them with his handkerchief. "No," he spoke softly, "Now that your eyes are open to this world, I would very much like to be a part of your life. If you are open to it?"

"I'd like that," Anna replied.

He smiled. It was genuine and warm. Anna could see some of her mother's features on his face.

Rupert reached into his blazer and placed two objects on the table. The first was a small silk pouch. The other was an ordinary-looking key. "I'd like you to have these," he said.

"What are they?" Anna asked.

"The pouch contains a protective charm bearing my symbol," he explained, opening the pouch to reveal a gold necklace with a coin-sized pendant. A seven-pointed star with two minuscule concentric circles in the centre gleamed on its surface. "Anyone familiar with me, or my work, will know you are under my protection while you wear this."

Anna turned the pendant in her fingers. The circles within the star followed her like an eye.

"It carries an enchantment," he continued, "If you need my help, simply say my name three times, followed by your predicament. I'll hear you no matter where you are. If the necklace is removed against your will, I'll be transported to your location."

Anna watched the magic radiating from the pendant. Though it was brand new, it felt like a precious family heirloom. She placed the charm around her neck.

"Thank you," smiled Anna.

"Thank *you*," countered Rupert, "Knowing you are wearing it will give me peace of mind."

"What's this?" Anna picked up the key.

"It will grant you entry to my home," answered Rupert.

"So, it's just a key?" Anna chuckled sceptically, turning it over in her hand. It didn't radiate magic like the charmed necklace but it felt heavier than it should.

"It will only work for you," Rupert explained, "My home is impossible to access without a key like that one. You are welcome to come whenever you'd like. Think of it as a second home."

Anna wasn't sure what to say.

"It seems our time is nearly up" Rupert checked his pocket watch, "I don't want you getting into trouble at work on my account."

He gestured for the waiter to bring over the bill.

"Do you have any questions?" he offered, "Before we part ways?"

"Why do you feel so familiar?" she blurted without thinking, "We've never met but I feel like we've talked before…"

Rupert seemed impressed by her question.

"When you and your sister were very young," he explained, "I used to visit your dreams. We would play games together and I'd tell you stories. You were a clever, creative, intelligent girl. I'm very proud to see the woman you've become."

"Why did you stop visiting?"

"A child's mind is more open than an adult's," he sighed, "As you grew up, and experienced new emotions, your heart and mind became more guarded. I would have had to force my way into your private thoughts, which I had no desire to do."

She nodded. It made an odd sort of sense.

"Does our family have any faerie in our bloodline?" She asked, "Like imp?"

"I'm afraid not," he frowned, "We're as human as they come. Why?"

"It's nothing really," Anna flushed, "People tend to forget me easily. Cassie thought it could be a faerie thing."

Rupert glanced away, looking guilty.

"That's my fault, I'm afraid," he said, "The most effective protective spells tend to make the subject largely imperceptible and forgettable. A predator cannot hunt the prey it doesn't notice. It will not stalk a creature it's forgotten."

Anna felt heat rising in her face. She'd spent her life believing she didn't matter because people never noticed her. They never cared about her. Because of him.

"Did you cast any other spells on me?" Anna tried to keep her tone even.

"No," Rupert assured her, "And the protective spells on you broke the second you died."

"What about Mum?" Anna asked, trying to remain calm, "Does she know about any of this?"

"No," Rupert answered firmly, "A long time ago, Diana asked that I remove all memories of magic and faeries from her mind. She didn't want to be a part of this and I respect her choice."

"So, no one in our family knows about magic but us?"

"Yes, and I must ask you to keep it that way."

Anna was tempted to argue but realised she had already made the same decision. She'd had the opportunity to tell her mother that magic was real and she'd chosen not to.

"Okay," she agreed. "But I'm not cutting them out of my life."

"I wouldn't expect you to," Rupert nodded, "It seems our time is up. Please don't hesitate to contact me. I'll be in touch. Be safe."

***

Anna walked back to the office in a daze. She wasn't sure what to make of her grandfather. He'd cast spells on her without her knowledge. Would her life be any different if he hadn't? Would she be popular and outgoing? Would she still be alive? Was her death part of some sinister plot for power? Was she killed so someone could get to Rupert? Or was he just supremely paranoid?

"Where'd you go?" asked Finn, as Anna sat at her desk, "We missed you at lunch."

"I had lunch with my grandfather" Anna answered absently.

"That's nice," Cassie smiled assuringly, "What's he like?"

"Um," Anna couldn't think of the best words to capture him, "Weird?"

"What?" laughed Cassie.

"He's-," Anna thought about it, "Smart. And caring…In his own way."

"What does *that* mean?" Finn's brow was furrowed.

"It's a long story," Anna replied. She nodded toward the temps as though they were the reason she couldn't elaborate. Both had noise-cancelling headphones on and obviously couldn't care less. Anna turned back to her computer and began typing. She embraced the mindless escape. Her phone buzzed a few times, but she ignored it. She didn't want to talk. She needed time to think. Too much had happened in the last few days and she needed time to work through it.

CHAPTER 13

Summer Storms

Anna took the next two weeks off work. Her nightmares weren't as strong when she slept during the day. It helped to journal her feelings. Getting everything down on paper stopped the negative thoughts from cycling over and over through her head. She cried a little less each day. She didn't know if that meant she was adapting or just getting better at ignoring her issues.

One evening, Cassie surprised Anna by showing up at her apartment.
"Finn's in the car," she smiled sheepishly, "Come I come in?"
Anna led Cassie to her room, silently grateful Finn hadn't come up and seen the state of Anna's hair after several days of not brushing it, not to mention the mess in her bedroom. She'd been in full *Wallow Mode*, where personal hygiene isn't high on one's list of priorities.

"It's not healthy to stay cooped up," Cassie chastised, opening the windows "But you know what's best for you so, as a compromise, come with us to pick up some Thai food. It'll take an hour at most. Sound good?"
"Okay," Anna was glad Cassie hadn't asked how she was feeling.
She splashed water on her face, brushed her hair, put on one of her new ensembles from Madam Oksana's, then followed Cassie outside.

A turquoise panel van waited for them on the kerbside of the quiet street. Anna smiled at Finn and she climbed into the front seat, "Where's Dex?"
Finn's smile faded as he let out an exasperated sigh.
"What?" Anna asked as Cassie pulled away from the kerb.
"It's just-" Finn grumbled, "Haven't you seen enough of him?"
"What?"
"Hasn't he been…teaching you his ways?"

"We only had that one session when I first turned," Anna had no idea what Finn's problem was, but he was acting strange.

Finn leaned into the front seat, "So, you haven't been with Dex at all recently?"

"Dex has been out partying every night," Cassie scoffed, "He's too busy hooking up to be teaching Anna anything."

"I thought Anna might have joined him," Finn clarified quietly. His ears had turned pink, "I thought they might have been doing things…together."

"I- No." Anna stammered.

"Finn!" Cassie laughed, "Did you seriously think Dex and Anna have been hooking up?"

"Is that so crazy?" Finn muttered, the rest of his face turning bright red, "They've both been off work since...it happened. Apart from the Monday when they both showed up tired-"

"Anna would *never* hook up with Dex!" Cassie assured, "Right, Anna?

Anna's eyes widened. She stared out the window with awkward determination.

"Right, Anna?" Cassie repeated with far less enthusiasm.

"Well…" began Anna, crinkling her nose. It would have been a great time to lie but she couldn't bring herself to do it.

"WHAT?!" Cassie exclaimed, jolting them forward as she hit the brakes by accident, "When?! Please tell me he didn't take advantage of you on your first night as a vampire!"

"It was nothing like that!" Anna assured, "We were getting ready to go out on Friday-"

"Before I came over?" Cassie asked.

"Yes," Anna confirmed, "And it was so… *Stupid.*"

"Do. Tell."

"There's not much to tell," Anna resisted the urge to look back at Finn, "I don't know what I was thinking. I was in a weird mood. And there was a *moment.*"

Cassie gestured for Anna to continue. Finn was silent.

"I kissed him," Anna confessed in a rush, "We made out a bit but then things got heated and he stopped it."

"*He* stopped it?" Cassie didn't bother to hide her scepticism, "Dexter Duke, voluntarily ceased hooking up with a willing partner? Why?"

"He knew I was looking for more than a hook-up," Anna shrugged, "And he's not the boyfriend type."

"Wow," Cassie pulled into the car park of the local Thai restaurant, "Were you upset? You guys seemed so normal when I got there."

"I mean, the rejection didn't feel great," Anna replied, "But thinking about it now, I couldn't be more grateful that he stopped it when he did."

"Really?" Finn blurted. Anna glanced back and caught his eye. His expression wasn't judgemental or angry, as she'd expected. It might have been wishful thinking on Anna's part, but he seemed optimistic.

"I was never under the illusion we had a lot in common," Anna continued, "I didn't even think of him that way until it was happening."

"Are you sure?" Cassie asked, looking concerned, "You don't have to put on a brave face for us."

"Dex is great," Anna assured, "He's fun and supportive. He's got this intoxicating vibe that makes you feel like anything could happen. But I can't imagine him being exclusive with anyone, let alone me. We're too different. And I want something real."

"Fair enough," said Cassie. "I can't believe I didn't pick up on it though. I'm normally so good with stuff like that."

The restaurant was a tiny hole-in-the-wall with no tables and only a few chairs lined along the walls. The counter was cluttered with tiny elephant statues and gold framed photos of Thailand. It stood in front of a beaded curtain, which partially obscured the busy kitchen. Aromatic spices wafted through the shop, tantalising Anna's taste buds. They ordered a generous amount of food from the girl behind the counter, who looked a little too young to be working, and then took their seats while the food was prepared.

"So Dex's been off all week too?" Anna asked.

"He tends to overindulge when he's stressed," Cassie nodded with a frown, "He usually comes good after a couple of days though."

"But it's been over a week," Anna looked from Finn to Cassie. They shifted uncomfortably in their seats.

"I'm sure he's fine," Cassie seemed to be assuring herself more than Anna, "I might just give him a call to check-in."

Cassie left the shop as she swiped through her contacts list. Anna used her vampiric hearing to listen as the phone rang. Dex answered with a slurred yell, "Helllooooooo!" There was techno music playing in the background and the chatter of a crowd. Where did people go to party so early on a weeknight? With an internal sigh, Anna supposed if there was somewhere in the city with round-the-clock clubbing, Dex would know about it.

"Sorry for that stuff in the car," Finn muttered, crinkling the take-away menu in his hands, "It's none of my business if you're with Dex or not."
"At least you think I'm capable of hooking up with someone," Anna half-joked, "Cassie couldn't have been more shocked."
"I think she was just surprised about it being Dex," he chuckled, "She's got it in her head that you're interested in...someone else."

Cassie was right but Anna wasn't about to admit to it. She tried to hide the colour rising in her cheeks by looking toward the kitchen. It was a convenient distraction. With a clamour of clicking beads, one of the cooks ducked through the curtain. He handed a plastic bag filled with food to the girl behind the counter. Anna collected their order and followed Finn back to the car where Cassie was pacing. She looked nervous, "Would you guys mind if I drop you off and then go check on Dex?"

"Sure," Anna glanced at Finn, hoping she wasn't cornering him into spending time alone with her, "Do you want us to come with you?"
"No, no," Cassie scratched under the back of her wig in distraction, "I don't want him to think we're teaming up on him or anything. I just want to make sure he's not going too hard."
Finn looked away. He seemed worried. Maybe he didn't want to stay with Anna. Maybe he had a bad feeling about Dex. Whatever it was, he didn't voice his concerns.

***

Once inside her apartment, Anna grabbed plates, cutlery and a large tray from the kitchen before heading into her bedroom. She arranged a picnic-like setup on her bed while Finn hovered in the living area.
"What's wrong?" Anna asked.
"Oh," he stammered, "Sorry, I wasn't sure if you were just grabbing something in there and we were going to hang out, um, out here." Finn gestured at the sofa. She must have looked so childish. Finn obviously

didn't restrict himself to his bedroom like she did.

"I don't usually spend much time outside my room," she explained sheepishly, "I never know when my roommates will show up...but we can stay out there if you want."

"No, no, I get it," Finn smiled, stepping into Anna's room, "Cassie's great, but sometimes I feel like she's hovering. I like the privacy of my bedroom too."

Anna closed the door behind him. The room suddenly seemed smaller than usual. Finn smiled politely, placing his hands into his pockets.

"Uh, welcome," Anna blushed. Her brain fired thoughts at her so fast they turned into white noise.

What do hosts normally do?

"Would you like anything?" She offered, "I could give you a- a tour?"

Stupid.

"That's okay," Finn laughed. His eyes moved from her ensuite to the wooden desk by her bed, then to the small TV sitting on her dresser, the movie posters covering the pastel blue walls, and the over-filled bookshelf in the corner.

"You've got a pretty good setup here," he smiled, gravitating toward the bookshelf.

"Thanks," Anna sat on her bed, feeling strangely exposed as she watched Finn inspect her collection.

"Oh! Can I borrow this sometime?" Finn asked, pointing to one of Anna's favourite graphic novels, "I've been trying to hunt down a copy for ages!"

"Sure," Anna felt a swell of pride, "Take it now if you want."

Finn carefully extracted the book from its shelf and held it to his chest. He shuffled back and forth on the spot before, finally, sitting on the bed. His cheeks had gone bright pink, matching his ears. "This is new," he chuckled awkwardly.

"The theme of my life," Anna laughed mirthlessly.

"Is it... Is me being here...okay?" Finn stuttered, "I can go if- if it's too weird."

"No!" Anna assured him, "It's only weird because I never have people over, so I don't know what I'm doing. I want you to stay. Unless *you're* uncomfortable! Then you can go if you want to. Obviously. I'm sure Cassie will come back if you call her. But I want you to stay... Do you want to stay?"

"I do," Finn smiled. There was a warmth in his eyes that made Anna's muscles relax. By the time they'd each had their fill of rice, curry and noodles, the nervous tension had dissolved. After Anna cleared the dishes away, she felt a jolt of delight to see Finn leaning against her pillows, looking quite at home in her bed.

"So," Finn said with purpose as Anna joined him on the bed, "What's going on in your head? I know you're not okay. Talk to me."

Anna tried to think of a concise way to summarise her feelings. She didn't want to overwhelm him with her problems. Once she started talking, however, words flooded like a broken dam. She described the whirlpool of emotions she'd had about death, secrets, and magic. The exhaustion from being unable to sleep. The horrors in her nightmares. Wishing she could remember being killed while simultaneously being glad she couldn't. She confided that she felt like her death was a punishment for being stupid enough to drop her guard in public. How her mother hadn't noticed anything wrong with her when they'd spoken, and how her grandfather had cursed her to be forgettable. She even found herself verbalising thoughts and fears she hadn't realised were there. Did she waste her life by playing it safe? Or would she have died that much sooner if she'd taken more risks? Why hadn't she cared that Rupert was a killer? Why had she wished he'd made her attackers suffer? Had her vampirism affected her morals? Or had this darkness, this rage, always been a part of her? Who was she becoming? *What* was she becoming?

Finn listened without any sign of judgement. When she began to cry, he wrapped his arms gently around her like it was the most natural thing in the world.

"...I guess you might say," Anna sniffed, "I'm feeling a *tad overwhelmed.*"

"I don't know how you're handling all that so well," he said with gentle reverence.

Anna shrugged, "No choice."

"I'm here, you know," said Finn, "For anything you need,"

"I think this is exactly what I need," Anna smiled, leaning into him.

He smelled like jasmine and firewood.

"What about you?" Anna asked, "I can see something's bothering you."

"That doesn't matter right now," he said quietly.

Anna raised her head, looking him in the eye.

"Of course, it matters," she frowned.

He shrugged and sighed, "My stuff is nothing compared to yours."

"It's not a competition," retorted Anna.

He looked at her apprehensively.

"Please?" She implored, trying to lighten the mood by pouting her lip with exaggerated puppy-dog eyes.

Finn smiled wearily, "Okay," he relented, "For starters…"

He leaned back and rolled up the left leg of his pants,and tugging off his prosthetic leg to reveal a tight sock with a metal bolt protruding from its base. He peeled it off, revealing red indentations in his skin, "This thing's been bothering me since lunchtime. It holds my leg in place but it's really uncomfortable."

Rubbing where straps had been digging in, he glanced at Anna, who had unfortunately winced at the sight of his grizzled scars.

"Sorry, it's gross," Finn quickly rolled his jeans back over his leg.

"No, it's not!" Anna stopped his hand.

He raised his eyebrows dubiously.

"It's just…*sobering*," Anna reiterated, "Seeing your scars makes me imagine how you got them. I hate thinking of you in pain like that…"

Fresh tears welled in her eyes. She felt stupid for crying over trauma that wasn't even hers. "I can't help picturing it," Anna crinkled her face apologetically, wiping a traitorous tear from her cheek.

"I didn't think about it like that," Finn looked bewildered.

"Your scars are proof that you survived something horrible," reiterated Anna, "You shouldn't be ashamed. I just wish it hadn't happened to you."

"Me too," Finn smiled sadly.

"So," Finn asked tentatively, "My leg, or lack-thereof, really doesn't bother you? Or my scars? Or the- the *werewolf* thing?"

"I'm literally dead," Anna scoffed, "Why would it?"

"But… I mean…" Finn looked away, "If you'd found out before…?"

"I would have found the werewolf thing extremely cool," she mused, "and I knew about your leg before. It never bothered me, why would it?"

"Right," he smiled sheepishly, "I just- I don't know… Compared to other guys, like Dex, or whatever… I'm…not *ideal*."

"Ideal for what?" Anna asked with a hopeful prickle in her chest.

113

Finn looked as though he was about to say something. Anna thought she saw a hint of longing in his eyes, but he pursed his lips and looked away. "Never mind," he answered, wrinkling his brow, "You're dealing with enough right now."

"I need a distraction," Anna coaxed, "I just word-vomited the darkest part of my soul all over you. Tell me what's going on with you. At the very least, it would be good to know I'm not alone with my inner torment." She gave a wry chuckle.

Finn looked away again, taking a deep breath, "Well, for starters I think Cassie went on her own tonight because she didn't want me there. I blamed Dex for what happened and he's taken it to heart."

"She didn't want me there either," Anna pointed out, "What else?"

Finn continued, "I'm not getting much sleep either. I get in my head with... stuff. I have nightmares."

"What about?" Anna prompted softly.

There was a glimmer of vulnerability in Finn's eyes. He furrowed his brow and closed his eyes, "That everyone I love is drowning and I'm stuck on the side of the pool, watching from my goddamn wheelchair. I can't get up. I can't move at all. I just watch everyone screaming and splashing until they sink. Then the water goes still and I'm left all alone."

"Oh, Finn," Anna whispered, taking his hand.

"It's obvious what it means," Finn continued, "I'm useless. I can't help anyone. The pack are doing stupid experiments and I can't stop them. But, if they hurt anyone, I'll feel responsible. Just like how I couldn't save you from being attacked because *I wasn't there*. I know how to fight, I could have taken those guys out. But, no. They hurt you. They're still hurting you with the trauma they caused. And I'm stuck on the sidelines watching. Again. I can't help you with vampire stuff. Dex is spiralling because *I blamed him* for not being there, so it's my fault he isn't helping you. I never should have blamed him. I wasn't there either. I was off turning into a literal monster. I'm such a hypocrite."

Finn blinked back tears. Anna pulled him close, just as he had done for her. It felt good to be the one offering support for a change.

"I asked Dex not to take you out that night," he confided in a whisper, "I told him I'd had a bad feeling but the truth is, I was jealous. I couldn't go with you and it killed me. Even if I'd been able to come, I would've just held you back. I get sore standing for too long. I fall over if I take a wrong step. Dex can spin you and dip you and jump around all night. I should've been happy that you were going to have a good time. Not bitter that it wasn't going to be with me..." Finn's face contorted as he pulled away from Anna. He sat on the edge of the bed, facing the wall, "I'm a fucking asshole."

"Don't be so hard on yourself," whispered Anna, "You're not a monster or an asshole. You're the kindest person I know. All you do is help people. You're helping me right now by just being here. By being you. By being honest."

"But I'm not *doing* anything," Finn sniffed, unconvinced, "I can't fix anything."

"I don't need you to fix my problems," she said, "I just need to know you care."

"I do care," his lip trembled slightly.

Before she knew what she was doing, Anna leaned in and pressed her mouth onto his lips. His face was hot. His breath caught. She felt his jaw tense under her hand. *Oh, crap.*

Had she completely misread everything? As she began to pull away, Finn let out a strangled sigh and pulled her closer, kissing her back ravenously. His breath quickened as Anna traced her fingers along his jawline. His hands shook as they moved along her back and into her hair. Her skin tingled at his touch. He pulled back and grinned, peppering kisses along her forehead and cheeks before returning to her lips.

Anna pushed her body into him. He pulled her closer, moving his hands down her spine to her lower back. Any space between them felt like too much. The intensity of his touch sent blissful shivers through her whole body. She wanted to live in this moment forever.

BOOM!

The room shook as a flash of lightning lit up the sky, followed by another explosive roar. Dizzy with a combination of exhilaration and shock, Anna jumped off the bed, "I- I should shut the windows," she flushed.

"I- uh- I'll help," Finn attempted to stand but jerked forward. Too late, Anna dove to catch him and they toppled onto the carpet in a heap. For a glorious moment, Anna was pinned under Finn's body. He pulled back and rolled onto his side, laughing, "I forgot-" he gasped between breaths,

"I forgot I took my leg off!" He covered his face with his hands, "I blame you!"

"What did I do?" Anna giggled impishly.

Finn grinned back at her. Anna no longer cared about the raging storm outside or the water showering through her open windows. Finn had stopped laughing. He gazed at her warmly, gently holding her hand as they lay side-by-side. Anna beamed at the gentle intimacy of his touch. Finn grinned back but then his smile faltered.

"What's wrong?" asked Anna.

"It's just," Finn laid on his back, looking toward the ceiling, "I haven't had a lot of experience...with s-sex."

"Me neither," Anna replied.

"Really?" Finn looked at her, relieved.

"Really." She confirmed.

"Do you think" he stammered, "I- I mean would you be okay if we… take things slow?"

"Of course," Anna replied, immediately replaying their kiss in her mind, wondering if it had been too much.

"It's not that I don't *want* to…" Finn went on, "Trust me on that. I really, *very much*, want to. And, I know most people our age are divorced with five kids, so they're pretty blasé about sex, but there's stuff from my past that I'm trying to work through. Stuff nobody knows. I- I don't know how to talk about it yet."

Anna took Finn's hand, "I'm happy to go slow," she whispered, "You don't have to explain."

Anna got to her feet and offered Finn her hands. He took them with a warm smile as she heaved him slightly harder than she needed to, pulling his body against hers. He held her in a tight embrace before they both dropped back onto the bed.

"I should get going," Finn murmured, showing no sign of wanting to, "I'm sure Cassie's on her way."

"Or, I could drop you home later," offered Anna, "Do you want to stay and watch some old episodes of Stargate with me?"

A playful grin spread across Finn's face, "Which season?"

They watched the show late into the night. So late that Anna suggested

Finn might prefer to stay over.

"If you don't mind?" Finn grinned sheepishly, "I don't want to outstay my welcome."

"Not possible," Anna replied as she searched her bathroom for a spare toothbrush, "I'm not planning on going to work tomorrow but I can drop you off."

"Cassie'll pick me up on the way," Finn was already typing. The screen illuminated his face in blue light, which seemed too bright compared to the warm string lights Anna had hung around her room. "She asked if you'd be up for a movie night on Friday. You could see our place. It'd be a low-key change of scenery." Finn tossed his phone onto the narrow shelf acting as a bedside table on the left side of the bed.

"Sounds good," Anna handed Finn a fresh toothbrush. Their hands grazed each other. A flutter danced along Anna's arm as Finn took her hand and stroked his thumb along her skin. They'd been friends for so long that a simple touch shouldn't have been so electrifying. But this was different. This was new. There were no screens between them now. There was nothing to stop Anna from losing herself in the warmth of Finn's embrace. Of all the times she'd imagined his touch, she'd never factored in the little details that made his presence deliciously real. His lightly calloused hands. The stubble on his jawline. The traces of herbal soap on his skin. Anna was more than happy to take things slow. Curled together in bed, the intimacy of holding each other was perfection.

***

Another storm erupted in the early morning, shrouding the sunrise behind dark clouds. Anna caught Finn's eye.

A wide smile spread across his face, "How long have you been awake?"

"Not long," she lied. She'd been feigning sleep for almost an hour, happy in their cosy bubble. Heavy rain tapped on the windows and the smell of coffee wafted from the kitchen.

"I suppose we should get up," he yawned. At some point during the night, he had kicked off his trousers. His cotton boxer briefs left little to the imagination.

"If you want," Anna stretched into his body, pleasantly aware that his eyes were resting on her bra-less chest, hidden only by a loose camisole.

"Hmm," he flushed.

Anna kissed him gently. His lips parted for hers with an indulgent groan. He pulled her close, sending fresh tingles down her spine. She brushed her fingers through the soft curls on his head. He grunted and pulled her on top of him. She straddled his hips with a giggle. His hands travelled slowly down to her waist, then under the hem of her top. She could feel him growing hard beneath her. The rain intensified, pounding on the windows like a drum roll. Finn looked imploringly into her eyes as his hands slowly traced their way upwards from her hips. He was asking for permission and she was more than happy to give it. She guided Finn's hands to her breasts and he let out a quiet moan. Craving warmth pulsed between Anna's thighs as he gently traced the curve of her nipples with his thumbs.

Anna gasped. His touch flooded her with shimmers of pleasure. She leaned forward, dragging another intense kiss from his mouth.

He moaned again, louder this time, pulling her closer, "I can't believe this is happening," he whispered.

"Me neither," Anna smiled, "and, to think, we spent all last night watching TV."

"Do you prefer this-" he kissed Anna's neck, "or Stargate?"

"Depends..." Anna smirked, boldly removing her singlet, "Which episode?"

His eyes bulged at the sight of her naked breasts.

"Is this okay?" She whispered, "We can slow down."

"God, no," he breathed, leaning up to kiss her, "This is very, very good."

Anna arched her back, moving her hips slowly. He buried his face in her breasts, stroking her left nipple while he ravaged the right with his tongue. Then switching. Anna had never been touched like this - intense enough to feel his lust yet gentle enough to know he cared for her. Her past experiences with men had left her feeling more like a masturbatory tool than a sexual being. Finn made Anna feel like a *very* sexual being.

Rolling Anna onto her back, Finn traced a finger over her cheek, "This is so much better than I imagined," he whispered.

"What did you imagine?" Anna breathed.

He pressed against her slowly. "Kissing you," he whispered, "Holding you. But it was never this good in my head. I didn't know it could feel so...this."

"We really should have been doing this the whole time," Anna agreed, "When Pam forced me to introduce myself, you should have just pounced on me right then and there."

"Oh, I wanted to," he laughed sheepishly.

"Really?" Anna grinned, sitting up.

"I obviously didn't know anything real about you yet," Finn brushed a stray hair from Anna's face, "but you were so- you *are* so fucking beautiful. I couldn't look away."

Anna knew he was exaggerating but she didn't care. She nestled into his arms. He wanted her. She wanted him. Nothing else mattered.

CHAPTER 14

Movie Night

Friday arrived quickly. A chattering cloud of bats glided through the pink and orange sunset as Anna waited outside her apartment with an overnight bag. Cassie and Finn arrived faster than expected.

"We left work a little early," Cassie admitted.

"I doubt anyone will notice," added Finn.

"As long as you don't get into trouble on my account," Anna tossed her backpack next to Finn as she ducked into the front passenger seat.

Anna loved watching the transition of scenery widen from apartment blocks and narrow townhouses to high-set, single-storey homes with wrap-around verandas, to large plots of wild bushland where people's residences were hidden among the trees. Leaving the confines of the city was freeing. Less people. More air. The way it should be.

They turned off the highway and followed a long dirt driveway through dense bushland until, finally, pulling into a green clearing with a single storey house sitting in an expansive garden.

"Welcome to The Grotto!" Cassie beamed.

Anna stepped out of the van. The sweet scent of jasmine wafted through the air while cicadas sang to the setting sun.

"Oh, look," Finn smiled, "You've got a new friend."

Anna followed Finn's gaze to a small brushtail possum cautiously approaching them.

"Hey, buddy," Finn said, pushing his wheelchair closer and offering his hand. The possum scampered over to him, sniffing gingerly.

"Wait there," Cassie called over her shoulder as she jogged inside the house. She returned moments later carrying a small bowl of assorted fruit slices. Finn offered a small piece of pineapple to the possum, who grabbed it with tiny paws and scurried away. Cassie handed Anna some mango with a wink.

"Wha-" Anna began, "Oh, hello!"

A bat swooped out of the sky and landed on the grass in front of her. Anna recognised it as the one she'd used as a messenger. "Nice to see you again, Calypso," Anna gave him the mango.

As juice dripped from his furry face, Anna felt a psychic swell of joy radiate from her little friend. More bats and possums appeared in the garden for feeding time. They chirped happily as they munched on bits of apple, mango and pineapple. When the bowl was empty, the animals disappeared back to their homes. Cassie and Finn went inside while Anna used her super-senses to track the various creatures back to their homes. She hadn't practised her new skills since her training night with Dex and had forgotten how fun it could be. She followed a stone path to the large wooden cottage. Warm light spilled from the open door, giving the entryway a welcoming glow. However, when Anna tried to step over the threshold, an invisible wall blocked her.

"Um, guys?" Anna called out, "Something's wrong, I can't-"

"Oh crap!" Cassie exclaimed from the bowels of the house. The sound of her hurried footsteps rushed toward the open doorway. She appeared with an apologetic smile, "Anastasia Green, you are welcome in our home, please come in."

Anna gingerly pushed her hand through the opening. The barrier had melted away.

"That was new," Anna winced, feeling heat colouring her cheeks as she walked into the house, "I haven't been blocked from anywhere before."

"The invitation rule only applies when the occupant considers the place to be their sanctuary," Cassie replied pensively, "It's the difference between a house and a home, I guess."

"I guess," Anna tried to hide her disappointment. She'd hoped the notion of vampires requiring an invitation into people's homes had been a myth. It made her feel like a monster.

"This place belongs to Finn's family, so our rent is super cheap," Cassie continued, walking Anna through the house, "Finn has the master bedroom but I use the guest bedroom as my study, so it's even. There's the lounge, where we'll be getting our movie marathon on, and over here we've converted the back patio into a greenhouse so all our herbs are closer to the kitchen."

"Are you expecting a blood delivery at your place tonight?" Finn enquired as he chopped fresh basil. Three balls of pizza dough sat on the bench. The kitchen smelled of onion and tomato.

"No, I've got the app now," answered Anna, pulling a full thermos from her bag, "I just order it as needed."

"Do you want me to add some of your blood to one of the pizzas?" Finn offered, then winced, "Not *your* blood. Obviously. I meant what's in your thermos."

"It'll be more sharable if I just drink it separately," Anna grinned, shaking her head with a chuckle.

"Pyjamas!" Cassie announced, disappearing into her bedroom.

Anna gave Finn a quizzical look. He smiled and shrugged. Cassie reappeared wearing a matching singlet and shorts set covered with illustrations of cats. "What are you doing?" she admonished. "We can't do movie night without PJs!"

Cassie shooed Finn into his bedroom then took Anna's backpack and led her into the spare bedroom. It was lined with bookshelves, each carrying mysterious tomes and strange artefacts. Crystals, feathers, candles, and tiny handmade dolls drew Anna's attention this way and that.

A small desk sat under a window facing the garden. A large notebook sat on one side of it while a sticker-clad laptop rested in the centre. A narrow bed had been pushed into the far corner. Cassie dropped Anna's bag on it and then left her alone to change. Anna didn't own any matching pyjama sets so she slipped on her usual sleep attire - a pair of loose yoga pants and a worn cotton shirt featuring a rock band from the 1970's. She opened the door to find Cassie waiting with fresh bedsheets.

"I'm glad you agreed to come tonight," Cassie said, pulling the dusty sheets from the bed.

"Me too," Anna smiled, helping Cassie stretch the fitted sheet over he mattress, "I needed to get out of my head."

"I think we all did," Cassie sighed.

"Sorry I've been so…" Anna struggled to think of the word. *Selfish? Brooding?* "Absent."

"We all need space sometimes," Cassie shrugged, "But too much can make things worse if you're not careful. I don't want you to feel like you're alone in this."

"I didn't mean to block you out," Anna sat on the bed.

"I never thought you did," Cassie put her arm around Anna, resting her head on her shoulder.

"How are you so good at this?" Anna sighed.

"I happen to know other introverted people who disappear when they're overwhelmed."

Anna could hear Finn moving around the kitchen, cutting ingredients and flattening dough.

"What happened between you two?" Cassie prodded Anna's side with an impish grin.

"He didn't tell you?"

"Annoyingly, no," Cassie rolled her eyes, "He's not one for sharing but he's been smiling like a goof since I picked him up so I'm guessing there's something to tell?"

"Well, we talked for a bit and," Anna felt her face getting hot, "one thing led to another…"

"He kissed you?!" Cassie prompted with delighted grin splitting her face.

"I kissed him," Anna felt like a schoolgirl, except when she was a schoolgirl nothing like this had happened to her.

"And he…*stayed the night?*" Cassie raised an eyebrow suggestively.

"He did," Anna admitted, "But not like that."

"Boo," Cassie pouted with a laugh.

"We're taking things slow," Anna shrugged.

"I'm glad. You both deserve happiness," Cassie nodded with a knowing smile, "Finn's always been a bit of a mystery in the *Sex and Romance department*. We assumed he was asexual, which would have been fine if he'd have just owned it, you know? He gets so uncomfortable talking about himself though. I didn't want to push but I also wanted him to find some confidence. It's a tightrope."

"I guess," Anna wondered what had stopped Finn from dating anyone in all the years he'd known Cassie. He'd said he didn't have a lot of experience. Maybe that meant none. But why? It sounded as though he'd never been interested but, as romantic as the idea was, Anna found it hard to believe he'd never been attracted to anyone else.

Cassie's jumped up, "We should go on a double date!"

"Oh, right," Anna had forgotten Cassie was seeing the bartender from the club, "How are things with, um…"

"Jedda," Cassie grinned, "*Quite* well!"

"That's great!" Anna smiled, "She seemed cool."

"She is!" Cassie gushed, "She's been really upset over what happened though. She keeps asking how you're going and whether you're adapting okay to being a vampire. I've told her you're dealing with things pretty well but it would help if she could see for herself."

"Sure," Anna nodded, "But I don't know if Finn and I are at a double-dating stage yet."

She didn't even know if they were officially dating. Were they a couple? Were they just friends who'd made out? Things were so new and she didn't want to let herself get carried away.

"Let me know when you think it's a good time," Cassie sat back on the bed, puffing the pillows, "But, for now, let's focus more on you."

"Me?"

"You've had a little time to grieve and adapt. How are you handling everything? Are you sleeping okay?"

"Not really," Anna gave a weary half-smile, "but I've already vented pretty hard at Finn."

"A different perspective might help," Cassie shrugged, "But it's totally fine if you don't want to."

Cassie's expression reminded Anna of Liz. She missed having a sister to talk to about anything and everything. Liz would never believe magic was real. Not without proof. Cassie didn't resemble Liz in looks or personality, but both were wise and cared for Anna like family.

"I died," Anna began, despite herself, "But I'm not, like, *dead* dead. I can't remember dying and I'm not sure I want to. But it feels like the memory's there, waiting to pounce out at me. Part of me wants to try and remember it now, to be prepared, while the rest of me wants to block it out forever."

"That sounds hard," Cassie nodded, "I can help you meditate on recovering the memories, if you like?

"No spells to fast-track the process?" Anna suggested half-heartedly.

"None that I'd recommend."

"I'd settle for a good night's sleep."

"That I can help you with," Cassie grinned, gesturing at the shelves surrounding them.

She started taking books off the shelves, "I don't think a simple sleep potion will do the trick. I have over-the-counter sleeping pills too, but I doubt they'd work with your new metabolism. They aren't working on Finn. He's not sleeping either. He won't talk about why but, based on the timing, it's not hard to guess. I've tried a couple of potions on him but his werebeast constitution is making it difficult."

"And a werewolf is a type of werebeast," Anna recalled, "Right?"

"Yup."

"What are the other types?"

"Depends on where they're from," Cassie answered, skimming through a spellbook called *Divining Your Dreams*, "Weredingoes are most common in Australia."

"And, they're not called lycanthropes or lycans?" Anna asked, disappointed her pop-culture education in magic had failed her.

"Lycans are what werebeasts aspire to be," Cassie answered, "They're the ones who stay in control of their actions while they're in beast form and they can shift when it's not a full moon."

"That's possible?"

"According to my research," Cassie shrugged, tossing a book aside, "But I don't have proof. I only know one werebeast and he doesn't like to talk about it. Ah-hah!"

Cassie held open one of the large tomes with a triumphant glint in her eye.

Unaccustomed to seeing magic in action, Anna was captivated when several books flew from the shelves and flipped open on their own. Each displayed the information Cassie wanted to see before stacking themselves into a neat pile. "Hmm, I thought so," Cassie murmured to herself. She pulled a wooden trunk from under the bed and extracted two balls of black wool, five candles and several thin branches.

"Care for a spot of magic before dinner?" Cassie offered, "I'll need your help."

Excited to see more magic Anna nodded.

"Everyone does magic a little differently," Cassie began, placing the items on the floor, "I connect my energy to the universe by calling on spirits and deities. If they're willing to help me, it adds power to my spells."

"How do you know if they're willing to help?" Anna wondered if she was about to see Cassie conjure a ghost.

"It's just a feeling I get," Cassie explained, "Like if you're carrying something heavy and someone helps lift it, you can feel the load get lighter. I don't know if they're conscious entities or not but I find it easier to imagine a *personified spirit* of the forest, representing the energy of a whole forest, rather than trying to focus on each tree and creature. Does that make sense?"

"Not really."

"Everything has an energy to it," Cassie elaborated, lighting the candles, "Rocks, grass, air, clouds, sunlight - everything. *Magic* is connecting yourself to that energy and shaping it to do what you want but there needs to be balance. It's a collaboration between the spellcaster and the universe. Fire won't turn to ice just because *you ask the universe nicely* but water might. You'd still need to do the heavy lifting though, energy wise."

Anna was lost again. The whole concept of magic had transformed from a whimsical delight into one of those maths formulas composed of letters instead of numbers.

She unfocused her vision so that she could see the wafts of magic in the air. An aura of pink and gold radiated from Cassie's chest. Tendrils of its light stretched out to the floating books. Pages flipped as Cassie placed candles at even intervals around a circular rug. The rug featured a five-pointed star that reminded Anna of the devil-worshipping scenes in horror movies. She wondered, with a chill, how much of those movies were fiction.

"The pentagram is a symbol of protection," Cassie explained in response to Anna's look of concern, "It blocks out any negative energies by harnessing the five elements of magic: earth, air, fire, water and spirit."

Anna watched as the gold from Cassie's aura expanded to the edges of the rug in a dome of shimmering light. Anna looked down, hoping to see her own aura. A horrifying swirl of dark purple and black swam under her skin. The only shimmer of light came from the skin tight shield emanating from the Sunlight Sigil tattoo on the back of Anna's neck.

"I'm going to call for help from *Asibikaashi*." Cassie said softly, "Her legend comes from the Ojibwe tribe, who lived in Northern America and Canada long before those lands were colonised. The tribe knew her as *The Spider Grandmother*, and she was extremely powerful, nurturing, and protective."

"Probably a silly question," Anna frowned, "But aren't we a bit far away for, uh, Abakashi to help us?"

"*Asi-bik-aashi*," Cassie corrected, "Her essence is universal so geography isn't an issue."

"Okay," Anna accepted, "But why her? Spiders aren't exactly relaxing."

"It's what the spiders make," Cassie winked as she placed the wool and slender branches into the centre of the rug. Moving her hands slowly over the items, Cassie began to chant under her breath. The branches entwined themselves into two separate hoops while the wool wove around them. Anna quickly recognised the webbed patterns emerging.

"Dreamcatchers," Anna smiled. Cassie nodded.

"According to the legend," Cassie whispered, "When the Ojibwe tribe grew so large that their *Spider Grandmother* was unable to protect them all, she created the first dreamcatcher using her sacred symbol - the web. It catches incoming visions and sorts them, allowing only good ones to pass through. The bad images remain trapped until the sunlight burns them away."

"Amazing." Anna stared at the talismans, floating in mid-air.

A sparkling blue light spiralled up from the centre of the pentagram, infusing the dreamcatchers with more magic. Looking closer, Anna realised the sparkles were tiny spectral spiders. They scuttled over the wool, filling the large gaps with thousands of minuscule webs.

"Now," Cassie smiled, "I need your help."

"What can I do?" Anna couldn't imagine how she could possibly be useful. She couldn't do magic, other than vampire *tricks*. If anything, her void of an aura might suck magic from Cassie's spell and ruin it.

"You and Finn both need a calming counterbalance," Cassie explained, ignoring Anna's concern, "Your fears are routed in the material world but so are your sources of safety."

"Right," Anna nodded, waiting for her role to become apparent.

"I'll need some of your hair," Cassie said, holding out her hand. Anna untied her ponytail and pulled some loose strands from her scrunchie.

"Wait here," Cassie stood up and left the room. The dreamcatchers kept hovering in the air, the golden tether extended out the door. Soon, Cassie returned with a hairbrush and sat cross-legged on the floor.

"You and Finn soothe each other," she began, pulling his copper hair from the brush.

"Okay," Anna accepted, "and our hair helps the spell...how?"

"Your *essence* will help power Finn's charm," Cassie placed Anna's hair on the rug, "and I'll use Finn's for yours. It'll hopefully boost the spell enough to overcome your supernatural defences."

Cassie held her hands over the items. Several short strands of auburn hair rose from the hairbrush and entwined with the thread on the left while Anna's hair wrapped itself around the right. The spectral spiders gathered the new materials and danced their way around the charms. One of the dreamcatchers glimmered with copper while the other turned caramel brown.

"Join me in the circle," Cassie reached out a hand, "I'm going to give you some of my magic so you can flavour it for the spell."

"What if I ruin it?" Anna glanced down at her dark anti-aura.

"Just remember how you feel when Finn's around," Cassie instructed in a calming tone, "When he makes you smile. Focus on that."

Anna nodded and crawled into the translucent dome. A comforting warmth washed over her like a bath. Gold light flowed around her. Closing her eyes, Anna focused on how she'd felt with Finn's arms wrapped around her. His heartbeat was steady under her. She was safe and happy. She opened her eyes to find that, while the dark swirls remained under her skin, a soft pink light had begun to glow in a ball over her chest. Careful to hold focus on the feelings that had conjured the ball, she willed it to expand. The dome turned rich orange.

"Perfect," Cassie murmured, taking Anna's hands, "Now push it into the dreamcatchers."

Anna followed Cassie's guidance as, together, they directed the glowing essence to infuse with the dreamcatchers. The dome returned to a soft gold and the blue light faded away.

"Harming none, the spell is done," Cassie clapped her hands and the candles extinguished.

The dreamcatchers fell softly to the floor. Anna felt suddenly cold without Cassie's magic surrounding her. Cassie handed the copper dreamcatcher to Anna.

"Hang this above your bed and you should sleep like a baby," Cassie instructed, getting to her feet, "I'll do Finn's now."

Anna flopped to the floor feeling drained. She hugged the dreamcatcher to her chest. It was still warm from the spell. Her eyes fell upon one of the open books. It had a picture of a handmade toy accompanied by information about the protective qualities of poppets. She wondered if her grandfather had put spells on any of her childhood toys. He seemed the type.

As though prompted by the thought of her grandfather, Anna's eyes caught on a familiar symbol. It was stamped into the spine of an old, leather-bound book. It was identical to the one on her pendant. Taking the book from the shelf, Anna read the title *the Morrigan's Shield.*

"What are you doing?"
Anna hadn't noticed Cassie's return.
"Sorry," Anna nervously thrust the book into Cassie's hands, "I didn't mean to snoop."
"It's not that," Cassie replied frowning, "You just seemed drawn to this book. Have you seen it before?"
"Just the symbol," Anna shrugged.
Cassie raised her eyebrows, running her hand over the cover, "These are stories about a wizard who worked for a supremely powerful faerie called *the Morrigan.* They're meant to be fiction."
"Is a male witch called a wizard?" Anna guessed.
"No," Cassie shook her head, "The terms aren't gendered. It's about how your magic works and where it comes from. Witches are born with a natural ability to manipulate energy. We study how to control and enhance the magic that's already flowing through us. Warlocks get their magic by making deals with more powerful beings, who share some of their power for a price. Fae folk, like elves and druids, are born with specialised kinds of magic. Umbrella terms for all magic users are sorcerer, mage, or magician. "
"What about wizards?" Anna prompted.
"Wizards are an urban legend," Cassie murmured. She didn't seem so sure, "They're meant to be incredibly powerful because they've studied obscure magic and found ways to bypass the limitations other mages can't overcome. Witches always have to consider the balance of nature. We can't do any magic that requires more external energy than we offer up from ourselves. The universe will only match our energy. It never does all the work. That's why we form covens when do bigger spells."

"You don't think it's possible to learn magic if you're not born with it?"
"Anyone can learn the *theory* of magic," Cassie tilted her head, "But

performing it is a different story. You can learn the theory of knitting but you can't make a scarf without any wool. Plus, a big part of learning magic is knowing your limitations. If you try to harness too much energy, it'll fry you from the inside out. Legends say wizards can channel limitless power…It's impossible."

"So, who was this *fictional* wizard?" Anna pointed at the book, "Why did this…*Morrigan* choose him?"
"It doesn't say," Cassie shrugged, "the stories mostly outline the things he did in her service."
"Like what?"
"Trick faeries," Cassie chuckled dismissively, "Capture beasts from new worlds and bring them back to serve his queen. Some stories say faeries disappeared because the Morrigan's Shield trapped them in a different dimension. Others say he conjured an army of monsters from a nightmare realm, and that's where the Underfae come from. One story says he could summon the souls of creatures from the Dead Realms and force them into living beings."

Anna swallowed. Cassie slid the book back onto its shelf.
"Did you say you've seen that symbol before?" Cassie raised an eyebrow.
Anna pulled the pendant from under her top.
"*Wha*- How long have you had that?" Cassie's eyes were wide.
"Since I had lunch with my grandfather," Anna said, "Apparently, it's *his* symbol."
Cassie looked stunned. She flopped onto the bed, patting the blanket for Anna to sit, "Tell. Me. Everything."
Anna recounted every detail of her meeting with Rupert. Cassie agreed that Anna was right to be disconcerted by Rupert's blasé attitude toward casting spells on people without their knowledge or consent. Most magic users, she assured Anna, did not work that way. She also confirmed Dex and Finn both came from royal faerie families, though she stressed how neither was *fancy like that*. As Rupert had said, Finn's family didn't believe in titles and rank while Dex wanted nothing to do with his royal upbringing.

When Anna and Cassie emerged from the spare room, the kitchen was filled with the delectable aroma of freshly baked pizza. Finn had changed into a green singlet and baggy tracksuit bottoms.

"Why am I the only one who owns proper pyjamas?" Cassie exclaimed in mock outrage.

Finn gave a sheepish grin and then nodded to Anna in solidarity. She smiled back and pulled out the hem of her oversized shirt in a mock courtesy. He laughed and gave a gentle bow with a twirl of his spatula.

Two massive pizzas were cooling on a coffee table in the lounge room. As Anna settled onto the sofa, Finn brought over a third pizza and a bowl of popcorn.

"What are we watching?" He asked.

"Creature features!" announced Cassie, "I know you're both fans."

"Nothing with vampires, please," Anna implored with a subtle smile.

"Or werewolves," Finn added.

"Jaws it is!" Cassie laughed, "then Jaws 2, of course. Then Alien and Alien 2 - aka *Aliens* - then Placid Lake, or maybe Anaconda? Ooh! Jurassic Park!"

"Do you *want* us to stay up all night?" Finn asked incredulously.

"I don't want you to," Cassie sighed, falling into a squishy armchair, "but since you probably will anyway, you might as well have some entertainment."

Cassie took a large slice of pizza and began the first movie. Finn joined Anna on the sofa. She tried to focus on the movie, rather than the electricity in her thigh as his knee gently grazed against hers. She wished he'd move closer. She missed the feeling of his arm around her shoulders.

Were they a couple? Just because they hadn't gone on any dates didn't mean they hadn't spent the better part of a year getting to know each other. Wasn't that the point of dating?

Finn handed Anna a slice of mushroom and pepperoni pizza. The toppings were sparse, but each was fresh and packed with flavour. It was the perfect combination of crunchy and soft.

"This is incredible!" Anna exclaimed, putting a hand to her mouth.

"Right?!" Cassie grinned, "Finn's pizzas are *orgasmic*. Better than sex."

Finn turned bright red. "Glad you find it, um, *satisfying*," he muttered through a blushing grin. Anna and Cassie both burst out laughing. Anna could swear Finn held her eye a fraction longer than he needed to before turning to face the screen.

They all spent the rest of the night making commentary on movie plot holes and yelling common-sense instructions at the frantic victims, who always did the opposite.

Anna couldn't remember falling asleep but, when she opened her eyes, the room was dark.

It took a moment to realise her head was resting on Finn's chest, which rose and fell gently as he slept. One of his arms curled around her waist while the other hung over the edge of the sofa. Cassie was nowhere to be seen but Anna suspected she'd had something to do with the large fluffy blanket that now covered them. She knew she should probably wake Finn so they could go to their respective beds but, instead, Anna allowed herself to drift back into a peaceful, dreamless sleep.

CHAPTER 15

Blood & Cycles

The next time Anna opened her eyes, the sun had risen. Finn was still asleep beneath her with a tranquil expression on his face. The sound of rustling paper drew Anna's attention to Cassie, who had returned to her armchair and was writing in a leather-bound journal.

"Morning," she whispered to Anna with a wink.
Anna blushed and gently extracted herself from Finn's embrace.
"What time is it?" Anna asked quietly.
"Still early," Cassie replied.
"Is it okay if I take a shower?" asked Anna.
"Of course," Cassie placed her book on the coffee table.
It had the same protective star symbol on the cover that they'd used during the spell, "I'll grab you some towels."

By the time Anna returned, the kitchen smelled of coffee. Cassie was busy transferring freshly baked chocolate croissants onto plates when Anna joined her. The sofa was empty.
"Finn's showering in his ensuite," Cassie explained, following Anna's eyeline.
"Oh, I wasn-" Anna stammered.
"Yes you were," Cassie interrupted with a grin, handing Anna a mug, "You take it milky and sweet, right?"
"Yes, thanks," Anna cradled the mug in her hands, "and with a dash of blood these days."
Cassie opened the fridge and poured some blood from Anna's thermos into the mug.

"I know it's gross," Anna apologised.

"*Gross* is subjective." Cassie shrugged, "Does blood taste different now you're a vampire?"

"I guess?" Anna considered how to describe it, "I'm picking up smells and flavours that I wouldn't have noticed before. There's still a coppery undertone but it's mild."

"Hmm," replied Cassie thoughtfully, "Does each delivery taste different?"

"Not that I've noticed," answered Anna.

"I've heard some older vampires will only drink from a specific person because their blood tastes better or something." Cassie mused.

"Maybe it takes time to tell the difference?" Anna suggested, "Or maybe, if I drank from someone directly, the taste would be more defined. I don't want to find out, though."

"You're not tempted?" Cassie asked, "Dex was pretty ravenous when he first turned, Finn wouldn't leave him alone with me in case he snapped."

A chill shot down Anna's spine. Dex had warned her to avoid being alone with Cassie. She'd forgotten all about it. However, he'd also said she'd be fine as long as she had access to blood. She took a large gulp of her blood infused coffee.

"No, I'm not tempted," Anna assured, "I've had some cravings for blood but it's more like wanting a greasy burger when you're hungry than, say, needing air when you're suffocating."

"That's good," Cassie nodded thoughtfully.

"How did Dex get over the bloodlust?" Anna asked, "He seems fine now."

"I think he still struggles," Cassie said, "But he had Markus to help him at the start."

"Markus?"

"Dex's sire," Finn said, entering the kitchen. His hair was still damp and he smelled like fresh rain on a herb garden. He thanked Cassie for his coffee as he grabbed one of the mugs on the counter.

"What's Markus like?" Anna asked, taking a sip of coffee. She wondered if Dex's sire might be willing to help with her vampire training but Finn and Cassie exchanged a dark look.

"He- he *was* a good man," Finn said delicately.

"Was?" Anna repeated with a sinking realisation, "Oh…sorry."

"You couldn't have known," Cassie shrugged sadly, "He was great. He helped Dex a lot."

Anna wanted to know what had happened but decided it could wait for another time. She wasn't about to drag down the mood with more talk of death. Not now that things were finally getting easier.

"I thought you had a pack meeting this morning?" Cassie frowned at Finn.
"Crap!" Finn jumped off his stool, "What time is it?!"
"Nearly ten," Cassie answered.
"I'm late!" Finn gulped down the rest of his coffee and dashed outside. An engine roared to life, speeding down the dirt driveway until it was out of earshot.

Anna turned to Cassie, "Like, wolf pack?"
"Not the kind you would have seen in shows with *alphas* and stuff," Cassie explained, "They're more of a support group for werebeasts. I don't think Finn likes them much."
"How come?"
Cassie shrugged, "He's always in a bad mood when he comes home from meetings but he never wants to talk about it. My best guess is they spend the meetings talking about how much it sucks to be werebeasts."
Is it really that bad?" Anna asked, biting into her croissant. Chocolate oozed onto her plate. She'd spent all her time adapting to what it meant to be a vampire that she hadn't asked Finn about werebeasts. She'd assumed it just meant Finn turned into a wolf during the full moon, but perhaps there was more.

"Werebeasts have similar gifts to vampires," Cassie sat next to Anna, picking pastry off her croissant, "Accelerated healing, heightened senses, amplified strength. But...those abilities change with the moon cycle. They come and go like the tide. Everything builds through the waxing phase until their power peaks at the full moon. The beast takes over and they have no control over what happens. Then, in the waning phase, their powers get slowly weaker until the night of the new moon, when they're as fragile and vulnerable your average human."
"Sounds exhausting," Anna grimaced, trying to imagine what it would be like to transition from human to vampire and back again on a monthly basis. Once was more than enough.
"Oh yeah," Cassie nodded, "Their bodies are in a constant state of change, which tends to make them... temperamental."
"Huh," Anna mused, "Reminds me of-"

"A menstrual cycle?" Cassie smirked.

"Yeah," replied Anna, "One day you're full of energy. The next, you feel helpless, the world is too loud and everyone's annoying for no reason."

"I have a theory that the women adjust better to becoming werebeasts because they're already used to living on a rollercoaster of bodily betrayal." She gave a dry laugh, "but it's just a theory. Finn works hard to keep a handle on his moods. I don't know, maybe I'm just...*barking mad*."

"Ha," Anna shook her head at the bad pun. "I had no idea he was going through all that."

"He doesn't like to *burden people* with his problems," Cassie rolled her eyes.

Anna could relate. The thought of dragging her friends down, just because she was suffering, seemed selfish and cruel.

On the other hand, venting her problems to Cassie and Finn had lifted a weight from her shoulders and they seemed happier for it. Glad to be trusted. And Finn had shared his problems with her in return. Perhaps that's why he didn't talk about these things with Cassie - she was great at helping with other people's problems but never seemed to have any of her own. It's easier to compare wounds than explain what pain feels like to someone who can't relate.

***

Anna and Cassie ate lunch on the porch watching butterflies and bees explore the garden. The tranquillity was wonderful. Living in an apartment was convenient but the noise was never-ending. Even before becoming a vampire, Anna had to constantly block out sounds from her neighbours, traffic, low-flying planes, people shouting on the street for no apparent reason, and more. She envied Cassie and Finn's little sanctuary in the forest.

Just as they decided to head inside, a roaring motorcycle sped down the driveway. It parked next to the van and its rider seemed to dismount in slow motion, like an advertisement for cologne. He wore a leather jacket, and tight blue jeans like a 1950's greaser. Anna did a double take when Finn's head emerged from the rider's helmet. She hadn't noticed Finn's clothing when he left but now, as he shrugged out of a leather jacket, her eyes drifted hungrily over the tight, white t-shirt as it hugged his muscular chest.

"Hi," Anna grinned stupidly from the shadows of the porch, "Nice ride."

"It's not very *me*," Finn grimaced, storing the helmet and walking toward them, "but it's good for driving through the bush."

"You go off-roading?" Dirt-biking also didn't seem his style.

"The pack meets in the middle of nowhere, right?" Cassie answered for him, "Even when they're not about to turn."

"Silverbark Ridge," Finn confirmed, "It's easier than getting everyone to agree on a different spot."

"Oh, right." Anna nodded, "Makes sense."

"Have you had lunch yet?" Cassie offered, "We left you some food and I thought, after you've eaten, you could give Anna a lift home?"

"Sick of me already?" Anna joked.

"I have some things to do in the garden," Cassie shrugged innocently, adding a secretive wink, "Besides I've been hogging your all time. It's Finn's turn."

"Sounds good to me," Finn smiled, "I stopped for lunch on my way back so we can go whenever you're ready."

"I'll just grab my bag," Anna dashed inside and then attempted to walk gracefully to the van while the sweltering sun blazed down on her. Her feet felt like they'd been coated in cement and she had to check her skin wasn't melting off. The air was so humid it was hard to breathe.

"Sorry to disappear all morning," Finn climbed into the driver's seat. Anna had a renewed appreciation for automatic transmission vehicles as Finn rested his prosthetic foot in the space where a clutch would normally be.

"It was good to catch up with Cassie," Anna smiled, doing her best to ignore the suffocating heat in the van, "How was the meeting?"

"Not great," Finn gave a weary smile.

"How come?" Anna turned the air conditioning to full blast.

"It's just dumb pack drama," Finn shrugged.

"Can you tell me about it?" Anna asked, "I might not be able to help but I'd still like to know what's going on, especially if it's bothering you."

"It's this guy, Dane." Finn shook his head bitterly, "He's one of the older members of my pack and he's been pressuring everyone to try shifting when it's not a full moon. It's extremely painful and, if you do it wrong, you can end up permanently stuck in beast form. Plus, turning more often obviously increases the likelihood we'll accidentally infect or kill someone. He's been targeting our youngest member, Toby, who's too afraid to stand up for himself."

"Why does he want people to shift?"

"He thinks it'll help us *control our beasts*," Finn sighed, "When we're forced to shift, we have no control over what we do. Sometimes we don't remember what happened, but a lot of the time it'll come back to us in bits. It's the worst kind of helplessness."

Anna placed her hand on Finn's knee as he continued, wishing she could do something more supportive.

"Dane's theory is," he continued, "if we embrace our beasts by letting them out regularly, we'll form a connection that lets us stay in control no matter what shape our bodies take."

"You don't think that's true?" Anna guessed.

Finn shrugged, "I don't think the risk is worth finding out."

"Why does he think it's possible?" Anna asked, "He must be pretty sure of himself to be forcing the idea onto other people."

"He heard the Elven army has a unit of lycan soldiers," Finn frowned at the road, "Apparently they enlisted a pack of werewolves and forced them to shift several times a day, every day, until they were all in full control - making them lycans. Rumour is, they're unstoppable. But I don't think it's true. The Elven Empire doesn't work with Underfae. They think we're beneath them and they definitely wouldn't want to train *unstoppable* lycans who might turn on them."

"Would Dex know anything about it?" Anna suggested, "Maybe he could set Dane straight?"

"I doubt it," Finn shook his head, "Dex grew up in the Elven court but he wasn't involved with secret military operations or experiments."

"What about Arik?" Anna suggested.

Finn's eyebrows shot up. "How do you know about Dex's brother?"

"He was at the club looking for Dex…that night," Anna answered.

"I didn't think they were on speaking terms," Finn said, looking pensively at the horizon.

"Dex wasn't happy to see him," Anna elaborated, "but he was pretty insistent about wanting to resolve things with Dex. He said something about a job."

They stopped in front of Anna's apartment. The journey had ended too quickly. Anna wasn't ready to say goodbye yet, and it seemed Finn wasn't either.

"Do you want to come inside?" Anna offered.

Finn hesitated, "You're not too tired?"

"Why would I be?"

"You didn't exactly go to bed last night," Finn rubbed the back of his neck sheepishly.

"Neither did you," Anna grinned, "Are you too tired?"

Finn smiled broadly, unbuckling his seatbelt.

CHAPTER 16

Experiments

Anna hung the dreamcatcher from Cassie over her bed. A magical feeling of comfort radiated from it. Finn reclined on her bed, watching her with a fond expression.

"So, um," Anna hovered by the edge of the bed, "What does *taking things slow* mean to you exactly?"

Finn sat up, his dimples disappeared, "Is everything okay?"

"Yeah," Anna joined him on the bed, "I just don't want to do anything that makes you uncomfortable."

He nodded with a relieved sigh and then looked away in thought.

"My first sexual experience ended badly," he whispered with a grim expression, "I've been trying to work though it - I've *experimented* - but I've never been able to go all the way..." he swallowed, "I'm a virgin."

Anna traced her fingers along Finn's cheek. He cast his eyes down and sniffed, "It's pathetic, I know. I understand if you don't want-"

She kissed him. His eyes snapped to hers in surprise.

"I just want to understand you better," she whispered. "I certainly don't think less of you."

Finn leaned his forehead against Anna's and sighed, "I don't deserve you."

"That's for me to decide," Anna replied with a soft smile.

He pressed his lips to hers, "I wish I could show you how much you mean to me."

"You do," Anna smiled, breathing in his gentle scent, kissing his neck.

"I can do more..." he nibbled her ear, "Like I said, I've *experimented...*"

Though she was poised to melt into his arms, Anna pulled back from Finn and tilted her head. She wanted to know more about his past. Especially if it explained why he was so insecure.

"But, you hit a wall?" she prompted, "Was it the act or the person? Or both?"

Finn leaned back against the pillows, running a hand through his hair, "I don't know if you want to hear about it. Me with other women…"

It was true. Anna didn't like the idea of picturing Finn with anyone else but understanding his past was more important than petty jealousy. She'd tapped into a part of Finn's life that not even Cassie knew about.

"Tell me. Please?"

"It was with someone in my pack," Finn began reluctantly, "We were around the same age and she helped me a lot when I first joined. I never had romantic feelings for her but we…tried things. She knew I wanted to work through my sexual triggers. I thought if I pushed my boundaries with a friend it wouldn't be so stressful. You know?"

Anna nodded and squeezed his hand to continue.

"I- uh- went down on her," he exhaled, avoiding Anna's gaze, "And I liked it. A lot. But she started to want more from me. Not just physical stuff but romantic too. We'd agreed it would just be physical experimentation but it turned out she'd had feelings for me all along. I think she was hoping I'd come around but I couldn't make myself want her the way she wanted me."

"What happened?"

"I ended it," Finn shrugged, "We still see each other when the pack meets. It was awkward for a while but I think things are okay now."

Anna didn't love that Finn and this mystery woman were still seeing each other every month. But she trusted him. And, more importantly, he'd trusted her with information he clearly felt he couldn't share with anyone else.

"You know," Anna curled into to him, "You don't have to brand yourself a virgin. A lot of people consider oral sex to be, well, *sex*."

"I feel like a virgin though," Finn ran a hand through his hair, "Saying I've had sex feels like a lie."

"If it helps," Anna rested her head on his shoulder, "I've only had sex twice and both times were so long ago I'm not sure they count anymore."

Finn looked confused, so she elaborated. "For the first, I was sixteen. I was so grateful a boy was interested in me that I was willing to do whatever he wanted just to keep him around. I didn't have a good time and he dumped me when I asked if we could wait a bit before we tried again."

"Yikes," Finn cringed.

"The other time, I was twenty-three," Anna continued, "I met a guy through a dating app and, even though the thought of meeting a stranger terrified me, I forced myself to go out with him. He seemed nice. We dated for a month or so and I thought we could be *something*...but after we slept together he ghosted me. Blocked me on everything. I never heard from him again."

"What?!" Finn exclaimed, turning to face Anna. "Why the hell would anyone do that?"

"I guess he got what he wanted," Anna shrugged.

She'd been a wreck when it had happened. It took years of reassurance from Liz that the guy was just a pathetic *Fuck Boy* before Anna believed his rejection hadn't been her fault. It had, however, put her off dating apps permanently.

"The woman I...you know-" Finn raised his eyebrows with a flush in his cheeks.

"Went down on," Anna prompted, feeling her cheeks redden too.

"As much as I liked it, it was nothing like being with you."

"Technically, you don't know that," Anna blushed, a sudden flush of warmth pulsated between her thighs at the thought of Finn exploring her with his tongue, "We'd need a direct comparison to be sure. For science."

"Hmm," a dirty grin spread across Finn's face, "That's true."

He leaned toward her, brushing a stray hair from her face. The loving way he looked into her eyes made her heart melt.

"You make my world brighter," he breathed. Anna smiled and pressed a slow kiss onto his soft lips. The dimples on his cheeks grew deeper as Anna moved her hand under Finn's shirt. She traced the soft contours of his chest with her fingers. He bit his lip and stroked his hand down Anna's spine until it rested on her backside. The warmth between her legs intensified. Tingles flew up her spine as Finn gently kissed the sensitive skin under her earlobe, "How would you feel about conducting an experiment," Finn growled seductively.

"I'm all yours," Anna sighed.

Finn slid off his shirt, exposing his exquisitely toned chest. There was a tuft of red hair between his pecs and his pale skin was adorned with freckles and thin, white scars. He took Anna's waist, guiding her to lay flat on her back. He kissed her again, greedily this time, before tracing his fingers along her collarbone and moving his mouth toward her chest. In a titillatingly sudden motion, he pulled down Anna's singlet. She gasped at the rush of cool air caressing her exposed nipples. Finn's tongue was quick to warm them as he grunted with pleasure, licking each in circular motions before continuing his excruciatingly deliberate journey down her torso. He massaged her thighs, kissing her navel until he reached the boundary of her pants. The fabric separating Finn's touch from Anna's naked body was unbearable. She unbuttoned her shorts, tugging them down just enough for Finn to get the message.

With a ravenous glint in his eyes, Finn slid Anna's pants past her ankles and dropped them on the floor. He moaned at the sight of her soaked opening, burying his face between her thighs. Waves of pleasure rippled through her body as he massaged her with his tongue. She cried out as he gave her nipples a gentle pinch before grabbing her ass, pulling her closer so his tongue could explore deeper. She shook with lust, stretching her knees apart and thrusting into him. The sight of his soft curls brushing against her pelvis was almost enough to send her over the edge. For a torturous moment, Finn pulled back, locking eyes with Anna as he licked his lips and grinned. He kept his gaze on her as he slowly petted her wet entrance with his index finger, "What are your thoughts on the experiment so far?"

Anna bit her lip. "Mmm, mixed," she moaned with a mischievous grin.
Finn raised an eyebrow, "Constructive criticisms are encouraged," he smiled as he continued to caress her.
"Well," Anna sighed, trying to hide the waves of pleasure provoked by Finn's touch, "Everything you're doing is very, very good," she grinned, "but it's making me want to fuck you so badly. And I can't even kiss you while you're all the way down there."
"Noted," he kissed his way up Anna's torso while his hand remained between her legs, "Your feedback is very important to us."

Anna chuckled as she pressed her mouth to Finn's lips, pushing his lips apart with her tongue. She could taste herself. It should have been

143

repulsive but the intimacy of the moment made it strangely pleasurable. Finn moaned as she wrapped her legs around his hips, pinning his petting hand in place. Finn looked down and smirked. He began wriggling his finger against her, driving her wild with desire.

"More?" His lips touched her ear like the brush of a butterfly's wing.

"More," begged Anna, letting her fingernails rake softly across his back.

The stubble on his jaw bristled across her shoulder as he slid a finger inside her. She moaned at the delicious feeling. She could feel his arousal pressing into her thigh. He nibbled her earlobe while he stroked her, massaging her g-spot with his index finger while his thumb circled her clit.

Anna's breath caught in a tsunami of pleasure. Her body jolted with euphoric spasms.

"You seriously think this isn't sex?" Anna panted.

"It's *sexy*," Finn beamed at Anna's unravelling.

"Your turn?" Anna stroked the bulge in Finn's pants.

"Not today," he breathed, kissing her softly, "Today, I want to explore your body. I want to touch you like I do in my fantasies. I want to make you come until you see stars."

His lips hovered over hers, barely touching. He guided her arms above her head, then lightly stroked her skin. He traced her arms, her breasts, her torso, and thighs slowly, ever so slowly, until his warm hands rested, once more, between her thighs.

He pulled wave after wave of orgasmic pleasure through her, each time watching her squirm with delight.

CHAPTER 17

Heroics

"Morning!" Anna chirped, handing Cassie a latte as she entered the office. She left Dex's cup on his desk before handing Finn a Dirty Chai with a coy smile. He returned it with a nod of thanks and a sneaky wink. There were two new temps sitting at the front of the room. One regarded Anna with casual disinterest while the other ignored her completely.

"Is Dex still taking time off?" Anna pondered aloud.
"I messaged him a couple of times," Cassie grimaced at her phone, "He hasn't replied,"
"We should check on him after work," Finn furrowed his brow.
"Do you think he's not okay?" Anna whispered, even though the temps were both wearing thick headphones.
"Probably just partying too hard," Cassie answered.
The coffee Anna had left on Dex's desk mocked her as a grim monument to his absence. How long had it been since she'd talked to him? When was the last time she'd seen that impish grin spread across his face? She'd been so focused on herself that she hadn't even considered Dex might need help.

***

There was no answer when Finn buzzed the intercom to Dex's apartment that evening. Cassie tried calling his phone twice but it went straight to voicemail, *"Hi, I'm not calling you back. This isn't the middle ages. Send a text like a civilised adult."* BEEP.
"He never turns his phone off," Cassie looked worried.
"Maybe he's not home." A crease appeared between Cassie's eyebrows.
"We need a way in to check," Finn looked around as though a solution

145

might appear. The building was five stories tall, surrounded by hedges.

"I have an idea," Anna announced, jogging back toward the street before taking a running jump at the building. On the night she'd trained with Dex, she'd cleared the trees in the park without even trying. How hard could it be to reach the roof of the building?
"Anna, what-?" Finn began, but she was already in the air. She was soaring toward the sky. She was going to make it. She was...

The world slowed to a stop. Adrenaline pumped in her ears as, too late, Anna realised she wasn't going to reach the roof. Her current trajectory was leading her into the cement wall. She put her hands and feet out like a cat, bracing herself for the impact.
CRUNCH.

She scrambled against the wall, desperate to get a grip on the flat surface. Impossibly, it worked. She tried to remember what Dex had said about vampires being able to scale walls. Nothing practical.
If it was anything like the other magic she'd experienced, she just had to focus on believing it was possible. She could sense the same pull in her hands and knees as when she walked on solid ground. Focusing on that feeling, she closed her eyes and told herself it was *just a floor*. A floor with windows. That's all it was. Ignoring a pulsing pain in her knees, Anna crawled toward the roof. It was working! She was doing it!

But then she opened her eyes.
Reality came rushing in. She slipped. Cassie screamed as Anna skidded a metre down the wall, regaining her grip just in time to avoid falling further. Her hands and knees stung with fresh wounds but she wasn't about to give up. Shifting her weight slowly, Anna imagined having a magnetic grip. She blocked out everything around her, focusing solely on her connection to the wall. Trusting the magic, she began to climb. She didn't feel weightless, by any means, but it was working. It was like rock climbing, except there were no handholds.

Finally, Anna made it to the roof. She forced her shaking legs to move across the corrugated metal to the side of the building where Dex's balcony overlooked the river and dropped onto it. His apartment was obscured by thick curtains but she heard movement inside.

"DEX?" she yelled, hammering on the sliding door, "DEX, ARE YOU IN THERE?"

"Bloody hell, calm down," his groggy voice moaned, "It's not locked."

Anna slid open the door and pulled back the curtain. The scene inside was not pretty.

The floor was littered with liquor bottles and dirty clothes. Two men and a woman lay naked on Dex's bed. Dex was on the floor wearing nothing but satin boxer shorts. He leant against his bed, eyes closed, cradling an empty gin bottle in his arms. Though everyone appeared to be unharmed, the bedclothes were stained with blood. The smell was overwhelming. A sudden thirst compelled Anna toward the humans. They were sleeping soundly. Their heartbeats beckoning her closer. Surely they wouldn't mind if Anna took a little taste. They'd obviously let Dex have his fill. A vibration in Anna's pocket brought her back to reality. She didn't remember stepping forward but she found herself hovering over one of the men. She dashed outside to centre herself. The fresh air helped but didn't eliminate the urge. When had she last fed? Lunchtime seemed a long while ago...

Holding her breath, Anna walked back inside.

"Watchoo want?" Dex slurred from the floor.

"We came to check on you," Anna made a beeline to the intercom, buzzing the others up.

"You don't need to," he murmured, "I'm *grrreat.*"

"Who are they?" asked Anna, gesturing at the people on the bed.

"Doesn't matter," Dex shrugged, "I'll get rid of them if you like?"

Without waiting for Anna to answer, he started banging on the bed.

"Oi!" he yelled, "Wakey, wakey kids! Time to go home!"

The strangers got up with glazed-over eyes and dressed clumsily. If it bothered any of them to be kicked out so abruptly they didn't show it. They barely noticed Finn and Cassie as they passed in the doorway. Finn left his wheelchair by the door while Cassie gawked at the strangers, "Is that guy okay? He looks- Oh my god, Dex you're a wreck!"

Cassie fell to her knees by Dex's side, wiping the air around him as though fending off flies.

Finn took Anna aside, "Please never scare me like that again," he whispered.

"What do you mean?" Anna wondered if Finn somehow knew how close she'd come to drinking human blood. The smell was still present but no longer overwhelming. The remaining blood was dry and unappealing, though Anna was sickeningly aware of Cassie's movements around the room.

"You nearly fell off a building!" Finn clarified in a muted yell.

"I made it onto the roof."

"You could have gotten hurt."

"But I didn't," Anna's knees were no longer pounding with pain. She silently thanked her vampiric healing for mending what had felt like severe gravel rash coupled with two shattered kneecaps. Especially before Finn had seen the damage.

"Just, please," Finn brushed his hand along her arm, "No more heroics?"

"No promises," Anna kissed Finn briefly on the cheek before walking over to Dex. It had felt good to throw caution to the wind. To take a risk without weighing the pros and cons. She'd *done something* instead of waiting for someone else to figure things out. Had it gone perfectly? No. But, thanks to her, they were all here to help Dex instead of milling about on the street outside.

Anna took the gin bottle from Dex and replaced it with a large jug of water from the kitchen. Finn began stripping the bed sheets. It seemed automatic, as though he'd found Dex like this many times before.

"I'm fine!" Dex insisted, "Can't I have some sodding fun without everyone jumping down my throat about it?"

"You're not fine," Cassie said gently, "When was the last time you slept?"

"Five minutes ago," he retorted, "before you lot barged in!"

"When was the last time you slept *sober*?" Cassie sighed.

Dex licked his lips and looked off to the side, thinking. "None of your business," he answered.

"What's going on with you?" Anna said, joining him on the floor.

"Nothing," he slurred, "I'm good. *I'm great!*"

Anna looked at him sceptically.

"I am *Dexter Duke!*" He announced savagely, "My life is one big party! Drinking, dancing and fucking. It might be all I'm good for but I'm exceptionally good at it." He gulped down the water as though it was something stronger.

"Never mind that I got you killed," he tipped his head toward Anna, "Or that I'm a constant worry to my friends-" He gestured to the others as they cleaned his wreck of an apartment, "Or that no one takes me seriously and my family's ashamed of me... at least I'm the *life of the fucking party!*"

"You didn't get me killed, Dex," Anna said quietly.

"I didn't bloody save you, did I?" He muttered.

"Has something happened with your family?" Cassie asked, "Something new?"

Finn stopped cleaning to listen.

"Arik's been hovering around," Dex growled, "Acting like he cares when I know he doesn't. It's all an act. Makes it harder to forget... I thought I was over it."

"Maybe he does care," Anna suggested.

"He's here on Mother's orders," Dex made a face, "He doesn't care about me. He cares about pleasing *her*."

"What orders?" Finn asked, sitting on the edge of Dex's mattress.

"I don't know," Dex tussled his already messy hair, "It's never simple with her. Arik said she wants me to be an intermediary between the Elven Empire and the vampires. *Ambassador*, he called it. But I know there's some catch. It's all bullshit."

"Are you sure?" Anna asked, "Maybe he's being sincere."

"They could get anyone for the job," he shook his head, "Someone who wasn't banished in disgrace. Someone who's not... How did Arik put it?... Oh yes, *an unreliable, superficial, selfish brat who would rather watch the world burn than miss a party*."

"He didn't say that, did he?" Cassie gasped.

"I may also have said some unkind things," Dex admitted, "We've always known how to push each other's buttons."

"Well, he's wrong," Anna said, "You're a kind, generous person. You've always been there when I needed you."

Dex raised his eyebrows at her. "If that were true," he hissed, "you wouldn't have fangs."

"Did I ask you to come into the alley with me that night?" Anna asked, frustrated.

"No, but- "

"Have you ever refused to help me when I asked for it?" she asked.

"Technically, no, but- "

"I left the club because I wanted to get some air and be *alone*," she said, looking from Dex to Finn and Cassie, "Everyone keeps blaming themselves for *not being there*. But another way of putting that is to say it's *my fault* for going out alone."

"It could never be your fault!" Cassie gasped.

"Exactly!" Anna agreed with exasperation, "Maybe those guys wouldn't have attacked me if we'd been together but it's still one-hundred percent *their* fault. They killed me. They're to blame. Fuck those guys. Stop. Blaming. Yourselves."

Anna stood up and continued cleaning where Finn had left off. No one spoke for several minutes while she aggressively threw bottles into Dex's recycling bin. Finn pulled Dex up to sit with him on the bare mattress, putting a thick arm around his narrow shoulders.

"Listen," Finn said quietly, "I know I've already apologised for what I said before, but I need you to hear me this time. I'm sorry I blamed you. It's not your fault. I should never have said what I said. I was projecting my shit onto you and you didn't deserve it."

Dex began to sob, leaning into Finn. "Everything's so fucked," Dex whimpered.

"It's okay," Finn consoled, "You're okay."

By the time Dex was calm and sober, his bedsheets and apartment were clean.

"Where's your phone, by the way?" asked Finn.

Dex patted the sides of his legs, forgetting he wasn't wearing pants, and then searched several nooks in his apartment before finally discovering his phone in the refrigerator. He turned it on to receive a barrage of notifications.

"Never let it be said I'm not popular," Dex cringed, clearing away all the messages without reading them.

"Dex!" Cassie chastised.

"Everyone who matters is here," he explained with a playful shrug.

A cool breeze wafted through the balcony door.

"Do you want to go out?" Finn suggested, "Get some fresh air."

"Nah," Dex smiled, standing up, "I'm pretty tired. I think I'll get some proper sleep. You guys don't need to stick aro-"

A heavy knock at the door interrupted.

Dex closed his eyes and slowly raked his fingers through his hair. "Who is it?" he called out, in a mockingly sweet tone.

"Open the door, please," a deep voice answered.

Dex stomped over to the door and pulled it open. Arik scanned the room as he stepped inside. He moved with the rigid grace of a ballroom dancer. "I didn't realise you had company," he said curtly.

"Well, I do," Dex replied curtly, "What do you want?"

"I-," he faltered. His expression softened. He took a step closer, "I came to see if you're alright. I called you several times. I'm worried about you."

"You're worried about *you*," Dex corrected, "You don't want to return to Mother having failed your little mission."

"That's not true," Arik said stiffly, "Mother's assignment was…" He cut himself off, pursing his lips.

"What?" Dex prompted.

"An excuse," Arik finished quietly, "I used it as an excuse to see you. She never asked for you specifically. My assignment is to find an ambassador to broker peace between the Elven Empire and the Underfae. I was the one who wanted you for the job."

The silence that followed made Anna wish she wasn't there. She considered excusing herself to the balcony or hallway but had a feeling it would only exacerbate the awkwardness.

"Why?" Dex breathed. If he was uncomfortable having this conversation with an audience, he didn't show it.

"I miss you," Arik replied quietly before glancing around the room and returning to his formal posture and tone, "And I thought you'd excel at the job. There was a time when you delighted in navigating the treacherous waters of diplomatic relations."

"I was a different person then," Dex said defensively.

"I know," Arik replied.

They stared at each other in a strange stalemate.

"I'm Cassie, by the way," Cassie stepped in and offered her hand, "and this is Anna and Finn."

"It's nice to meet you, Cassie," said Arik, shaking Cassie's hand before nodding at Finn, "Henry and I are well acquainted. We used to spar together, though it seems a lot has changed since I last saw you."

"Yes," Finn nodded back, "It feels like a lifetime ago."

Arik turned to Anna. His pale blue eyes lingered briefly on her pendant before he spoke. "Anna is a lovely name," he smiled gently, "I see you're no longer Lax. I hope the transition hasn't been too disorienting for you. How are you finding things?"

"I'm doing well, thank you," she said politely, "I've had a lot of support. From Dex especially."

"I'd expect nothing less," Arik looked at his brother with pride, "Please let me know if I can assist you in any way."

"That's a very kind offer," Anna matched his polite tone, "Maybe we can keep in touch?"

"Of course!" Arik gave a genuine-looking smile, withdrawing an unnaturally clean mobile phone from his internal blazer pocket and handing it to her. Anna entered her details and handed it back.

"Thank you," he smiled.

"Well, this has been swell," Dex said, rounding everyone toward the door, "Thank you all for coming and caring but if you wouldn't mind buggering off so I can shower, that'd be great."

"Okay," Cassie hugged him goodbye, "but please *look after yourself*, and get an early night! We'll see you at work tomorrow, right?"

"Right," He smiled appreciatively before closing the door.

As they approached the van outside the apartment block, Cassie turned to Arik, "Do you need a lift anywhere?"

"No, thank you," He began to walk away but stopped, turning back with a frown. "I-," he stammered, looking from Cassie to Finn, "I'd like to thank you for looking after him. Today and…When I couldn't…When I wasn't there. "

They both nodded sombre comprehension.

"Any time," Cassie replied.

"Always," Finn added.

On the way home, Anna received a comically formal text message.

Arik: *Thank you for sharing your details, Anna.*
       I hope in time we will become good friends.
       Sincerely,
       Arik Faeregina

"Faeregina?" Anna read aloud, "Not Duke?"

"Dex changed his name when he left," Finn explained, "He didn't want to be associated with his old self."

"I guess that makes sense," Anna said, "It just seems a bit extreme."

"At the time," Finn said slowly, "Extremes were necessary."

"What does that mean?" Anna asked.

"It's not my story to tell," replied Finn apologetically, "Dex will share all the details when he's ready." Finn put a reassuring hand on Anna's shoulder. She rested her cheek on it.

"I'll check on him again later tonight," she promised, "Just to make sure he's really okay."

CHAPTER 18

Blood & Monsters

The night air was blissfully cool on Anna's face as she ran through the city. It was surprising so many people were out and about at midnight on a Monday. Cheers and clinking glasses sounded from pubs as she passed. The scent of battered food wafted from greasy hole-in-the-wall food vendors. Giddy laughter echoed off the empty office buildings as groups of drunk revellers stumbled from one place to another.

Dex's place was dark. Meaning he was either sleeping or had decided to go out. Anna climbed onto his balcony. She was getting the hang of her powers. She only slipped on the vertical climb once and didn't even scrape her knees this time. Dex's curtains were closed but the balcony door was still open. She heard a steady heartbeat and rhythmic breathing coming from the direction of Dex's bed. His sweet citrus scent wafted through the open door. He was sleeping. Good. She climbed up to the roof to watch the stars under the waning moonlight before heading home. It was beautiful. Peaceful. Though not as quiet as she'd have liked...

A house party blared its music a few blocks away. Anna used the opportunity to hone her skills at focusing on individual conversations, blocking out all competing noise.

"...best place to get booze," one voice said, "They never check ID. I got all these for $30!"

"...And then David said he wasn't going to ask her out," said another, feminine voice, "but now they're, like, fully dating and Paul was like..."

Anna chuckled. The one-sentence stories gave her a tiny window into people's lives. It was like switching channels on a TV.

"...Where are we going?" slurred a slightly panicked female voice. Anna sat up.

"Just trust me," replied a young male, "it's too crowded in there."

The girl giggled nervously as footsteps crunched through dry grass.

"Brad!" gasped the girl, "Brad, stop! Someone will see…"

"Aw, come on, babe," he soothed, "No one's around."

"Seriously," the girl pleaded, "Not now. Not here."

"*Seriously*," mocked the male voice, "You know I can't resist you in that skirt."

"No, really," the girl struggled, "I don't want to!"

Blood pounded in Anna's ears as she listened to the exchange.

"Brad, STOP!" the girl whimpered, "Get off me!"

Anna had heard enough. She leapt from the rooftop, landing silently on the street before dashing toward the sound of a scuffle. She saw two figures wrestling in the shadows of a nearby park. To the rest of the world, they were obscured in darkness but she could see them with perfect clarity.

"Stop squirming," complained Brad, "You know you want it."

"No," the girl cried, "Not again, Brad, please! You promised you wouldn't-!"

"Fuck, you make me so hard!"

"No, *please!*"

"Just stay still!"

Anna ripped the man off the girl. She threw him into the trunk of a nearby tree. He crumpled like a ragdoll, coughing and sputtering. The girl screamed and hastily covered her exposed bra with shaking hands. Her singlet was in shreds.

"He didn't mean it!" She cried.

"He did," Anna growled, pushing her foot into his chest.

"Ge'roff me, bitch!" Brad choked, "Mind your fuckin' business!"

Anna pulled him up by the neck. He was taller than her but seemed unable to find his footing as he scrambled in vain to assert dominance. He cursed again, spitting blood in her face.

The smell was intoxicating. Overpowering.

Like a frenzied shark, Anna drove her razor-sharp fangs into his soft, pulsating flesh. The gush of warm liquid pouring down her throat was euphoric. Better than anything she'd ever tasted before. The fresh blood tingled and exploded through her whole body. It satisfied a hunger she'd never known she had. It filled an emptiness that had existed long before she'd died. She'd never felt this alive. She was free. She was powerful. She was divine. Nothing could stop her. She devoured life itself. She...

The dizzying high ended as quickly as it began. Anna returned to herself to find her face pressed against Brad's sweaty neck. The toxic fumes of cheap body spray choked her nostrils. She gagged, letting his lifeless body fall to the ground. The girl was screaming again. Anna stared in shock at the pale body of the man she'd just killed. *What the fuck have I done?*

"Nice work," a voice purred from the shadows. A set of glowing eyes emerged from the darkness. As the figure approached, her telltale fangs became visible. Her hair had two bright streaks of red flowing through it, and had been fixed into two tight buns. Heavy, black eyeshadow emphasised her monolid eyes and dark lipstick shone like oil from her mouth. Her clothes were covered with torn holes, held together with shining safety pins.

Disturbingly unperturbed by what she'd just witnessed, the vampire approached the screaming girl, placing a hand on her cheek, "Hush now," she soothed the girl with unblinking eye contact, "Be calm. You're safe now."

The girl stopped screaming. The anguish in her face faded into an expressionless stupor. The vampire smiled triumphantly at Anna but then frowned, "Why do you look freaked?"

Anna didn't know what to say. She'd just killed someone. His lifeless body was sprawled at her feet. How else should she look?

"Oh," the woman's tone softened, "You're new to this, aren't you?" She wrapped her arm around Anna's shoulder, "It's all right. We've all been there. I'm Roxy."

Anna blinked.

"Wait here," said Roxy, lifting the man's limp body and tossing it unceremoniously over her shoulder, "I'll get rid of this piece of shit, then we can talk."

Roxy disappeared into the night. Though she was small and slender, she carried Brad's hulking figure with ease. Anna looked at the dazed girl. She no longer seemed worried about her torn clothing.

"Are you okay?" Anna's voice shook.

"Yes," the girl replied mildly, "I'm safe now."

"What's your name?"

"Laura."

Anna nodded. She didn't know what else to say. They stood in silence for the few minutes it took for Roxy to return.

"Where did you take him?" Anna choked. Her chest felt tight.

"One of the drop-off points," Roxy answered conversationally, "The VA'll sort things out from there."

"What does that mean?" Anna whimpered, dropping onto the grass. Her shaking knees had given up on her.

"The Vampiric Alliance expects us to kill," Roxy explained, "as long as we don't cause a public panic, they'll take care of any mess left behind."

"I'm a murderer," Anna felt bile rising in her throat, "He had a family and friends-" She glanced at Laura, "he had a whole future that's just...Gone now..."

"Like I said... Mess," Roxy shrugged, "It'll be fine. You're not in any trouble. Those fucked up human laws don't apply to us."

"Human laws aren't *fucked up*!" Anna snapped, "Murder is wrong! He was practically a kid!"

He had looked about twenty-five but it was impossible to be sure. Laura couldn't be older than sixteen. It sounded like they'd been dating a while. Maybe they were in the same year at school...

"He was a rapist!" Roxy exclaimed, "It doesn't matter how old he was! Fifteen or fifty, once they think they're entitled to sex whether the other person wants it or not, there's no going back. The world's better without him in it, *and you know it*."

"But the law-"

"Laws exist to protect the men who write them. They aren't a marker for what's right or fair. It wasn't too long ago that slavery was legal and *freeing a slave* was a crime. Laws on rape are weak because lawmakers think it's more likely they'll be accused of rape than become victims of it."

"Why don't you just hypnotise the lawmakers then?" Anna asked.

"Most have covens of witches protecting them," Roxy said, raising a pierced eyebrow, "Or they're already being controlled by vampires. Not all of us care about protecting the innocent. There's a reason the cliché image of a vampire is a rich old white dude."

"But…" Anna wanted to cry.

None of this felt real.

"It's just a shame that fucker died feeling good," Roxy lamented.

"What?" Anna blanched. She'd been violent. She'd knocked him around and held him by the throat. How could Roxy think he'd had a good time?

"Our bite puts people in a euphoric state," Roxy explained, "Keeps them still while we feed, which is convenient unless you want them to suffer."

"I didn't want him to suffer," Anna retorted, wrapping her arms around her legs, hating that it wasn't true. "I didn't mean to kill him."

She hadn't…had she? She'd wanted to stop him. To punish him. To make sure he never touched another woman like that again…Had she wanted him to die? No. He couldn't learn a lesson if he was dead. She'd wanted him afraid. Not dead.

"Look…" Roxy softened, "My first kill was a fuckin' train wreck. At least you saved that girl's life. You should be proud."

"He wasn't going to kill her," Anna mumbled.

"Oh, *nooo*," Roxy tittered, "Not *kill*. He'd just traumatise her. That's all! Just defile her and chuck her away like trash when he got bored of her. Then he'd go on to do the same to countless others. And, even if he got caught - and miraculously found guilty - they'd slap him on the wrist and send him back into the world to fuck up more lives. Because he has *such a bright future that shouldn't be tarnished*…But, you're right, he wouldn't have *killed* her. So I guess you're the monster here."

"Maybe we're all monsters," Anna said quietly.

"Maybe," Roxy tilted her head, "But I'd rather be a monster who kills other monsters than one who hurts innocent people. What about you?"

"I don't want to be a monster at all," Anna began to cry.

Roxy patted Anna's shoulder, "I'm guessing you didn't ask to become a vampire?"

Anna shook her head.

"Me neither," Roxy sighed, looking at the stars, "How did you die?"

A flash of memory blasted into Anna's mind. Hot, beer-saturated breath engulfed her. Bellowing laughter of gargantuan men reverberated all around. Meaty hands pawed at her skin. Huge fists shattered her bones with wet, dull cracks and pops. She cried out under a putrid, sweat-covered mass as it pushed itself onto her- *into* her unwilling, broken body.

"Anna?" Roxy's voice seemed very far away, "What's wrong?"
Anna was trapped in the memory.
She didn't know how to get back.
Everything was too loud.
Too bright.
Too much.
She couldn't breathe.
She couldn't think.
The sky was spinning.
The ground was caving in around her.
Suddenly Roxy's voice was everywhere, echoing in Anna's mind and sending chills down her spine.
"Breathe," Roxy compelled, "Tell me what you need."
"Finn," Anna gasped, "I need Finn."

***

Anna observed events unfold around her from a deep, dark place in the back of her mind. She was absently aware of unlocking her phone and handing it to Roxy. Of being scooped into the woman's arms. Of wind in her face. Her apartment floated into view. The elevator to her floor.
Visions of the men in the ally flashed around her.
Then she was in her bed.
She felt rough brick grating her skin.
Then the sheets were soft, surrounding her.
Deep sadistic laughter.
Roxy's panicked whispers.

"Anna?" The quiver of fear in Finn's voice tugged Anna back toward reality.
Salty tears stung her eyes as she reached for him. His arms wrapped around her, surrounding her in comforting warmth.
"Finn-" she whimpered.
He stroked her hair while she sobbed against his chest like a child.
"I'm going to take off," Roxy said gently, "I added my number to her phone. Reach out if you need anything."

159

"Thank you," Finn answered.

"Anytime," Roxy nodded.

Anna cried for what felt like a long time before finally speaking in a hoarse whisper, "His name was Brad."

"I know," Finn whispered.

"I'm a monster."

"I don't think so," Finn stroked her hair.

"The universe thinks so."

"What do you mean?"

"I killed someone and," Anna closed her eyes, allowing another tear to escape down her cheek, "it made me remember...everything."

"Oh." Finn held her tighter, "Do you want to talk about it?"

"No."

"Do you want me to go?"

"No."

"How can I help?"

"I don't know," Anna whimpered, "Just don't go."

Finn kissed Anna's forehead, "I'm not going anywhere."

Her eyes fell onto the dreamcatcher hanging over her pillows. Nothing was strong enough to block out her nightmares anymore.

"Your memories aren't a punishment for what happened tonight," Finn said gently, "They were bound to come back sooner or later."

"I killed someone," her hand shook against the curve of Finn's back, "I'm a murderer. How can you even look at me now?"

Finn paused, "Because I'm a murderer too."

CHAPTER 19
Guilty

Anna stared. Had she heard correctly?

"I don't want to burden you with my past," Finn continued quietly, "You've got enough on your mind."

"Tell me," Anna wasn't just curious to know, she was desperate. She needed to hear what happened. She wanted to know she wasn't alone. That it was possible to survive the guilt and shame, currently corroding her soul like acid. Finn wasn't the sort of person to lose control like she had. It must have been while he was in wolf form.

"Remember how I said my first sexual experience went badly?" He whispered.

Anna nodded.

"The night I got bitten..." Finn's muscles tensed, "There are versions of the story that people know and then there's one that's true."

He hesitated. Anna took his hands in hers and tried to smile reassuringly. She was still shaking a bit but it seemed work nonetheless.

"The first story is the one the Unseeing community believes," he began, "where I got attacked by a feral dog while camping with my school friends. It was the easiest lie. My high school was mostly just humans so we couldn't give too much detail. As far as they know, no one else got hurt."

Anna could understand that logic. Wolves weren't exactly common in Australia so saying it was a feral dog made more sense.

"The second story," Finn continued, "The version everyone else believes, even Cassie and Dex, is that I was attacked by a *rogue werewolf.*"

"And the truth?" Anna prompted.

Finn closed his eyes and took a long, shuddering breath.

"I was sixteen," he whispered, looking at his hands, "and I knew all about werebeasts so, when my Unseeing friends wanted to go camping, I made sure we picked a safe spot with lots of people around. Nowhere near any of the fields where a pack might transform. I'd been dating this girl, Jade, for a while. We were in a *teenage romance* sort of love. And we'd made... *plans*."

Finn swallowed and looked up at Anna, as though he was unsure whether he should continue. Part of her hated imagining him in love with someone else but now wasn't the time for immature jealousy.

"Plans," she squeezed his hand knowingly, "Go on."

"So, um," his voice wavered. "It was going to be the first time for both of us and we wanted things to be special. Roses and full moon and all that. And things were good. We were having a good time but then...then- "

Finn's heart began to pound.

"You don't have to keep going," Anna soothed, stroking his back, "It's okay."

"No," he gasped, "I need to get this out. No one knows about Jade. Everyone thinks that when we got attacked... they think I killed a werewolf *defending my friends*. Everyone said I was- that I was a hero for k-killing it. Killing *her*."

Anna gasped, raising a hand to her mouth. Finn's face contorted into heartbreaking anguish. He began to shake as tears streamed down his freckled cheeks.

"She didn't even know about werebeasts!" he cried, "I saw the scratch on her arm. She said she couldn't remember how she'd gotten it. It looked like nothing! Just a tiny mark. Barely even a scratch. I didn't know until... Not until...and when she turned it was *so fast*. We'd started- We were... she- I- we... It was meant to be our first time."

Finn sucked in air like he was drowning, "I killed her," he cried, "She was a werewolf but she was still *Jade*! She didn't know what she was doing. But I couldn't let her attack our friends. Or the families at the campsite. And I was so- so scared. I was naked and terrified and I thought I was going to die! And I- I couldn't- there wasn't another way."

Anna held him as he bawled into her shoulder. She was crying too, not for herself anymore but for Finn. He must have tortured himself with this guilt for years.

"So now you know," he whispered.

"You did the best you could do in a horrible situation," consoled Anna.

"She never changed back," he said darkly, "Did you know that when a werebeast dies in beast form, they stay that way? Just a dead animal. One minute she was with me and we were happy and then she was just…gone."

"That's awful" Anna wiped the wetness from his cheeks, "What about her family? Did they think she'd run away or something?"

"At first," Finn leaned his face into her hand, "But the Alliance have ways of identifying werebeasts, regardless of form. When they figured out that she was Unseeing, they gave her family some story about her being in a car accident. They said the car exploded so no one questioned why her remains were cremated."

"At least they got closure," Anna pointed out, "They're not hoping she'll show up one day."

"It's still my fault she's dead," Finn frowned.

"No it's not," Anna frowned, "You said it yourself, you didn't have a choice."

"I just told you I killed my first girlfriend," Finn sniffed, "After everything you've been through…How can you stand to look at me?"

"Because you haven't told me anything that changes how I feel about you," replied Anna, "You were in a life-or-death situation. You didn't want her dead. You didn't follow her into an alley and force yourself on her. You didn't kill her just because you could."

Finn sighed heavily, dropping onto the pillows.

"Killing Brad felt powerful," Anna admitted quietly, "I didn't *have* to kill him. I just…couldn't stop myself."

"Why?" he asked, pulling her onto his chest.

"What do you mean?" Anna asked.

"What was driving you to kill him?" Finn elaborated, "What happened?"

"I don't know…" Anna mumbled, "He spat blood in my face and I lost it."

"There was blood?"

Anna nodded.

"It sounds like your bloodlust took over," Finn frowned.

"I guess," Anna was glad Finn couldn't see her face when she whispered, "But I liked it."

Finn paused before replying, "What did you like about it?"

There was no judgement in his tone.

"I don't know," Anna stammered.

He rubbed her back. "It's okay," he soothed, "You can tell me."

"The blood was-" she felt flustered just remembering it, "So, so good. And when I realised he was dead...I was terrified but also...I felt almost... empowered?"

"You lost control," Finn mused, "Vampires and werewolves have that in common. I don't usually remember what I've done in wolf form, which is terrifying for other reasons, but when I do remember it's always coupled with feeling free and powerful. That's the scariest part. I have nightmares about tearing into rabbits and possums where I relish the hunt and the kill. They get mixed up with memories of Jade... It's awful."

"It sounds awful," Anna sniffed, "How do you handle it?"

"I remind myself that I can only control so much." A line formed between his eyebrows, "I separate myself from the general population when the moon is full but I can't control what happens outside of that. If humans come to our part of Silverbark Ridge during a full moon they'll die - the pack would kill them, not turn them - and I have to accept there's nothing I can do about that. It doesn't excuse it. I'm still responsible for my actions but I have to accept I can't plan for everything. You know?"

"Should I isolate myself?" Anna didn't like the idea of separating herself from the world but, if it meant she never killed again, she was willing to try it.

"For you, I'd recommend the opposite," Finn replied thoughtfully, "Now you know how powerful your bloodlust can be, and how quickly it takes over, you should practice overcoming it. Dex and I can help restrain you while you practise, if you want."

"I hate knowing I could snap," Anna fretted.

"It won't be forever," Finn assured, "Dex got control of his bloodlust and you can too."

"Is it safe for us to be together right now?" Anna fretted, "I know you're strong but I don't want to hurt you. What if you get a cut or a nosebleed and I can't stop myself?"

"My blood won't tempt you," Finn assured, "Dex says it smells like putrid meat. Apparently, if a vampire drinks werebeast blood they get sick. Like, *gastro* sick."

"Weirdly, that's actually a big relief," Anna chuckled morosely as she pushed away the mental image of a vampire with food poisoning, "I wish I'd focused more on this stuff before last night. Maybe Brad would still be alive."

"I'd love to tell you it'll get easier," Finn put his arm around Anna's shoulders, "but you took a life. The guilt will always be there."

Anna nodded, "It all happened so fast."

"It won't happen again," Finn promised, "Not if I can help it."

CHAPTER 20

Hypnotic

Even with Finn's calming presence, Anna didn't sleep well. Her dreams were plagued by visions of the graffitied alleyway stretching on forever while enormous, blood-stained zombies with Brad's face chased her. They laughed and bellowed at her. She could sense them catching up, reaching for her just before she jolted awake, covered in sweat.

When her alarm went off the next morning, she and Finn both called in sick. Anna was vaguely concerned that she'd taken too much leave already but the thought of leaving her bed for anything more strenuous than a shower seemed exhausting.

Finn smirked at his phone, handing it to Anna.

Cassie: *Did you seriously disappear for a booty call on a Monday night? Who even are you?!*

"I guess she found my note," Finn chuckled.

"What did it say?" Anna raised an eyebrow as she handed back his phone.

"Just that I'd gone to your place," he shrugged, "and not to worry if I wasn't back by morning."

Anna laughed.

"In hindsight, it was a bit misleading," he blushed.

"Wait," Anna mentally replayed the night from Finn's perspective. "You got a call in the middle of the night from a random vampire and you just did whatever she told you to?"

"She called from *your* phone," Finn reminded Anna, "I could hear you in the background. You needed me. I came."

"My hero," Anna laughed as she swooned into his arms.

"I'm not kidding," he said, looking serious as he cupped Anna's cheek in his hand, "Whenever you need me, I'm there."

"I'm not kidding either," Anna replied, leaning up to kiss him softly, "You saved me last night."

Shortly after nine o'clock, Anna and Finn received identical messages.
Dex: *Hypocrites! Have fun ;)*

They spent the morning napping through Firefly reruns. After lunch, they talked for hours on topics ranging from pop-culture to philosophy. Finn seemed determined to keep things light but Anna's mind kept straying to darker subjects.

"Do you think it's okay that vampires are legeally allowed to kill people?"

"It doesn't matter what we think," Finn sighed with a troubled expression, "The VA doesn't exactly have a feedback box."

"They seem pretty good in other ways," Anna opened the blood delivery app and submitted a new order.

"For vampires, sure," Finn scoffed, "They support their own. The rest of us…"

"I don't suppose you can form a union?" Anna mused, "Demand equal rights?"

"I've heard rumblings that some factions are trying to do that," Finn raised his eyebrows, "but they're working in secret for obvious reasons."

"They'd kill people just for wanting to be treated fairly?" Anna gasped.

"Maybe," Finn shrugged, "More likely, they'd make it known that anyone involved in the union is no longer protected by the Alliance. The High Fae would do the job for them. We may not get a lot of support from the VA but at least they don't see us as vermin."

"Aren't your family High Fae?" Anna couldn't understand why people couldn't just leave one another alone to live in peace.

"They're the exception," Finn scrunched his nose, "Most High Fae look down on the Tree Folk for consorting with Underfae. During the last war, my family protected anyone who asked for it. It didn't matter what side they were on. Our forest was a sanctuary for anyone who wanted peace."

"They sound great," Anna smiled.

"They are," Finn beamed, "Which reminds me…"

Finn scrolled through his phone, hitting a few buttons before looking up, "Check your email."

A forwarded message popped into her inbox. It had an animated graphic of people wearing flower crowns and dancing around a bonfire. The text below read:

~

You're invited to the annual
Finnegan Family BBQ!
Celebrate the Summer Solstice
with good food and great friends.

Saturday, December 22
Finnegan Farm
Entry via Granite Arch,
Girraween National Park, Stanthorpe

BYO
Appetite, good vibes and
any friends you wish
the more the merrier!

~

"Will you come?" Finn asked, running his hand through his hair, "It's my family's version of Christmas but it's more like a big music festival."
"Sure," grinned Anna.
"You should know," Finn added with a slight frown, "My parents are polyamorous so when I introduce you to my *aunts* and *uncles*… They aren't literally aunts or uncles."
"Noted," Anna tilted her head, "How does that work exactly? With your siblings and everything. Sorry, is that rude to ask?"
"No, no," Finn gave a welcoming smile, "My parents are in an open marriage. They'll form relationships with other people, sometimes it's just romantic, often it's just sexual too, occasionally it's both. A couple of my siblings are from those relationships but we don't qualify each other as half-siblings or anything. We're all family. It'll make more sense when you meet them. If you still want to?"
"Of course I do," Anna hopped off her bed and marked the paper calendar above her desk.
"Old school," Finn laughed.

"I never remember to look at digital calendars," Anna explained.

Glancing at the mess on her desk, her eyes fell on the plastic bag of reading materials she'd taken from the hospital. There were flyers from tattoo parlours offering discounts on enchanted inking and a signup form for the VA's blood bank service. There were brochures for group therapy sessions: *Dearly Departed, support for the recently dead* and a pamphlet labelled *Coping with Cravings ~ Resist your bloodlust in 6 easy steps!* The first step was to make sure you always had access to blood, the second was to limit your exposure to humans. The third was to *accept little trip-ups - they're bound to happen!* Anna tossed it aside. Finally, there was a thin booklet titled *Welcome to the Family! An introduction to Vampirism. Proudly brought to you by the Vampire Alliance.*

"What's that?" asked Finn.

"Stuff from the hospital," Anna answered, flicking through the book. "I forgot about it until now."

She skimmed the table of contents:

FAQ ... (page 4)
Fact vs Fiction ... (page 5)
Your Sire & You ... (page 6)
Special Abilities & Bloodlines ... (page 8)
Bloodlust & Cravings ... (page 14)
Vampiric Laws ... (page 16)
Important Numbers ... (page 22)

The Bloodlust and Cravings page matched the messaging on the flyer, telling her to accept that she'd kill a few people before she mastered the art of controlling herself. It was hardly helpful advice.

Flipping the Special Abilities section, Anna was pleased to find she'd mastered many of the skills listed as *Common*. The only one she hadn't tried from the list was hypnotism.

"Do you want to try it on me?" Finn asked.

"What?" Anna blushed, "No! I don't want to force you to do anything."

"I trust you."

"I shouldn't-"

"It's important to know what you're capable of," Finn insisted.

"How will I know if it's working?" Anna read through the instructions.

"I'll do what you say, even if I don't want to," Finn shrugged.

"I hate that," Anna frowned, "What would I even tell you to do?"

"Whatever you like."

"Kiss me!" Anna laughed. She hadn't followed the instructions at all but Finn complied.

"Point made," he chuckled, "Tell me to do something I wouldn't *normally* do. I'll try to resist."

"Like what?"

"Anything."

Anna looked Finn in the eyes, "Slap me."

Finn took a shocked step back from her, "Anna, I don't want to hurt you!"

"You won't," Anna said, "But clearly that didn't work."

"Nothing violent, Anna, please," Finn stammered, "Pick something else?"

"We don't need to do this," assured Anna, "I don't want to take people's free will away. Especially not yours."

"It could save your life one day," Finn frowned, "And, if you can't control it, you might do it to someone without meaning to."

Anna bit her lip, "Fine."

Taking a deep, focused breath, she looked into Finn's eyes again. Unlike the previous attempt, Anna felt a connection. It wasn't the usual comforting bond she had with Finn. This felt dominating. She was in control. Finn stared at Anna with a dazed expression, awaiting instruction.

She could take away his insecurities. She could remove his guilt. She could make him forget Jade entirely. But then who would he be? Not Finn.

"Tell me three secrets," she compelled, "Nothing that betrays anyone's trust - nothing serious - just stupid things you weren't planning on telling me."

Finn swallowed and took a breath, blinking.

"I used to practice talking to you in the mirror," he cringed.

Anna felt ill. If he'd admitted this freely she would have found it adorable but the compulsion of it felt wrong. Why had she chosen three? She should have just asked for one secret and gotten it over with.

"When I was fourteen," Finn continued, "I stole a chocolate bar from the supermarket on a dare... and..." Finn struggled against the compulsion, "I- I sometimes masturbate to a photo of you."

He covered his quickly reddening face and dove onto the bed.

"I'm sorry," Anna crawled next to him, stroking his back, "I shouldn't have done that."

Finn "I asked you to."

"Still."

"Why secrets?"

"It's all I could think of," Anna grimaced, "I thought you'd just tell me the code for your phone or something. Not sexy stuff."

"You think touching myself to your photo is *sexy*?

Anna smirked. Finn raised his eyebrows. His lips were pursed but the corners crept upward.

"Which photo was it?" Anna asked peevishly.

Finn reached for his phone. His face was still bright red.

"You don't have to show me," Anna laughed.

"I feel like I should," he replied with a coy grin.

Finn had saved several pictures from Anna's social media accounts.

"This one," he held up an older photo of Anna. She'd been at a pop-culture convention in her late twenties, dressed as Arwen from Lord of the Rings. The costume wasn't designed for someone with Anna's curves so the gown pressed tightly against her breasts and hips.

"Huh," it was Anna's turn to blush.

Finn reburied his face under the pillows and gave a muffled cry.

"Here…" Anna held up her phone, showing a photo she'd saved of Finn. He was lying on the grass with a book next to him. Dappled sunlight played gently across his face and his cotton shirt was unbuttoned just enough to see a few of his chest hairs.

"Why are you showing me this?" Finn asked quizzically.

Anna raised her eyebrows.

"Oh," Finn's eyes lit up, "Now, that's hot."

Anna laughed.

Finn pulled her close, "It's good to see you smile."

"I shouldn't be smiling." Anna frowned as a sinking feeling took over. For a moment, she'd forgotten about last night…What she'd done to Brad. She'd killed someone, hours ago, and now she was relaxing in bed. Laughing.

"Guilt comes in waves," Finn assured, "It's like grief that way. Let yourself feel happy when you can. You made a horrible mistake. You can't take it back so the best you can do is not repeat it. That doesn't mean you can't have a life and be happy."

"I guess," Anna sighed. She wished there was something she could do to earn her happiness. Right now, she didn't deserve it. Not after what she'd done. Despite her instinct for self-preservation, she pushed her mind back into the alley. The gargantuan men were waiting for her, ready to play.

"What are you doing?" Finn interrupted her morbid meditation.

"Nothing." She lied, sending the sickening memories back into the dark recesses of her subconscious.

"I don't know where you went just now," Finn stroked her cheek, "But forcing yourself to be unhappy isn't going to help anyone. Please don't torture yourself over this. I know I'm a hypocrite for asking but...Please?"

"I just..." Anna sighed, "I don't know what to do now."

"Just take each day as it comes. It'll get easier to balance your life with the pain and guilt," Finn promised, "And I'm here for you. Whatever you need."

"Same," Anna nestled into Finn's chest, hoping he was right about things eventually getting better, "Tell me when you're struggling too, okay?"

"I will," Finn promised.

CHAPTER 21

Lessons in Magic

"... Rarer abilities are limited to the elders of specific vampiric bloodlines. For example, elders of the Narcissa bloodline can create weather events such as localised fog and rain. While powerful members of the Ferosha line have been known to transform into bats, ravens and even wolves..."
Anna paced her bedroom reading from the Vampiric Alliance booklet.
"...Your sire will advise which bloodline is yours and instruct you on the best way to hone your talents."

"What's wrong?" Finn watched from the bed. Anna slumped into his arms, showing him the book. "It sucks being an orphan vampire. What if I can control the weather and I don't even know it?"

"Maybe there's a test to find out who your sire is," he suggested.

"I doubt it," she smiled weakly.

"Does it really matter either way?" he gave her a reassuring hug, "You've already got more powers than most of the X-men."

"It's not really about the powers," Anna replied, "It's feeling left in the dark. I keep stumbling on information that's common knowledge to everyone else. I don't know what I don't know, so I can't ask about it."

"Give it time," assured Finn, "No one expects you to be an expert overnight."

"I just feel so clueless," Anna sighed, "You, Dex and Cassie all grew up in this world."

"And we're all here for you," Finn stroked Anna's hair, "You're putting too much pressure on yourself."

"I just wish there was someone who could teach me magic who didn't grow up around it," Anna pouted, "Someone who knows what it's like to start from complete ignorance."

Finn tilted his head and looked out the window.

"What about your grandfather?" Finn suggested.

Anna had forgotten about Rupert.

"He's a bit…" Anna tried to think of the best word to use. *Paranoid* seemed too judgemental but *cautious* was an understatement, "Protective."

"Is that a bad thing?" Finn asked.

"I guess not," Anna said thoughtfully. "What would I tell him about last night?"

"Nothing," Finn shrugged, "Who you tell is your business. I won't tell anyone, not even Cassie or Dex."

"Thank you," Anna said, "but I think if I'm going to ask him for help, I should be honest about why I need it."

"Do you want to call him now?" Finn prompted, "I can leave, if it's easier."

"No," Anna suddenly felt nervous, "Would you stay?"

"Of course," Finn smiled.

Rupert answered on the second ring, "What's wrong?" he sounded concerned.

"Nothing," Anna replied in a higher pitch than was natural, "Why would you think something's wrong?"

"It's the middle of the afternoon on a work day," he replied.

"I just wanted to ask you about magic stuff," Anna felt childish, "Like bloodlines. Vampire bloodlines, that is. Not our family bloodline. Although, I would like to know more about that too, come to think of it, but I was mostly calling about the first thing- the vampire bloodlines. And whether you have any advice about how I can learn more about my abilities without a sire…and stuff."

Finn smiled fondly, shaking his head as she rambled. She hit him with a pillow.

"Would you like to come over for tea?" Rupert offered, "It might be easier to speak in person."

"Uh, sure," Anna replied, "Can Finn come too?"

"If you trust Mr Finnegan, he is welcome."

"I do," said Anna, "What's your address?"

"Do you still have the key I gave you?"

"Yes."

"Hold the key near any door and you'll find your way. See you soon." he hung up.

Anna looked to Finn for some sign of comprehension but his confusion mirrored her own. She took the key from her handbag and approached the bedroom door. She waved the key over the door like a wand, hesitating as she opened it. As usual, the kitchen and lounge room were on the other side. She shrugged and closed the door again, sitting next to Finn on the bed. She stared at the door. The paint was chipped in the upper corner and the silver handle and lock were tarnished with- wait. *The lock?*

Anna's bedroom door didn't usually have a lock. Anna's heart pounded as she pounced from the bed and slid the key into the anomaly, turning it with a satisfying click. The door shimmered with magical energy.

Anna opened her door once more, this time revealing the foyer of a regal, old house. Books and papers were stacked along the dark wood-panelled walls while strange metal devices littered every surface. A grand staircase blocked Anna's view of the manor's depth but a large window on her left showed a vast jungle of tropical trees outside. She glanced over her shoulder to Finn, whose eyes were wide.

Anna cautiously stuck out her hand, wondering if she'd be able to pass over the threshold without an in-person invitation from Rupert.

The temperature inside the mansion was much cooler than Anna's bedroom. With no magical barrier blocking her, Anna stepped into her grandfather's house.

"This is wild," Anna whispered.

Finn nodded as he followed her into the dimly lit entryway.

Metallic footsteps clanged against the hardwood floor, announcing the arrival of a small robot that toddled through a doorway to the right of them. Its copper head resembled an upturned plant pot and its cylindrical body had flexible limbs like a vacuum hose. It had two large cameras for eyes and a smile-shaped speaker for a mouth.

"Greetings, dear guests," it chirped, "I am Boggle, please follow me!"

Boggle continued down the central corridor behind the stairs. Anna raised her eyebrows at Finn, who shrugged and nodded as if to say, *"We've come this far."*

They followed the little robot into a vast library. The musty smell of books was entrancing. Leather-bound tomes lined the walls while dozens of immense bookshelves divided the space into narrow aisles and spacious reading areas.

"Wait here, please," Boggle gestured toward an arrangement of sofas, which sat under a glowing chandelier. Anna and Finn lowered themselves onto the soft leather of a chesterfield. Boggle bowed and left.

"What was that?" Anna whispered.

"No idea," answered an astonished-looking Finn.

Rupert entered the library carrying a large tray with three cups and an ornate teapot. Boggle followed at his heels carrying a plate of biscuits.

"Welcome to Morrigan Manor," Rupert smiled as he placed the tray on a coffee table, "Apologies for not greeting you myself. You must be Mr Finnegan, correct?"

"Yes, sir," Finn stood nervously, shaking Rupert's hand "I'm Henry. Or Finn, most people call me Finn. It's an honour to meet you, sir."

"The honour is all mine, Finn, and please call me Rupert," he replied, picking up the teapot, "What would you like to drink?"

"Whatever you've got is fine," Finn answered with a perplexed look on his face.

"I've got it all, dear boy," smiled Rupert, "What's your favourite?"

"Chai," Finn answered with a challenge in his eyes.

Rupert turned the lid of the teapot like the dial on a safe before pouring a serving of perfectly brewed Chai tea into Finn's cup. He placed it on a saucer with two shortbread biscuits and handed it to a very impressed Finn.

"And for you, Anna?" Rupert held up the teapot, "I'm afraid it can't conjure human blood...Yet."

"Oh, uh," Anna wasn't a fan of tea, "Can it do hot chocolate?"

"It certainly can," he grinned as a stream of sweet cocoa poured into Anna's cup.

Rupert poured himself some black tea and took a tentative sip, "So, tell me how you're struggling with magic."

"I feel like I don't understand the basics," Anna explained, "Like, how was I able to enter your home when I couldn't cross the threshold to Finn and Cassie's place? They invited me to stay before we got there, just like you did, but I couldn't cross the barrier until Cassie invited me from inside the house."

"The key I gave you bypasses all magical protections, including vampiric wards," Rupert said, "It's attuned to you, meaning only you can use it, but you're welcome to bring anyone with you, provided you trust them. You should know, even an elder vampire would have asked the same question. You are not as behind as you think."

Anna nodded thoughtfully. Boggle mimicked her silently.

"What is he?" Anna asked with her eyes on the robot.

"One of my creations," Rupert said affectionately, "I've developed a hobby of combining robotics with spellwork. It's a fascinating but largely untapped field."

"Enjoy your tea!" exclaimed Boggle.

"Thank you Boggle," Rupert smiled, "That will be all."

Boggle gave a tiny bow and then trundled out of the library.

"Incredible," remarked Finn as he watched the robot leave.

"I am quite fond of him," Rupert agreed, "But you're here to learn about the vampiric bloodlines, correct?"

"Yes," Anna confirmed, "Is there a way to find out which one I belong to?"

Rupert held a finger to his lips as his eyes darted across the book-laden shelves.

"I have several volumes on the subject of vampiric clans and bloodlines, which you are welcome to read anytime," he gestured to the far corner of the library, "However, I am not aware of an official test to determine one's bloodline. I suspect the fastest way to discover this information would be to attempt the magical abilities unique to each line and see which comes most naturally to you."

"She'll *only* be able to do magic from her bloodline, right?" Finn pointed out, "And wouldn't it take centuries before she can even try? I thought only elder vampires could perform bloodline magic."

"All magic follows the same set of rules," Rupert explained, "The thoughts in your mind are currents of energy passing through organic matter. With practice, you can direct that energy to manipulate the subatomic particles surrounding you, thus modifying physical and atmospheric matter. Neither age nor race has any impact on one's ability. Only one's level of determination, dedication and focus."

Anna stared at him blankly.

"Anyone can bend the world to their will," he summarised, "But it's not easy."

"I've never heard magic described that way," Finn said faintly, "I learned it was all about feeling your connection to nature and harnessing your natural abilities."

"That is another way of putting it," said Rupert, stirring his tea, "The religious call it *prayer*, mages call it *spellwork*, atheists call it *the placebo effect*, scientists call it *quantum physics*. The titles are irrelevant. The results are irrefutable."

"But… I'm a vampire," Anna frowned, "When Cassie did magic she used this golden aura of energy that came from inside her to move things around. I don't have anything like that inside me. I just have darkness. *Nothingness*…How can I channel nothing into something?"

"I didn't know you could see magic like that," Finn gasped.

"Can't everyone?" Anna replied. Dex had pointed out the Veil of Unseeing on a guy like it was normal to see the fog hanging around people's heads.

"Maybe it's a vampire thing," Finn mused, "I can't see auras or magic. I can only feel them."

"Fascinating" Rupert raised his brows, "The ability to see motes of magic will no doubt help you manifest your will more easily. *Seeing is believing*, as they say."

"You think I'll be able to do magic?" Anna asked sceptically, "Real magic?"

"Oh, yes," Rupert smiled, "We'll just need to find a technique that works for you. It sounds as though Miss Nakamura used herself as a primary source of power in her spellwork. A common practice among witches. You simply need to learn how to draw power from external sources instead."

"But vampires can't…right?" Finn's eyes were wide, "Everyone has their own type of magic and magical limitations."

"You come from a line of druids, dryads and nymphs," Rupert sipped his tea, "Is that correct?"

"Yes," Finn answered, "So we can only do earth magic."

"Have you ever tried any other form of magic?" Rupert prompted.

"I can't do anything else," Finn said quickly.

"Are you positive?" Rupert raised his eyebrow.

"I- Yes?" Finn looked at Anna, who shrugged.

"While you would certainly be *best attuned* to earth magic, I believe you can learn to do any form of magic," Rupert mused, "With the right mindset and training."

"But…" Finn floundered, "That's impossible!"

"Says who?" Rupert asked, sipping his tea.

"Everyone!" Finn exclaimed.

"Exactly!" Rupert grinned with a twinkle in his eye, "The magical community can't seem to agree on anything except that certain powers are limited to specific bloodlines. Yet, to my knowledge, no one has been able to explain the obvious flaw in this theory."

"What's that?" Anna asked.

"The Lax," Rupert sipped his tea as though his point was obvious, "Or are we calling them *Unseeing* now? I can never keep up with these things…"

"What about them?" Anna prompted.

"They're very good at magic considering they *aren't supposed to have any*," he smiled conspiratorially, "The Veil of Unseeing, or *Fog of Ignorance* as it was once called, is a powerful spell. Yet almost all humans, with no magical bloodline to speak of, have managed to cast it without even trying."

"No, but-," Finn stammered, frowning against Rupert's logic, "That would mean…"

"I was born as a Lax human," Rupert continued, "I have no faerie in my bloodline and I've yet to find a spell I cannot master."

Finn opened his mouth, raising his finger as if to make a point but he seemed to counter the argument in his mind before it reached his lips. He stared into the middle distance with wide eyes, lost in contemplation.

"If we're all capable of doing *any type of magic*," Anna frowned, "wouldn't more people have figured it out?

"The two greatest killers of progress," Rupert sighed wearily, "are assumption and apathy. Before the invention of the light bulb, people believed oil lamps were the pinnacle of artificial lighting. They assumed there would never be a better option and had no interest in spending their time trying to figure out a new or better way. It only takes one person to prove the impossible is possible for the world to change forever."

"By that logic, I should be able to do magic from all the vampiric bloodlines," Anna mused.

"Indeed," Rupert answered, "But, just as Finn is predisposed to perform earth magic, you will find the magic associated with your vampiric bloodline easier to master."

"Where do we start?" Anna felt a spark of hope in her chest. The possibility of learning more magic excited her. The possibility of learning *all* magic was intoxicating.

"Study, of course," A large tome flew from the stacks into Rupert's outstretched hand, "I want you to read this page," flicking the book open, "tell me if any of the descriptions or abilities resonate with you. Remember, you are trying to determine which bloodline is influencing you, not the one you would prefer to call your own."

Anna took the ancient book from Rupert. The pages were made of impossibly thin, yellowing parchment.

"Though the origin of the Vampire is unsubstantiated, seven distinct bloodlines (see also: Clans) have been proven to exist. After centuries of internal conflict, the Seven Clans formed an alliance during the Old War, claiming sovereignty over all Underfae and eliminating the possibility of a unified Fae society. A summary of each clan's bloodline can be found below, with further elaboration in subsequent chapters.

Line of Helena: *Known for their debilitating beauty, these creatures inspire such obsession and lust that their victims will do anything to please them, including the most heinous of acts.*
It is said Helena vampires can mesmerise victims into a fugue state, whereupon victims have woken to find several years have passed during their servitude. Reports also indicate these creatures can boil the blood of their victims and absorb heat from a targeted area until occupants freeze. Capable of drawing power from the sexual energy of their audience, vampires of the Helena clan are drawn to performative roles and opportunities for fame.

Line of Jaynus: *Masters of stealth and disguise, a Jaynus vampire can mimic any humanoid form and disappear into the smallest shadow. These creatures take pleasure in stealing both life and lifestyle, taking on their victim's identity after killing them. Easily restless, these creatures will not remain in one place for long. They crave change and have been rumoured to initiate riots, and even wars, simply for amusement.*

Line of Ferosha: *Bestial and untamed, these creatures have fearsome stamina and primal predatory instincts. They are nearly impossible to kill and have a strong kinship to beasts of the night, often calling on swarms of bats, rats, and insects to do their bidding. Though unsubstantiated, several rumours indicate rare members of this clan can transform into beasts such as bears, leopards, snakes, and wolves. They are drawn to physical acts of aggression and will not run from a fight.*

Line of Midas: *This clan will stop at nothing to grow their collection. Whether they value money, antiquities, exotic animals or something more sinister, only a fool would come between a Midas vampire and their treasure. Skilled in the art of illusion, they can force vivid hallucinations into their victim's mind. While rumours suggest these beasts can breathe fire and turn the bones of their enemies into gold, the Midas clan is paradoxically known to be the most personable. Many have formed long-term relationships with humans, preferring peaceful negotiations over bloodshed to build their wealth.*

Line of Morpheus: *These creatures can spend decades, or even centuries, in slumber. While they have been known to consume vast amounts of blood upon waking, Morpheus vampires primarily feed upon astral energy. They corrupt dreams into nightmares so frightful that their victims never wake. It is believed this traps the victim in the astral plane, allowing the Morpheus vampire to devour the victim's spirit, piece by piece.*

Line of Narcissa: *From pulling the strings of government to mastery over weather, there is nothing a Narcissa vampire does not aim to control. Drawn to positions of leadership, it is believed they can draw power from admiration and fear. Some have even been known to lead churches and cults, saying the 'taste of blind faith' offers a banquet beyond compare. Reports indicate these creatures can read minds and transform into mist, teleporting short distances to avoid attack.*

Line of Tantalus: *Known as 'The Insatiable Ones", these creatures often lead self-indulgent, debaucherous lifestyles. It is said that a single Tantalus vampire can drain an army of blood without becoming full, go for weeks without rest, and survive any poison. Rumours suggest these creatures can also gain remarkable abilities depending what, or who, they eat. For example, excessive consumption of spiders may give a Tantalus vampire the ability to create webs. They may acquire new skills from human victims, such as acrobatics, code-breaking, or even mastering a foreign tongue."*

Anna looked up from the text. She didn't feel particularly drawn to any of them. They all sounded horrific. Rupert and Finn, deep in conversion, hadn't noticed she'd finished reading. Returning her focus to the page, she decided to try using the process of elimination.

"Debilitating beauty..." Nope.

"Drawn to positions of leadership..." Definitely not.
None of the options described her.

She slammed the book on the coffee table in frustration clattering the tray of teacups and saucers.
"Are you alright?" Rupert asked.
"I don't fit in anywhere." Anna growled.
"Have you tried the process of el-" Finn began.
"Yes," she huffed.
Rupert smiled patiently and nodded, taking the book from the table.
"This volume," he sighed, "gives an excellent summary of each vampiric bloodline's abilities but the author's bias against vampires does tend to pollute the facts. You need to read between the lines."

He skimmed over the text, "Since becoming a vampire," he asked, "have you found yourself more attuned to the emotional states of others?"
"No?" Anna replied.
"Have you found yourself sleeping more than you usually would?"
"No."
"Have you found yourself wishing you were someone else?"
"Uh, no."
"Have you developed a kinship with any nocturnal animals?"
"N- oh, yes," Anna answered, "but just in the normal way."
"How's that?" Rupert asked.
"Dex showed me how to send a message using a bat," she shrugged.
"But it remembered you when you came to our place," Finn added, "Animal messengers aren't normally loyal like that."
"Interesting," Rupert said, then asked, "Was your residence the bat's original home?"
"No," Finn answered.
"Dex and I were practising in the Botanic Gardens," Anna explained, "It was one of the animals that came to me when I called out for assistance."
Rupert's mouth twitched. "One of the animals?" he repeated, "More than one came to your call?"
"Yes," Anna said slowly, "A whole bunch, actually."

She'd forgotten Dex had been impressed by the number of animals who'd answered her call.
"I don't pretend to be an expert on what is normal for vampires," Rupert

admitted, "but it is my understanding that most require a great deal of focus to attract even one creature to them. Particularly for those who are new to magic."

"Do you think that means I might be from the- what was it? *Ferosha* line?"

"I do," he smiled, "Especially if the bat you chose showed loyalty to you long after your connection should have naturally severed."

"I think that's just because I was feeding him" Anna blushed, feeling foolish, "Finn was bonding with him too, right?"

"Not like you," Finn smiled, "I can connect with animals and plants because of my druid background but Calypso cares specifically for you."

"*A vampire will typically only connect to an animal long enough for it to complete its task,*" Rupert read aloud, "*at which point the animal will return to its life as normal, forgetting the vampire completely.*"

Anna reached for the book, flipping back to reread the passage about her bloodline. Her insides twisted at the monstrous description, "I'm not, *bestial and untamed*...right?"

"Subjective twaddle," Rupert waved his hand dismissively, "No different to historical texts referring to native people as *primitive savages*. It characterises the author more than their subject matter. Don't let problematic language distract you from the relevant facts."

"Which are?" Anna was feeling frustrated again.

"*Fearsome stamina, primal predatory instincts and nearly impossible to kill,*" he read, "Indicates you likely have superior senses and healing abilities, even for a vampire. The part about *beasts of the night* suggests magic involving animals will come most easily to you."

"It says I'm drawn to physical acts of aggression," she argued.

"You sort of were," Finn said quietly, "last night."

"That was-," Anna couldn't reasonably argue that he was wrong.

Interrupting an attempted rape was not something she would have done as a human. She'd been too cautious, so scared of getting hurt, that she would never have considered running toward someone crying for help in the middle of the night.

"Something happened last night?" Rupert asked with concern.

Anna walked Rupert through the events of the night before, grasping Finn's hand as she confessed to taking a life. Rupert listened without interruption, resting the tips of his fingers together in silent contemplation.

"I understand your moral distress," he stated with sincerity, "But it would be hypocritical of me to condemn you for your actions, given my reaction to your attack."

Finn choked on his tea, "That was you?!"

"It was, I'm afraid," Rupert showed no hint of remorse.

Finn bit his lip. He looked pale.

Rupert placed his tea on the table, "Would you have done any different in my place?"

Finn swallowed. He looked as Anna with a resolute expression but didn't answer.

"Don't you care that I murdered someone?" Anna asked.

"Of course," Rupert replied, "It pains me to know you are suffering from the worst kind of guilt there is and I feel for the young man's family. However, we humans tend to place a disproportionately high value on the lives of our species over others. We think nothing of killing a cockroach. If a dog bites a child, it's life is ended without question. Yet we fall aghast at the notion of killing a man who poses a far greater threat to society than either of those. It is arrogance, plain and simple."

"I broke the law!" Anna couldn't believe what she was hearing, "I murdered someone!"

"Firstly," Rupert smiled kindly, "Legally speaking, you didn't *murder* that man. Murder implies forethought and the intent to kill. By human laws, you committed *involuntary manslaughter*."

Anna shook her head. The semantics were irrelevant.

"Secondly," Rupert continued, "Under *vampiric law*, what you did was no different than a farmer killing a chicken for its meat. Morality is subjective, and highly changeable in the context of culture."

Anna blinked and took a sip of her chocolate. It was cold. Finn took her hand, squeezing it gently. At least *he* understood right from wrong.

"I never want to hurt someone like that again," Anna whispered, "I need to learn how to control my bloodlust."

"I understand," Rupert said gently, "I will research the topic and help you however I can. In the meantime, I recommend you seek council from your fellow vampires. They may have more practical advice than I can offer."

"Thank you," Anna couldn't help but feel frustrated. Was Rupert good or bad? Unlike most people, he really would do *anything* for his family. But was that a good thing? She'd learned she could count on him for unwavering support, no matter what atrocities she'd committed, but did that mean he expected the same?

Rupert stood, "Shall we get started in expanding your magical skill set?"
"Right now?" Anna put down her drink. She was eager to start but felt suddenly apprehensive. Was Rupert the best choice for this? What if he taught her dark magic that made her indifferent to killing? Would that be better than not knowing any magic at all?

"I don't want to be in the way," Finn stood awkwardly.
"Not at all!" Rupert exclaimed, "The offer was to both of you. I'm rather interested to see how quickly you take to performing the Druidic spells of another element."
"I- what?" Finn gaped.
"It would be easiest to track your progress with the element of fire," Rupert led them out of the library, "but I think, for the sake of my possessions, we ought to try water first."

Anna and Finn followed Rupert through the manor, careful not to lose him as he glided past room after room of intriguing trinkets and curiosities. Glowing artefacts housed in glass domes sat on shelves next to oil paintings that moved. Anna caught a glimpse of herself in one of them and paused to investigate. There were likenesses of almost everyone in Anna's family, each with a metal plaque under it. Instead of listing their names, however, they said things like *Reading (Office), Anxious (Bruce Highway),* and *Eating (Kitchen).*
The only pictures missing were from her father's side of the family.
Anna smiled at the plaque for her niece, Clara: *Inventive (Bedroom).*
Her own plaque read: *Exploring (Morrigan Manor).*
"I like to know you're all doing well," Rupert appeared at her shoulder with a wistful look in his eyes, "I regret it wasn't enough to save you."
"I didn't realise you cared so much," Anna said feebly, "Mum- we all thought you were too busy for us."
"That is for the best, I'm afraid," he replied sadly, "Shall we...?"

They entered a large circular room with polished hardwood floors. Runic markings decorated the wood in fine, silver lines. Strange equipment rested against the walls, leaving an empty space in the centre.
"I use this space for magical experimentation." Rupert declared, indicating

the protective symbols and markings, "No magic performed in this room will harm us, nor can its effects spill into the world outside."

Finn let out a low whistle.

"Don't get too excited," Rupert warned, "This session will be an introduction to the basics. I don't expect you'll need this level of protection, however, one can never be too careful."

Anna ventured into the room, unsure where to stand in the vast space. Without any furniture to interact with, she felt strangely exposed. Finn followed her to the centre of the room but his eyes darted eagerly from one piece of equipment to the next. Rupert extracted a pocket watch from his vest and spoke quietly into it, "Boggle, would you be so kind as to bring me Tabitha and a pot of damp soil from the conservatory?"

"Coming right up!" Boggle's voice chimed from the watch.

"While we wait," Rupert smiled, "I'd like to start with a simple meditation technique." He made several calculated gestures with his hands, as though performing complex sign language. The floor lurched up. Finn grabbed Anna, taking in a defensive stance as the wood shifted into a spongy cushioned mat beneath their feet.

"Please make yourselves comfortable," Rupert instructed, "and close your eyes."

Anna helped Finn lower himself onto the mat and then sat cross-legged next to him. His knuckles grazed her knee reassuringly. She closed her eyes, awaiting further instruction.

"Now," Rupert spoke softly as he padded around them, "This meditation technique is an exercise in focus. Simple in theory. Difficult in practice. Like any exercise, it will become easier with repetition. I want you to count backwards from one hundred in your mind, visualising each number as you go. If you find your mind wanders, you must start again from the beginning. Go."

Easy. Anna began to count backwards in her mind, picturing the numerals as she went:

100, 99, 98, 97, 96, 95, what if we finish before Boggle gets here? Oh, damn. 100, 99, 98, 97, 96, 95, 94, 93, 92, 91, I bet Finn is ahead of me now, I wonder what number he's up to. Crap! 100, 99, 98...

Anna restarted several times before Boggle's arrival.

"What was your personal best?" Finn whispered.

"56," Anna grimaced, "You?"

"83," Finn chuckled, "I never realised I was so easily distracted!"

The ground deflated like a punctured air mattress until it regained its original rigidity.

"Would either of you like a chair?" Rupert offered.

Anna looked at Finn, planning to mimic his answer.

"I'm fine, thanks," Finn replied, stretching his legs out.

"Me too," Anna smiled.

"Alright," Rupert said, placing an item in front of each of them, "Each of you will be focusing on a different challenge, based on your natural abilities."

Anna looked at the wicker picnic basket she'd received. It began to shake and growl.

"Tabitha does not like to be contained," Rupert said in answer to her puzzled expression, "If you'd like to let her out, you'll find she's quite friendly."

She glanced at Finn, who stared quizzically at the pot of dirt Boggle had placed in front of him. She looked back at the basket and opened the lid. A fluffy, round-faced cat stuck its head out of the basket. Its large golden eyes assessed its surroundings before settling on Anna.

"Anna," Rupert crouched next to the basket stroking Tabitha's head affectionately, "I'd like you to repeat the process you used to bond with your bat friend except, instead of asking Tabitha to send messages for you, I'd like you to focus on what it feels like to be her."

"Like, how it feels to be a cat?" Anna asked.

"Yes," Rupert said, "Emotionally and physically. The sensation of having claws and fur, the sensory advantages of her tail and whiskers, her feelings toward birds compared to those of dogs. That sort of thing."

"Okay," Anna reached out to Tabitha with her mind. The cat jumped out of the basket and stretched gracefully before climbing onto Anna's lap.

"Hello," Anna directed her thoughts to the cat, *"Would you mind helping me with something?"*

"I heard Papa's instructions," purred the cat in Anna's mind, *"I will allow you into my mind if you will do me a favour."*

Anna wasn't expecting such a coherent response. She supposed a house cat's experience with human language is quite different to that of a wild animal.

"*What sort of favour?*" Anna asked.

"*Please tell Papa I don't like the tinned tuna,*" Tabitha instructed, "*He seems to think it's a special treat but chicken is my favourite.*"

Anna chuckled and relayed the message.

"Noted," smiled Rupert, inclining his head toward the cat.

"*Thank you,*" Tabitha purred, "*Would like to venture into my mind now?*"

"*How do I do that?*"

"*How should I know?*"

Anna focused on Tabitha's enormous, golden eyes. She imagined them as doors and felt a sense of calm, welcoming acceptance. Stepping through the doors, Anna felt as though she was sharing Tabitha's body. The cat's heartbeat was much faster than her own. Its fur made her feel protected, both a comforting shield and a finely tuned sensor for subtle changes in airflow. Her whole body began to vibrate with a satisfied purr.

"*It's nice in here,*" thought Anna.

"*Thank you,*" replied Tabitha.

Tabitha began extending and retracting her claws into the fabric of Anna's jeans. The sensation of her kneading paws reminded Anna of being at the beach with soft, warm sand between her toes. Mildly aware of the tiny pinpricks nagging at her leg, Anna pushed further into Tabitha's mind. She saw a vision of Rupert, *Papa*, gently stroking her fur with one hand while holding a book in the other. In another vision, Boggle ran ahead of her holding a string with chiming bells attached to it - her excitement piqued. She dashed and pounced trying to catch the jangling prey. In a final vision, she was a kitten, abandoned in a soggy cardboard box next to a dumpster. Rain poured into the box, flicking her tiny whiskers and drenching her fur in filthy water. A looming figure appeared over the box. A monstrous hand scooped her up and held her close to his chest. It was warm. She felt safe. She looked up to see a younger version of Rupert.

"*Papa has given me a lovely home,*" Tabitha purred.

Anna returned to her body, smiling. She gave Tabitha gentle scratches under the chin as she allowed the cat's mind to separate from hers. Tabitha smiled and drifted off to sleep. Finn, on the other hand, wiped droplets of sweat from his brow as he frowned at the pot of mud.

"Remember," Rupert spoke calmly, "The barrier to this magic exists only in your mind. If you can train your thoughts to *know* it can be done, rather than merely hoping it's possible, the power will flow through you easily."

"I can feel that there's water in the soil," Finn sounded strained, "I can feel the potential for new growth it brings, but I can't separate it from the soil. I *can't sense it on its own*. It's like trying to find a flashlight in the dark…I know it's there, but…ugh!"

Finn sat back in frustration.

"Don't fret," Rupert reassured, "You'll get there eventually. We simply need to try different methods until one of them clicks. You've both made wonderful progress for the first session."

Finn looked over to Anna and the sleeping cat on her lap.

"Can we switch?" he said with an exasperated laugh.

"Nope," Anna laughed.

"Anna's next task will be more demanding," Rupert assured, "But it's getting late. Would you like to stay for dinner?"

Anna hadn't realised how much time had passed. Finn looked exhausted.

"Thanks, but we should get going," Anna replied politely.

"Thank you for all your help," Finn added, looking relieved.

"You're welcome," Rupert beamed, "Please come back any time. Use the library and practice space whenever you please, even if I'm not here. Make yourselves at home."

Rupert led them back to the foyer where he showed Anna how to return to her bedroom. "Any door you've passed through while holding this key will be accessible from this door," he explained, "you simply need to put the key in the lock and picture the location clearly in your mind."

After the door closed behind them, Finn fell onto Anna's bed in a heap.

"That was great," he sighed, "but also *a lot*."

Anna climbed onto the bed, lifting Finn's head to rest on her lap. "Your thing was harder than mine," she said, "I just played with a cat."

"But you played like a pro," Finn chuckled, closing his eyes, "I was meant to be summoning the water out of that pot but I can only manipulate earth elements. I don't think it's possible."

"I could see your magic connecting with the soil," assured Anna, "Maybe the soil is the problem? You could try connecting with water on its own and see if that helps."

"When you say you could *see* my magic," Finn seemed confused, "What did it look like?"

"Swirling green light flowing from you into the pot," Anna replied, "It's beautiful. It's a shame you can't see it."

Finn tilted his head, "I can *feel* my magic...sometimes I visualise it in my head but I never actually see anything."

"Well, I struggle to feel the magic," Anna played with Finn's earlobe, "I have to see it first and even then it's more like my senses are responding to what I see."

"I guess that's what Rupert means about us needing different techniques to learn."

"I thought that was because I'm on *Beginner Level* and you're on *Expert Mode*."

"I'm hardly an expert," Finn sighed, "I just sat there, staring at a pot of dirt for hours."

"Don't be so hard on yourself," Anna crooned, "If your task was to move the soil, or make something grow from a seed, could you have done that?

"Yeah," Finn shrugged half-heartedly.

"That's amazing!"

"Everyone in my family can do that," he shrugged.

"Well, I think it's deeply impressive," Anna brushed her hand through Finn's hair, "You're being too hard on yourself."

"It's not just that," Finn exhaled, "I- I'm not great at being spontaneous. It's kind of related to my leg... I need to know plans in advance so I can plan which mobility aids I'll need. I get stressed when things happen out of the blue, even if I end up just sitting around like today, because I don't know how much energy I need to preserve."

"I didn't even think about that," Anna gasped, "I'm sorry."

"Don't be. It's not your fault," he rolled onto his side, "I just wish I was better at doing things impulsively. We didn't do much today but I'm still tired from it. It sucks."

"It's just a *thing*," shrugged Anna, "We all have *things*. Sunlight drains me, that's one of my things. I hate feeling invisible but I freeze when too many people are looking at me. I can't stand coriander-"

"I'm boring," Finn grimaced.

"Ha! *What?*" Anna scoffed, "You are many things, Henry Finnegan, but boring is not on the list."

"But there's so much stuff I can't do!" he complained, "Some of it is because of my leg but most of it is just me. I've never been outgoing or charismatic. I spend all my time hidden away, watching shows and reading books."

"You literally just described me," Anna played with Finn's hair, "And you said you didn't think I was boring. Were you lying?"

"No," he looked at her with a twinkle in his eyes.

"I think it's boring when someone has no interest in imagining a world outside their own reality." Anna couldn't pinpoint the moment she'd stopped feeling inadequate for her interest in stories but she suspected Finn's support had been a key factor, "You're interesting and wise. Anyone who doesn't see that is an idiot."

"How do you do that?" Finn smiled.

"What?"

"Make me feel like…like I'm enough."

"Enough?"

"For anything," he blushed, "For…you."

Anna laid next to Finn on the bed, resting her hand on his cheek.

"You are more than enough," she said quietly, "You're kind, strong, funny, smart, supportive, and very, very hot."

He snorted.

"And humble, to a fault," she continued with a grin, "And, for some reason, you want to spend your time with me. I have a pretty great imagination but I could never have thought up someone as wonderful as you. Because you're better than perfect. You're real. You're you. Please don't ever let anyone make you feel like you're not enough. You are the best person I know."

He leaned toward her. His lips hovered close to hers, barely brushing against her skin at first before pressing against her with an intense passion that flushed Anna's cheeks.

"You're the best person I know too," Finn breathed against her mouth.

Anna nuzzled closer to him, kissing him softly. He ran his fingers along her figure, resting his hand on her lower back.

"Can we stay like this forever?" she breathed.

"I'd like that," Finn smiled, "but I'll have to go home eventually."

"Not yet though?" Anna coaxed.

"No," Finn let his eyes drift shut, "Not yet."

CHAPTER 22

Practice Makes...

"Anna?" Dex whispered over the gentle taps of several keyboards being typed upon.

"Mm?" Anna responded.

"Why are you purring?"

Anna snapped back to reality. She had been following Rupert's instruction to meditate on the feeling of being a cat. The ultimate goal was to manifest something physical, like growing a tail or whiskers, but until then it made a relaxing change to her normal typing stupor.

"What?" she coughed, "I... wasn't."

Dex grinned and raised his eyebrows, "Don't stop!" Dex chuckled, "It's cute."

"Shut up," she whispered, glancing to check the others hadn't heard. Dex sniggered then turned back to his screen and resumed typing.

"So...Finn, eh?" Dex muttered. He spoke so softly only someone with vampiric hearing could pick up his words.

Anna glanced again to where Finn was sitting. He showed no sign of having overheard.

"What about him?" Anna matched his volume.

"You know," Dex waggled his eyebrows.

Anna smirked.

"Was there a question?" She asked, resuming her typing with a grin.

"I just didn't think you'd be into the mysterious, stoic type."

"He's not stoic."

"I'm not criticising, love, I think you two are *adorkable* together!"

"So, what's the problem?"

"No problem, I just want the hot goss. Give me details! The when, the where, the how, the what..."

"The *what?*"

"What sort of relationship is it?"

"...Romantic?"

"No, love, are you friends-with-benefits or a couple? Exclusive or open?"

"We're a couple...But, I guess we haven't defined anything."

"You should probably do that," Dex advised, "you know what they say about assumptions and asses."

Anna rolled her eyes.

Her relationship with Finn wasn't casual. He'd been pretty clear about Anna being the only one he wanted. Just because they hadn't specifically said they were exclusive didn't mean they weren't on the same page. Finn didn't look at her like she was just a *friend with benefits*. He treated her the way a boyfriend would. Surely he thought of them as a couple.

Or did he?

Finn grew up with polygamous parents. His idea of a *normal* romantic relationship might be different from Anna's. Had Anna taken it for granted that she and Finn were exclusive? He'd said he didn't have much *sexual* experience but hadn't said anything about his *romantic* endeavours. What if he had a long-distance girlfriend? Plenty of women would be happy to *take things slow* with a sweet, kind man like him.

Anna couldn't concentrate on her work. She wished she could see into Finn's mind and figure out what he wanted without the embarrassment of asking. After her recent magic lessons from Rupert, she was sorely tempted to try. People were animals, after all, and she'd visited Tabitha's mind several times now. She quickly dismissed the idea. She'd never betray Finn's trust that way. Not to mention, Tabitha had always invited her in. Anna had never tried to enter the mind of an unwilling creature.

She forced her mind back to focus on her meditations. She was a carefree feline, covered in soft fur...What if Finn assumed they were in an open relationship?

The thought made her insides squirm. Maybe she could find a way to be alright with sharing his affections with someone else. She didn't own him, after all. He should be free to do whatever made him happy. But the thought of someone else made Anna nauseous. And angry. She deserved better than a shared romance. She wanted to be the only one. She...No, wait... *She was a cat.* A calm, carefree cat...Who definitely didn't care about human to human intimacy or the exclusivity of certain relationships...

With a strange scratching sound, followed by an electrical pop, her keyboard exploded under her fingers. Deep claw marks dug into the desk, cutting the keyboard into shreds.

"Holy crap!" Dex was staring at Anna's hands, which had semi-transformed so that her palms remained human but her fingers were now furry and elongated with razor-sharp claws.

Anna marvelled at the claws, slashing through the air as though she was fighting an invisible foe. Testing their strength, she gently scraped the tip of her pointer finger along the top of her desk. It carved through the wood like butter.

"Um, Anna?" Cassie interrupted Anna's amusement, "Whatcha doin'?"

Anna looked up to see all three of her friends staring. Dex looked awestruck while Cassie seemed shocked and Finn was impressed.

"Look at these!" Anna exclaimed in a hushed tone.

"Yes," Dex nodded emphatically, "We see them. Very impressive but may I ask *what-the-actual-fuck*?"

"Rupert's been helping me with magic," Anna shrugged.

"So, you did this on purpose?" Cassie confirmed, looking at the damage to Anna's workstation.

"Not entirely," Anna shrugged.

"What were you trying to do?" Cassie frowned.

"Embrace my inner feline."

"Good job," Dex laughed, "Do you think you can *un-embrace* it before you freak out the temps?"

The headphone-wearing temps sitting in front of them hadn't turned around but it was only a matter of time before they noticed their colleague had claws. Or, because of the Veil, would they see her holding knives? Either way, it wouldn't be good.

"Um," Anna had a sobering thought. She didn't know how to change the claws back into fingers. She briefly thought of calling Rupert but was certain he would expect her to figure this out for herself, or at least attempt to. *Okay, you did this. So, undo it.*

"Are you okay, Anna?" Finn's voice was filled with concern.

"Give me a second," Anna closed her eyes, trying to remember the sensation of having normal hands but her mind kept drifting back to the claws.

"Go away." She thought desperately toward her furry fingers. *"Be normal."* She opened her eyes. Nothing had changed.

She sat at her desk and took several steadying breaths. Finn rubbed her back. She counted backwards from one hundred. When she reached zero, she felt calmer.

This is my body. I control it.

She set aside the idea of *normal hands* and instead remembered the sensation of touching things with fingers. The cold surface of her phone screen. The soft, silky fabric of her favourite dress. The gentle warmth of Finn's face. His soft curls. The pinprick scratches of the stubble on his jaw.

She knew she'd succeeded before she opened her eyes. She smiled as she looked upon her first, intentional, transformation.

That wasn't so hard.

"Sorry about that," she said sheepishly.

"All good," Dex frowned with a smirk. "Not sure how we're going to explain your desk to Pam though."

***

Anna's progress with magic was frustratingly erratic. Just when she thought she'd mastered something, like transforming her hands into claws and back again, she'd lose focus and fail. Then she'd have to start from the beginning. Some days she could summon her claws without thinking about it while, on other days, the task required hours of meditation and visualisation.

On a good day, Anna could touch the strands of magic surrounding her and easily manipulate them into shapes. On other days they'd avoid her touch or zap her fingers when she reached for them. If her confidence wavered the spell would always fail, so her primary challenge was maintaining faith in spite of failure. She could feel when the magic didn't want to cooperate. Sometimes it just needed some gentle coaxing. Often it needed bribery. With no life force to offer up, she'd found elemental offerings helpful. Cassie's explanation of balance made more sense now. Different forms of magic required offerings of a similar *temperament.*

To make something happen quickly, fire worked best. If she wanted something to last a long time, earth was the better element. Her favourite spell thus far had been making a pencil levitate by offering up air from her lungs. She blew onto the pencil as she folded the magic around it. Watching it hover in the air filled her with satisfied pleasure. She finally felt like a mage. She could make things fly!

Finn made some progress too. It had taken several weeks but he'd finally managed to manipulate water. The revelation that he could, in fact, perform magic outside his innate abilities had ignited a childlike enthusiasm in him. "I can do anything," he whispered with wonder, swirling a ball of water in the air, "This is incredible!"
However, his excitement was short-lived. Each new spell came with its own challenges. Rupert worked with him but Finn's patience for progress was lower than Anna's. He was used to magic cooperating. When it didn't respond quickly, or easily, he gave up.
"You're not being persistent enough," Anna chastised during one of their practice sessions.
"It doesn't want to cooperate," Finn frowned at his bowl of water.
"Try bonding with it first," she suggested, "Earn its trust before you ask a favour."
"Yeah, I guess," Finn looked tired.

They decided to call it a day and headed back to Anna's bedroom.
"You don't have to do this, you know," Anna squeezed his hand.
"Neither do you," Finn gave a weary chuckle, "I like struggling over magic together."
"As long as you're not just doing this for me." Anna didn't like the idea of Finn pushing himself past his limits. She was glad she didn't have to chose between practicing magic and seeing him but suspected he was only coming to these lessons for her. He was always exhausted by the end of them and rarely made much progress.

"Have you talked to Dex about your bloodlust yet?" Finn hoisted his backpack onto his shoulder.
Anna had been putting off reaching out to Dex. The only way to overcome her bloodlust was to face it head-on but she had no desire to put any more people in danger. However, as Finn kept reminding her, it was better to lose control under supervision than when no one was around to stop her.

The whole thing put a pit in her stomach.

She kissed Finn goodbye as he mounted his motorbike. She watched him drive away, promising herself she'd ask Dex for help when she got back inside.

As she sat on her bed, however, she couldn't bring herself to unlock her phone. Suddenly, it buzzed. She nearly dropped it in surprise.

Roxy: *Hey, hope you're dealing okay. Hit me up if you need anything.*

A tingle ran down Anna's spine. She barely knew Roxy. They'd met once on one of the most traumatic nights of her life but, for some reason, Anna wanted to take her up on her offer. Roxy had been there when Anna lost control. She'd seen Anna at her worst and accepted it. She clearly had more experience at being a vampire. Maybe she could help. To Anna's surprise, her fingers had already typed a reply.

Anna: *I need help controlling my bloodlust.*

Anna watched the animated dots blink on her screen as Roxy formed her reply.

Roxy: *Too easy. Meet me this Saturday night at U4ria.*

Anna did a quick search on the location. It was a private gallery specialising in tech-based artwork. Their current exhibit included interactive projections of classic paintings. Anna couldn't imagine how this setting would be helpful but wasn't about to question Roxy's choice. In a sudden wave of guilt, Anna messaged Dex to see if he'd mind coming along. She should have asked him first. He was her friend and Roxy was a stranger. What had she been thinking?

Dex: *I'm near your place. Fancy a visit?*

***

"When did you meet her?" Dex asked with a quizzical expression as he reviewed Roxy's message.

197

"Pretty recently," Anna answered evasively.

"Well, aren't you just the social moth." Dex winked, "Get it? Like a butterfly but for night-time?"

"Hah," Anna rolled her eyes, "Can't you just hypnotise me into not having bloodlust?"

"Vampires can't hypnotise each other," Dex sighed sadly, "Only sires have that kind of control but they use it sparingly. They feel when their ward is suffering. It's for protection, not control."

"Yes, yes," Anna pouted, "Sires are great."

"At least Roxy knows her stuff," Dex shrugged, "I was thinking of taking you to the same place. They have special feeding nights where hospice patients can come for an escape. A lot of new vampires learn to control their feeding there."

"I don't want to kill anyone, Dex," Anna frowned.

"Well, you might," Dex replied with a serious expression, "The volunteers know the risks. If you succeed, they'll get a nice high from your bite. If you fail, their pain will be over for good. It's the best way to learn. I know it's scary but maybe it won't be as bad as you think. You've had great control so far."

Anna sighed. She had to tell him the truth about how she'd met Roxy. It was bound to come up on Saturday. "The truth is…" she hesitated. Dex had never hurt anyone drinking blood. Would he understand? It was a risk she had to take, "I've already killed someone. By accident. The bloodlust took over and it happened so fast. Roxy was there and she helped me."

Dex's eyebrows shot up. He sat on the edge of Anna's bed and rubbed his forehead pensively. It was a strange contrast of worlds to see Dex, in his gothic mesh singlet and torn jeans, perched on Anna's cheerful sunflower patchwork blanket.

"Shit," Dex frowned, "I should have helped you with this sooner. Who else knows?"

"Finn," Anna joined Dex on the bed, "And Rupert."

Dex nodded slowly, "That's good. Don't tell Cassie. I love her but she won't understand. Some things are unimaginable…*unforgivable*…until you've been put in that position yourself."

"You seem to be handling it okay," Anna crossed her legs.

"I know the power of bloodlust," Dex qualified, "There's no doubt in my mind that, without Markus helping me, I would have killed a lot of people when I was newly turned. You said your granddad killed the bastards who murdered you, so he knows what it's like to cross that line. And Finn does too, of course-"

"What?" Anna gasped. Finn said he'd never told anyone about Jade.

"I thought you knew?" Dex frowned, "Finn took out the werewolf who attacked him. He doesn't like people mentioning it but I though he'd have told you. I've seen the anguish in his eyes when folks praise him for *besting a werewolf with his bare hands*. They forget that werewolves are people too."

"I knew," Anna confided with secret relief, "I...I thought you didn't."

"He's my family," Dex said with a shrug, "We've been through some shit together. I'm glad he's finally talking about it with someone."

Dex didn't linger after their conversation. He disappeared into the night shortly before Anna's daily blood delivery arrived. She wondered how many vampires subscribed to the service compared to those who preferred a fresher source. Dex had said it was too much hassle to drink fresh blood regularly but he didn't have human roommates. Anna shook the thought from her mind. Even if she could control herself, even if her roommates came home regularly, they would never agree to let her drink from them. As she gulped down blood from her thermos, one thought was inescapable. *Fresh blood tastes better.*

***

By Saturday, Anna had worked herself into an anxious mess. No matter how many worst-case scenarios played through her head there was nothing she could do to feel prepared. Her only consolation was knowing she wouldn't be alone. She clung to Dex's arm as they waited outside the gallery. The building was a collection of grey cubes, stacked at varying angles, with blacked-out windows. The door was hidden around the side of the building with a keypad entry. There was no signage to confirm they'd found the right place but Dex assured Anna he'd been there before.

"It creates a sense of exclusivity," he assured, "and, in tonight's case, it stops people wandering in."

Roxy emerged from the door, ushering Anna and Dex inside. She handed Anna a red wristband before attaching a black one to Dex's wrist.

"I feel like I've seen you before," she squinted at him.

"I've seen your band play," Dex nodded, "You're good."
Roxy smiled. Her pearly fangs emphasised by her dark lipstick.

The reception area reminded Anna of a high-end spa. The lighting was low and candles adorned every surface. The air was scented with lavender. Calming music played through unseen speakers and lapping ocean waves were projected onto the curtained wall behind the front desk. The receptionist nodded to them as Roxy led them through the curtain.

They emerged into a long corridor, painted black and lined with doors like a hotel. Each door featured a large touchscreen monitor, housed in an antique-looking gold frame.
"We're in *The Starry Night*," Roxy pointed at the nearest screen showing a stylised cityscape with swirling blue brush strokes.

The room inside had an impossibly high ceiling. Subtly animated projections of the painting illuminated all four walls and the floor, making it feel as though they'd stepped inside the painting. A black recliner sat auspiciously in the centre of the room with smaller cushioned seating surrounding it. An attendant greeted them, offering fruit-infused water before excusing herself to bring in their first *guest*.

"I don't know if I can do this," Anna paced back and forth.
"We'll start slow," Roxy assured.
"You can just watch this first one, if you like." Dex offered, "You don't have to do anything."
Anna nodded and sat on one of the cushioned chairs. The attendant returned wheeling an elderly woman into the room. After helping her shuffle into the recliner, the attendant gave a small bow and left.

"Hello," smiled the woman. She had arthritis in her fingers but otherwise seemed quite healthy.
"Hi," Anna swallowed.
The woman leaned slightly toward Anna, "Is this your first time, dear?"
Anna nodded.
"Don't worry," the woman offered her wrist, "You'll do fine."
"I-" Anna glanced at Dex, "I don't know…"
Dex stepped forward and sat with Anna, taking the woman's wrist, "I'll start and then you can try to take a sip, okay?"

Anna nodded again. The woman inclined her head toward Dex, "There's a good lad."

Dex's fangs pierced paper-thin skin on the old woman's wrist. The hypnotic smell of blood made Anna want to push Dex aside. She dug her nails into her palms to distract herself. The woman closed her eyes as a blissful expression spread across her face. Her knobbly fingers stopped shaking and her body loosened. She sighed.

"Your turn," Dex whispered, holding out the woman's limp hand.

The open wound made Anna's mouth water. She couldn't resist. She snatched the wrist from Dex and began to drink. The warm liquid was velvety smooth with an intoxicating play of sweetness and acidity. Anna's body tingled with warmth as echoes of fruit and spice enticed her to drink more.

And more.

And more.

A light buzzing tickled her ear like a fly zooming in and out of range. Feathers stroked the skin on her jaw.

And more.

And more.

Roxy's voice cut through the dream, "Anna, stop!"

Razors ran along Anna's spine as she released the woman from her grip. Dex held Anna's head in a stranglehold while Roxy pulled the old woman's hand away. Dex loosened his grip, seeming out of breath.

"That was close," he murmured, "Couldn't you hear me yelling?"

With ice pumping through her veins, Anna listened for the old woman's heartbeat. It was slow but, thankfully, still thumping.

"She did it though," Roxy smiled reassuringly, "She stopped. Eventually."

Anna began to shake. How long had they been trying to stop her?

What if she'd resisted them for five seconds longer?

Roxy pressed a button on the wall near the door and a new attendant appeared. They helped the woman shift dreamily back into her wheelchair, then took her away. A few minutes later, another guest was shown into the room. This one was younger. He looked around Anna's age but had dark circles under his eyes, sallow skin and thinning hair. He slouched into the armchair as though the effort of walking across the room had exhausted him.

"Can't our blood heal him?" Anna whispered into Dex's ear.

Dex shook his head, "Our blood only accelerates the natural healing process."

Barely glancing at the vampires surrounding him, the man extended his arm. It was pale and bruised. Anna took it gingerly. She closed her eyes and sunk her teeth into the warm flesh. Blood spurted into the back of her mouth, soaking her tongue in the delicious elixir. Once more, Anna lost herself to the sensations. She couldn't stop. She didn't want to stop. The buzzing returned. Ribbons, once again, brushed her skin. She swatted them away. She deserved to be happy. She deserved this one indulgence. She'd spent her life denying herself pleasure. Playing it safe. Worrying about how she was perceived rather than how she felt. None of that mattered now. She felt good. She felt powerful. She felt-

"Stop!" Roxy brought Anna back to herself once again.

The man in the chair was grinning, lost in a sea of elation. Attendants took him away and replaced him with another. The cycle continued three more times before Roxy decided to try a new approach.

"We're not going to stop you this time," she announced as attendants ushered in another volunteer, "sink or swim - this one's all you."

Anna looked from Roxy to Dex, "You're not serious?"

"You're relying on us to stop you," Dex frowned, looking unsure, "You'll never learn self-control that way."

Anna wanted to argue but knew they were right. She hadn't been afraid of hurting anyone since the first woman. She'd known her safety net would catch her so she'd allowed herself to fall.

"Okay," Anna took a deep breath, "I can do this."

The woman in the chair looked frail. She was easily the eldest of the volunteers they'd had thus far. "What's you name?" Anna asked, thinking it would help her to restrain herself.

"Edith," the woman replied in a light, husky voice.

Like the others, Edith seemed to be well accustomed to the procedure. She held out her arm for Anna to drink. As the warm liquid flowed into her mouth, an immediate rush of vitality shot through Anna's body. The world faded away, replaced by changing blends of flavours from sweet and rich to earthy and bitter. Each sip heightened Anna's craving for more.

It was more than intoxicating, it was transcendent. She could taste the essence of Edith's memories and emotions within each drop. Joy, fear, lust, agony - Anna was drinking life itself. She was powerful. She was free.

Her heartbeat matched the pulse of her prey as it transferred life into her with each beat. Time slowed down. The wait between pulses took longer and longer. Anna bit down harder, hoping to elevate her victim's adrenaline but it had the opposite effect. With a final gulp, Anna felt Edith's heart beat for the last time. Far too late, Anna frantically pushed the limp wrist away. She'd killed again.

"I-," Anna's chair clattered to the floor as she stumbled away from Edith's body. "I didn't mean to."

The swirling projections of The Starry Night loomed down on her. The room was spinning, the floor tilting and turning. Anna crumbled in the corner, holding her knees and rocking as tears ran down her face. Dex slid down the wall next to her, "I'm sorry. I thought you'd be able to stop on your own."

"You'll get it next time," Roxy said gently as two attendants removed Edith's body. She had an expression of joy plastered to her face, though her skin was grey and lifeless.

"There won't be a next time," Anna shuddered. "I'm done."

"But what if-"

"No." Anna stood up. Her legs felt like jelly as she paced to the door, "I'm done."

CHAPTER 23

Broken

"I can't feed on people without killing them so I just won't feed on people."
Anna curled up to Finn on his bed.

"You didn't mean to feed on Brad," Finn pointed out, "What if something like that happens again?"

"If someone else spits blood in my face," she replied savagely, "they'll get what they get."

"You don't mean that." Finn knew Anna would hate herself if she killed anyone else, regardless of the circumstances. "You're allowed to be upset about what happened but I don't think you should give up."

"I just..." Anna groaned in frustration, "I don't want to learn how to control myself it means killing more people. That defeats the whole point!"

"I know," Finn soothed, stroking her hair, "We'll find another way. I agree you shouldn't try Roxy's method again but please don't give up all together, okay?"

Anna nodded, "How can you be so supportive?"

"I know how much this is torturing you," Finn answered, "How else should I be?"

"I've killed two people." Anna sniffed, "I'll probably end up killing more. I'm a monster and you're kind and lovely."

He deserved to be with someone better. Someone who didn't accidentally murder people. Someone who didn't consider, however briefly, reading Finn's thoughts instead of asking him simple questions. Someone who wasn't constantly wallowing in her own drama.

Finn laughed darkly, "I'm not as good as you think."

Anna looked at him sceptically, "Care to elaborate?"

He leaned over the edge of the bed. It felt like a long time before he spoke.

"Part of me loves this," he muttered under his breath, "A good person wouldn't feel this way."

"What do you mean?" Anna followed him to the edge of the bed, watching the muscles tense in his jaw as he stared at the ground.

"Part of me," he whispered, "was glad when you got killed because now, you're not just awake to the magical world...you're also *broken like me*. I hate seeing you struggle. I hate it. But there's this tiny feeling that won't go away. It's happy I finally have a kindred spirit. We already had so much in common before... I've never been able to talk with anyone so easily, or felt so- so *seen*."

Finn turned to Anna. A tear rolled down his cheek.

"I can open up to you in a way I never have before," he said, "Cassie and Dex are my best friends but they've never been able to relate to the things I love or fear or hate. They understand me on a theoretical level but you...you *get it*. You talk about fictional characters as though they're real, like I do. They live in your heart because their stories are more than entertainment, they're an experience. A chance to live another life. An exercise in empathy. A way to understand the world better."

Anna nodded. He was right. She felt it too. There was a connection between them that Cassie and Dex simply couldn't touch. More tears trickled down his face.

"It killed me that I couldn't tell you everything," Finn wrinkled his nose, "I wanted to be honest with you about magic but I was scared you'd be afraid of me if you knew what I was. I kept wishing you'd find out by accident so it'd be out of my hands. And then I got my wish! Lucky me, right?"

Finn aggressively wiped the tears from his cheeks. He stared at his lap with a guarded expression, awaiting Anna's response. Anna placed her hand gently on the side of his face and leaned in, touching her forehead against his. He let out a quiet whimper.

"How monstrous that you want me in your life," Anna stroked his earlobe with a light smile, "What a twisted mind you have to recognise the good parts of a horrible situation."

Finn looked at Anna incredulously.

"You think I haven't noticed how much better my life is?" Anna went on, "I can do magic, I have superpowers, and best of all - I finally feel like I *belong*. I'm not just trying to fit in anymore. The world finally feels real to me and that's largely thanks to you."

"But the bloodlust…the killing…the way you died?"

"All awful things."Anna agreed, "I'm not saying my life is perfect but, if I got to choose, I wouldn't go back to how things used to be."

Anna hadn't assessed her life this way until now. It surprised her as much as Finn, who gazed at her with disbelief and admiration.

***

Anna channelled her bloodlust frustration into her magic lessons. There was power in strong emotions like rage and fear. They attracted strong magical energies that needed a degree of mental juggling to control.

After a lifetime of anxiety, constantly planning what could go wrong at every turn, it was easy for Anna to focus on several things at once.

She could predict the way magical elements would interact and when to cut her losses. Sometimes the air had too much humidity. Sometimes lighting was too bright or the temperature was wrong. Rupert commended her when she articulated these observations, "Most mages study weather charts and moon cycles in the hopes of guessing the right time and place. They cannot judge the time or place for their spellwork by instinct alone."

She was glad to hear it until she remembered that most mages could draw on their own life force for spellwork. If they were anything like Rupert or Cassie, their magic flowed freely and they only needed to consider external elements for larger spells.

The more Anna tried to channel magical energy through the dark void where her life force should be, the more she exhausted herself. If she used too much magic, she'd get hot, dizzy and nauseous. Sometimes she'd get awful headaches or her skin would turn red like she'd been burned.

Rupert warned her to stop whenever she reached this barrier, "Heatstroke is a sign you are pushing the magic too far. Ease back. Rest."

Anna didn't want to rest. She couldn't control her bloodlust but at least with magic she was only putting herself in danger. Rupert didn't understand. Nobody did. She needed to be good at *something*. She needed to feel in control of her life.

***

A few weeks later, Roxy stopped by Anna's apartment to check in. They sat on the roof, enjoying the starlight and warm breeze.

"Sorry for the way things went down," she murmured, picking at a stud in her eyebrow, "I shouldn't have made you fly solo so fast."
"I could have refused," Anna hugged her knees. Edith's face hovered in her mind like a ghost.
Roxy tilted her chin, "It's been a long time since I was turned. I don't remember how intense it was."
"You don't remember the bloodlust?"
"I remember what I did because of it," Roxy cringed, "it's what stops me from giving in now. My sire was the *sink or swim* type of teacher."
"What happened?" Anna wasn't sure she wanted to know. Roxy seemed indifferent to murder, so whatever she'd done must have been horrific to still affect her.
"I killed my family." Roxy crossed her arms and swallowed, "My parents, my little brother and sisters, even my grandmother. Once I'd started, I couldn't stop myself."
"I'm sorry," whispered Anna. She couldn't imagine how it must have felt to find herself surrounded by her freshly slaughtered family. To lose everyone she loved in an instant. She was grateful she'd never been tempted to drink from Rupert or Cassie. It made her hopeful she'd be able to restrain herself around the rest of her family too. She didn't want to avoid them for the rest of their lives but she'd have to if she couldn't get a handle on her bloodlust.
Roxy shrugged, "Not your fault. It was a long time ago."

"Do you forgive me for the other night?" Roxy seemed genuinely concerned.
"Of course," Anna replied. A wave of relief washed over them. The stars seemed to shine brighter.
"Next time'll be better," Roxy promised, "Just bear with me, okay? I'll ask around. There has to be a better way of doing it."
"I'm not in a rush to try again," Anna grimaced, "But, if you find anything, let me know."
"Will do." Roxy smiled at the moon, "Just, please don't beat yourself up about that old lady. She's in a better place now."

Anna nodded as a cool breeze sent a chill up her spine. The night was peaceful. Edith's face faded from Anna's mind, replaced by the twinkling stars.

CHAPTER 24

Don't Panic

Anna's phone buzzed across the surface of her new desk. Pam had been surprisingly unconcerned about replacing all the office equipment Anna had destroyed with her claws.

Roxy: *Come check out my band at Greaser tomorrow night!*

Anna smiled. She felt a sudden itch to go out. She'd earned it after all the magic lessons and meditation work she'd been doing in her spare time.
"Do you guys have plans after work tomorrow?" Anna looked from Dex to Cassie and Finn.
"Nope," Cassie replied brightly.
"Me neither," Finn answered.
"Depends on your offer," Dex smirked.
"Roxy's band is playing," Anna said, avoiding eye contact. She didn't know how the Dex and Finn felt about the vampire who'd enabled her to kill again. Even Anna couldn't explain why she liked her, "It's at a bar called Greaser."
"I know the place." Cassie smiled. "Sounds great."
Dex leaned back in his chair, "Count me in." If he had a problem with Roxy, he wasn't showing it.

Anna looked imploringly at Finn,
He pulled his wheelchair closer to the desk, "Sure, yeah," his smile didn't quite reach his eyes.
"What's wrong?" asked Cassie.
"Nothing," Finn resumed typing, forcing a weak smile, "It'll be fun. We could all use a night out."

Cassie raised her eyebrows and shrugged at Anna. Anna turned to her phone.

Anna: *Hey, talk to me, what's wrong?*
Finn: *Nothing. It's dumb.*
Anna: *If it matters to you, then it's not dumb. Is it Roxy?*
Finn: *No.*
Anna: *Then what?*
Finn: *I shouldn't go.*
Anna: *Why not?*
Finn: *I can't dance all night. I'll get tired. It'll ruin things for you.*
Anna: *This is a bar, not a club. No dancing required!*
Anna turned to watch Finn reading her last message. His face brightened.

Finn: *I suppose we can't always hang out in your room practising magic.*
Anna: *Don't worry, we can still take plenty of 'study breaks' ;)*
Finn grinned as his ears turned pink.

***

The following night, Anna and Finn entered the laneway to Greaser. The bar was at ground level but Finn still needed help from Anna to get his wheelchair over a couple of small, inconveniently placed, steps.
"You shouldn't have to help me," he muttered.
"There shouldn't be a step there," Anna replied, kissing the top of his head. After all the times he'd been there for her, it felt good to be the one helping.

A small group of people dressed in punk outfits emerged from the entrance. One of the men laughed at something another said and the stench of beer on his breath stung Anna's nostrils. Before she could react, her chest turned to ice. She couldn't breathe. Scenes from her nightmares played before her eyes. Gasping for air, her legs gave out. The Brad-zombie-ogres were back, surrounding her, but there was no waking from her nightmare this time.

"Anna?!" Finn's voice echoed in the darkness, "Just breathe, I'm here."
The world was suffocating. Her heart pounded.
"Can you count backwards for me?" Finn's voice seemed far away.
Anna shook her head.

She couldn't meditate right now.

She couldn't think.

She couldn't breathe.

"Okay," Finn replied, "Can you tell me my name?"

"Finn," gasped Anna, gulping down air.

"Good," replied Finn, squeezing her hands, "What colour are my shoes?"

Anna forced her eyes open to see Finn crouched by her side.

"Brown," Anna answered.

"What's your sister's name?"

"Liz."

"What's her husband's name?"

"Mark."

"What's their daughter's name?"

"Clara."

"Can you count backwards from ten now?"

The distraction had worked. Anna could breathe again.

"Anna!" Roxy rushed down the laneway, "Shit! Are you okay?"

"Yeah," Anna slid up the wall on shaky legs, "I'm fine."

"What just happened?" Roxy demanded with concern.

Finn sat back in his wheelchair, eyeing Roxy with suspicion, "Panic attack," he replied.

"The beer smell," Anna winced, "Maybe coming to a bar was a dumb idea."

"Do you want to go home?" Finn offered.

"No," Anna wanted to cry. Or punch a wall. Or both. "I should be able to go out without it turning into a shit show. I need to do this. If I don't go into that bar... then they've won."

"That's the spirit," Roxy patted Anna on the back.

"Who's won?" Finn frowned.

"The guys who killed me," Anna muttered, "Every asshole who treats people like me as disposable playthings. The assholes who blame the victim for being in the wrong place at the wrong time. You know...*them*."

"I understand," Finn rested his hand on Anna's shoulder and gave a reassuring squeeze.

"You're not a helpless little lamb anymore," Roxy said firmly, "You don't have to hide in the herd and hope the wolves show you mercy. You're gonna go in there-" she pointed at the entrance to the bar, "and you're going to have a *fuckin' great time*. Don't let your past, or your fear, control you. The fuckers who killed you are nothing but red stains on the sidewalk. You never have to think about them again. You can do this."

A tingle shot down Anna's spine. She *could* do this. What's the worst that could happen? She'd already experienced the worst-case scenario. She stood up with a renewed sense of confidence. Head up, shoulders squared. "See you in there," Roxy winked before jogging back to the street where a group of women were unloading a large amp from the boot of their car.

"Anna," Finn whispered, "I get where you're coming from but you can't just walk off a panic attack. We can go home and try another time. You don't have to prove anything to anyone."
"I'm feeling okay now," Anna assured Finn, "Really. I want to go in."
Finn frowned but nodded in support.

Passing through the doorway, a red neon sign greeted them with the words *I'd rather be dead than cool*. She laughed sardonically. Roxy was right. Anna wasn't a helpless lamb anymore.
But she wasn't a wolf either.
The thugs who'd killed her were the wolves, stalking women like prey as though it was a god-given right. But the tables had turned. It wasn't safe for the wolves anymore. *This lamb had fangs.*

Anna grinned, walking with purpose through the dimly lit rooms of the bar. The place was packed. Mismatched seating from cushy velvet armchairs to hardwood bar stools were occupied by various groups of people, all having a good time. Gallery walls featuring framed images of rock'n'roll legends covered the raw brick and metal pipes ran along the low ceiling. The rich smell of onion rings overpowered the scent of beer. Though Roxy's band hadn't set up yet, a small mosh pit of fans hovered by the small stage.

Cassie waved from the line at the bar and then pointed to Dex, who had somehow managed to claim a table.
"Not enough chairs," he grumbled as Anna and Finn approached.
"We can improvise," Anna shrugged, impishly sliding onto Finn's lap. She had always hated public displays of affection but, until now, she'd never been a participant.
Dex raised his eyebrows with a proud grin, "Okay, then."

"Is this okay?" Anna whispered into Finn's ear.

"Are *you* okay?" He whispered back, wrapping his arms around her protectively, "For real?"

"I'm great," she kissed his cheek.

"Okay," he maintained a look of concern but didn't push the matter.

"Which one is your friend?" Cassie appeared with a jug of cider and four glasses. She gestured at the band, who'd begun setting up on the stage.

"Roxy," Anna pointed, "with the high buns."

"I feel like I've seen her before," Cassie squinted.

"Probably at Rock Bottom," Dex held up his phone, showing Cassie photos of the band playing. "Her band plays there a lot."

"I don't think that's it," Cassie scrunched her face.

Roxy spotted Cassie staring and stepped off the stage, weaving through the crowd toward them.

"Cassie, right?" Roxy grinned, "You're Jedda's girl?"

"You're Jedda's roommate!" Cassie's face exploded into recognition.

"Yeah, me and Jeds are tight," Roxy nodded, "She won't shut up about you."

Cassie blushed, "She would've come tonight but she's-"

"Working," Roxy laughed, shaking her head, "As always."

"ON IN FIVE, ROX," The guitarist yelled from the stage.

Roxy nodded and then turned to Anna, "Mind if I steal you for a sec?" she asked.

"Sure," Anna replied, sliding out of Finn's arms.

They walked into one of the more secluded areas of the bar.

"I'm okay now," Anna preemptively answered, "You don't need to worry."

"That's the thing," Roxy glanced around, suddenly serious, "I've been worrying about you a lot. And tonight, I *knew* something was going down before I saw you on the ground. Something weird's going on, right?"

"I don't know," Anna had to admit she felt unusually close to Roxy for someone she'd only talked to a few times, "Maybe?"

"I'll talk to Jedda about it," Roxy said, more to herself than Anna.

"Do you think she'll know anything?"

"Witches know everything," Roxy shrugged, "At the very least, she'll have a theory."

"Maybe," Anna doubted Jedda had any answers.

"Anyway," Roxy checked her watch, "I've got to get on stage but I'm glad you're doing okay. Hit me up soon, yeah? We'll get to the bottom of this."

"Yeah, thanks."

Anna slid back onto Finn's lap, giving him a light peck on the cheek.

"What was that about?" he asked quietly.

"She was just checking in-" Anna began, but was interrupted by an ear-splitting roar.

"WE'RE THE BANGIN' BANSHEES!" Roxy yelled into the microphone, "TIME FOR SOME NOISE! ONE- TWO- THREE- FOUR- !"

The music was deafening but exhilarating. Soundwaves reverberated through Anna's chest.

"Fuck, yeah!" Dex yelled over the din, grabbing Cassie's hand and pulling her into the mosh pit. He began aggressively head-banging while Cassie bounced to the beat, punching the air.

"Go join them," Finn offered, "I'll mind the table."

"I can smell the sweat from here," Anna crinkled her nose, "No, thanks."

"You don't need to make excuses to stay," Finn smiled, "Really. Go have fun."

Anna wrapped her arms around him, "You're the only person I want to rub up against." She pressed her lips to his, parting them just enough to taste the sweet cider on his breath.

Finn touched his forehead to hers, "And you're feeling okay now?"

"I am," Anna smiled, "I promise. I feel great."

"You don't find that weird?"

"I'm choosing not to question it," she turned to face the show, leaning back to rest her head against Finn's shoulder.

"Roxy told you not to let your past control you," Finn whispered in her ear, "And now you're surrounded by triggers, completely fine."

Anna turned to look into Finn's eyes, "She couldn't be my sire."

"Why not?"

"We didn't meet until later."

"That you know of..."

Anna watched Roxy dance around the stage. Could she be the one who saved Anna from death? If so, why keep it a secret? Roxy seemed just as perplexed about their connection as Anna. But there was a connection.

Anna glanced around the room. There were plenty of hulking groups of men guzzling beer. She could smell their breath. The walls were made of the same earthy bricks that lined the alley where she'd died. But she felt indifferent to all of it. No fear. No panic. She was having a good time, just as Roxy had instructed. *Could Roxy be her sire?*

If so, why did it seem like Roxy didn't know about it either?
Was she lying? What would be the point?

***

Anna didn't have a single nightmare that night.
Or the ones that followed.

CHAPTER 25
Party Time

"I still don't know why we have to go to this," Dex muttered, fiddling with his pocket square as the elevator carried them up. The annual Kingsley & Laurant Christmas Party was held in the rooftop gardens of the corporate tower, "It's not like any of the *Suits* care about rubbing shoulders with us meagre peasants."

"Because we work here too," Cassie said, adjusting a loose curl on her wig, "We deserve to drink champagne and eat whatever stupid, tiny, fancy food they're serving. Just like the rest."

"Well, when you put it like that..." Dex chuckled, "Do you think they'll have brandy? I do love a nice brandy."

"That's the spirit!" Cassie giggled.

She had already ingested some cocktails, "Get it? Spirit? Like, booze!"

"Oh, dear," Dex rolled his eyes affectionately.

Cassie poked out her tongue.

"Are you sure this thing's straight?" Finn touched his bow tie with a cheeky smile.

"Let me check," Anna grinned, playing his game. She leaned down to adjust it, kissing him lightly on the cheek as she did so.

"Have I told you how beautiful you look tonight?" Finn whispered, stoking the fabric of her emerald silk dress.

"You have," She grinned, "but I'm not complaining."

"...And then we all got diabetes," Dex narrated, rolling his eyes with an affectionate smile.

"Sorry," Finn blushed, taking hold of Anna's hand as she straightened up.

"I like it," Cassie smiled, "It's a vast improvement from brooding Finn and shy Anna."

"True," Dex agreed, "But it's hard to make conversation when your faces are all smushed together."

"Fine," Anna sighed, "We'll tone it down."

The elevator opened onto the roof of the building. Glittering streamers and fairy lights had been strung across the barbeque area and raised garden beds. A transparent glass railing surrounded the perimeter. It gave Anna the unnerving feeling someone could just walk over the edge. The view, however, was spectacular.

"Hello, my dears!" Pam hiccuped merrily, "So glad you could make it!"

"Thanks," Cassie grinned, grabbing a flute of champagne from a passing waiter.

Dex made a beeline toward the bar. More elevator doors opened. A new group stepped out. "Hello, my dears!" Pam exclaimed again, "So glad you could make it!"

"Well, I feel less special now," Cassie laughed, "Shall we?"

They mingled for about an hour. Cassie knew several people, greeting them warmly and making polite small talk before moving on to the next group. Anna and Finn were better at the *Silent Nod* method of networking, following Cassie around the party like a pair of ducklings. Eventually, they found a quiet place to sit, away from the big-wigs boasting about their corporate wins, the tipsy admin staff who tried to hook up with anyone who stood still long enough, and the overly excited interns who weren't used to being offered free food and alcohol.

"This is the life," Anna smiled, downing her third glass of Champagne.

"If only we didn't have to go back to work on Monday," Cassie pouted, "They should have the Christmas Party on the last day before the office shuts for the holidays. Then it'd be a real celebration."

"But then we'd have to miss it," Finn pointed out, "We'll be driving to Stanthorpe next Friday night, remember?"

"Oh, right!" Cassie giggled, "Next year, though! They should make the party on the last day, next year, for sure."

"Agreed," Anna toasted.

"You are both drunk!" Finn chuckled.

"But not for long," Anna smirked, "Because now I have a fast *me-tab-o-lism*."

The effort she'd made to pronounce the word correctly did little to hide her inebriation.

"You do," Finn crooned with a chuckle.

"Because I'm a vampire!" Anna whispered, though not as softly as she intended.

"You are," Finn laughed, "But you don't need to whisper, look around."

Anna had grown used to seeing magical beings wherever she went. She barely noticed pointed ears, horns, fangs or even tails anymore. Looking around, however, there was a much higher number of vampires at this party than she'd seen anywhere before. Almost no one here was Unseeing.

"Now *I* feel less special," Anna hiccuped, "How come everyone's Unseeing? Lax? What's the difference again?"

"Lax is the more common term," Cassie answered, over-articulating her words, "but people don't realise it was originally a slur that implies people who can't see magic are from lazy families who couldn't be bothered maintaining their ancestor's traditions. It's saying they deserve to be in the dark."

"Harsh," Anna raised her eyebrows.

"It's especially dumb," Cassie continued, gaining volume, "because anyone who's skimmed a history book knows people usually lose their cultural traditions due to invasions and war. Not laziness! Look at how Christianity spread across Europe. Killing anyone who wouldn't convert, stealing sacred artwork and burning any books that contradicted their mythology. Books filled with valuable ancient knowledge of science and magic! It's amazing anyone held onto their culture at all!"

"And yet, we persisted," Finn toasted.

"Here, here!" Anna chuckled, "Is there a bathroom up here?"

"Next level down," Cassie pointed toward the lifts. Anna wobbled as she stood.

"Do you want me to take you?" Finn offered.

"No, I'm good," Anna giggled, "High heels are stupid, though."

Anna attempted to walk gracefully to the elevator. She wobbled a bit but didn't' stumble or fall so she counted it as a success. She'd never been on the uppers floors before, and not seeing any obvious signs pointing her toward the toilets, she picked a random direction and hoped for the best. She was drunk enough that even this little adventure felt like fun but sober enough to know how out of place she looked wandering around. The glass-walled offices formed an infuriating labyrinth. Anna quickly saw through several offices to where the bathrooms were located but couldn't find a direct route to access them.

She wandered up and down the corridors, pausing to peruse the varying decor choices in the spacious executive offices. They reminded her of school dioramas. One looked as though King Midas had fondled every piece of furniture, with gold covering everything from the shining desk to the glittering rug. Another seemed to have been stolen from the set of a futuristic space movie. Screens and keyboards covered the walls, illuminated by coloured LED lights. She lingered in front of a particularly huge office lined with bookshelves. An ancient parchment was displayed on the wall behind the desk. It had a strange poem printed on it in runic lettering that shifted to English as Anna eyes traced over them.

From thy world, thy must depart.
Claim the mighty lycan's heart.
Fires dance upon the air.
Sacrifice a virgin fair.
Trust thy foe with love most pure,
Pain of loss thy must endure.
Thy mirror's captive set unbound,
The missing damsel must be found.
Seek thee out an ancient beast,
Imbibe night's power with a feast.
Blood to blood, repair the rift.
Almighty power is thy gift.

"Can I help you, Miss?" A deep, gravelly voice spoke from behind her. Anna turned to see a middle-aged man with large fangs and dark eyes. It had been months since Rufus had given her his business card. He wore the same pinstripe suit and superior expression. Anna couldn't tell whether he remembered her or not. She couldn't imagine why he would. She'd been human when he'd seen her last.

"I was trying to get to the bathroom," Anna shrugged awkwardly, pointing through the glass walls to where the toilet doors mocked her.

"I'll show you the way," he offered with a smirk, "Follow me."

It occurred to Anna, with no one else around, this was exactly how all the true-crime horror stories began. A young female employee finds herself alone in the office with her powerful boss. Sure, Anna had vampiric strength, but so did he. To her surprise, however, Anna wasn't afraid. Whether it was the booze or her new found courage, she was curious to see what would happen next.

"I'm Anna, by the way."

"I know," Rufus smiled over his shoulder.

"You remember me?"

"I never forget a face," Rufus glanced at her, "Which department are you in, again?"

"Data entry."

"Ah," smiled Rufus, "that would explain why you haven't been up here before."

"Yeah, they don't let us out much," Anna joked.

"They should," he said, "You're a breath of fresh air compared to the rest. Do you know how long it's been since someone's come to me with a problem as simple as finding the bathroom?"

"Two minutes?" Anna smirked, "Though, technically, you came to me."

"I love a technicality," he gave a gruff laugh, "You'd make a decent lawyer."

"Isn't that an oxymoron?" Anna laughed.

"Seems to be," Rufus chuckled.

Rufus led Anna past the elevator, in the opposite direction to the path she'd taken. The bathrooms were immediately around the next corner.

"Thanks," Anna smiled, "See you up there?"

"You certainly will," Rufus replied, walking away.

Several mimosas later, Anna watched the stars twinkling while a lipstick-stained Dex described the adventures of his evening thus far.

"Who knew PAs could be *so spicy*," he fanned himself with his hand, "She really couldn't get enough of me."

"And I'm sure you didn't encourage her at all?" Cassie smirked.

"She was wearing skin-tight satin!" Dex exclaimed, as though that closed the matter.

The dinging of glasses signalled that it was time for speeches.

"Thank you everyone for coming!" Pam beamed with ruddy cheeks. She was one of the few Unseeing people at the party, "At Kingsley & Laurant, we are a family and I hope you've all had a wonderful year! We're so lucky to have one of our founding partners here tonight, and I know he's excited to say a few words so I'll stop gas-bagging and clear the stage for Mr Rufus Kingsley!"

Holy shit.

Anna's stomach dropped as Rufus stepped onto the raised platform. She'd assumed he was in a managerial position but never considered he might be one of the founders of the company.

"Thank you, all," Rufus grinned, "I hope you're all having a great time tonight. You've well and truly earned it. From our exceptional finance team-" Several people gave loud cheers, toward which Rufus smiled and inclined his head, "The unbeatable sharks in legal-" A huddled group on the other side of the roof raised their drinks, looking haughty, "Our incomparable marketing department-" A team of women howled like coyotes then burst out laughing, "Acquisitions-" Another group yelled in drunken excitement. The list of departments went on for a while. Anna zoned out, wandering where the trays of food had gone. She supposed the waiters had been asked to pause service for the duration of the speeches.

"And let's not forget," continued Rufus, "the members of our team who don't get nearly as much praise but who work just as hard. This company would fall apart without them. So, thank you to our admin, our HR team led by the wonderful Pam-"

Everyone gave a cheer for Pam, who promptly started to weep and hugged the person standing nearest to her.

"The team in data entry-"

Dex gave a loud wolf whistle amongst the polite applause. Rufus caught Anna's eye and gave a nod of acknowledgement. His list continued to include the janitorial staff, security and interns.

"Finally," he said, "I'm afraid I have to disagree with one of Pam's earlier messages because, as much as we care about one another, we're not family. Your family are the people you see when you're not here, whose quality time gets cut short every time you put in extra hours here at work. So, to the spouses who've come tonight, I offer my final, and most grateful, thanks. Thank you for putting up with the late nights and stressful days. We try our best here to ensure everyone has a good work-life balance but when that doesn't happen, you are the ones to remind your spouses to take a step back, book a holiday, eat something, and get some rest. I see you and, from the bottom of my heart, thank you. Happy holidays to you all!"

***

Anna revved the engine of Cassie's van. She'd stopped drinking an hour ago and, thanks to her super-metabolism, was now completely sober.

"That was quite fun," Dex smiled from the passenger seat, smelling the lipstick on his collar.

"I can't believe I didn't know Rufus owns the company," Anna cringed, pulling onto the road.

"He could have told you but he didn't," Dex yawned, "Equally rude."

"I doubt he sees it that way."

"He seemed pretty cool though," said Finn, holding up Cassie in the back seat, "I liked his speech."

"Try not to drive so windy-ly" Cassie hiccuped, "I get car sick when I'm not driving!"

"You should have thought of that before you got blotted," Dex laughed.

"Shush," Cassie poked the back of Dex's head, "or I'll aim at you when I puke!" Five minutes later, she was snoring on Finn's shoulder.

The original plan had been for the group to continue celebrations at The Grotto but no one was in the mood. Dex carried Cassie into her room before passing out on the spare bed. Anna drifted into Finn's bedroom, barely glancing at his book-covered wall or the massive arched window surrounded by plants. She loved Finn's room, with its pale green walls and sweet herbal scents, but right now she was more focused on the man himself.

"Did I tell you how sexy you look in that suit?" Anna whispered, straddling his lap. Only four thin layers of fabric separated their naked bodies from touching. It was an excruciating pleasure. Finn wrapped his hands around her waist, sensually stroking the fabric of her bodice. Anna pressed her mouth against his soft lips.

"That dress," he moaned, tracing his hand up her thigh, "you know it drives me crazy."

"Maybe I shouldn't wear it then," Anna grinned, untying the halter neck, "to save your sanity."

The silky fabric fell away from her chest, exposing her naked breasts. Finn's eyes widened at the sight of Anna's firm nipples. He caressed them gently with his tongue. Ripples of ecstasy rolled from Anna's chest into the lower region of her body. Hidden from view, under the skirt of her dress, Finn traced the lining of her underwear with his knuckles. She squirmed toward his touch, desperate for more. Her trembling fingers tripped over the buttons on his shirt in her rush to undress him. He leaned back, taking her hands and kissing them before slowly revealing his chest button-by-button, "Should we move this to the bed?" He whispered, his lips brushing against Anna's earlobe. A sizzle ran down her spine. Fighting her primal urge to remain wrapped around him, Anna pushed herself from his lap, letting her dress fall to the ground before climbing onto the soft, cotton sheets.

Finn was quick to join her. He pressed his lips to her forehead and then looked deeply into her eyes, "You're incredible," he whispered, bringing Anna's lips to his. His fingers traced light circles around her nipples. She moaned at his sizzling touch. She needed more.
Pushing him onto his back and straddling him once more. The buckle of Finn's belt bit her thigh. She gasped and drew back, unfastening the clasp. The bulge in his pants was tantalisingly eager to escape its prison. She stroked him through the fabric, running a fingernail along the closed teeth of his zipper. It didn't take more than an imploring look from Anna for Finn to unbutton his pants, allowing her to slide the zip down.

He fumbled with the straps of his prosthetic on the edge of the bed and cursed, "Nothing sexier, right?" He glanced at Anna with an exasperated sigh.

Anna slid onto the carpet and pushed his hands away. She detached the false limb, along with his tangled pants, kissing the scars on his knee.
"Nothing sexier," she smiled as her lips travelled up his thigh.
"F-fuck," Finn moaned breathlessly as she reached his penis, kissing it softly on the tip before wrapping her mouth around it. His hands trembled as he stroked her hair.
She teased him with her tongue, lapping like a lollipop and then sucking him to the back of her throat. Her hands explored him, seeking out the parts that made him squeal and grunt.
"I need you," he growled, lurching forward and pulling her face toward his mouth. She wrapped her legs tightly around his waist. No belt buckle blocked her this time. Only Anna's lust-saturated underwear separated their naked bodies from intertwining.

"Are you sure?" Anna breathed.

"Fuck, yes." He rasped, "Do you want to…?"

"Finn," Anna whispered, slipping the last bit of fabric down her legs and kissing his neck, "Please fuck me."

A longing growl escaped Finn's throat. He pulled Anna forward, cradling her neck with one hand while the other pulled her waist closer. His movements were slow. Measured. He savoured every moment. He kissed along her collarbone. She sighed with pleasure, spreading herself on the bed. His eyes swept ravenously over her naked body.

This was it.

Anna pulled him onto her, kissing him greedily as his hand slid between her thighs. She purred with delight as his fingers sank inside her. She thrust herself onto him, urging him deeper. His breath quickened. His measured touch morphed into a passionate frenzy. Anna squirmed and convulsed under Finn's electric touch. It was a dizzying pleasure to feel him all around her, on her, inside her. His sweet, earthy scent engulfed her. His fingers played her like a instrument of pleasure. She gasped and moaned. She ran her tongue along his cheek, tasting his desire. He nibbled at her earlobe, sparking chills throughout her body.

She squealed and gripped his erection with trembling fingers. He grunted with desire, letting Anna guide him toward her opening. A glint of gold flashed through the green of Finn's eyes. He jolted forward, grabbing her arms with primal intensity. Suddenly, his breath caught in his throat. His expression changed from longing to shock. He scrambled backwards.

"Finn?" Anna could see beads of sweat forming on his forehead.

He leaned over the edge of the bed, shaking. "I- I can't breathe," he panted, blinking rapidly, "I can't breathe! Fuck! *I can't breathe!*"

He dropped to his knees on the floor. Anna froze. She was desperate to help but what if going to him - touching him - made things worse?

"Finn," Anna hovered.

"I can't," Finn slid off the bed onto his knees, "I- Fuck."

Anna couldn't stand watching Finn suffer.

She joined him on the floor, "It's okay," she soothed, hopelessly rubbing his back, "You're okay. Just focus on breathing."

"I'm so sorry," he gasped for air, "I'm so fucking sorry."

He grabbed her hand, clutching it tightly to his cheek, "Please don't give up on me," he winced.

"Just breathe," she whispered, cradling his head against her shoulder, "I'm here."

He nodded and closed his eyes, leaning into her as he swallowed a slow, shaking breath.
Then another.
And another.
Until, finally, his breathing returned to normal.

"I'm sorry," he whimpered, "I just- I-...I-"
"It's okay," Anna stroked his back, "You're okay."
"I ruined everything."
"No, you didn't," assured Anna, taking a glass of water from the nightstand and lifting it to his lips. He drank slowly and then sat with his back against the bed, staring blankly at the wall.
"You shouldn't be with me," he said flatly, "You deserve better than my bullshit."

Anna held his face with both hands, forcing him to look at her.
"There is no one better," she said, "Not to me."
"But-"
"No!" Anna wasn't having it, "You're the only one I want. You're my perfect person."
Finn grimaced, gesturing toward the bed, "That was hardly perfect."
"It was until it wasn't," Anna shrugged, "But even then, you let me in. You could have pushed me away but you didn't. Sex isn't the only way to be intimate with someone."
Finn looked at her with a strange expression.
"What?" Anna frowned.
"Only you could take this moment and make it beautiful," he said with a weary smile.
"Do you want to talk about what happened?" Anna offered.
"I..." Finn looked away.
"You don't have to," Anna qualified, taking his hand, "But...I'm here.

"It felt like my wolf was about to take over or something," Finn's voice rasped, "Then Jade popped into my head. Not *Jade* Jade, wolf-Jade. I felt like I was about to lose control. I just wanted you so badly. I mean I always want you but usually it's less...Primal. And, with the wolf...I'm scared of what could happen. The thought of hurting you…It just…It freaked me out."

"Were you about to transform?"

"I don't think so," a crease grew between Finn's eyebrows, "It felt more like my wolf was talking to me… Or acting through me…That's never happened before."

"Understandably unnerving," Anna nodded.

"I never want to hurt you, Anna," Finn said seriously.

"You won't," Anna replied.

"How do you know?"

"Because I know you," Anna replied, "I trust you."

"Even after what I did to Jade?"

Anna sighed.

"Have you ever considered," she spoke carefully, "that Jade would've preferred things go the way they did?"

"What?" Finn looked aghast.

"If you hadn't stopped her," Anna elaborated, "she'd have killed you and everyone else at the campsite, right?"

"Probably, but-"

"You knew her," Anna persisted, "Would you say she was the sort of person who would want to survive if it meant her friends, her boyfriend, and a bunch of innocent people would die?"

Finn opened his mouth to argue but stopped, He sighed, looking at Anna with dejected gratitude.

"No," he whispered. "No, she would have done anything she could to save us. Even if it killed her."

"What happened to her is awful," Anna stroked Finn's hand, "But it's not your fault. You were a victim that night too. Please try to stop blaming yourself for surviving."

"I- just," Finn gave a half smile, "Thank you."

"Cold shower?" Anna suggested.

"Cold shower." Finn nodded.

CHAPTER 26

Connected

The following week at work was a blur. An avalanche of forms appeared in the office, all needing to be digitised before the three-week break. Anna tried typing at super speed but the computer's operating system couldn't handle it. Even Dex started focusing on his work. It didn't help that some sort of electrical fault with the lights had plunged half the office into darkness. The brightness of Anna's screen against the shadows made her eyes sting.

She paused her magic training, too exhausted after work to do anything other than collapse in bed. Staring at the ceiling of her bedroom in pre-sleep meditation, Anna willed herself to fall asleep. She'd replaced the counting exercise with a more pleasant version where she pictured herself canoeing along a peaceful river, covered by the shade of trees. Every time an unwanted thought entered her mind, she'd simply let it fall into the water and wash away.

She had just begun to drift off when a jolting spark of horror exploded through Anna's chest. She was bound in wire netting and sinking through dark, murky water. A group of rippling figures looked down on her from a glowing bridge. She recognised it. Victoria Bridge. The figures were laughing. Blood drifted through the water like red smoke as she sank deeper. Deep cuts stung all over her body. Her black hair drifted like seaweed above her, the red streaks barely visible as the darkness closed in around her. *Wait...Black hair? Red streaks?* Anna bolted upright. *Roxy.*

Running at top speed, Anna arrived at the bridge in time to see six men with small horns and cow-like tails watching the water with sickening glee.

She could smell fresh blood in the air. Roxy's blood. Claws out, Anna hurled herself at the men, slashing the throat of one before the rest realised they were under attack. One of the men landed a punch to her face. Blinking away stars, Anna threw him across the road. His head hit a metal bar with a satisfying crunch. Someone kicked her in the stomach with a cloven hoof. She grabbed his leg and twisted it until it cracked. The man screamed and pulled out a gun, firing two shots.

The first missed but the second hit Anna in the stomach. Excruciating pain burst through her. She choked, clutching at the burning wound as blood oozed from it. *Too much blood.*

Anna focused on slowing her heart. She needed to limit her blood loss. The man on the ground trained his gun on her again but, before she could react, another slammed her into the ground, Her arms were pinned under his barrel-like legs. "Fuckin' leeches," he spat, pulling a wooden stake from his leather vest. The men huddled around in a horrifyingly familiar formation.

No. Not this time.

Anna used all her strength to lift her torso. Two loud cracks, followed by a searing pain in both of her shoulders meant her arms were fucked. But it was worth it. Her fangs sank into the femoral artery of the man's thigh, draining him in seconds. She felt a surge of power as the man's lifeless body tumbled off her. The gun fired again. Searing heat punched her in the back. She coughed up blood before pushing past the barrier of men. She jumped over the railing and into the inky water below.

The chaos of the city disappeared in a rush of bubbles. Three more shots pierced the water above Anna's head. She didn't dare breach the surface. Putting all her focus into stilling her heart, Anna swam down. Her shoulders screamed in pain. Stars danced in her vision as she fought the instinct to breathe. *I'm in control of my body.*

Anna released the air from her lungs. They whined like spoilt toddlers. Despite the cold water, her bullet wounds burned. It felt like she'd been stabbed by white-hot pokers. There was nothing she could do about that now. The pain in her arms slowly retreated until a series of sharp clicks told her whatever she'd broken had healed.

A school of fish dashed past Anna in the murky water. Their sudden appearance was a sobering reminder to her that anything could be lurking in these waters. She wasn't safe. She wasn't alone. Anna closed her eyes, focusing on Roxy. A pull in her chest told Anna which direction to swim. It called to Anna like a beacon.

Roxy's arms were pinned in chicken wire and her feet had been encased in a cement block. She was trying to bite through the wire when she saw Anna approaching. Her eyes widened. Anna used her cat claws to slash through the layers of thin steel and then helped Roxy pummel the cement into pebbles. They swam along the riverbed toward the southern bank before breaching the surface of the river like a pair of Gothic mermaids.

"How- the fuck- did you- find me?" Roxy panted as they climbed over rocks, sand and silt.
"No idea," Anna gulped in fresh air and collapsed onto the grass, "Who were they?"
"Sex traffickers," Roxy scowled, "Didn't take too kindly to us helping *their property* get out of town."
"Us?" Anna asked, sitting up on the grass and then wincing in pain.
"I'm in a gang," Roxy explained, checking over her injuries, "We help the helpless, and all that."
"Where are the others?"
"Driving the girls to the airport. That was their job."
"And you?"
"Operation Distract the Fuckers," Roxy smirked, then coughed up water.
"You *wanted* them to attack you?" Anna wasn't sure if she should be concerned or impressed.
"I'd be lying if I said things went according to plan," shrugged Roxy, " but I needed to keep them focused on me while the others escaped, so...I'll call it a win."
"Has anything like that ever happened to you before?"
"Nope."
"Were you scared?"
Roxy looked at Anna with a curious frown, "I think you know I was."

"Could you feel me too?" Anna asked.
"When you were on the bridge, for sure," Roxy answered, "Before that...I don't know. I felt like I wasn't alone. Like I knew someone was coming. We have a weird *thing*, don't we?"

"Yeah, I think we do." Anna agreed, cringing as she examined her injury.
"They'll stop bleeding soon," said Roxy, "Those dickheads use silver
bullets so your gunshot wounds will take a few weeks to heal properly.
You'll know they're nearly done when the bullets fall out of the holes. It
helps that you got a fresh feed in, though."
"You saw that?" Anna asked.
Roxy nodded, "Sometimes I dream about what you're doing. But because
I sleep during the day you're usually just-"
"Working?" Anna finished.
"Yeah," Roxy laughed, "Kinda boring, as dreams go. I keep thinking about
you, though. Wondering if you're okay. It's weird."
"Did you talk to Jedda?" Anna asked.
"Yeah," Roxy frowned, "she told me about the night you died. She's really
cut up about it. I've never seen her like that. I forget she hasn't been around
much death, being human and all."
"Were you anywhere near Rock Bottom that night?"
Roxy shook her head, "I was in Melbourne. Why?"
"No reason."

CHAPTER 27

Summer Solstice

"We're only going for the weekend, right?" Anna eyed the small mountain of luggage Dex had stuffed into the van, "I'm only bringing a backpack."
"One can never be too prepared," Dex stated emphatically, "There might be a fashion emergency!"
"Half the people will be naked!" Cassie sounded exasperated, "What sort of fashion emergency could there be?"
"It's a party," Dex replied, as though that explained everything.
"Every year you bring a truckload of stuff," Finn laughed, "and you lose half of it in the forest."
"Call it an offering to the gods of fornication," Dex grinned wickedly.

Anna's bullet wounds had become swollen, purple and sensitive to touch. She tried to hide her discomfort, subtly pushing the seatbelt away from her shoulder.
"Are you okay?" Finn whispered, looking concerned.
"The seatbelt's just digging in," Anna tried to look nonchalant. It wasn't technically a lie. She hadn't told Finn about her rescue mission with Roxy. He didn't want her running into danger but that's exactly what she'd done. And she'd killed again. This time, however, the guilt of taking a life hadn't plagued her at all. Was it because he'd been a sex trafficker? Because he'd shot her? Or was she becoming desensitised to sucking the life out of people? She wasn't ready to answer those questions.

"Anyone for *car-aoke*?" Cassie called from the front seat.
"Hell yeah!" Dex plugged his phone into the sound system, "I've got the perfect mix, hold on…"
You Give Love a Bad Name exploded from the speakers. Embracing the

distraction, Anna forced a laugh and sang along with the music.

The world outside the window changed from urban to rural. Huge expanses of farmland passed by. The grass was yellow and dry under the setting sun. They wove through the dense rainforest in a high mountain pass. The distinctive song of the bell birds serenaded them as a damp earthy scent wafted through the van. More farmland was waiting on the other side of the mountain. This time green and lush. Industrial sprinklers rained on perfect rows of crops. A small mob of kangaroos raced them for a short stretch, bounding into the bush when they got bored. Finally, Cassie pulled the van into a motel car park just outside Stanthorpe.

Anna gazed wearily at the moon, "Are you sure it'll be safe to transform tomorrow night?"
"The farm's always set up for that," Finn replied, "I'm more worried about what'll happen during the day. Whenever different packs get together, they always try to show off and get into fights."
"Your pack's a rowdy bunch, then?" Dex pulled an overnight duffle from his pile of luggage, leaving the rest in the van.
"Not all of them," Finn shrugged, "But this one guy, Dane, has a way of riling people up."
"They're not your responsibility," Cassie said firmly, "Just focus on *your* good time."
"Right," Finn agreed, looking apprehensive.

Cassie followed Dex into the room. Anna pulled her bag from the car, wincing at the weight of it on her bruised shoulder.
"What's going on?" Finn asked with a tone that told Anna she hadn't fooled him in the car.
"It's fine," Anna dropped her bag and shifted her shirt enough to show him the bruising on her stomach and back, "I just had a…thing."
"A thing?" Finn exclaimed, gaping at her bullet wounds, "What does that even mean?"
"I may have…gotten a bit… shot," Anna couldn't think of a gentler way to put it.
The colour drained from Finn's face, "W-What the actual fuck? Who shot you?!"
"Sex traffickers. It's a long story," Anna answered, "Can we talk about it later?"

"If I got shot would you be okay with *talking about it later?*" Finn challenged.

"What's going on?" Cassie reappeared with Dex at her side.
Finn looked at Anna pointedly.

"I got shot," Anna sighed. She told them about her dream of Roxy, the river and the horned men with guns.
"Wow," Dex looked bamboozled, "What happened to shy little Anna?"
She died.
"I didn't ask for it to happen," Anna shrugged, "I'm still me."
"Did you check Roxy was actually away on the night you turned?" Cassie looked pensive, "This would all make sense if she's your sire."
"Her band's social media pages show them performing at different places in Melbourne for the whole month," Anna replied, "She was there."

"What if the sex traffickers find out who you are?" Finn worried aloud.
"They won't."
"What if they do?" Finn wasn't dropping it, "What if they kill you next time?"
"I don't know," Anna picked her bag off the ground with irritation, "I guess I'll die! What do you want me to say?"
Finn swallowed and gently took Anna's bag.
"Let me train you to fight," he offered, "Ask Rupert to teach you protective magic. Anything to keep you safe. Please?"
"Fine," Anna agreed, "Can we get back to our nice weekend now?"

The motel room was minimally decorated with two queen-sized beds, a small kitchenette, and an even smaller bathroom.
"What time are we waking up?" Dex unplugged the lamp next to one of the beds, using the outlet to charge his phone instead.
"Dawn's at five," Cassie yawned, "But we need to head out earlier so we're there for the opening ceremony and sun-welcoming rituals."
"Can't we skip all that guff?" Dex fell onto on of the beds, "When's the party actually starting?"
"Not usually until ten or so," Finn answered, dropping a large suitcase near the other bed.
"Well, I'm getting up at four," Cassie said resolutely, setting her alarm and shoving Dex aside, "Jedda's dad is one of the elders performing the smoke

232

ceremony this year. I want to see it."

"Why didn't Jedda come down with us?" Anna asked.

"She had to work this weekend," Cassie sighed, "Again."

"That sucks," replied Anna, "It would have been great to see her."

"Yes, yes, very sad," Dex rolled his eyes, "But back to the plan. What if Anna and I hang back until a less horrific hour? You two can take the van and we'll jog over when the party's in full swing. That way, you can get your spiritual jollies, Finn can catch up with his family *sans-G-F*, and us vampires won't have to stand around awkwardly while folks worship the same sun that's actively trying to burn us to ash."

"How does that sound to you?" Finn turned to Anna.

She was torn. On one hand, she'd never been a fan of the pomp and circumstance that ceremonial gatherings always required and, like Dex, would prefer to get some extra sleep. On the other hand, she didn't want to seem rude by skipping the formal part of the day and only joining for the fun. She looked back at Finn, hoping for some guidance in his expression. His face was frustratingly neutral.

"Will your family think I'm rude for showing up late?" Anna sat on the bed, rubbing her bruised shoulder.

"People trickle in all day," assured Finn, "You should get some extra rest."

"Are you sure?"

"Of course," Finn smiled, kissing her lightly on the forehead.

"Perfect!" Dex exclaimed. He'd already changed into satin pyjamas, "Lights out in ten, everyone!"

Despite the early bedtime, Anna had no trouble falling asleep. Exhausted from the week and nestled in Finn's arms, it felt like she'd barely closed her eyes when Cassie's alarm began blaring.

"See you later," Finn whispered into Anna's ear, "I love you."

"Love you too," she slurred back, groggily pecking him on the lips before rolling over to go back to sleep. The sound of the van's engine had faded from the car park before Anna's brain processed what had just happened.

She sat bolt upright.

"Dex?" Anna climbed to his bed. It was still warm where Cassie had slept. Anna nudged Dex's arm as he shifted away from her, "Dex, wake up."

"Hmmrsph," Dex groaned.

"Dex!"

"What?"

"Finn just told me he loved me."

"That's nice."

"For the first time."

Dex rolled onto his back. He didn't open his eyes but smiled, "Did you say it back?"

"Yes."

"WoooOOooooh," he teased, opening his eyes reluctantly.

"Shut up!" Anna blushed.

"Why do you look like you're in shock?"

"It's just...I was half asleep! I didn't realise what he said, or what I said, until he'd gone."

"Did you mean it?"

"Yes."

"Then what's the problem?"

"I don't know..."

Dex leaned up on his pillow, "Did you imagine the moment would have more gravitas?"

"I mean… I wasn't even looking at him."

Dex smirked, "He gave you the option of pretending to be asleep if you didn't want to say it back."

"Or maybe he didn't mean to say it, and it just slipped out?"

"Finn's an overthinker. Words like *I love you* don't just slip out of his mouth by accident."

"I just wish I reacted properly, you know?"

"You reacted honestly, which is as proper as it gets."

"I suppose."

"Tell you what," Dex yawned, "Go back to sleep. When you see him later you can run into his arms say it right to his big ol' freckled face."

Anna smiled, imagining the cinematic scene.

"You just want to go back to sleep," she grinned.

"Correct."

"Okay, fine," she sighed, "Goodnight."

"G'night, love."

Anna got back into her bed.

"Anna?" Dex's voice was quiet.

"Yes?"

"I'm happy for you."

***

Anna woke to an overcast sky. The humidity clung like a sticky sweater but at least the cloud cover meant she and Dex could run at full speed without too much exhaustion.

"Did you bring your cozzy?" Dex asked, holding up a pair of black swimming trunks.

"Do you mean *togs*?" She smirked, pulling a bikini from her backpack.

"Whatever," he laughed, "Put them on now. We'll want to dive into the lake as soon as possible."

"Do you think it'll be that bad?"

"The Summer Solstice is a celebration of the longest day of the year," he answered, "The sun's at the peak of its power. So, yeah. It won't be great."

"Why do you go every year, then?"

"For family," Dex shrugged, "The Finnegans took me in when I had no one."

"Do you think they'll like me?" Anna couldn't imagine they'd be overjoyed at the idea of their son dating a blood-sucking vampire.

"They'll love you," Dex smirked, "But they love everyone so don't let it go to your head."

Anna squeezed into the tiny bathroom to put on her bikini, followed by a pair of denim shorts and a white peasant top. She tied her hair into a high ponytail and applied blush and peach lipstick. She looked pale, as always, but at least now she didn't look quite so dead.

"Damn," Dex lowered his sunglasses as she emerged from the bathroom.

"Girlfriend material?" Anna posed.

"Defs," chuckled Dex.

On their way to the Granite Arch, Anna and Dex stopped to buy cold drinks, food and ice. Anna had wondered about the large Esky Dex had brought with his luggage. It contained several bottles of blood.

"We can put all the cold stuff in here," he said, topping up the ice in the Esky, "hopefully no one will confuse a can of beer with a bottle of O-neg."

"If they do," Anna smiled wickedly, "They won't do it twice."

"Depends on who, or *what*, they are," Dex winked.

The heavy blanket of clouds over the national park enriched the scents of wattles and eucalyptus. Light rain gently pecked at Anna's skin as she followed Dex over huge granite rocks, passing small creeks and waterfalls. It was beautiful. A handful of tourists were exploring the area, most of whom were Unseeing. A few, however, looked as though they were also headed to the Solstice celebrations.

"Penny?" Dex called to a young woman with deer antlers sprouting from her honey-blonde hair. She had glitter on her cheeks and goat-like hooves peaked from under her flowing skirt. She turned and, upon seeing Dex, grinned widely.
"Dex!" she dashed over, "Sunny Solstice! I hoped I'd see you again this year."
"Sunny Solstice," He hugged her, "This is Anna, she's new to the fold."
"Great to meet you!" Penny hugged Anna like they were old friends.
"This is Penny," Dex explained, "She's a yoga instructor from Sydney. And a faun, FYI."

"Oh," Penny drew back from the hug. Her eyes were wide, "You're, like, *new* new?"
"Yeah," Anna shrugged, "Nice to meet you."
"The pleasure is all mine!" she exclaimed, linking her arm with Anna's as they continued along the dirt track, "I've never met anyone who lost their Veil before. What was it like? Scary? Liberating?"
"Both, I guess." Anna answered, "Sometimes I think I've gone crazy and this is all a dream."
"And other times?" Penny was enraptured.
"I'm embarrassed that I believed magic wasn't real."
"Why? It wasn't your fault!"
"It's a bit like..." Anna paused to think, "As a child, I believed in magic. It was an instinct. But, somewhere along the way, I stopped believing. The concept of magic was regarded as a joke. I felt stupid for holding on to the belief as long as I did so I pushed my instincts aside."
"I get it," Penny nodded.
"But then, when I found out magic *was* real," Anna continued, "it was overwhelming but also...validating? Like, I was never crazy or childish for being drawn to stories about magic and fantasy. It was my gut trying to tell me something all along. And I'm embarrassed that I let society tell me what to think. Does that make sense?"
"Totally," Penny nodded.

"I didn't know you felt that way," Dex mused.

"You know I love stories," Anna shrugged.

"Yes," he smiled, "you are quite the connoisseur of tales."

"You *have* to meet Henry Finnegan, then!" Penny bounced down the path, "He'll be there today and he loves stories too! He's usually off reading somewhere but if you can pull him away from his books, he's really nice." Dex snorted.

"What?" Penny frowned.

"Anna knows our boy quite well already," Dex winked, "Quite. Well. Indeed."

Anna blushed.

"Shut up!" Penny squealed, clapping her hands, "That's awesome! So, you'll already know the Finnegans too, then?"

"No," Anna could feel her cheeks burning, "I only know Finn- uh, Henry." She realised calling him *Finn* among a throng of Finnegans might get confusing.

"*Henry*," Dex imitated Anna's voice, wiggling his eyebrows. Penny giggled.

"Don't worry about meeting the Finnegans," Penny assured Anna, "They're lovely."

Three blockish boulders made the doorway of the Granite Arch. Anna couldn't help but imagine a giant placing them into formation. Perhaps that's what had happened? A perfect stone frame sitting in the middle of the forest seemed unnatural, and yet, not out of place. A family of Unseeing tourists were posing for photos with the monument. Anna, Dex and Penny hovered nearby until the family moved on.

"Sunny Solstice!" Penny called, disappearing as she skipped through the archway.

"Magic words," Dex winked, nodding at Anna to go ahead. Anna stepped forward.

"Sunny Solstice!" she shouted, feeling a little foolish. The view through the archway rippled as though a thin sheet of water covered the opening. Anna held her breath and ran through.

A rush of air washed over her as she stepped onto a massive field of lush, green grass.

The blaring hot sun pummelled own. She squinted against its blinding light. Rupert's lessons echoed in her mind. She needed to harness the energies surrounding her. Make them work in her favour. She took a breath and allowed her vision to relax until she could see the magic surrounding her. Bright beams of powerful sunlight were attacking the darkness of Anna's vampiric aura. Even with her Sun Sigil protecting her, whatever necromantic magic kept her alive was slowly withering. The grass, on the other hand, reached up for the sun's rays, thirsty for it. Anna focused on redirecting the beams toward the grass. They seemed willing to cooperate, for now. The sunlight bent around her, casting her in shadow.

With the sun's impact reduced, Anna took in her surroundings with more interest. The huge field, surrounded by dense rainforest, hosted a village of festive tents and picnic blankets. She gazed at the revelry with awe. Spicy aromas permeated the air. Hundreds of colourful butterflies danced overhead like confetti caught in a breeze. Crowds of faerie folk were cooking and laughing. Anna was used to seeing strange-looking people in the city, but some of the people here were truly fantastical. There were fur-covered children with long, rabbit ears blowing bubbles and then dancing around to catch them. A group of stocky dwarves sat around a cauldron, bickering about how much hot sauce to add to their stew. Green women with flowers growing from their skin did acrobatic yoga in a circle.

A granite archway stood behind her. It was almost identical to its twin but this one had been covered with painted handprints of orange, red and yellow. The opening in the archway rippled for a moment before Dex burst through.
"Blimey! That's the sun, alright, " he groaned.
He dropped the Esky and withdrew two thick parasols from his backpack.

He handed Anna a yellow one and kept the black for himself, popping it open with a theatrical flourish.
"Where's Penny gone?" Dex scanned the crowd.
"Over there," Anna pointed. The faun was getting her face painted by a wild-looking man with flowers in his hair.
"Ah, well," he shrugged, adjusting his mirrored sunglasses, "We'll catch up later."

Already feeling dazed by the brightness, Anna and Dex rushed past the tents to the opposite edge of the field. The forest welcomed them with its cool, shaded paths. They followed a narrow, winding track to a second clearing. It had several cabins along the treeline to their right, a large bonfire in the centre, and a huge sparkling lake to their left. Cheers and laughter filled the air, along with the alluring smell of cooking meat. Several of the swimmers had gills running from their necks to their collarbones. Scaly fish-tails flapped out of the clear water, spraying whoever was nearby.

"Merrow," Dex explained, "You'd know them as mermaids and mermen."

Anna watched one of them slide onto the grassy shore and transform from merman to man. As the sun touched his scales, they fell away like glittering sand. His fins split, forming feet. And then shins, knees, thighs, and...

Anna averted her gaze from the naked man, only to realise most of the people sunbathing and dancing on the grass were similarly exposed.

"Pretend it's an art class," Dex smirked at Anna's hastily reddening face, "Bodies aren't inherently sexual, you know."

"I know," Anna muttered, lowering her parasol to hide her face, "I've just never been around quite so many naked people before."

"Welcome to the Solstice, love!" Dex chuckled.

Anna followed Dex past the lake to a long, wooden table laden with fresh fruits, salads, cheese, bread, honey cakes, and several colourful foods she didn't recognise. Barrels of alcohol sat either side of the banquet.

Large ice-filled tubs had been scattered around, filled with every drink imaginable. Dex planted his Esky next to one of the barrels and passed Anna a bottle of ice-cold blood from the bottom. The exhilarating rush flooded through her body, boosting her energy.

"What do you fancy first?" Dex asked, wiping his mouth, "Quick dip in the lake? Or we could continue our tour. They have orchards and mazes, a gorgeous waterfall, though that's a bit of a hike...Oh! What about the Fighting Field?"

"I'd like to find Finn and Cassie if we-," Anna started, "Wait, why is there a *Fighting Field*?"

"It's not as sinister as it sounds," Dex laughed, "It's where the werebeasts'll go to turn. The rest of the time it's for combat training and sport. Finn wanted to try LARPing on it, but he couldn't get enough nerds together. Want to check it out?"

"Do you think the others will be there?"

"No idea," Dex looked around the crowd. "Oh! Finn's Dad's on the spit.

He might know where Cas and Finn have gotten to…"

"Wha-" Before Anna could stop him, Dex strode toward a huge, burly man with a shaggy, grey beard and heavily tattooed skin. Slowly rotating a massive pig over flickering flames, he wore a frilly pink apron and nothing else. "DEXTER, MAH BOY!" boomed the man's voice, clapping Dex on the back "Was wonderin' when ya'd get here. How the hell are ya?"
"Bill!" Dex beamed, clapping the man on his hairy shoulder, "I'm great! How've you been?"
"Getting into trouble, as always," winked Bill, "Who's your wee lassie there?"

Dex waved his hand for Anna to come closer. She could see hints of Finn in Bill's broad smile, the constellation of freckles on his nose, and his kind green eyes.
"This," Dex gestured with a bow, "Is none other than Miss Anastasia Green."
Bill's bushy eyebrows shot up with excitement.
"Anna?!" Bill exclaimed, "*The* Anna?"
"It's nice to meet you, Mr Finnegan," Anna smiled timidly, extending her hand.
"None of that here," Finn's father laughed, slapping her hand aside and pulling her into a surprisingly gentle hug, "You call me Bill, alright, Missy?"
"Okay, Bill," she smiled, patting his fuzzy, tattooed back. It was like hugging a sweaty bear but Bill was so contagiously jubilant that Anna found it comforting.
"Hold on," Bill turned and called toward the cabins, "ELLIE, MY LOVE! ANNA'S HERE!"
Several people turned to look at Anna with curiosity. It occurred to her that, while Bill and Dex were behaving casually, she was about to be introduced to the Queen of the Tree Folk.
"Ah, here she comes," Bill grinned.

Anna couldn't see anyone at the cabins. She looked curiously from Bill to Dex, who looked pointedly at the treeline behind the row of wooden huts. A massive elm tree tilted as though it was about to fall onto the clearing. It swayed back and forth before shrinking from view. Seconds later, a larger-than-life woman glided out from between the cabins. Her hair was an afro of dark green and her skin was mottled white and brown like the bark of a tree. She wrapped a linen gown around her curvy body as she approached. "Anna," Her voice was deep and smooth as honey. "It's a pleasure to meet you."

"It's a pleasure to meet you too," Anna replied, wondering if she should curtsy, "You've raised a wonderful man."

"Henry's a good boy," Elowen replied proudly, "But we can't take credit. He's been a kind, loving soul since the day he was born."

"Not like our other little scallywags," Bill nodded at a rowdy group of adults emerging from the trees across the clearing.

The group was led by an impossibly tall woman with perfect blonde hair and red lipstick. A cricket bat rested on her shoulder as she laughed hysterically at something the woman behind her had said.

The second woman was larger than the first. She had heavily tanned skin, grass-stained overalls and wild hair.

They were followed by a spectacled man who carried a thick binder and a duffel bag. He appeared to be arguing with a stout pair with matching blonde hair, freckled skin and identical wrestler-thick bodies. The woman had slightly longer hair than her brother but, otherwise, they were identical. They laughed as they bumped the spectacled man around. He retaliated by hitting them with his binder.

Another thickset man entered the clearing who, apart from his thick beard, looked uncannily like Finn. He jogged casually, waving a phone in the air, playfully mocking someone out of view. Seconds later, Finn appeared in the clearing. He was using a cricket bat as a cane while reaching for his phone with his spare hand. A grin was plastered to his face. Someone less trained in the subtleties of Finn's expressions might have thought he was enjoying the good-natured ribbing but Anna could see the strain in his smile. He was hiding his exhaustion.

"Just give me the passcode," laughed the bearded man, "and we can settle this once and for all."

"I don't want you looking through my messages!" Finn exclaimed.

"Or photos..." Chided the man, "What saucy secrets are you hiding?"

Finn rolled his eyes.

"Is Hen-Hen still going on about his *very real* girlfriend?" The female twin called out, gesturing for the bearded man to toss the phone to her. He did.

"She *is* real," Finn replied, his compliance with the joke faltering.

"Sure," chimed in the male twin, joining the game, "A *stunningly beautiful* vampire who just so happens to love all the same nerdy shit as you, doesn't care about your anti-social tendencies, and is *definitely not made up*?"

"SHE'S NOT!" Finn yelled, losing his temper, "You saw her photo! She's real!"

"Calm down," the female twin chuckled, "We're just teasing."

"So you believe me?"

"I believe you have a photo of a cute girl on your phone," smirked the woman with a shrug, "Whether or not she knows you exist, however..."

"For fuc-" Finn stopped himself, regaining composure, "This behaviour is childish. Grant, may I please have my phone?"

"It's childish you made up a girlfriend to impress us," chortled the bearded man, Grant. He impishly tossed Finn's phone higher and higher into the air, "My boys lie about having girlfriends too. But, they're six, so it's less embarrassing for them."

"I did *not* make her up!" Finn bellowed.

"Prove it!" Grant laughed, gesturing around theatrically.

Anna gave Dex, Elowen and Bill a quick farewell nod before dashing across the clearing and springing into the air. She caught the phone at the peak of Grant's toss and landed gracefully at Finn's side.

"Hi, honey. Sorry, I'm late," she smiled, kissing Finn on the cheek. "Did I miss much?"

Finn's face split into a massive grin, "We were just debating the nature of reality."

He wrapped an arm around Anna's waist, whispering, "My hero."

Anna smiled at Finn's siblings, who stared back in silence.

"What?" Finn narrowed his eyes with suspicion.

"Right-o," said the man with the binder, "Pay up, you lot."

Some of them laughed, while others groaned, as they handed various amounts of cash to him.

"Excuse me, Wallace," Finn raised his eyebrows, "Did you make bets on the status of my love life?"

"Technically," Wallace held up his finger, "They *made* the bets, I simply took them knowing full well you are not a liar. You're welcome."

"Thanks?" Finn cocked his head.

"Don't you think Finn should get a cut of that money?" Anna asked pointedly.

Wallace considered her for a moment and then smiled, "I suppose so," he sighed, handing Finn a few of the notes, "A cut for *Finn*, it is."

"Hey, I'm *Finn*," Grant snickered, "Where's my cut?"

"Oh, please don't start the Spartacus thing again!" The male twin rolled his eyes.

"Sorry, I should have specified " Anna put her hand affectionately on Finn's chest, "*My Finn* deserves a cut, for putting up with you."

"Ooh, I like her," grinned the female twin, "She's got boss energy."

Finn put his arm around Anna's shoulder and kissed her temple.

"Let me introduce you to my *dear* siblings," he said, pointing at the man with the binder, "Wallace is the oldest, then Quinn - the glamorous blonde - is over at the buffet with Fern-"

The giant woman had just taken a huge bite of burger and coughed cheese into her unruly hair. She wiped her hands on her overalls before taking a piece of fruit and holding it next to her left ear. A tiny sugar glider poked its head out of Fern's nest of hair, grabbing the fruit before disappearing again.

"...Jen and Jed," Finn continued, pointing at the twins. They each wore tight, matching activewear and began juggling beer cans, laughing whenever one of them got hit.

"And, finally, Grant."

"Good to meet you," Grant shook Anna's hand, "No hard feelings, eh?"

Anna shook Grant's hand and smiled, baring her fangs a little more than she needed to, "We'll see."

"Haha, Respect." Grant nodded.

Grant and the twins jogged over to the buffet table and began stuffing their faces. Wallace rolled his eyes, consulting his binder, "There's no point eating yet," he muttered, "the roast will be done any minute now."

"Why did you all think I made Anna up?" Finn asked Wallace with a curious smile. He seemed to find the joke funny now that it was over. Wallace raised his eyebrows and glanced at Anna.

"Do you not recall the *Hermione* incident?"

"No-," Finn blushed, "Shut up!"

Wallace turned to Anna with a playful grin and explained, "Before the movies came out, Henry drew a picture of what he imagined his favourite Harry Potter character looked like. He carried it with him everywhere and insisted they were in love."

"Should I be worried?" laughed Anna.

"I was eight!" Finn exclaimed, "That can't be the reason you didn't believe me."

"Honestly, we were just dicking around." Wallace shrugged, "Usually nothing gets to you. It was hard to resist a bit of poking."

"Right," Finn shook his head with disbelief.

"Have you met Mum and Dad yet?" Wallace scanned the crowd.

"Yeah, Dex introduced us," Anna pointed to the spit where Dex, Bill and Elowen waved back.

"Oh, no," Finn laughed nervously, "Dad's naked, isn't he?"

"Yup," Wallace nodded with a resigned expression.

"He's wearing an apron," Anna shrugged diplomatically.

"Oh, jeez," Finn scrunched his face, "I'm so sorry!"

"Don't be," Anna laughed, "Bill's great."

"Still though," said Finn, "My Dad's bare ass is not something I want locked in your memory forever."

"Are you worried I'll ditch you for the original model?" Anna joked.

"Well, now I am!" Finn laughed.

"ROAST IS READY!" Bill's voice boomed over the music and laughter in the clearing, "COME AN GEDDIT!"

CHAPTER 28

Fight and Flight

A flood of people crowded around the spit for a serving of freshly cooked pork. Wallace scuttled over and quickly arranged them into a line, which all of Finn's siblings joined while still chewing on their previous helpings of food. Finn limped over to the queue, masking the pain in his leg as he leaned heavily on the cricket bat. He had grass stains all over his clothes. Anna wondered if he'd been running around since dawn.

"Would you mind you finding us a nice shady spot to sit?" Anna asked, not-so-subtly taking his place in line, "I'll grab the food."

Relief spread across Finn's features. "Sure," he smiled, kissing her forehead before turning away. Anna watched him disappear into a patch of trees by the lake. She turned back to find Elowen smiling at her. She handed Anna a wicker basket containing a large bowl of roast pork, a can of cider and a large salad.

"Wow, thanks!" Anna gushed.

"You're very welcome," Elowen led Anna away from the line.

"Aren't you eating?" Anna asked, adding a bottle of blood from Dex's Esky to the basket.

"Today, I prefer to absorb my nutrients from the sun," Elowen smiled serenely, "I'm quite full from basking all morning."

Anna looked at the vast forest, filled with trees spreading their leaves to the sun like millions of hands reaching upward, "I never thought about trees and sunlight like that. It's beautiful."

"You have an open mind and a righteous spirit," observed Elowen, "An excellent combination."

"Oh, uh…" Anna didn't know how to respond. She didn't think she'd demonstrated either quality.

"I particularly enjoyed watching you stand up for Henry just now," she mused, "His siblings tend to take advantage of his selfless nature."

"It was all in good fun," Anna blushed.

"I suppose so," Elowen gave Anna an evaluating gaze, "May I tell you a story?"

"Of course," Anna finished packing the picnic basket and walked with Elowen toward the lake.

"Several years ago," Elowen began, "on a Solstice celebration like this, several strangers cut in front of Henry for a helping of Bill's famous slow-roasted pork. Henry had been looking forward to it all year but, assuming their need was greater than his, he chose not to question those who'd pushed in. Seeing weakness in his kindness, more people did the same. Soon, Henry found himself at the very back of the queue, despite being one of the first to join it. He missed out that year."

"That's horrible," Anna grimaced, "No one shared with him?"

"None of us knew what had happened until it was too late," explained Elowen, "He ran to the forest and cried. He was very young."

Anna frowned. Her heart was breaking for little Finn.

"Is that why you made him a basket?" Anna guessed.

"I don't make one every year," answered Elowen, "He doesn't like to feel singled out but he was looking particularly weary so I thought I'd spare him the discomfort of standing in line. It seems you had a similar idea?"

Anna nodded.

"I'm glad he's found you," smiled Elowen, "He looks out for others so much, he forgets to care for himself."

"I care."

"Exactly." She gave Anna a warm hug before walking back to the spit to help Bill serve the guests.

Anna found Finn resting against a smooth rock in a cool, heavily shaded patch. He sat up as Anna approached with the picnic basket. His eyes widened at the generous serving of roast meat Anna had secured.

"Compliments of your mum," Anna grinned, placing the bowl on his lap.

"She must really like you," he grinned, "Try this-"

Finn scooped some of the succulent pork onto his fork and offered it to Anna. The meat was so tender it fell apart in her mouth. Rich flavours danced on her tongue. The only thing Anna loved more than the taste of the meat was the way Finn's face lit up as he watched her enjoying it.

"I'm surprised so many people are meat-eaters here," Anna mused, "I'd have thought everyone would be vegan or vegetarian."

"Some are," Finn shrugged, talking between bites, "I certainly understand the desire to change how the meat industry treats animals. But we're more traditional around here."

"How so?"

"We follow the balance of nature," Finn continued between bites of pork, "Every living thing consumes other life forms in some way. Herbivores kill plants for their energy and nutrients while Carnivores can only get their energy and nutrients by consuming other animals. Omnivores, like us, are generally healthiest when we consume both plants and meat. Plants consume sunlight but also need nutrients from the soil, which typically come from decomposed plants and animals. Plus there are carnivore plants...And don't get me started on mushrooms..."

"So, *Circle of Life?*" Anna concluded.

"Yup," Finn wiped a dribble of sauce from his chin, "As long as it's done respectfully, there's nothing barbaric about eating what your body craves."

He scooped a huge pile of the juicy meat into his mouth.

"Did you say you can communicate with plants?" Anna asked as she looked guiltily at the cherry tomato she'd just speared with her fork, "How does that work?"

"Plants are more primal than animals," Finn explained thoughtfully, "They have a spirit that I can connect to, or maybe *essence* is a better word...in any case, they don't have the same sense of self."

"So, this salad...?" Anna prompted.

"It's not in pain," Finn assured, "Cutting leaves and berries from a plant is a bit like shearing a sheep. It gives us something we need while making room for new growth. The berries themselves feel a sense of loss when they're removed from the mother plant but don't have a sense of fear or self-preservation past that. By the time we eat them, most are excited that their essence is about to transform into something else. They don't have nerves, like animals, so they don't feel pain the way we do."

"Oh, good," Anna popped the juicy berry into her mouth.

When the basket was empty, Anna lay next to Finn on the cool grass. The sun glinted peacefully through the leaves. Sounds of splashing and laughter from the lake lulled Anna into a happy, sleepy stupor. Finn rolled onto his side, placing his hand affectionately on Anna's hip. Though it was hardly a suggestive move, the intimacy of it made Anna's heart leap.

"When you left this morning…" Anna began, "You said a *thing*."

"Did I?" Finn looked amused.

"And I said it back," Anna looked into his eyes. They glowed like sun-dappled leaves.

"I noticed," he nodded.

"Do you- …could you say it again?"

Finn smiled.

"I love you, Anna," he whispered, "I love your kindness and your passion. I love that we can talk about anything and everything. I love the way I feel when I'm with you. I love everything about you. My heart is yours, now and forever."

"I love you too," Anna beamed, kissing him softly on the mouth, "For all those reasons and more. I'm addicted to you, in a non-creepy way." She wrinkled her nose, "I wish I was better at saying things poetically, like you."

"I liked it," Finn chuckled.

"My heart is yours too," she added, "I hope you know that."

"I do now," Finn kissed her cheek, "I just wish I could show you how much I adore you."

"You do," replied Anna, confused.

"I mean, *really*," He gave her a pointed look, "I appreciate how patient you've been but we're not teenagers. Losing my virginity shouldn't be such a big deal."

A twig snapped from the shadows nearby. They both jumped. Anna had forgotten they weren't alone in the forest.

"I don't want you to think about it like that," Anna whispered, "I don't expect you to wake up one day and *stop being traumatised*. We have amazing chemistry and it'll be great when we get there but I'm not in a rush. You make me happy."

"But," Finn blinked slowly, "We were so close last time. It could have been so amazing-"

"It *was* amazing," Anna placed her hand on his cheek.

"Until I ruined it," Finn grimaced.

"Until you had a panic attack," Anna corrected, "which isn't your fault."

"It doesn't change the fact that I can't, you know, fully satisfy you." Finn shrugged sadly.

"The stuff we've done together so far has been *extremely* satisfactory," Anna blushed.

Finn's ears turned pink. He grinned and traced the details on the waistband of her shorts before slowly travelling upward to the bare skin under her shirt. She melted under his touch.

"I think you'll find the orgy pit is a couple of kilometres west," Dex's impish voice popped their bubble of intimacy as he and Cassie trudged into the hideaway.

"Thanks," Finn sneered, "We'll keep that in mind."

"Now, now," Dex wiggled his finger, "No need to be testy! We come bearing gifts."

He sat down and placed a platter of honey cakes and fruit on the grass before uncorking a bottle of wine. "Cheers," smirked Dex, sipping from the bottle and then passing it to Cassie.

"I've had such an amazing day," chirped Cassie, taking a sip, "The dawn rituals were breathtaking and I've met so many interesting people!"

She handed Anna the bottle. Anna took a tentative sip. It wasn't as sweet as she liked her wine to be, but it was tolerable. She took a second sip before handing the bottle off to Finn.

"Some guy is looking for you, by the way," Cassie said to Finn, "I think he said his name's Toby. He looked a bit lost."

"Where did you see him?" Finn furrowed his brow. Cassie pointed to the cabins through a gap in the trees. A dozen people stood in a tight circle. One was a short man with thick black hair, who had his hand firmly on the nape of a young man's neck. The younger man, slender and dark-skinned, looked deeply uncomfortable. They were talking to a tall, heavily scarred elf with salt and pepper hair who wore a formal military-style uniform. A shockingly familiar elf stood silently beside him.

"What's Arik's doing here?" Anna asked.

"I assume he's part of the Elven envoy," Dex rolled his eyes.

"You haven't talked to him?"

"Arik's here in an official capacity," Dex scoffed, "He can't be seen talking to a banished embarrassment like me. Besides he's here with Bass, who's the actual worst."

"Bass?" Cassie squinted toward the group, unable to see their faces clearly with her human eyesight.

"Captain Bass," Dex sang, "With a stick up his-"

"Colonel," Finn interjected.

"I was going to say ass," Dex chortled, "But if he's got a stick up his colonel, he's kinkier than I gave him credit for."

"No," Finn sighed, "He's *Colonel* Bass now."

"Urgh," Dex pouted, "He suuucks."

"What's so bad about him?" Anna asked.

"Let's see…He's boring," Dex listed on his fingers, "malicious, prejudiced, power-hungry and racist. As far as he's concerned, there are elves and there are *lesser beings*. Nothing else."

"Then why is he talking to a pack of werebeasts?" Anna frowned.

"Good question," a pronounced crease formed between Finn's brows, "I'll be right back."

He made a beeline towards the group. Before he reached them, one of the women sniffed the air and turned with a smile. She broke away from the pack and pulled Finn into a tight hug.

"She seems friendly," Dex raised his eyebrows, "Any idea who she is?"

"Another member of Finn's pack, I guess," Anna tried to sound unconcerned but couldn't take her eyes off them.

The woman was slender, tall and tanned with dark hair and deep brown eyes. She smirked toward the lake as though she knew Anna was watching. She kept her arm around Finn, flipping her hair as she whispered into his ear. Blood pounded in Anna's ears.

Why is he letting her touch him like that?

"Let's talk about something else," Cassie suggested stiffly, "What have you been up to so far today?"

"Yeah, fine," Anna answered absently. Her eyes were glued to Finn. Cassie sighed and took Anna's shoulders, turning her away from the group at the cabin.

"Do you trust Finn?" Cassie asked.

"Of course, but-"

"Then stop acting like you don't."

Anna was about to argue that it was the woman she didn't trust…but Cassie was right. This woman didn't matter. Finn would never do anything to hurt Anna. He'd literally just said he loved her.

"Well, I've been having a great solstice," Dex smiled mischievously, "I wasn't kidding about the orgy in the woods. I've made lots of new friends."

"Good for you," Cassie laughed, "I've had a pretty great time too. Jedda's dad taught me a lot about the history of their tribe. There's so much I didn't know about aboriginal culture!"

"Sounds like you've both had busy mornings," Anna fanned herself with her hand.

"So have you," Dex said, "Meeting all the Finnegans at once is not a task for the faint-hearted."

"Ooh! Did you meet Fern?" Cassie exclaimed, "She does incredible earth magic and she's great with animals."

"Was she the one with the overalls?" Anna laughed, "I think she had a possum in her hair"

Cassie nodded, "That's her!"

"I'm surprised you didn't ask about Jed," Dex smirked, then explained to Anna, "Cassie used to fancy him. She'd follow him around like a lovestruck little duckling."

"Which one was he?" Anna struggled to connect the name to a face.

"One of the twins," Cassie answered, blushing, "He looks a bit like Channing Tatum."

"I always thought he resembled a young John Cena," shrugged Dex.

"Whatever," Cassie retorted, "Dex used to have a crush on Quinn."

"Used to? She's a total Glamazon!" Dex grinned, "Barbie, but huge enough to lift a car. Hot. If you're going to crush on anyone, she is the correct choice."

"That's not how crushes work," Cassie punched Dex affectionately, "You don't get to pick who you're attracted to."

"Speak for yourself," Dex lowered his sunglasses, gazing at a glistening merrow in the lake. She winked at him and then disappeared under the water.

"Anyone fancy a swim?" Dex asked.

"Not if you're about to sully the water," Cassie snickered.

"Fine," Dex sighed, lying on the grass, "I guess I'll slum it here with you two."

"Gee, thanks," Anna smirked, glancing back to the cabins, "They're gone!"

The group had disappeared from the clearing. Finn was nowhere to be seen.

"Hmm?" Dex was picking bits of grass out of his hair.

"Finn said he was coming right back," Anna tried to hide her concern, "Did you see which way they went?"

"Why are you so worried?" Cassie asked.

"Finn said Dane's been bullying the pack," Anna explained, "He wants to make them all turn when it's not a full moon. Maybe he thinks the Elven army can help."

"Way to bury the lede!" Dex sat up.

"Yeah, what the hell?" Cassie frowned, "Why would he want to do that?"

"To control their inner beasts," Dex said flatly.

Anna and Cassie stared at him.

"Bass used to boast about taming werewolves," he said, "I always thought he was full of it, everyone shows off at parties, but ...maybe not?"

"Do you think he's going to help them?" Cassie asked.

"I think he's going to recruit them," Dex stood up purposefully, "The Elven army wouldn't help werebeasts if there was no tactical advantage in it for them."

"Where do you think they went?" Cassie sounded nervous.

"The Fighting Field, probably," Dex said, "He'll want to see what they can do."

"He wouldn't make them all shift in broad daylight, right?" Anna jumped to her feet, "Not with so many people around."

"I guess we'll see," Dex took off toward the north-western field. Anna ran close behind at top speed. Cassie would have to catch up. Passing over a line of rune-covered rocks, Anna felt a wave of energy pass over her. At least the magical barrier was functioning. If the pack transformed into savage animals, they wouldn't be able to pass through the boundary.

Anna spotted Dex having a heated discussion with Arik and Bass. She slowed to a stop. The pack had formed a loose circle around Finn and Dane in the centre of the field.

"...can't force us to do this!" Finn exclaimed.

"We're never going to have this chance again!" Dane barked, "Do you have any idea how many favours I had to cash in to get him here?"

"I don't care!" Finn retorted before turning to the group, "Anyone who doesn't want to do this can leave with me right now."

Several people moved to follow him but the other members stopped them, physically holding them back and looking at Dane for further direction. Dane smirked at Finn triumphantly.

"Let them go," growled Finn, "I don't want to have to hurt you."

"Go ahead," Dane took a step closer, a smirk growing on his lips, "You may be bigger and stronger than me but make no mistake, I'm the one with the power here."

In one swift movement, Dane pulled out a syringe and stabbed it into Finn's neck, injecting him with shimmering grey liquid. Anna screamed and ran to Finn but the damage had been done. As Finn pushed him away, Dane's followers began attacking their peers with identical syringes. Finn shook his head wildly against the potion's effects. Several members of the pack fell to the ground. The wet, cracking noise of bones breaking filled the air as their bodies morphed into beasts. Dane stepped past Finn and grabbed Toby's neck.

"No, please," Toby begged.

"This is for your own good," Dane muttered. He produced two more syringes from his pocket, forcing the contents of one into Toby's veins before injecting himself with the other.

Finn resisted the potion better than his peers, whose pained screams had turned into howls as their jawbones cracked into elongated muzzles. Most of them transformed into massive dingoes but one, who Anna recognised as the merman she'd seen earlier, roared in agony as he shifted into a seven-metre-long crocodile. Finn fell to the ground on all fours, retching. He looked in Anna's direction. His eyes were wide with horror, "Run!" he choked before transforming into a huge, three-legged wolf.

Anna didn't move. She was frozen with fear. The wolf growled at her but the look in its eyes was not wild. There was recognition in them. Finn was still in control. He bared his teeth at an oversized Tasmanian devil, which snarled at him with its fangs bared. Just like Dane, this beast was smaller than others in the pack but looked twice as savage. Dane charged at Finn. The two monstrous beasts collided with a dull thud. Finn overpowered Dane easily but the frenzied yelps from the Tasmanian devil summoned half the dingoes to his aid. One sank its fangs into Finn's throat. Another clawed at his face. Finn bucked them off with a strained whimper, blood trickling from a deep gash above his eye. Finn lunged at Dane again, pinning him to the ground. Dane thrashed and snapped his maw, twisting and squirming until he was in a position to bite into one of Finn's front legs with a sickening crunch. Finn howled in agony.

He picked Dane up in his mouth and threw him across the field. The other werebeasts ran after Dane, away from Finn. Bleeding from the head and trying to stand on only two good legs, Finn's footing stumbled. Dane scrambled to his feet across the field and turned to his pack with wild fury. He gave an ear-splitting, guttural screech and then grunted savagely at Toby, whose dingo form cowered. Dane snarled at the rest of the pack, bending them all to his will. They began to nip and howl at Toby, provoking him into a wild frenzy. Toby's whimper transformed into a manic howl as he sniffed the air in Finn's direction with savagely absent eyes.

"Stop it!" Anna screamed. No one responded.
Finn toppled onto the grass, looking dazed. Anna flew to his side, gently touching the gashes on his temple and leg. His fur was soft but sticky where thick blood from his wounds oozed onto it. She wished she could do something to help him. His eyes shot ahead with sudden focus and he let out a guttural snarl, lowering his ears in preparation to pounce.

Toby bounded ferociously toward them. There was no humanity in his eyes. No sign of the scared, innocent boy Anna had seen moments earlier. Finn pushed her behind him, bracing for the impact of the rampaging dingo. A dark resignation flashed in his eyes. He was ready to kill. Anna couldn't let Finn suffer the guilt of taking another life. Not like this. Not for her.

Before he could react, Anna leapt over Finn's crouched form and ran to meet Toby head-on. She reached into the dingo's mind. There was no cognitive thought. Only a swirl of manic confusion and fury. The instinct to hunt. To tear flesh. To destroy. She tried to push her voice into his head to calm him, but it was like screaming into a hurricane.
She desperately pulled magical energy from wherever she could - the grass, the sun, and even the pack itself. The force of her will didn't wait for the universe to cooperate. She took what she needed.
She was absently aware that the field had fallen into shadow. The grass was dying, crunching under her feet as Toby pounced at her with his fangs bared. With everyone moving in slow motion around her, Anna ducked easily out of the way, grabbing the massive dingo by its neck in mid-air. The power inside her burned like an inferno.

"STOP!" She roared, slamming Toby into the ground. An explosion of magical energy surged from Anna's body, firing down her arm and into her fist. As it hit Toby, he transformed back into human form. The magic rippled outward like an invisible wave, returning the rest of the pack back to themselves before crashing at the rune-warded boundary like waves on a cliff.

Shocked silence radiated through the field.

The sun had returned but the grass had disintegrated into dust. Half of the pack sat dumbstruck on the dirt while others hurried to grab their clothes, hastily covering their naked bodies from the gawking crowd.

Dane stared at Anna with terror in his eyes.

Anna stumbled back to where Finn crouched in the dust, regaining his breath.

"Are you okay?" she whispered.

Finn's eyes were wide, "What did you do?"

"I- what do you mean?"

There was a deep cut above Finn's eyebrow. His blood carried the stench of putrid meat, making her gag. The field faded in and out of Anna's vision.

"Time to go, love," Dex took Anna's waist and lifted her away from Finn.

"I'm not leaving him!" Anna struggled weakly against Dex's arm. The world was spinning. Her legs crumbled like the dry grass underfoot.

"He'll be fine," Dex muttered, "Right, mate?"

"Yeah," Finn nodded, looking fearfully at the crowd gathering outside the runic border, "Get her out of here."

"But-"

"Anna, please. Go."

With a final, confused glance at Finn, Anna let Dex pull her away. She stumbled past the crowd. The ground lurched forward. Dex scooped her up like a doll. With her head safely against his chest, Anna allowed the world to fade away.

CHAPTER 29

Sanctuary

"What's going on?" Anna pushed herself up from the stiff motel room pillow.

"We need to get as far away from here as possible," Dex was tossing Anna's things haphazardly into her backpack.

"Why?"

"Anna," Dex stopped, grabbing her shoulders, "You just did magic no one has ever done before. Do you have any idea what this means?"

"No?"

"It means..." He sighed, rubbing his eyebrows, "It means you're not safe."

"What?" Anna's throat burned. She was desperately hungry and the room around her tilted back and forth like a boat on wavy seas.

"I'll explain it better when I can think," Dex handed her backpack over, "We need to get somewhere no one will find us...where the fuck can we go?! Shit."

"What about Rupert's place?" Anna suggested.

"Can we trust him?"

"I hope so."

"It'll have to do," Dex looked distractedly out the window, "How far away is it?"

"Not far," Anna replied, taking out her magic key and using the bathroom door to transport them into Rupert's mansion.

***

Dex gave a low whistle as they stepped into Rupert's manor.

"Safe enough for you?" Anna asked.

"It'll do," Dex whispered with a look of astonishment.

A familiar clanging noise approached them. Boggle appeared with Rupert walking silently behind, sipping on a cup of tea.

"Welcome," he greeted them warmly, "Sunny Solstice! I wasn't expecting-" he stopped at the less-than-festive expressions on Anna and Dex, "What's happened?"

He handed his tea to Boggle who promptly toddled away.

"Well, I-," Anna looked at Dex, "I'm not really sure…"

"Anna just turned a full pack of werebeasts back into humans," Dex said, "In front of everyone at the Finnegan Solstice Festival."

Rupert's eyebrows shot up. Anna thought she saw a hint of pride on his face before he removed his glasses and cleaned them with a serious expression, "Follow me."

He led them up the sweeping staircase and then along a carpeted corridor into a lavishly decorated guest bedroom.

"There's a similar room across the hall," Rupert gestured, "You're both welcome to stay as long as you'd like."

"Thanks," Anna smiled weakly, "This is Dex, by the way."

"Mr Duke," Rupert smiled, shaking Dex's hand, "Anna has spoken highly of you. Please, call me Rupert."

"It's a pleasure to meet you, Rupert," Dex said, "I can't thank you enough for your hospitality."

"Not at all," Rupert bowed, "I would like to hear more details when you're settled. For now, however, would either of you like tea or coffee? Or blood?"

"Blood, please!" Anna replied, giving up any pretence of strength as she toppled onto the bed.

"Coming right up," Rupert rushed from the room.

Dex threw Anna's bag on the bed, "How are you feeling?"

"Fine," lied Anna.

"I can see that."

"I'm just a bit dizzy," Anna closed her eyes, "Blood should help."

Her stomach groaned. Her throat felt like sandpaper.

"I know you said your grandfather was a wizard," Dex gripped the bridge of his nose, "but I had no idea he's, like, a fucking *actual wizard*."

"What does that mean?" Anna asked

"You realise we're in a pocket dimension right now?" Dex asked.

"A what?" Anna wasn't sure she cared. She just needed to stay conscious until the blood arrived.

"This place!" Dex exclaimed, gesturing around wildly, "It's attached to the world but not part of it. Didn't you think it was weird that you could access this place from *any* door?"

"Isn't that how we got to Finnegan Farm?" Anna shrugged.

"The Granite Arch in Stanthorpe is a specific doorway that links to matching stone arches around the world. If you wanted to get to Finn's place without magic it would be possible - extremely difficult, but possible. You can't do that here."

Dex walked to a large window and pointed emphatically. The jungle outside was infinite. There were no houses, roads, mountains, or landmarks of any kind. The sun had almost disappeared behind the horizon. The stars twinkling in the indigo sky weren't quite right. There were far too many of them, and they shone too brightly.

"Huh," Anna felt like nothing could phase her at this point, "Is that bad?"

"I don't know," Dex fell onto the bed, "It means we're cut off from everyone. No phone signal. I guess that means we're safe though."

"Safe from *what*?" Anna asked for what felt like the hundredth time.

"It's a who, not a what."

"*Who* then?"

"Anyone who likes things the way they are." Dex grimaced, "You just broke an unwritten rule of the universe. Vampires aren't meant to be able to do proper magic. You're a threat to the status quo."

"I just wanted to help Finn, is that so horrible?"

"It wasn't horrible," Dex answered, "It was *impossible*, which is worse. Some of the greatest mages in history have dedicated their lives to curing the Werebeast Curse. None have even come close."

"I didn't cure them," Anna defended, "They're still cursed."

"Are you sure?" Dex asked, raising his brows, "Will they turn tonight?"

"I assume so?" Anna furrowed her brow. She hadn't considered the possibility that what she'd done to Finn and his pack might be permanent. Dex stared, "You don't know?"

"I didn't plan what happened!" Anna felt close to tears.

"Look, I grew up learning magic," Dex said gently, "Elves are sort of the opposite of vampires. We're connected to nature. Magic flows through us. Or *them*, I should say. I lost it when I turned. It still feels like a huge part of me is missing."

"I'm sorry," Anna whispered.

"This isn't about that," Dex waved his hand dismissively, "The point is, I learned magic in steps. The most basic level is channelling your energy into lesser magic like protective shields. Then you learn how to increase your power by incorporating magically charged ingredients in your spellwork. Then you learn how celestial events affect your powers and whatnot. It all becomes very technical and complicated."

"Sounds like it," agreed Anna.

"But it's all founded on the notion that magic is fuelled by the spellcaster's *lifeforce*," Dex frowned, "and it's meant to be limited by how much energy a person can channel without it killing them."

"But I'm already dead," Anna interjected.

"Exactly," Dex placed the back of his hand on her forehead, "You're not looking great but you're alive."

"Thanks."

"You know what I mean," Dex smirked, "You're in danger because one of two things is true. Either you're an exception to the rule that vampires can't do magic or you're an example for others to follow. In either case…" Dex looked at Anna apprehensively.

"They'll want me dead," Anna focused on filling her lungs with air.

"Don't get me wrong," Dex sighed, "what you did was bloody badass. I just wish you hadn't done it in front of quite so many people."

Rupert opened the door carrying a tray of blood-filled wine bottles and his special teapot.

"I've done some cursory investigating," he began, "Word of your magic has spread rather quickly, I'm afraid. The rumours haven't identified you by name yet but, as it's just a matter of time, I suggest we gather some things from your home in case you need to stay here for a while."

"You think I'll have to hide?" Anna's hands shook as she gulped down the blood.

"It's not a matter of hiding, but rather *limiting access*," Rupert said, "Once your identity is known, you will be something like a celebrity. Werebeasts wanting to be cured will seek you out. Others will want to learn the limits of your power. Some may try to kill you out of fear."

Dex gave Anna a pointed look.

Anna's chest tightened, "What about Finn? Is he alright?"

"Officially," Rupert said, cleaning his glasses, "Colonel Bass has placed everyone under quarantine, including Finn's pack. No one is permitted to enter or leave the Solstice festival."

"And Unofficially?" Dex prompted.

"Bass is trying to limit the number of people looking for you," Rupert answered, "He wants to find you first and knows he can use Finn as a hostage, if necessary."

"What about Cassie?" Anna finished her fourth bottle of blood. It was far more than she normally drank but at least the room felt less wobbly.

"I'll see if I can contact Miss Nakamura," Rupert soothed, "But first, we should collect your things. The longer we wait, the more likely we'll encounter unwelcome company."

"Fine," Anna growled, "Let's go."

With Rupert's magic and the strength of two vampires, it took less than an hour to transport all of Anna's things to Rupert's largest guest room.

"Where do you want the TV?" Dex asked, dumping her books in a pile next to the bed.

"Wherever," replied Anna, "I can't use it here anyway, right?"

Dex probably thought she was pouting over the lack of reception but she didn't want things set up properly. This was *temporary*.

Her apartment might not be grand like Rupert's manor but it was *hers*. She didn't want to get too comfortable here. She wanted to go home.

"What about my roommates?" Anna asked Rupert as he placed her sunflower pillows on the bed, "I can't even warn them. Will they be safe?"

"Once it's clear you're no longer residing there, I expect everyone will leave the building alone," Rupert answered evenly, "However, I've put up some protective wards so your roommates should be protected from intruders."

Anna dropped to the floor, "I hate this."

Rupert sighed and sat beside her, "You did a brave thing," he sighed, "Unfortunately, leaders tend to punish the brave. Heroes cannot be controlled."

Anna sniffed.

"We'll work this out," he assured, "You're not in this alone."

***

After a compulsory nap, which lasted far longer than intended, Anna went downstairs to find Rupert in the kitchen. He wore welding goggles and a thick, leather apron as he flipped metal toggles on a clock-like machine. It sparked a few times before launching a chain reaction of mechanised wonders. Cream-coloured liquid travelled through intricate pipes from the refrigerator, across the splashback and into the rangehood before pouring small, round portions of batter onto the iron stovetop. It wasn't long before perfect, golden pancakes were flung from the stove onto a nearby dinner plate. Boggle carried a basket of fresh eggs in from the terrace. Sizzling bacon engulfed Anna's senses.

"Evening!" Rupert grinned at Anna's arrival, "How do you feel about breakfast for dinner?"

"Yeah, good," Anna mumbled, too distracted to be impressed by anything happening in front of her, "Have you heard from Cassie yet?"

"Not yet," answered Rupert handing Anna a mug of warm blood, "The message I sent her emphasised the importance of discretion. I suspect she's waiting until she is alone to reply."

Anna huffed, looking absently out the window.

"She may be also waiting until Mr Finnegan is permitted to leave," Rupert continued, "My message offered both of them sanctuary but he'll be in no position to reply until dawn."

"Assuming the pack changed tonight," added Dex, entering the kitchen.

"What if they didn't?" Anna frowned.

"Then Bass'll want to keep them forever?" Dex shrugged, "To *study*."

"I'm sure they're fine," assured Rupert, "Patience is a virtue."

Anna took a large gulp from her mug. It gave her the usual energising rush. Her mind felt sharper and the final traces of dizzying weakness finally disappeared. Not that it mattered. She was stuck in the manor with nothing to do but hide.

"I just feel so useless," Anna muttered, bouncing her leg, "Last time I saw Finn, he was bleeding from the head and I don't even know what happened to Cassie."

"Finn's been through worse scrapes," Dex assured, "On a full moon, he heals almost as quickly as we do."

"And Cassie?" Anna prompted.

"She had the sense to stay outside the Fighting Field's wards," Dex answered, "I'm sure she's just lying low."

Anna nodded, feeling guilty. If anything bad was happening to Finn and

Cassie, it was her fault. After barely tasting her pancakes, a familiar tingle on the back of her hand sent a bolt of excitement through her body. Cassie's handwriting scrawled across her skin in black ink, *"Ready when you are."*

"Oh, thank fuck!" Anna bolted from the table, reaching Rupert's front door before the others had time to react. She focused on a vision of Cassie and opened the door, only to find the front steps of the manor and a footpath leading into the jungle. Closing the door, she rushed back to the kitchen, showing Rupert her hand. He smiled, dabbing his mouth with a serviette, and standing. He removed his apron and goggles before leading Anna back to the entryway. He opened a small metal box next to the door that contained a series of toggles, dials and a raised keypad marked with runic symbols.

"If Cassie has followed my instructions correctly," Rupert explained, pressing buttons and flicking toggles, "She will have drawn a specific set of symbols on whichever door she wishes to use as a gateway. We simply need to enter the same code on our end to bridge the connection." He pulled down a large lever and the runic symbols glowed blue. The lock gave a loud click and the light under the door changed. Rupert placed his hand on the doorknob and turned it slowly.

"Hi," Cassie waved apprehensively from inside a small wooden cabin. She looked exhausted but, thankfully, unharmed.
"Hello, Cassandra, I'm Rupert Bolt," Anna's grandfather bowed, "Please, come in."
Cassie shifted the large backpack on her shoulders and stepped into the manor. When Rupert closed the door, the lock clicked back into place, the runes disappeared, and the warm light under the door returned to darkness.
"Thanks for the escape," Cassie said quickly.
Anna rushed forward, hugging Cassie tightly.
"Woah, too strong!" Cassie coughed.
"Sorry!" Anna pulled back, "Are you okay?"
"I'm fine," Cassie tilted her head, assessing Anna, "How are *you*?"
"I'm okay," Anna replied, pulling the heavy backpack from Cassie's shoulder, "Freaked out... but okay."

They returned to the kitchen where Dex prepared a plate of food for Cassie. She reported information between bites, "After you left, word of what happened spread crazy fast. Everyone was looking for you. Bass is furious you got away. He put everyone under quarantine saying your magic could have *pushed the curse* into anyone. No one believes that though. And it's kind of bitten him in the ass because he can't bring in reinforcements to stop anyone coming or going. There are guards posted on every stone archway in the world but he's only got Arik to guard the one at Finnegan Farm. Elowen's refusing to put a magical barrier around the farm so people have been sneaking in and out through the forest all night."

"People are sneaking *in*?" Anna asked, puzzled, "Why?"

"To see if the pack transformed," Cassie replied, taking a bite of her pancake.

"And?" Dex prompted.

Cassie bobbed her head, exaggerating her chewing, and then swallowed, "Varied results," she answered, "Some of them turned faster than normal, some took a while, and some haven't turned at all. At least, they hadn't when I left."

"Finn?" Anna asked quietly.

"He didn't turn," Cassie answered, "Bill said it looks like they've all *mastered their beasts*. So, basically they're all lycans now."

"A valid hypothesis," mused Rupert.

"Bass won't agree," Dex said gravely, looking at Anna, "He needs to catastrophise this so he can keep Finn as bait for you."

"And he wants to use the rest of the pack as test rats," Cassie grimaced, "I heard him saying he wants to know if they'll be able to transform in daylight, without the Wolfsbane potion this time."

"Is that what they were injecting yesterday?" Anna clenched her fist.

"Yup," Cassie said, "Bass supplied them. Apparently, he's claiming Dane said the whole pack had agreed to take it."

"Funny, then, how he didn't seem bothered by their obvious lack of consent," glowered Dex.

"In any case," Cassie continued, "He's acting like he's doing everyone a favour, *offering magical aid and expertise on behalf of the Elven Empire*."

"He can hardly keep them under any other pretence," Dex rolled his eyes, "Politically speaking, Elowen's hands are tied...for now."

"Oh yeah. They're all playing nice," Cassie agreed, "but you can cut the tension with a knife."

"What happens if Bass oversteps?" Anna asked, recalling the fear in Finn's face when he'd told her to run.

"You don't fuck with the Tree Folk in the middle of a forest," Dex smirked, raising his brow, "But Elowen won't start a conflict with the Elven Empire unless she has no other choice."

"Not to mention the Shadow Tribunal are involved now," Cassie added.

"Who?" Anna frowned.

"Leaders of the Vampiric Alliance," Rupert explained, "Each member represents one of the seven bloodlines. Have they made an appearance?"

Cassie nodded, "Elowen said a few turned up after sunset."

"It's unusual for them to congregate in public," Rupert frowned, "Things are progressing faster than I anticipated."

"But they'd be on our side, right?" Anna's stomach writhed.

"It depends if they see this as an opportunity or a threat," Rupert cleaned his spectacles.

"They wouldn't hurt the pack though, right? " Dex grimaced, "The VA is meant to protect the Underfae."

Cassie looked weary, "No one's safe while Bass is there."

"I should go back," Anna stood, "It's me he wants."

"No!" Dex sprang out of his chair, "Bass'll kill you before you can become a proper threat to the Empire. You can't go back there, Anna, please."

"I agree with Dex," Rupert said evenly, "To free Finn *and* keep you safe, we need to devise a more strategic plan than having you simply surrender yourself."

"Oh! I nearly forgot!" Cassie squeaked, pulling a letter from her pocket and handing it to Anna, "Arik slipped this to me when Bass wasn't looking. I don't think they're working together."

"Better not be," muttered Dex.

Anna opened the letter and silently read the parchment.

Dear Anna,

I'm certain my brother is keeping you safe, for which I am both proud and grateful. I must humbly apologise for failing to intercede in recent events. I cannot question a Colonel's orders, even when I believe those orders oppose the core duty of an Elven soldier, which is to protect the innocent from harm.

I intend to make things right. However, I need your help to do so. As you may recall, I have a pre-existing assignment from the Empress. I believe we may be able to dissolve all tensions if I were to present you directly to

the Empress as a potential candidate for the role of Elven Ambassador.
Please let me know your decision at your earliest convenience.

Sincerely,
Arik Faeregina

Anna read the letter to herself once more before laying it on the table for the group to read. Silence followed as three sets of eyes devoured the words on the paper.

"Are you going to go?" Cassie asked.

"It's our best option, right?" Anna replied, looking up.

Rupert and Dex shared a look of concern.

"Arik's been clever," a crease grew between Dex's eyebrows, "The Elven Realm has ancient laws protecting guests from harm. Mother would be honour-bound to ensure your safety while you're there."

"Appealing directly to the Empress would be our best chance at removing Bass from the equation," Rupert agreed, "But it's risky. You don't know the customs and breaking even one rule will negate the Law of Hospitality, allowing the Empress to hurt or kill you as she pleases."

"Let's assume she wants to kill me," Anna replied flatly.

"Bass does," Dex corrected, tilting his head, "*Mummy Dearest* may have other plans for you. Especially if she thinks she can use your power to her advantage."

"So, should I let her think she can control me?"

"Of course not!" Cassie interjected, "You should just tell her what's going on. She's probably only getting a highly biased, half-accurate account from Bass. If it seems like she's going to be unreasonable then come back and we'll make a new plan."

"That sounds too easy," grimaced Anna.

"You'd be amazed how many wars have been averted by a simple, civil conversation between political leaders," Cassie insisted.

"But I'm not a leader," Anna pointed out, "I'm nobody."

"You've never been a nobody," Rupert patted Anna's shoulder, "but I'm afraid your days of living in anonymity are over."

Anna hated the idea that everyone's safety hinged on her ability to say and do the right thing, but what choice did she have? How long would it take to come up with another plan? Every second she wasted could be making things worse. At least this way she'd have Arik to help get the Elven Empress on their side. Assuming he wasn't about to double-cross her, "Okay," Anna decided, "Let's do it."

CHAPTER 30

The Elven Empire

"We won't be able to come," Rupert warned, "The invitation was for you alone."

Anna nodded, feeling queasy.

"Keep your pendant on you at all times," Rupert prompted, "Remember, if you need help, say my name three times and explain what you need."

"Thanks," Anna tried to ignore the scorpions doing battle in her stomach, "How do I tell Arik I'm in?"

"I can send him a hand-scrawl memo?" Cassie offered, "Like I did for you."

"We can't risk Bass seeing the message," Dex shook his head, "If they're together when writing appears on Arik's hand, we're fucked."

"I'll arrange for him to discover a note in his pocket," Rupert offered, "as I did for you, Cassie. One that is only legible to his eyes."

"We *need* to talk after all this," Cassie grinned at Rupert, "I have so much to learn."

Anna wrote a quick letter back to Arik. She agreed to join him but didn't make any promises about taking the ambassador role. While Rupert performed the magic to send the letter, Anna went upstairs with Cassie and Dex to get ready. Cassie helped her put together an outfit worthy of meeting royalty while Dex gave her a crash course on the basic rules and customs of the Elven Empire.

"The Elven Realm is in another pocket dimension," Dex explained as he applied mascara to Anna's lashes, "It mimics weather from the Northern Hemisphere so try not to feel disoriented."

"Okay."

"And be careful about what you agree to," he continued, "You know those fairytales where someone gets caught in a magically-binding verbal contract? Mother loves those."

Anna felt the colour drain from her face.

"Arik will watch out for you," Cassie assured, wiping some blush across Anna's cheek.

"Yeah, he's a good person," Dex agreed, "Don't tell him I said that."

Cassie braided Anna's hair with green ribbon to match her dress.

"Remember, you're not one of her subjects," Cassie instructed, "She can't order you to do anything."

"And don't let this stuff with Finn's pack become a quid pro quo," Dex added, "Werebeasts aren't her subjects either. They aren't even High Fae. They already have a right to their freedom. You are simply reminding her of that fact."

"Without being aggressive," Cassie added.

"Right," Dex agreed, "She needs to believe you're on her side or she'll find a reason to kill you."

"Great." Anna fidgeted with her pendant.

"Don't worry," Cassie soothed, "You'll be fine."

"Totally," Anna took a steadying breath, "Is there anything else I should know?"

Cassie gave Dex a strange look. He clenched his jaw before shaking his head, "Nothing relevant," he spoke in a higher pitch than normal.

Not entirely filled with confidence, Anna hugged them and left to meet Arik.

***

Stanthorpe's main street was buzzing with people. The shops had stayed open late in the countdown to Christmas. Tourists and locals alike rushed to buy last-minute gifts for their loved ones while carollers, wearing festive singlets and shorts, sang in roaming groups. Anna had completely forgotten about the holiday. As though conjured by the thought, her phone buzzed.

Mum: *Hi, honey! Can I put you down to bring potato salad to Xmas lunch? We're all looking forward to meeting Finn. Xoxo*

Anna's heart sank. It might not be safe to see her family this Christmas. Or any Christmas. Tears welled in her eyes as she typed back.

Anna: *Hi Mum, I think I'm coming down with something so we might not be able to make it. If we can, I'll defs bring the potato salad. Love you! Xoxo*

She hated lying but couldn't dwell on that right now. Her insides squirmed as she headed toward the agreed-upon meeting spot. Arik paced back and forth under the clock tower of the post office. He rushed forward to greet her as she approached.

"Thank you for agreeing to come with me," he greeted her quickly, "Are you ready to go? We mustn't spend too much time in the open."

"I'm ready," Anna glanced around. Anyone could be stalking them in this crowd.

Arik offered his arm, "Shall we?"

Anna took his arm gingerly, not sure what to expect. He led her into a nearby dress shop.

He took a random dress from one of the racks and made a beeline for the changing rooms.

"We need a mirror," he explained quietly, ushering Anna into the small cubicle. He hung the dress on the wall then focused on the mirror.

"Bloody Mary," he spoke in a low voice.

"Are you serious?" Anna scoffed.

"Shh," he continued, "Bloody Mary, Bloody Mary."

At first, it seemed nothing had happened. Anna stared into the mirror, waiting for Arik to admit he was playing a prank to lighten the mood. Then, to Anna's horror, long scaly fingers appeared behind Arik's shoulder. He clenched his jaw as the fingers caressed his neck before wrapping firmly around his arm. Anna gasped, looking away from the mirror to where the creature should be standing. She saw nothing.

"We seek passage to the realm of Elves," Arik's voice was calm but Anna could hear his heart hammering.

"On who's authority?" replied a rasping voice.

Anna felt a claw-like hand grip her shoulder and looked back to the mirror to see a horrifying face emerge between her and Arik. An inky, wet curtain of hair concealed half the creature's face. A crooked smile bearing shark-like fangs was visible through it. It, or *her*, scaly skin was pale blue and patched with algae. Her sharp fingertips were stained black. Anna tried to grab the creature's wrist but her hand passed straight through. This creature could touch them but they couldn't touch her. Mary tilted her head, staring at Anna with unnervingly black eyes.

"Her Majesty Empress Aiyana," Arik answered, "We claim the right of safe travel, in accordance with the Treaty of Alvara and-"

"Yes, yes," Mary sniffed them hungrily, moving her hand to the small of Anna's back, "Passage granted."

Mary shoved Anna toward the mirror with incredible strength. She fell through the glassy surface into black, freezing water. Tiny bubbles whirled in all directions as Anna flipped through a maelstrom of infinite darkness. Dots of colour flared in her periphery. She squeezed her eyes shut, helpless against the rushing current, but opened them again when a wave of nausea frothed in her chest. Finally, a dim light flickered into view, expanding as Anna hurtled toward it. Bracing for impact, she burst through the opening, landing on a bed of snow with a soft crunch.

A shimmering turquoise aurora danced through thousands of blinking stars. The scent of roses danced through the brisk air. Anna stumbled to her feet, completely dry, in the courtyard of an opulent palace. Perched on a mountaintop, the magnificent gardens overlooked a vast city. Unlike human cities, the buildings wove through giant trees, incorporating them into beautifully organic architecture.

Arcane magic rippled in the circular opening of a moon gate behind her. A second crunch of snow announced Arik's arrival. He landed gracefully beside Anna, though he looked pale.

"Welcome to Tiranoir," Arik whispered into the still night, "Capital city of Alvara, the realm of the elves. I hope you-"

"Bloody Mary! Really?!" Anna shouted, pushing Arik harder than she'd intended. He toppled into the powdery snow. She was surprised he'd fallen so easily. He was a soldier, after all.

He's not a vampire, though.

Arik remained on the ground, "I'm sorry," he spoke in the calm voice of someone trained to defuse volatile situations, "I should have warned you. She's the gatekeeper between our worlds. No one gets in or out without her."

"It's fine" Anna huffed, offering her hand, "I just wasn't expecting...*that.*"

He accepted her help, dusting snow off his clothes as he stood.

"I truly am sorry," Arik reiterated, "I've never brought an outsider into our realm before. I'm used to everyone knowing about her."

"I'm sorry too," Anna shivered from the cold, "I shouldn't have freaked out on you."

"Let us put this moment behind us," Arik bowed his head. With a strange flourish of hand gestures, he conjured two thick cloaks, placing one around Anna's shoulders. The fabric was soft and radiated warmth. She hugged the cloak to her chest and followed Arik toward the towering palace.

Two guards greeted Arik cheerfully as he led Anna through the pointed archways. It was warmer inside, but not so much that Anna was willing to remove the cloak. Orbs of light hovered in the air, illuminating vines of pure gold, which wove around tall marble columns. Exquisite tapestries adorned the walls and flower arrangements embellished every surface. As they ventured deeper inside, the lights dimmed and the atmosphere fell into tranquil silence.

"Where is everyone?" Anna whispered.

"Sleeping," replied Arik, escorting Anna up a grand, sweeping staircase and through several long corridors, "It's quite early in the morning here."

They passed two more guards and then entered a large room with hardwood floors and a huge, arched window. The lights of the aurora washed the room in rippling green light. The imposing silhouette of a pointed throne dominated the far end of the room. A slender woman sat upon it wearing a tall, sharp crown.

"Is this the vampire I've heard tales about?" Her serene voice echoed through the chamber.

"Yes, your Majesty," Arik stepped forward and bowed, "I present Miss Anastasia Green."

The Empress stood, gliding toward them. Her steps were so light Anna could barely hear them against the polished marble floor. Arik took a step backward. Anna wasn't sure what she was meant to do. She gave a clumsy curtsy, hoping it was right.

"It-It's a pleasure to meet you," she stammered, "Your Majesty."

"You may call me Aiyana, Miss Green," the Empress circled Anna like a shark.

Her pleasant expression filled Anna with inexplicable dread.

"That's very kind of you, *Aiyana*" Anna replied, "Please, call me Anna."
"Tell me, *Anna*," smiled Aiyana, "Why do you believe my son has chosen you as a candidate for the Elven Ambassador position?"

Anna blinked. She hadn't prepared for an actual job interview. The whole ambassador thing had just been an excuse to come here.
"Uh, because I'm a vampire?"
"Is that all?" Aiyana glanced at Arik, "Are my son's standards so low that he would pick any common vampire for such an important role?"
Shit.
She was making Arik look bad after he stuck his neck out for her.
"I'm unbiased," Anna added, scrambling for any relevant qualities, "I don't think vampires are superior to anyone. I grew up as an Unseeing human so I'm learning everyone's customs and laws from a fresh perspective. Most importantly, I want everyone to coexist peacefully."
"Admirable," Aiyana inclined her head, "Is there anything else that sets you apart from an average vampire?"
"Uh," Anna looked to Arik. His expression was emphatically neutral but Anna knew what Aiyana wanted to hear. She may as well get to the point, "I can also do magic outside the normal vampire, uh, *skillset.*"
Aiyana raised her eyebrows with an unconvincing air of surprise, "Is that so?"
"It is."
"Tell me," Aiyana took a step closer, "Did you dispel the Curse of the Werebeast from an entire pack under the sun of the summer solstice?"
"I-," Anna paused, glancing back at Arik whose head gave an almost imperceptible shake, "I think the rumours you've heard have been a bit exaggerated."
"By all means," Aiyana's unblinking eyes bore into Anna, "Set the record straight for me."

"I didn't *cure* them," Anna wanted to choose her words carefully but found herself rambling under the Empress's penetrating gaze, "They're still werebeasts. They still have the curse. I think I just dispelled the effects of the potion they got injected with... *Wolfsbane*, I think it was called? Colonel Bass gave it to this guy named Dane who forced half the pack to transform against their will. The other half transformed too, but they did it willingly. Anyway, when the whole pack was transformed, Dane got them into this frenzy and attacked my boyfriend, Finn. He's part of the pack too. He was against them turning and everything Dane was trying to do. Especially forcing people to turn against their will. So Dane attacked Finn. Then, when he failed, he got his other guy to do it. Toby. He's just a kid. Things got out of hand… The magic I did…It was never meant to *cure* them. I just wanted them to stop fighting. I wanted them to be themselves again...and that's what happened."

Heavy silence sat in the air.

"I see." Aiyana spoke softly.

Arik cleared his throat and stepped forward, "Your Majesty, if I may?"

The Empress turned to him and nodded.

"Colonel Bass has insisted on quarantining the werebeast pack and all those present," Arik reported, "However, all tests have shown the only lasting effect on the pack is a higher-than-average level of control over their ability to transform. They have reached Lycan status but remain well within the parameters of the Werebeast classification. As such, I believe they do not pose a significant threat to themselves or others and should be free to return to normal activities."

"Your assessment has been noted," replied Aiyana, "The Council of High Fae are meeting at first light. Nothing will be decided until then. I would like you both to attend."

"Of course, your Majesty," Arik bowed.

"Is the meeting about the pack?" Anna stammered. Arik shifted uneasily. It seemed the Empress wasn't usually questioned.

"I expect we will discuss whether further observation is necessary moving forward," Aiyana answered, "However, our primary agenda is regarding you and your abilities."

"What do you mean?" Anna swallowed.

"Whether you cured the Werebeast curse or the effects of a simple potion, the magic you performed is unprecedented for a vampire," Aiyana explained, "The Council would like to hear the facts first-hand, as I did."

"Is that all? Anna prompted suspiciously.

Aiyana gave a placating smile. The beauty of her sharp cheekbones and piercing blue eyes made her all the more terrifying, "I do not presume to know how the other council members will react," she said, "If the Council agrees your gift is worth nurturing, you may be invited to study magic at one of our academies. You would certainly be granted access to Alvara's schools, as Elven Ambassador."

"*If* I'm offered the job," Anna clarified, "And *if* I accept it. I don't know enough about the role, or the Elven Empire, to know whether I'm right for the position."

"Indeed," Aiyana replied, "By all means, ask any questions that will help inform your decision."

Anna had been through enough interviews to know the essential questions to ask for any job.

"What are the specific requirements of the role?"

"Each day would be different," Aiyana replied, "Your goal would be to promote relations between the Elven Empire and the Underfae, particularly among your fellow vampires. This may involve speaking on behalf of the Empire in meetings where only vampires are permitted, attending formal events, and corresponding with leaders on both sides. The responsibilities would change as needed. You may find you need to employ advisors and assistants, which would add a managerial role to your list of responsibilities."

"Who would be my boss?"

"You would be paid by the Empire," Aiyana answered, "So your reports would come to me. However, your actions would be self-directed and any of the monarchs of Alvara may come to you seeking advice."

"Alvara has other monarchs?"

"Alvara has several provinces," explained Aiyana, "Each province is ruled by a monarch. I am responsible for the Empire as a whole."

Anna nodded. It was just like any corporate structure. The CEO is at the top, followed by district managers, then office managers, and workers at the bottom.

"Why don't you appoint someone from Alvara for this job?" Anna asked.

"As I mentioned," Aiyana clasped her hands together, "part of the role requires access to vampire-only meetings. I believe the Underfae are more likely to listen to arguments made on our behalf by one of their kind."

"Are you saying no one from the Elven Empire has ever become a vampire?"

Arik made a strangled cough. The were dangerously close to discussing Dex.

"You know the answer to that question," Aiyana raised an eyebrow, but her tone remained calm.

"If you banish your people from the realm for becoming vampires," Anna frowned, "Why have an ambassador at all? Why would you want to promote relations between our kinds?"

"No one has been banished from this realm for simply becoming a vampire," contradicted Aiyana, "Though I will not pretend they find a welcoming environment among the people of the Elven Empire. It is named as such for a reason. We elves prefer the company of our own kind."

Dex had never explicitly told Anna why he'd been exiled. She'd assumed it was because he'd switched from High Fae to Underfae. What else could it be? Despite Arik's warning, she decided to simply ask, "Why did you banish Dex?"

"*Dexter Duke?*" Aiyana glanced at Arik, "Surely you already know what happened. It was my understanding the two of you are quite close."

"He's my best friend," Anna said defensively, "I trust Dex with my life."

"Yet, he hasn't told you why he was banished?" Aiyana asked with raised eyebrows.

"I didn't ask," Anna admitted.

"He killed my daughter," Aiyana replied with stone-faced composure, "He robbed the Elven Empire of an heir to the throne, forcing me to extend my rule until I can produce another."

Anna stepped back, shaking her head in disbelief.

"Dex has never killed anyone," Anna argued, faltering in her sureness, "I thought *he* was meant to be the heir to the throne. And wouldn't Arik be next in line?"

It occurred to Anna that, as the older brother, Arik should have been first in line.

"The bloodline of the Empress flows from mother to daughter," Aiyana said coolly, "The heir must have a functioning womb to bear the crown. We cannot bear responsibility for the lives of our people until we know the pain of creating a life."

Anna glanced at Aiyana's pointed crown and then back at Arik. His eyes were cast to the ground and his jaw was tight.

"Follow me," Aiyana walked through a small door to the right of the throne. It led to a narrow hallway, lined with several generations of royal family portraits. They passed paintings displaying Aiyana as an infant in

her mother's arms, then as a child, adult, and mother. Aiyana stopped at a portrait of herself holding a newborn baby wrapped in an ornate gold and white blanket. A young boy stood at her knee. All three wore serene smiles. The engraved plaque under the photo read:
Empress Aiyana, Princess Victoria, and Prince Arik of the Faeregina line.

"Where's Dex?" Anna asked, "And their father? The…King?"
"Their father was not a king," the Empress explained, "He was my consort. He passed before Victoria was born." Aiyana blinked as a subtle flash of sadness crossed her face.
"I'm sorry," whispered Anna.
"Yes, well," Aiyana recovered her composure quickly, "What's done is done."
They moved forward. With each painting they passed, Anna observed Princess Victoria's progression through life. As a child, Victoria grinned for the artist, posing in frilly ballgowns and gem-encrusted tiaras. As she reached adulthood, however, her expression became dull. Her smile never reached her eyes. There was something about Victoria that felt eerily familiar. It was as though they'd met in another life.

"In your realm," Aiyana spoke softly as she walked, "Women are seen as little more than incubators. They are oppressed, belittled, and denied bodily autonomy. Men speak of *spreading their seed*, as though women are nothing more than patches of dirt to be ploughed and planted. Their leaders do not value life because they will never understand what it takes to create it."
Anna walked in silence, wondering what this had to do with Dex.
"In truth," continued Aiyana, "if a woman's womb is a garden, then her ovum is the seed and a male's contribution to life is nothing more than the indiscriminate rain that happens to fall upon the rich, fertile earth where the seed awaits."

Anna hated when people used analogies to rationalise hateful ideologies. People weren't gardens. Yes, she came from a patriarchal society where, even in modern times, women were undervalued and treated poorly. Yes, it bothered Anna how quickly old men sent young ones to war as though they were nothing more than pieces on a chessboard. But it seemed the Elven Empire had simply flipped oppression in the other direction. Anna wondered if taking the ambassador job could help push things toward true equality. She would have a voice among the leaders. Whether they listened, however, was another matter entirely.

"My line can be traced, womb-to-womb, to the alphafae, Titania." Aiyana continued, "She had god-like magic and blessed only a few with her gifts. My ancestors are among those few."

Aiyana stopped at the final portrait. Princess Victoria was a fully grown woman. She was exceptionally beautiful but for her sunken, empty eyes.

"*Dexter Duke*," Aiyana scowled, "Put a dagger in the heart of my only heir. Elves do not fall pregnant as easily as humans. Creating another will take decades. It may not even be possible. *That* is why he was banished."

Anna suddenly realised where she'd seen those eyes before. They were Dex's eyes. His cheekbones. His nose. His lips. It wasn't just a family resemblance. The sadness in Victoria's eyes matched the expression Dex had shown on the morning of his birthday.

"Dex...was Victoria?" Anna whispered, feeling numb.

A single tear rolled down Aiyana's cheek. She flicked it away like a bothersome fly.

"I'll leave you to contemplate how well you know your...*best friend*," the Empress glided away in silence.

Anna stared at the portrait.

How could he not tell me?

It was none of your business.

I thought he trusted me.

"I've arranged a room for you," Arik appeared beside Anna, "Dawn is a few hours away. I suggest you get some rest. May I escort you?"

"Uh-" Anna turned away, wiping her eyes, "Sure. Thanks."

Arik paused. "I take it you weren't aware...?" he trailed off, looking at the portrait.

"No," she said quietly, "Dex didn't tell me he's transgender."

Arik sighed.

"The only thing he and Mother agree on is this farce that *Victoria is dead*," muttered Arik, shaking his head, "Sometimes I wish that were true."

"How can you say that?" Anna asked, shocked.

"If my sister had simply died," he spoke quietly as they walked through the palace, "There would be a diamond statue of her in the city centre. People would leave fresh lilies at its base every dawn and light candles for her at sunset. Those of us who loved her would be allowed to share stories about her. We'd be *encouraged* to remember her."

The sound of footsteps made them turn. Two guards passed them in the corridor, nodding with respectful indifference. Arik glanced around before continuing the journey in silence. When they reached the lavish bedroom, Anna pulled Arik inside.

"I've seen you with Dex," she whispered urgently, "I don't believe you'd prefer him dead."

"Of course not! That's not what I-" Arik stammered, "I love Dex…It's complicated."

"Explain it to me," Anna demanded.

"I can't," Arik shook his head, "My wording will be inadequate. You'll decide I am a transphobic person, which I am not. At least, I don't believe myself to be... This is already going poorly."

"I promise not to get offended or judge you," assured Anna, "I just want to understand."

Arik nodded and swallowed, clenching his jaw. Anna closed the door and guided him to a small sofa near the window.

"As children," he began, sitting stiffly, "We were as close as siblings could be. There are so few children in Alvara, for several decades we had only each other -"

"*Decades?*" Anna was sure she'd misheard.

"Elves age slowly compared to humans." He explained, "It takes around fifty years to mature physically and we aren't considered adults until we've acquired at least a century of experience."

"Right," Anna had a multitude of questions but didn't want to get off topic, "So, you and Dex were close when you grew up…?"

"That's the problem," Arik furrowed his brow, "I didn't grow up with *Dex*, I grew up with *Victoria*. I know they are one and the same, but Dex talks about his past as though he was never *her*, as though she's a stranger who died and he popped into existence at the same time. As though the memories we made together as brother and sister are shameful."

Arik's lip quivered despite his stoic expression. Anna rested her hand reassuringly on his.

"I suppose it's just selfishness on my part," he whispered, "I cherish my childhood memories. Victoria and I had wonderful adventures together.

She was happy, confident, kind, bright, and courageous. She was an inspiration. She was my inspiration."

Anna recalled the genuine joy depicted in the royal portraits of Dex, or *Victoria*, as a small child.

"Do you think a butterfly denies its time as a caterpillar?" Arik pondered.

"I don't know," answered Anna.

"We all transform throughout our lives," he mused, "Growth without change is impossible.

But Dex, if he allows me to speak of our shared childhood, would have me use masculine pronouns when recounting stories of our youth, simply because he's male *now*. As though Victoria never existed. As though my memories are false. He claims her very name is dead. He would have me never utter it again. But to do so feels dishonest. Back then, *Victoria* identified as a girl, so her stories should remain about *her*."

"But if using masculine pronouns makes him more comfortable-" began Anna.

"Then it doesn't matter if I'm *uncomfortable*." Arik nodded with resignation.

"I- I didn't mean it like that," breathed Anna.

"It's true nonetheless," Arik shrugged, "What I want doesn't matter. It never has. My rank as a soldier is valued more highly than my royal title. I was raised to serve and protect my mother and sister. If I hadn't joined the Amorian Guard I'd have been married off to a King or Queen of a lesser court the second I reached maturity."

"That's horrible," consoled Anna, "No one should be forced to marry someone they don't love."

"It doesn't matter," Arik shrugged, "I don't get a say. Not even when we're talking about the words that come from my mouth or the memories that live in my mind. I know my place."

"What you want matters," breathed Anna, "You matter, Arik."

"You are kind to say so," Arik smiled meekly.

"I'm sure Dex agrees," Anna consoled, "He just doesn't want you to think of him as a *her*."

"I don't think of him as a woman," Arik sighed, "He is my brother. He's become a great man. But, he was once my sister. And, sometimes, I miss my sister."

"When he left," he whispered, "I questioned whether our bond was ever real. He hadn't talked to me about any of it. I'd seen Victoria struggling and knew she wasn't happy. I assumed she was simply feeling the pressure of her upcoming coronation. But she was already Dex by then, of course. I just didn't know it yet. He didn't trust me enough to confide in me."

"Who did he confide in?" Anna whispered.

"The skills of a socialite are tactically no different to that of a spy," Arik rubbed his eyebrows, "Being raised for politics, Dex can charm dignitaries for hours without divulging any information of national importance. He can flatter sensitive information from people without them realising it. Most importantly, he knows the best way to keep a secret is to *never speak of it.*"

"So, he didn't talk to anyone about it?" Anna couldn't imagine how alone Dex must have felt.

"As far as I know, the first person he told was our mother," Arik grimaced.

"Oh, no," Anna frowned.

"She told him the price of leadership is sacrifice," Arik continued, "She said only commoners had the luxury of changing their sex."

"No," Anna whispered.

"She didn't think he would defy her," Arik's voice was hollow, "but he escaped the realm and found a coven willing to transform his body to match his soul. She ordered the guard to return him to the palace. The magic used to change his gender was reversible, after all. She planned to force him into a body, and a life, he didn't want so, I-"

All pretence of composure left Arik. His hands shook as he wiped tears from his cheeks.

"I sent him a warning," he confessed, his voice breaking, "I told Dex what her plans were and, in response, he- he made sure he'd never be fit for the throne."

Aiyana's words echoed in Anna's memory, *"Dexter Duke put a dagger in the heart of my heir."*

"He became a vampire," Anna breathed.

"Which is why both Dex and Mother say Victoria died," Arik's face was wet, "But he was already Dex when he died. *She'd* transformed into *him*, the caterpillar became the butterfly."

"He still loves you," Anna soothed.

Arik shook his head, "I don't think he does."

"He does," Anna assured, "Trust me."

"Thank you," he allowed Anna to hug him for several seconds before he stood, straightening himself into his original, formal posture.

"I shouldn't have fallen apart like that," he said, raising his chin and briskly wiping his face, "You are a guest here. I'm sorry."

He dashed from the room before Anna could reply.

CHAPTER 31

The Council of High Fae

Anna paced the length of the bedroom, occasionally glancing at the green and blue lights dancing across the sky. Too anxious to sleep, thoughts raced through her mind. Dex's past had thrown her for a loop but, she needed to focus on the council meeting.

Would they genuinely want to help her learn magic? It seemed unlikely. Besides, she didn't want to learn magic at an Elvish academy, separated from the world and surrounded by strangers. She couldn't imagine a better magic teacher than Rupert. *Rupert.*

Anna inspected the pendant. He'd said if she needed help, she could call on him. Did this count? A council meeting was hardly life and death. But if things went badly, she may not get another opportunity to contact him.

"Rupert?" she whispered into the necklace, "I need your help."

The necklace felt warmer and the circles in the centre blinked twice.

"The Council of High Fae are meeting soon," she said, hoping Rupert could hear her, "The Empress wants me there to tell them what happened…I'm scared."

The eye blinked again before returning to its original static state. Anna took a deep breath, hoping she'd done the right thing. A few hours later, the aurora faded into the purple and pink hues of sunrise.

A gentle knock at the door signalled Arik's return.

"Are you ready?" Arik held out his arm. He was dressed formally in a blue doublet with gold trim, like a prince from fairy tales. Anna took his arm, flattening the bodice of her dress. They retraced their steps to the Throne Room. Sunlight bounced off the white and gold marble. The gentle tranquillity of the night before was gone. The palace was alive with guards and servants rushing about to fulfil their duties. Many of them greeted Arik warmly, cheerfully waving as they passed. Some glanced curiously at Anna but most paid her no mind.

"The Council Chambers have been set up in the Throne Room," Arik explained as they hurried through the halls, "They've conjured a Circle of Truth, so you won't be able to lie once we're inside."

"I wasn't planning to," Anna mumbled.

"I wasn't implying-," Arik stopped, "I recommend you keep your answers short and simple. Choose your words carefully, and remember you can elect to say nothing."

"Got it," Anna's palms were sweating again.

"Just because no one can lie in there," Arik continued, "Doesn't mean they'll be entirely truthful. Everyone has an agenda."

"But, you'll be with me. Right?" Anna clutched Arik's arm.

"As much as I am permitted to be," he placed a protective hand on hers.

"How many of them are there?"

"Seven," Arik stopped short of the door, "It's a magically relevant number. One for each faction of High Fae."

"Which are?" Anna was feeling woefully unprepared.

"The Elven Empire," Arik listed, "Folk of the Mountains, Seas, Air, Fire, Trees-"

"Tree Folk?" Anna prompted, "So, Elowen's in there?"

"Yes," Arik smiled. A rush of relief wash through Anna's chest. At least one friendly face would be there.

"What's the last one?"

"Court of Cunning," Arik answered. Something about his tone made Anna suspect he was holding back an eye-roll, "They represent urban mages."

"What does that mean?"

"It means they do not represent *all* witches," Arik replied diplomatically.

Two soldiers guarded the door to the Throne Room. The meeting had already begun. When Arik and Anna approached, one of the guards knocked loudly.

"Enter," Empress Aiyana's voice echoed from the room.

The guards pulled open the doors. The tall, arched window had been covered by a thick, velvet curtain. Spotlights illuminated the council, who sat upon ornate thrones matching Aiyana's. Each wore a crown of unique design. A blue, glowing ring surrounded them on the floor. As Anna and

Arik passed over its threshold, spotlights shone upon them too.

"Presenting Sergeant Arik Faeregina and Miss Anastasia Green," one of the guards announced with a low bow.
"Prince Arik," beckoned the Empress, "Please present your report and personal observations concerning the act of magic performed by Miss Green during the solstice."

Arik stepped forward and gave his statement. It was a clinical yet accurate account of what happened, including Colonel Bass's insistence that Finn's pack remain under supervision. As he spoke, Anna's eyes drifted over the Council of the High Fae.
Elowen sat to the right of Aiyana, a crown of flowers and vines woven through her curly hair. Next to her, a man wearing an abundance of eyeliner and a navy suit embroidered with stars and runic symbols picked at his painted nails. His obsidian crown had a crescent moon sticking up in such a way that he seemed to have horns. Anna guessed he must be the mage.

On the far right sat a woman whose veins glowed red like lava under her brown skin. Her crown was an array of long ruby shards. A fire-tipped tail twitched behind her back as she listened to Arik's account of the Summer Solstice. *Fire Folk.*
To the left of the Empress sat a middle-aged dwarf with an eyepatch and thick, black beard. His angular crown was steel grey and featured a large, black opal on the centre peak. *Mountain Folk.*
Lounging next to him was a woman with pale bluish skin who held a shining golden trident. Her long, braided hair held a coral tiara and her sharp collarbone bore scars where gills would emerge underwater. *Sea Folk.*
On the far left sat a man with ivory white skin and hair that floated like dense clouds. Feathered wings protruded from his shoulders and his crown shone like a silver halo. *Air Folk.*

"Your statement has been received," announced Aiyana, "You are dismissed."
Arik returned to Anna's side.
"You are *dismissed*," Aiyanna repeated, raising her eyebrows.
Arik glanced apologetically at Anna before leaving the room. She resisted the sudden urge to grab his arm and cling like a toddler.

"Miss Green," Aiyana began, as the council turned their attention to Anna, "Do you accept the testimony of Prince Arik as true?"

"Yes." Anna felt uncomfortably exposed. Her face was burning. She hoped the council couldn't hear the twinge of fear in her voice.

"You did perform the act of magic Prince Arik described?"

"Yes."

"Was this magic performed with the aid of a coven?"

"No."

"Were you, to the best of your knowledge, granted temporary powers by another mage to boost your magical abilities for the duration of the spell in question?"

"No."

"Please explain to the council your account of the events in question."

Anna swallowed. She was determined not to embarrass herself again.

"The man I love was in danger," she began, "He and his pack were drugged with a potion that forced them to transform into their bestial forms. I believe the magic I performed was a manifestation of my desire to keep everyone safe. It negated the effects of the potion but, as far as I'm aware, they are still werebeasts."

The silence that followed felt as though it lasted an eternity.

"What if all vampires are capable of such magic?" The man in the suit spoke with a thick Irish accent. He seemed more intrigued than concerned.

"If that's the case," replied the man with feathered wings, "Nothing would stop them from overthrowing us. The Alliance took dominion of the Underfae with only sharp teeth, quick wits and parlour tricks. Imagine what they'd do with real magic on their side."

"Let's not overreact," Elowen said evenly, "This is one instance of *accidental* magic."

"That makes it all the more impressive," countered the Irish man.

"Perhaps she is not a true vampire?" The dwarf had a strong Russian accent, "It would explain her abilities. They say she has no sire."

The council looked expectantly at Anna.

"I don't know who my sire is," admitted Anna quietly.

"Whether she's truly a vampire or not doesn't matter," said the mermaid in a smooth, deep voice, "The entire Fae community is talking about her incredible power. My people fear an uprising in her name! How am I to calm them?"

"I propose we keep her here until we know more about her unusual abilities," announced Aiyana.

Several of the council members nodded in agreement.

"Unfortunately," a gravelly voice spoke from behind Anna, "It's not up to you."

All eyes darted to the shadows, where Rufus Kingsley appeared with a smirk on his face.

The guards jumped to attention, pointing their swords at his throat.

"Rufus?" Aiyana's face was pale, "Mr Kingsley, how did- this is a *closed meeting* for the Council of High Fae. What is your business here?"

"I'm here to represent Miss Green," he replied coolly, "As a member of the Underfae, she is entitled to counsel of her own."

"She is not on trial," Aiyana replied.

"And yet you seek to imprison her," countered Rufus, "Whether she's on trial or not, any member of the Underfae standing before the Council of High Fae is entitled to bring private advisors."

The Empress inclined her head stiffly to affirm his statement as true. The guards returned to their posts at the door.

"Some of us are not *entirely satisfied* that Miss Green is a vampire at all," the Empress added curtly, "If she is nothing more than a well-disguised sorceress then her alignment, and right to council, would be in question. And, of course-" Aiyana looked in Anna's direction, "We shall require a copy of the relevant paperwork to prove Miss Green has employed you to represent her if you intend to speak on her behalf."

Shit. Shit. Shit.

Anna didn't have any paperwork. How was she supposed to know she'd need it?

"Actually," Rufus walked forward holding a thick contract in the air, "I've employed her. She's worked at my firm for several months. As such, she is entitled to the best legal services Kingsley & Laurant has to offer, regardless of alignment or faction."

"I see," the Empress did not look pleased.

"Let us begin," Rufus strutted across the floor, "by establishing Miss Green's status as a vampire. Just so we're all satisfied. Miss Green?"

"Yes?" Anna squeaked.

"Do you drink blood for sustenance?"

"Yes."

"Do you require a protective sigil to walk in sunlight?"

"Yes."

"Have you altered your appearance, magically or otherwise, to look like a vampire?"

"No."

"At some point over the course of your existence, have you died?"

"Yes."

"Are you a vampire?"

"Yes."

Rufus smirked and held up a manilla folder. "If anyone would like to review Miss Green's death certificate, signed registration to the Vampire Alliance, or statements from several witnesses that she is, in fact, a vampire, here they are."

The dwarf reached for the folder, placing a thick monocle over his good eye as he skimmed over the documents.

"Accepted," announced the dwarf, "but this does not explain how Miss Green was able to perform such powerful magic."

"Miss Green is not High Fae and therefore under no obligation to appease your concerns or answer any of your questions," Rufus raised an eyebrow, "However, as you seem to believe it is a matter of international security, I have secured an expert witness who is prepared to offer some insight on this matter."

"And who might this expert of yours be?" Aiyana asked indignantly.

"Professor Rupert Bolt," Rufus announced.

Each member of the council's eyes grew wide.

"the Morrigan's Shield?" whispered the Irish man, practically bouncing in his seat, "You found him? He's here?"

"He is waiting outside this room," Rufus confirmed, "Would you like to hear what he has to say?

Aiyana swallowed before gesturing to the guard at the door. As Rupert strolled into the room, the council broke out into whispers. Rupert did not acknowledge Anna as he passed her, instead staring directly ahead as he approached the line of High Fae leaders.

"Your Majesty," said Rupert with a slight bow, "It has been too long."

"In- Indeed," Aiyana's voice faltered but she quickly regained her regal manner, "How did you come to be involved in this matter, Professor Bolt?"

"I have been following Ms Green's journey with interest for quite some time," said Rupert.

"Why is that?" Aiyana prompted.

"My reasons are my own," Rupert answered simply, walking toward Rufus, "However, I believe the council may find this relevant to the matter at hand."

Rupert pulled a worn piece of parchment from his blazer and handed it to Rufus, who promptly read it aloud in his husky voice.

"A Sireless vampire born under the full moon
shall usher forth a golden age of magic.
They shall bring an end to the Ancient War,
blessing the worthy with gifts beyond imagining
and cursing the wicked to unbearable torment.
When they bear the crown of the Forgotten Deity,
the broken worlds will come together as one."

"A prophecy?" Aiyana whispered with furious disbelief.

"It appears to be," Rupert nodded.

"And who made this prediction?"

"It was written by Cassandra's hand," replied Rupert.

The Empress looked as though she'd been slapped. The rest of the council whispered excitedly. The woman with lava glowing under her skin exclaimed with awe, "The great oracle herself!"

"Do you believe Miss Green is the vampire referenced in this text?" Aiyana asked, ignoring her peers.

"I'm certain these words were written with Miss Green in mind," Rupert replied.

A sudden ringing echoed in Anna's ears. How long had Rupert known there was a prophecy written about her? She tried to focus on what the council was saying while her heart pounded against her ribcage.

"According to her death certificate," the dwarf flipped through the folder Rufus had provided, "Miss Green was, in fact, turned during a full moon."

"It seems she is a special case then," Elowen smiled at Anna, "Not a threat, but a blessing. If the prophecy is to be believed, she may yet unite all Fae in peace."

"Or it may not refer to Miss Green at all," Aiyana scoffed, "Professor Bolt could be mistaken. The prophecy may be false. Its relevance to this matter is inconclusive."

"Aiyana," said the dwarven king quietly, "You've questioned prophecies before and it did not serve you well."

"Thank you, Tritus," the Empress cast a cutting glare at the dwarven king, "I am well aware."

"Professor Bolt," the Irish man spoke with reverence, "Do you have any idea how Miss Green was able to perform magic, from a technical perspective?"

"All vampires are perfectly capable of performing magic, Magnus," stated Rupert, "Given the Court of Cunning is dedicated to magical research, I would expect you to know this. I've written several papers on the subject."

"Vampires lack the life force required to weave magic into the world," countered Magnus.

"Rufus?" Rupert turned, "How did you arrive in this place?"

"Shadow walking," Rufus replied with an air of smugness.

"Is that not a form of magic?" Rupert directed his question to Magnus.

"It is an *ability* he inherited from his vampiric bloodline," Magnus shook his head, "Admittedly, it is an extremely rare and impressive one-" Magnus inclined his head toward Rufus, "But it's hardly the same as casting a unique spell."

Rupert shrugged. "It seems we have different beliefs on the subject."

Magnus looked as though he'd just been handed an exciting puzzle to solve. He looked at Anna with a glimmer in his eye.

"Any further questions for Professor Bolt?" Aiyana asked.

The council looked at one another expectantly. It was clear they wanted Rupert to stay longer but couldn't think of any relevant questions to keep him there.

"You are dismissed," Aiyana waved her hand.

With a polite bow, Rupert walked back the way he'd come, giving Anna a subtle wink as he passed.

"Next on the agenda?" Rufus prompted.

"We have yet to make a decision regarding Miss Green," Aiyana responded with a stony expression, "I would *prefer* that she remain in Alvara until we are able to shed more light on the origin of her powers."

"With all due respect, *Your Majesty*," Rufus spoke with an eerie calmness,

"Your preferences are irrelevant. You have no claim to Miss Green. She is protected by the Vampiric Alliance. Holding her here, against her will, would be seen as an act of war against the Underfae."

A wave of tension rippled through the room.

"How dare you threaten us with war!" she said sharply.

Rufus held up open palms, "I'm simply reminding this council of the facts," he raised his brows, "Your people are not the only ones whispering about a *vampiric sorceress*. You must realise the Shadow Tribunal will not tolerate Miss Green being sequestered by the Elven Empire for much longer. They have questions for Miss Green too."

Aiyana looked shaken.

"And," Rufus continued, "They were not pleased to hear that one of your colonels has attempted to conduct unsanctioned experiments on a pack of werebeasts, under your instruction."

"He was *not* acting under my orders."

"Are you saying you've lost control of your military?"

"Of course not!"

"The pack in question are currently being held hostage to ensure Ms Green's continued cooperation with this council...Or I have been misinformed?"

"They're being *quarantined*." Aiyana defended.

"How thoughtful," Rufus said coolly, "However, if a quarantine is required, it will be arranged by the Vampiric Alliance. This matter involves werebeasts and vampires. Neither falls under this council's jurisdiction."

The other council members looked at Aiyana. Each was notably silent.

"Very well," Aiyana's fists were clenched so tightly her knuckles were white, "I shall recall Colonel Bass from his post after this meeting concludes."

"I must say," Rufus spoke casually, "After his previous failures with the young Prince of the Tree Folk, I'm surprised your *Colonel Bass* still has his job. Or his head, for that matter."

"What do you mean by that?" Elowen asked.

"My Apologies, Your Majesty," Rufus bowed to Elowen, "I meant no disrespect."

"None was taken," Elowen replied quickly, "To which failures are you referring?"

"Surely, you're aware," Rufus raised an eyebrow, "that your youngest son was under the watchful eye of the Elven Empire when he was attacked and infected by a werebeast? My sources tell me Bass was in charge of the operation. Strange, given his obsession with werebeasts, that he failed to keep the boy safe from one. Particularly one from the European timber wolf genus. They are exceptionally rare in Australia. One might wonder how such a conspicuous creature managed to find its way into a heavily populated area without being spotted by any of the trained soldiers who had eyes on your son. The poor boy lost half his leg, didn't he?"

"He did," Elowen stared daggers at Aiyana.

"We investigated the attack and found no one at fault," Aiyana said sharply.

"You're not the only one who did some investigating," Rufus countered, "Would you like to hear *my* findings, Your Majesty?"

"This is neither the time nor place," Aiyana snapped, "We called an emergency council session to discuss the magic performed by Miss Green, which we have now done. As such, I suggest we call an end to this meeting. All in favour?"

"Agreed," the council replied robotically.

At the sound of their voices speaking in unison, the glowing blue circle faded from the floor and the curtain covering the window opened as though pulled by invisible hands. Bright sunlight filled the room, warming the space in both temperature and atmosphere. Anna had never been happier to feel the draining waves of light touch her skin.

"That went pretty well," Rufus stood at Anna's shoulder.

"Thank you," gushed Anna, "I don't know what I would've done without you."

"Anytime, Kiddo," Rufus winked like a proud uncle.

The Empress stormed from the room without so much as a glance in Anna's direction.

"She'd better be on her way to summon back Colonel Bass," Elowen appeared at Anna's side, staring after Aiyana, "It would not be safe for him to be present when I return."

"Do you think he had something to do with Finn- uh- Henry's attack?" Anna asked.

"I didn't know Aiyana had him under surveillance," she answered, shaking her head, "It makes me question what else she's been hiding."

"I must apologise again, Your Majesty" Rufus bowed deeply to Elowen, "I *truly* didn't mean to blindside you. I know the Tree Folk are friendly with werebeasts and assumed you were aware of the rumours surrounding

Colonel Bass."

"I'm afraid not," Elowen said, "I would like to hear the results of your investigations when you have time. And, please, call me Elowen."

"Certainly," he said, "If you would allow me to escort you back to the moon gate, perhaps I can give you a summary on the way?"

The other council members drifted out of the Throne Room. Some looked at Anna with interest but none approached. Arik appeared in the doorway, bowing several times as the stream of royalty passed him. He looked at Rufus with confusion.

"Are you ready to return home?" he offered his arm to Anna.

"Yes, please," Anna took his arm, glad for the support. Her legs were jelly.

"I hope to see you soon," added Elowen with a warm smile, "*Very* soon."

Anna nodded. She couldn't wait to see Finn again.

Steering clear of the crowd, Arik led Anna through the palace's scenic route to the gardens.

"I wish you could visit our realm under better circumstances," Arik lamented, "Alvara is a wonderful place."

"Maybe I'll be back one day," she suggested, "You could show me around."

"That would be wonderful," Arik sighed, "Though I suspect Her Majesty wouldn't allow it."

"Do you think I'm still allowed to call her Aiyana?" Anna grimaced, "I have a feeling I've lost first name privileges."

"She already asked that you call her by her name," Arik smiled mischievously, looking more like Dex than ever, "She acknowledged you as an equal. She can't take that back, so I suggest you keep using her name whenever possible. If nothing else, it will remind her not to underestimate your power."

Anna looked around before whispering, "I don't have any power."

Arik stopped, "What do you mean?"

"The magic I did on the solstice was kind of a fluke," she confided.

"There's more than one kind of power, Anna," Arik whispered back, "Yes, you performed magic unprecedented for a vampire, and that's impressive, but your real power - the power my mother fears - lies in your ability to inspire people."

"Oh, no," Anna laughed, "No. I-I'm not good with people."

"You're better than you think you are," Arik smiled, "You listen to people. You genuinely care. That's rare."

"Not *that* rare," Anna retorted, "Everyone here seems to like you."

"Not my mother," Arik scoffed.

"Does she like anyone?" Anna smirked.

Arik opened his mouth to answer but closed it and raised his eyebrows, "You know, I don't think she does."

They walked down the sweeping stairs into the grand entrance. Finely dressed courtiers milled about, spreading into the gardens and beyond in small groups. Some perked up when they saw Arik approaching with Anna at his side. Several whispered behind lace fans while others didn't bother to hide their interest, gossiping openly.

"It's been quite the procession this morning," one of the guards rolled her eyes at Arik as they paused, overlooking the courtyard gardens.

"I can't remember when the full council last met in our realm," Arik nodded with a smile, "Not to mention our potential ambassador. Kira, this is Anna. Anna, this is my good friend Kira."

At the mention of her name, a bashful grin spread across Arik's face. It was a dazzling change to his otherwise serious demeanour.

"Hi," Kira tossed a stray dreadlock over her shoulder. She was pretty. Her armour contoured her figure, shining silver and gold, "I've never met a vampire before. I thought you'd be... scarier? Sorry, is that offensive?"

"Not at all," Anna laughed, "Though I'm afraid I may have ruined my chances at the ambassador job."

"No matter what happened in the meeting just now," he assured, "you're still the best choice."

"Because I'm the only choice?" Anna guessed.

"You're also extremely well suited to the role."

"I don't think I could work with Aiyana," Anna crinkled her nose, "If you were Emperor, I'd take the job in a heartbeat."

A nearby courtier giggled behind his fan. Arik glanced around anxiously.

"I could never be Emperor," Arik muttered, "That's not how it works here."

"Maybe not, but where I'm from we vote for our leaders," Anna made a point of not lowering her voice. It wasn't like the Empress could hate her more, "And, if I could, I'd vote for you."

"It would be an interesting answer to *The Conundrum*," Kira whispered in agreement.

"The what?" Anna frowned.

"The Conundrum, my dear," a lady of the court leaned into their conversation. The skirts of her gown rustled as she moved, "If Her Majesty The Empress is unable to produce a female heir then who shall lead the empire when she is gone?"

"It's not for us to decide," Arik pulled Anna toward the moon gate.

"Of course not," winked the courtier, then added with an impish grin, "Not yet anyway."

Arik conjured glowing shapes in the air around the moon gate. His fingers moved with inhuman speed as he worked his magic. He flicked completed glowing symbols onto the smooth, round frame until they were evenly spaced on the stone. They glowed for a few seconds before the world beyond the gate disappeared into a shimmering surface, which quickly stilled to show their reflections.

"Leaving so soon?" Mary appeared behind them with a fanged grin.

"I'm afraid so," Anna replied, shrinking from Mary's stick-like fingers at her waist.

"Allow me to escort you back," Arik offered.

"I'll be okay," Anna patted his shoulder as they unlinked arms.

"Don't worry," Mary winked, pushing Anna back through the void, "I'll keep an eye on her."

Summer heat engulfed Anna like a sticky blanket. *Home, sweet home.*

The shop was dark and empty. Orange street lights cast eerie shadows through the display window. Anna approached the locked entryway with Rupert's manor key in her hand. She'd never tried using this magic on a locked door before but the window's glass turned opaque as she drew closer, which was a good sign. A second, familiar-looking, lock appeared under the existing one and Anna sighed with relief as she turned the key.

CHAPTER 32

Faerie Land

Cassie pounced on Anna as she walked into the manor, "What happened? Did the whole *prophecy* thing work? Rupert had me write it out in such a rush, I was worried I misspelled something! Can you imagine?"

"You did what?" Anna blinked.

"We made up the prophecy," Cassie explained with a mischievous grin, "Rupert and Rufus came up with the wording but I wrote it out. They said that was important."

Anna began to laugh. It was fake. An invisible weight lifted from her shoulders.

"They can't touch you now," Cassie smiled triumphantly.

"Don't you think people will realise it's not true?" Anna frowned, "Like when I don't...what was it? *Bless the worthy with gifts beyond imagining?*"

"You don't age," Cassie shrugged, "So it could refer to things that won't happen for two thousand years. Plus, it's all very subjective. Like, helping Finn's pack control their transformations could count as *gifts beyond imagining.*"

"I guess," Anna was glad the prophecy wasn't real but hated the idea that people would be watching her for the rest of her life, waiting for greatness to happen. "Where's Rupert?"

"Not sure," Cassie shrugged, "He's probably gone to check things are safe for the *Chosen One.*"

"Please don't call me that."

"Don't worry," Cassie grinned, "You'll be a hot gossip for a while and then something else will happen and everyone will forget all about you."

"I hope so," Anna mused, "Where's Dex?"

"Upstairs," Cassie's smile faded, "As soon as you left he- well, he kind of freaked out. Did his mother, or anyone, say anything to you...about him?"

"Yeah," it was clear Cassie already knew that Dex was transgender. Of course, she did. They had a long history together. Anna felt childish that it hurt to be the only one he hadn't trusted enough to tell. They'd barely known each other a year. It only felt like longer because so much had happened.

"You guys need to talk," Cassie surmised.

"I'll go find him," Anna sighed. She had no idea what to say to Dex.

"I'll be in the library when you're done," Cassie called as she headed down the hall.

As Anna made her way up the stairs, a crippling wave of exhaustion engulfed her. Was it possible to have jet lag from inter-dimensional travel? If so, she was feeling it. Her legs were like stone and she was sorely tempted to sneak into her room for a nap instead of entering yet another emotionally draining conversation. Pausing outside the door to Dex's room, a wave of frustration washed over her.

Why hadn't he told her about his past? Surely he knew she'd find out when she met his mother. He'd seen how anxious she'd been about going to the Elven Realm. He knew how much pressure she'd been under to successfully navigate the politics of his world. Aiyana's look of condescending triumph flashed through Anna's mind as she opened the door to Dex's room. He looked up from the bed with an unreadable expression.

A moment of silence hung in the air.

"So," he said quietly, "You met my mother."

"I did," Anna replied, the heat rising in her face.

"And...?" There was a sharp edge to his voice.

"Remember before I left," Anna said slowly, "I asked if there was anything I should know?"

"She told you," Dex spoke with a hollow voice, staring at the floor.

"Yes," Anna crossed her arms.

More stagnant silence.

"Okay fine!" Dex spat, springing from the bed with a crazed look in his eyes, "So you made out with a *fucking freak*. Deal with it."

Anna blinked. "I- what?"

"I wasn't born with the penis you were rubbing up against that night," he hissed, "So I'm a *disgusting abomination*, right?! But guess what? If I'd known you'd freak out about it, I wouldn't have kissed you back!"

"I'm not freaking out!" Anna held up her hands, "*You're* freaking out! I don't care that you're transgender-"

"Clearly, you do!"

"I really, *really* don't."

"Tell that to your face!" Dex retorted, "Why else would you be shitty?"

"Because you let me walk in there with *no idea*!" Anna exclaimed, "I stood up to your mother, *the Empress of a fucking Empire*, on your behalf! I told her we're best friends, that I trust you with my life, and then she dropped this bomb in my lap! I felt like a fucking idiot!"

"Oh, I'm *so sorry* my trauma made *you* feel foolish," Dex sneered, "I guess I should get *Tranny* tattooed on my forehead so everyone knows, lest they be caught out too!" Tears formed in Dex's eyes.

"That's not-," Anna took a steadying breath. "Dex, I'm sorry. It's not fair to blame you. I just...I wish I hadn't found out from your mother. I wish you'd trusted me enough to tell me yourself. But I understand why you didn't."

Dex's indignation faded. He fell onto the bed. "I wanted you to know," he sighed, "that's the stupid thing. For most people, it's none of their bloody business. But for people that are important to me, like you... It's a cosmic joke that I only want to tell people whose rejection will hurt the most. I didn't want you to look at me like *she* did. I don't want you to hate me too."

"I don't," Anna put her arm around him, "You're the same old Dex to me, I promise."

"I'm not old," Dex sniffed with a wry chuckle.

Anna smiled.

"I shouldn't have let you walk into the viper's nest blind," He said, leaning on Anna's shoulder. "I hoped it wouldn't come up. Or maybe I wanted someone else to tell you so I wouldn't have to. I don't know."

"Have I ever made you feel like I wouldn't be okay with it?" Anna asked gently.

"No, but that doesn't mean much," Dex rubbed his arm. "For most of my life, I thought my mother loved me *unconditionally*. When I realised why

I'd been depressed for so long, I went to her for help and it took her all of three seconds to reject me." Silent streams ran down his cheeks. "It was like I flicked a switch and her love was gone. I had to leave my home. I had to leave my whole world behind. I had nowhere to go, no money. Nothing."

"What did you do?" Anna breathed.

"Appealed to the mercy of the one person I knew who lived outside Alvara," Dex smiled nostalgically, "My ex-husband-to-be, Prince of the Tree Folk, Henry Finnegan."

"What?" Anna clapped her hand to her mouth.

"Oh, yes," Dex chuckled, "Finn and I were betrothed when he was born. We hadn't met but, when he was old enough to write, we sent each other letters."

Anna imagined how a young Finn, engrossed in his fantasy books and romance novels, might have liked the idea of being destined to marry a mysterious, Elven princess.

"When Finn became a *dirty werebeast*," Dex rolled his eyes, "Mother decided he was unworthy of my royal hand. Imagine his surprise when I showed up at his door seeking refuge."

"Why. Do. I. Not. Know. This?" Anna punched Dex playfully on the arm with each word. He grinned.

"The Finnegans took me in," his smile faded, "They helped me in ways I can never repay. They gave me a home and a family. They showed me what unconditional love actually looks like. When we got word my mother was planning to force me to come home, and change me back... I- I tried to end things, permanently..."

"To become a vampire?"

"No," Dex confessed, "That was a last-minute redemption. I was desperate and I couldn't see any other way to escape her for good. I didn't want to die but when you have to choose between living in a cage or dying free..."

"That's horrible," Anna hugged him. She couldn't imagine what it must have felt like to be in that position. None of the awful things that had happened to her had come from someone she trusted. She admired Dex for his bravery. She couldn't say she'd have made the same choice. As a human, she'd done everything she could to avoid death. She probably would have lived in a cage of misery for the rest of her life rather than risk oblivion. He was far braver than her.

"It all worked out," Dex pulled back with a sniff.

"What about Arik?" Anna asked quietly, "Do you want him back in your life?"

"I don't know." Dex tensed his brow, "I can't trust him while he's on Mother's leash."

"He looked out for me at the palace," she said, "He misses you a lot."

"He was groomed to be my personal protector," Dex smiled sadly, "I didn't think about it at the time but he lost everything when I left. His knighthood, his social status-"

"His best friend," Anna finished, "He said you were everything to each other once."

"I'll make more of an effort to let him in," he promised with a sigh, "How did the rest of your visit go?"

"Just your standard witch trial," Anna shrugged, "I met the whole High Fae Council."

"What?"

"Don't worry," Anna smirked, "I'm *the chosen one* so they can't hurt me."

"Okay, back up," Dex pinched his nasal ridge, "Start from the beginning."

***

By the time Anna and Dex joined Cassie in the library, Anna's adventure to the Elven Realm seemed like nothing more than a crazy dream.

"Hungry?" Rupert appeared with a tray of scones and two large bottles of blood.

"Starving!" Anna rushed forward and began gulping down blood. Her fatigue was momentarily silenced as the liquid spread through her body.

"When did you get back?" Dex asked, taking a sip from the second bottle of blood.

"Just now," replied Rupert, "I had some loose ends to tie up with Rufus."

"How did you know he'd help us?" Cassie asked, piling jam onto her scone.

"He's not a fan of High Fae at the best of times," Rupert sighed, "But he has a particular hatred for the Elven Empire."

"Because he's a vampire?" Anna guessed.

"He believes they imprisoned his lover," confided Rupert, "Technically, she's trapped by a magical contract, not imprisoned, but I understand the distinction is insignificant to him."

"What contract?" Dex asked, handing the rest of his bottle to Anna. She gulped it down hungrily.

"Marielle volunteered to partake in a ritual that would stop the Faerie Realm from accessing any other realm. Her physical presence is key to the barrier."

"So, what? She's like a cork in a bottle?" Dex scoffed.

"In a manner of speaking."

"How long has it been?" Anna asked, remembering Rufus's cavalier attitude with the council. If he'd been enraged, he hid it well.

"Hundreds of years," replied Rupert, "Long before Aiyana was born."

"Can't we do anything to help?" Cassie asked, looking alarmed.

"I'm afraid not," Rupert sighed, "Only the Elven Empress can release her but that would likely mean undoing the spell entirely. While it's regrettable, I cannot fault Aiyana for keeping Marielle in place."

"Is she in pain?" Anna whispered.

"I don't believe so," smiled Rupert sadly.

"What's the big deal about letting the spell drop?" Dex scoffed.

Rupert took a long sip of tea before answering, "What did your Elvish education teach you about Faeden?"

"It's the name of Faerie Realm," Dex frowned in thought, "Alvara used to be part of it, but there was a war or something, so we left."

"Faeden was once part of *our world*," Rupert explained, "or rather, the Mortal Realm was a part of Faeden. Early humans learned how to live off the land from faeries. Like the gods and goddesses of old mythology, they were neither good nor evil but divinely powerful. Some loved mortal creatures and helped them thrive while others delighted in playing tricks. Eventually, humans began to upset the balance of the world, taking from nature without giving anything in return. Arguments over what to do about them turned into a war. Some faeries wanted to control the humans, treating them as pets and slaves, while others felt extinguishing our species was the only way to protect the natural balance."

"That's horrible!" Cassie gasped, holding a forgotten bite of scone halfway to her mouth.

"If termites are eating your house," Dex stretched across the sofa, "your priority isn't going to be the wellbeing of the termites, is it?"

"But slavery or death seems a bit extreme," Cassie muttered.

"Three extremely powerful faeries, known as *alphafae*, felt the same way," Rupert nodded, "It's said the sisters Titania, Mab and Morrigan took pity on the humans. Titania was the Queen of light, earth and fire. Mab ruled over darkness, air and water. The youngest, Morrigan, was the Queen of Twilight. She controlled the elements of life, death and spirit, which allowed her access to other planes of existence. Working together, the sisters created a new realm where humans could thrive without impacting Faeden's ecosystem."

"The Mortal Realm," Anna guessed.

Rupert inclined his head with an affirming nod.

"Did Alvara leave at the same time?" Dex asked.

"Not quite," Rupert shook his head, "My research indicates the Elven species was borne from a union between Titania and early humans. The human ancestry in elves made them seem weak in the eyes of other faeries. Because of this, elves avoided faeries and humans alike, living on an island known as *Alfheim*. After the Faerie and Mortal Realms separated, the war didn't end. It had become a competition of superiority between the Seelie courts. The elves found themselves attacked on all sides. Even though they lived in perfect balance with nature, many Fae argued they should be banished to the Mortal Realm to live with their human cousins."

"And that's when we left?" Dex prompted.

"I believe so," Rupert nodded, "Though accounts of how they managed it vary, all agree Alfheim was renamed to honour the sacrifice of the elven mage Alvara Orchidtree, who remained behind to perform the spell that would separate Alfheim from Faeden."

"How did she manage it?" Cassie frowned sceptically, "If creating the Mortal Realm required three god-level faeries, I doubt she did it alone."

"Perhaps the elves made a deal with the three sisters," Rupert answered, "Her sacrifice may have been a small component in a larger ritual."

"Hmm," Cassie sipped her tea, deep in thought.

"What does this have to do with Rufus's wife?" Anna asked.

"Not wife," Rupert corrected, "They never married. Furthermore, Marielle has refused to see him for quite some time. He didn't want her to participate in the ritual and was not pleased when she did it anyway. He acts as though she was stolen from him but, from what I can tell, he drove her away."

"But how is she blocking the realms?" Anna prompted, "I thought the sister had already done that."

Rupert began cleaning his glasses, "The Mortal and Elven realms were separated from Faeden but not *inaccessible*. Faeries found their way into the Mortal Realm via hidden portals. Some came as refugees from the war, but others came to steal humans and use them as slaves, soldiers, spies and breeders. A few Fae even crossed over in the hopes of claiming dominion over the new realms."

"So the Elven Empire corked the bottle?" Dex surmised.

Rupert nodded.

"And they *needed* Marielle to do it?" Cassie grimaced, "There was no other way?"

"All magic has a price," replied Rupert, "Just as Alvara Orchidtree was forced to remain in Faeden to separate the realms, Marielle must remain in place to keep the barrier active."

"Why would faeries want humans at all?" Anna questioned, "Aren't humans weak compared to faeries? Why have a human spy when you could have a...pixie or something?"

"We have many appealing qualities," Rupert smiled, "Firstly, faeries cannot lie, which makes mortals invaluable in plots of subterfuge. We are far more fertile than most of the High Fae species so, in addition to producing heirs for them, we can produce vast armies. We are easily controlled by enchantments, so make loyal minions. Even in death, our remains take on magic unlike any other. After we fall, soldiers can be brought back to fight as-"

"Vampires?" Dex choked.

"And zombies, ghouls, mummies, et cetera," Rupert confirmed, "All undead creatures were created to serve as soldiers in various faeries armies."

"What about werebeasts?" Anna asked, "They aren't undead."

"Interestingly, werebeasts seem to be a natural phenomenon originating in the Mortal realm," Rupert mused, "The strongest fighters of a village used to invoke the primal power of their local spirit guardians to help keep the community safe. Most attacks happened after dark, under the light of a full moon, so that became the most common time for these warriors to transform."

"How did it become a curse?" Cassie prompted.

"I'm not convinced it is one," Rupert answered lightly as he buttered a scone, "As new generations were born with the warrior's gift, I suspect some didn't want it. Perhaps they chose to repress the animal guardian residing within them and, as they passed the spirit on, via wound or womb, the spirit learned to behave more like a caged animal than a respected ally."

"So that Dane guy was right," Dex surmised, "Letting out the beast more often helps you control it."

"Not necessarily," contradicted Rupert, "His goal was *control*, not mutual respect. Accepting one's beast as a part of oneself, trusting it, embracing it, shouldn't require transformation."

"Speaking of…" Anna jigged her leg anxiously, "When can we go get Finn?"

Rupert took a strange-looking device from the pocket of his blazer and dropped it to the floor. It bounced once on the carpet before exploding into Boggle's round, metallic form.

"Hello!" Boggle greeted everyone, "How may I help?"

"Please call Mr Henry Finnegan," Rupert said.

"You have phone service?" Dex leaned over to inspect Boggle's eye-like cameras.

"Yes!" Boggle reported, "I relay data to and from cellular towers in the Mortal Realm."

Anna could hear quiet ringing in Boggle's head. No one was answering.

"Can you connect our phones?" Dex looked from Rupert to Boggle.

"It will take some time," answered Rupert thoughtfully, "But, yes."

The ringing stopped and clicked over to Finn's voicemail recording, *"Hi, you're calling Henry Finnegan. Sorry, I can't answer the phone right now, but if you leave your name and number after the beep, I'll get back to you as soon as possible."*

Rupert gestured for Boggle to hang up.

"Do you think he's okay?" Anna frowned.

"I'm sure he's fine," Rupert assured, "He's with his family."

"I need to see for myself," said Anna, standing.

"I imagine there will still be quite a crowd at Finnegan Farm," Rupert warned.

"Does that mean I can't go?" Anna challenged.

"I'm not going to try to stop you from doing whatever you want to do," Rupert, lowered his teacup, "but you should be prepared. You won't be able to pass through crowds unnoticed anymore."

"I'll be careful," promised Anna.

"And you won't be alone," Dex smirked, standing with Anna.

"I'm just bringing Finn back here," Anna shrugged, "I'm sure I'll be fine."

"Well, I need to get my van," Cassie said, licking jam from her fingers and then standing, "And our stuff is still at the motel."

"Fine," Anna sighed, "Anyone who's coming, let's go!"

"Be careful!" Rupert called as Cassie and Dex followed Anna from the room.

CHAPTER 33

The Shadow Tribunal

Anna scowled at the mess of clothes and toiletries in the motel room.

"This is going to take forever," she complained, "Why couldn't we go straight to the Finnegan's cabins?"

"Elowen lifted a lot of protective enchantments to allow me to get to Rupert's the way I did," Cassie explained, "And she only did it because the Granite Arch was being guarded. Gaining access again would take longer than going back the normal way. "

"It won't take long to shove all this into bags," Dex added, scooping up a pile of clothes.

Anna packed Finn's overnight bag and pulled it onto her back, wincing at as her bullet wounds throbbed under the weight. The straps smelled like him. She removed the bag and hugged it to her chest, breathing him in. They'd be together soon.

The moon looked full, with only a tiny sliver of darkness to hint the waning cycle had begun.

"I'll get us checked out," said Cassie, locking the room. Anna watched Cassie jog across to the main office. Dex tapped Anna on the shoulder, "Scissors, paper, rock?"

"Why?" Anna wasn't in the mood for games.

"We have to decide who's giving Cassie a piggyback ride to the van," he smirked, "Unless you'd rather wait for an Uber to pick us all up?"

"I'll do it, it's fine," Anna growled impatiently.

Dex sighed and put his arm around her shoulders.

"I know you're worried about Finn," he said quietly, "But, you're not the only one who cares about him. Imagine what all this has been like for Cassie. Her best friends are in trouble, like life-or-death shit, and the only thing she could do to help was write a fake letter."

"That letter helped a lot," Anna argued sheepishly. She knew that wasn't the point. Cassie might be a witch but she was human. The powers involved in this, political and magical, were beyond her. She'd been the one to take Anna under her wing on that first day in the office. Now Cassie was the one being left behind.

Dex sighed, "Do you honestly believe anything bad's happened to Finn?"

"I just-," Anna blinked back tears. She was exhausted. She was *almost* certain Finn was fine but she couldn't relax until she saw him, "Why didn't he answer his phone?"

"We'll ask him when we see him," Dex assured with a smile, "In the meantime, scissors, paper or rock?"

Anna rolled her eyes and then beat Dex on all three rounds.

***

Cassie screamed into Dex's ears for the entire run to Girraween National Park. When they passed through the Granite Arch, they found most of the tents had vanished. The grassy expanse seemed larger than it had before. The hairs on Anna's neck rose as they crossed the open space.

Anyone could be watching from the treeline, hidden in darkness. Though she couldn't see anyone, she felt sure at least one set of hidden eyes followed their progress.

Conscious of her conversation with Dex, Anna let Cassie set the pace. They crossed the moonlit field quickly but their progress slowed to a snail's pace on the forest path. Dex and Anna could see the rocks and tree roots in the shadows but it was pitch black for Cassie She shuffled slowly through the rough terrain using the torchlight on her phone. She stumbled a few times, grabbing Anna's shoulder for balance. A murmur rustled through the trees. Cassie couldn't seem to hear the whispering but a subtle glance from Dex told Anna that he could. Like an eerie game of *Red Light Green Light*, silence would fall whenever Anna turned to find the source of the muttering. When she, Dex and Cassie reached a fork in the pathway, a young ghostly-looking girl, who couldn't be more than five years old, approached the group.

"Are you the magic vampire everyone's talking about?" asked the girl. She had the round, yellow eyes of an owl and talon-like feet.

"I guess so," Anna crouched down to the girl's height, "I'm Anna, what's your name?"

"Libby," smiled the girl, "Is it true you fought off an army of werebeasts?" Dex snorted behind her.

"Not at all!" Anna replied, "Werebeasts are my friends."

"Aren't they scary?" asked Libby, "Mumma said to stay away from them."

"Have you ever seen your Mum get mad?" Anna asked the girl.

"Yeah," the girl nodded.

"I bet *she* can be pretty scary, right?"

The girl nodded again.

"Werebeasts are like that," Anna explained, "They *can be scary*, like anyone, but the rest of the time they're mostly nice."

"Oh, okay" smiled Libby, "Here you go." Libby handed Anna a wildflower and then ran back into the forest. A gust of excited whispers and giggles washed around them in the darkness.

"That was adorable," smiled Cassie.

Anna put the flower in her hair and continued down the path toward the cabins.

"There ya' are!" Bill's booming voice greeted the group as Anna, Dex and Cassie emerged from the treeline. Anna couldn't see Finn among the people in the clearing but she spotted Wallace flicking through his brick-like binder near the bonfire. Elowen stood at the lake's edge with some members of Finn's pack, including Toby. Small groups of strangers, mostly vampires, hovered around the tree line.

Bill strode toward Anna, Dex and Cassie, embracing all three in a warm hug. He'd changed into baggy, cotton pants and a loose singlet.

"Welcome back," Bill greeted the group, then whispered to Anna, "How're ya doin' kiddo?"

"I'm alright," Anna replied, "How's Finn?"

"We just got him to lie down," Bill answered, jerking his head toward one of the cabins.

"Can I see him?" she asked.

"I doubt anyone in the world could stop you," he chuckled with a wink, "But you should know, Ellie made him a cup of her infamous *Sleepy-Time tea* so, if he's managed to stay awake, he'll be groggy as a frog in beer."

Anna turned to Cassie and Dex.

"We're fine out here," Cassie smiled, "Go."

Anna ran to the cabin. The room inside was sparsely decorated, as though anyone might claim it for a night or two and then move on. Finn slept peacefully on the bottom level of a bunk bed in the far corner. Drool trickled from the corner of his mouth onto his pillow. With a grateful sigh, Anna dropped his backpack on the floor and crouched by the bed.

"Finn?" she whispered. He had a pink scar above his eyebrow where he'd been bleeding the day before. She traced it with her finger, "Finn?"

"Anna?" Finn's eyes fluttered in his sleep, "Don't trust them...Anna, don't..."

"I'm here," she said softly, stroking his hair, "I'm here with you."

"I'll keep you safe," he took her hand and hugged it like a teddy bear, "My Anna."

Anna kicked off her shoes and crawled into Finn's arms, "I'll keep you safe too," she whispered.

"I love my Anna," Finn whispered.

"I love my Finn," Anna smiled, closing her eyes and finally allowing sleep to take her.

***

"Anna?" Finn's voice roused Anna awake, "When did you get here?"

"A few hours ago, I think," she said, checking her watch. From the smell of smoke and dim light outside, it seemed the bonfire was still going.

"Mum told me what happened," he frowned, "Sounds like the Elven Empress is not your biggest fan."

"At least she didn't kill me," Anna grimaced.

Finn's arms tensed, "I don't know what I would've done if she had."

"You could always go back to your *ex-fiancé*," suggested Anna with a wink.

"My *what?*" Finn frowned incredulously.

"You and Dex used to be betrothed, did you not?" Anna smirked. She didn't want to focus on serious things now that she and Finn were together again.

"Oh, right," Finn nodded with a grin, "I take it you and Dex had *The Talk.*"

"We had to after *Her Majesty* spilled the beans."

"Oh, jeez, I didn't even consider that," Finn wrinkled his nose, "What happened?"

"She blindsided me with it...so I'd question my judgment, I assume," Anna frowned, "But it only made me question hers. I'm glad he had you

308

back then, even though it's weird to think of you two being a couple."

"That's why I kept Jade a secret," Finn whispered, "I wasn't meant to be dating."

"Your parents don't seem like they'd force a marriage on you," Anna frowned.

"They wouldn't," Finn agreed, "To them, the betrothal was more of a *possibility* than a finalised agreement. But the Elven court made it clear to me that they took the arrangement seriously, and I should too."

"Rufus said Bass had you under surveillance," Anna recalled.

"What?" Finn sat up.

"During the meeting," Anna elaborated, trying to remember exactly what had been said, "Rufus said Bass shouldn't have a job anymore because he'd had people watching you around the time you were attacked and did nothing to stop it."

"But he has lycans under his command," Finn blinked, "He'd recognise a werewolf."

"I think that was the point."

"What do you mean?"

"Didn't you say Jade only had a scratch on her?" Anna asked gently, "And she couldn't remember how she got it?"

"I-" Finn closed his eyes, the colour drained from his face, "Yes."

"Even if Jade didn't know about werebeasts I doubt she'd forget being that close to a *huge wolf*. And how did she get away with only a scratch? For a werebeast to show that level of restraint, it would need-"

"Self-control," Finn blanched, rubbing his forehead.

"They could have scratched Jade while she was asleep," Anna suggested, "Or used magic to make her forget it happened, right?"

"Bass used Jade to attack me," Finn looked like he might throw up, "She was a threat to the betrothal. Fuck."

"Fuck is right," Anna agreed. She couldn't imagine how he must be feeling right now. They stared at each other.

Finn pulled his prosthetic from under the bed, attached it, and began pacing the room.

"What are you going to do?" Anna asked.

"Nothing," Finn raised his eyebrows. He was strangely calm. The air was charged like the moments before a thunderstorm explodes.

"Nothing?" Anna stared, "Aren't you angry?"

"Of course I'm angry," Finn seethed, "But I don't have the luxury of showing it. People would take it as proof that all werebeasts are monsters. At the very least, I'd just be another *jacked douchebag* who can't control his temper. I can't let people see how furious I am. Not ever."

"I'm not *people*," Anna insisted, "You can be honest with me. Get mad. Break something! It's fine."

The tips of his fingers grew into claws and his ears began to elongate, growing a layer of short fur.

"What do you want me to say?" he growled, "That I want to kill him? That I want to watch him suffer for what he's done to me? *To Jade?!* Because I do. But we both know I'll just do nothing."

"Bass was probably following Aiyana's orders anyway," Anna replied. She didn't know whether she should keep encouraging Finn to express his anger or try to calm him. The latter felt hypocritical but the former could get him killed.

"So what?" Finn muttered, "Bass is still responsible for what he did. He could have rejected the orders. He could have said *I draw the line at killing and mutilating innocent kids*, but he didn't."

"The entire Elven military would come for us if we kill him," Anna argued.

"If *I* kill him," Finn corrected.

"*We*," Anna emphasised. There was no way she'd let Finn go on a rampage alone. If he wanted revenge then she was going to help him.

Finn stopped pacing and turned to Anna. His expression softened and his wolf-like features faded.

"I'd never put you in that sort of danger," he assured.

"They already want me dead," Anna shrugged, "Everyone's just being polite about it…for now."

"Hunting down Bass would be dumb," Finn sighed, falling back onto the bed.

"So, what do you want to do?"

"Just…" Finn frowned at his lap and then looked up at Anna with a resigned sigh, "Just be with you. Live my life. Put all this shit behind us. Revenge won't change anything. I have everything I need right here with you, it would be stupid to risk it. "

"Okay," Anna took his hand and kissed it.

Cassie's laughter sounded faintly through the cabin door. Beer bottles clinked together.

"Tell me about last night," Anna prompted, "Cassie said only some of your pack turned?"

Finn let out a deep sigh.

"By the time the moon was out," he began, "a huge crowd of spectators had gathered to watch. The other werebeasts had to use the same field because there was nowhere else for them to go-"

"I forgot about them," Anna gasped.

"Normally on a full moon we'd be naked in anticipation of the change," Finn continued, "but with everyone watching, taking photos and stuff…most of us opted to stay dressed and deal with the ripped clothes afterwards."

"Understandable," Anna cringed.

"When the other packs transformed," Finn sat on the bed, "I didn't feel the push to change like I normally do. It was more like a nudge. I didn't want to turn, so I didn't. I think the ones who did just wanted to feel normal. Or maybe they wanted to escape the stress of being there. Things feel simpler in beast form. The other packs stayed away from us. Their beasts could tell we were different."

"I'm sorry I made everything weird," Anna murmured, "I just wanted to help."

"Don't be sorry!" Finn smiled, "You set us free."

"But you're still werebeasts, right?" Anna said, "What if it wears off?"

"We'll keep meeting up at the full moon, to be safe," Finn shrugged, "but this feels permanent. It's like…I can sense my wolf all the time now but we understand each other better. It's hard to explain."

"What about the rest of your pack?" Anna asked, "I did magic on them without their permission. I changed them in this huge way and I don't even know them."

"They're just as grateful as I am," Finn assured, sniffing the air, "Some are still outside. Come and meet them. You'll see."

***

"They have RISEN!" a heavily intoxicated Dex cackled, throwing his arms around Anna and Finn as they emerged from the cabin. Several people around the bonfire laughed and whooped drunkenly.

"Is that barbeque I smell?" Finn smiled sheepishly, taking Anna's hand and heading toward the giant buffet table where only two chafing dishes remained. One was filled with sauteed mushroom and onions and the other with beef patties and sausages. A small collection of bread rolls sat to the side, covered by mesh tents to discourage flies. As Finn loaded up his plate, Dex handed Anna a red party cup filled with a mixture of blood and cherry liqueur. As she drank it, something stirred in her memory. She couldn't figure out if it was deja vu or a clue to a riddle she'd forgotten about but she tucked the thought away as she helped herself to some sausages.

Three figures came into view as Anna followed Finn to the lake. One was a dwarf with a long, braided beard and partially shaved head. He stood between Toby and the annoyingly beautiful woman who'd been overly affectionate with Finn the day before. The woman gave Anna a sour look as they approached.

"Toby, Zach, Gemma," Finn smiled, ignoring the woman's scowl, "This is Anna."

"Hey, hey!" Zach the dwarf grinned, extending his hand, "All hail the Lycan Queen!"

"Oh god. No one's calling me that, right?" Anna crinkled her nose as the dwarf shook her hand firmly.

"Not yet," he laughed, "I'm hoping it'll catch on- Ooh! Where'd you get that sausage?"

Anna pointed back toward the food table, which was partially obscured by the bonfire. Zach ran toward it at full speed.

"Bye, then!" Finn laughed, shaking his head at Zach's retreating figure.

Toby shuffled forward, "Um, thanks," he mumbled, shifting his feet uncomfortably, "Sorry for attacking you and stuff..."

He was dark-skinned with a broad nose and dark, curly hair. He was taller than Finn but hunched over like a wilting flower so they stood at roughly the same height.

"It's okay," Anna smiled encouragingly, "It wasn't your fault."

"He had a bruise on his neck, you know," Gemma said coolly, "Where you clotheslined him."

"I'm sorry about that," Anna said sincerely, looking at Toby, "How are you feeling now?"

"I'm all good," Toby shrugged, shrinking away from the attention, "Don't worry about it."

"Do you want to grab some food?" Finn said gently, putting his hand on Toby's shoulder.

"We'll wait here," Gemma smiled at Finn, linking arms with Anna, "Hurry back now."

"Oh, uh, okay," Finn cast a concerned look from Gemma to Anna. Anna nodded that it was fine. If Gemma had something she wanted to say to Anna in private, it may as well be now.

"Do you want anything, Gem?" Finn offered.

"No, thanks," Gemma smiled sweetly.

The second Finn and Toby were out of earshot, Gemma pulled her hand away from Anna. "I'm not going to thank you," she muttered quietly.

"Okay," Anna raised her eyebrows.

"Things were fine before."

"Sorry I ruined things for you, then."

Gemma glared at Anna, "You don't get it, do you?"

"I guess not."

"You're ruining his life."

"Do you mean Finn?"

"I mean *Henry*. His name is fucking *Henry*! Not Finn."

"Fine, how exactly am I ruining *Henry's* life?" Anna asked incredulously.

"He loves you," Gemma answered sternly, "But you're going to outlive him by centuries. He'll devote his whole life to you. He'll put aside everything *he wants* to make *you* happy and in three hundred years you won't even remember his name. He deserves better than you."

"Like you?" Anna guessed.

"He doesn't want me," she scowled, "but I still care about him and want him to be happy. And that's just not possible with you. He's sacrificing who he is and what he wants just to make things work with you."

"I would never ask him to sacrif-"

"He wants kids."

The words hung in the air between them.

"What?" Anna whispered.

"Henry's greatest wish," Gemma said slowly, "for as long as I've known him, is to be a father. The fact that he hasn't told you speaks volumes, don't you think?"

Anna stared. It felt as though a shard of ice had pierced her heart. It was just like Finn to put his needs last. To withhold his aspirations from conversation in case they caused conflict or discomfort.

"You say you'd never ask him to sacrifice anything for you," continued Gemma with a judgemental sneer, "but he's already doing it and, in your ignorance, you're letting him."

Anna wanted to contradict Gemma. She wanted to say she and Finn would get married, have a family, and live happily ever after… But Gemma was right. Finn hadn't told her he wanted to be a Dad. Knowing him, he'd chosen to keep it from her because he knew it was impossible. Could vampires reproduce? Anna had a feeling the answer was no. Her body may be generally functional but she hadn't menstruated once in the months since she'd died.

"Henry should be with someone who can give him the life he wants," Gemma reiterated, "I know it won't be me but it shouldn't be you either. The longer you're together, the worse things will get for him. If you love him, leave him be."

Gemma stalked away leaving Anna to stare into the empty lake.

"Penny for your thoughts?" said a gentle voice.

"Can vampires get pregnant?" Anna asked absently before looking up. A stunningly beautiful woman raised her eyebrows at Anna. She wore a long, corseted gown with lace trim. Her dark hair was fashioned into a crown of braids and her red lips stood out boldly against her snow-white skin. Her fangs were subtle but her dark brown eyes glowed like a cat's in the moonlight.

"Oh, sorry," Anna stammered, "I didn't realise- Forget I said-"

"It is exceedingly rare for a vampire to fall pregnant to a mortal male," the woman graciously interrupted with a voice like honey.

"But it's not *impossible*?" A tiny spark of hope flickered in her chest, "If, someday, a vampire *hypothetically* wanted to…"

"It's possible," confirmed the woman with a knowing smile, "Though this *hypothetical vampire*, would be wise to seek magical assistance when she's ready."

"Noted," Anna nodded awkwardly, "Thanks."

"You are most welcome," the woman smiled back.

"I'm Anna."

"I know," nodded the woman, "My name is Ambrosia Laurant."

"You're my boss!" Anna blurted, "And you're on the council for the

Vampiric Alliance."

"The Shadow Tribunal, yes," Ambrosia nodded, "I cannot see my fellow council members here but I'm sure their spies have been observing you since your arrival."

Anna followed Ambrosia's gaze to several moving shadows in the forest. More cat's eyes flashed in the moonlight.

"Well, that's creepy as hell," Anna frowned, "Why don't you just pull me into a meeting like the Council of High Fae did?"

"There's no point in asking a person if they intend to be a threat," Ambrosia mused, "they will always refute the idea. Observing one's behaviour is far more telling of their character."

"So...you don't have any questions for me?"

Ambrosia smiled. She was so ethereally beautiful that it was almost painful to look directly at her.

"Are you worried about the prophecy?" she asked.

"Oh...no," Anna stammered. She couldn't divulge that it was a fake but didn't feel right lying, "I- I don't believe it's true."

"Don't make the same mistake as Aiyana," advised the vampire, "She once refuted a prophecy made about her."

"What happened?" Anna asked in a hushed whisper.

"The prophecy foretold Aiyana would be the *last Empress of her line, bearing only sons*."

"Oh."

"She was terrified, as you might imagine," Ambrosia sighed, "but when she gave birth to a female-presenting child, it was cause for great celebration in her realm. Aiyana arrogantly proclaimed the prophecy was false and the Great Oracle, Cassandra, was a fraud."

"But then, Dex...?"

"Yes," Ambrosia nodded with a conspirational smirk, "it quickly became clear Aiyana was too quick to dismiss her destiny. It's a sore subject for her, to say the least."

It occurred to Anna that Rupert probably knew all this. If he hadn't, Rufus certainly would have. They'd come up with their plan to use a fake prophecy because no one would dare question its validity, especially Aiyana. It was a smart move. Cruel, but smart.

"Is it true your prophecy mentioned the Forgotten Deity?" Ambrosia asked, adjusting her skirt as she perched on a nearby log. Anna joined her, watching gentle ripples slide across the surface of the lake. She'd thought that part of the prophecy was made-up gibberish, "Yes," she answered, "What does that mean?"

"The Forgotten Deity is the personification of all gods and spirits who remain undefined or have, over the years, been forgotten," explained Ambrosia, "If you imagine each known deity as a single star in the sky-" she directed Anna's gaze to the glittering stars above them, "the Forgotten Deity is the void between those stars. It's the god people pray to when their religion betrays them. It's the *greater power* one feels without being able to name its origin."

"So, what does it mean to *wear the crown* of this Forgotten Deity?" Anna whispered.

"I would guess," Ambrosia pondered, "It is to master the power of the unknown. Chaos magic. Dangerous but powerful." She narrowed her eyes in thought, pouting her full lips before continuing, more to herself than to Anna, "There is a ritual, written thousands of years ago, to evoke such power."

Why would Rupert have written a line about this in the fake prophecy? Was it dumb luck? Had he read the name Forgotten Deity somewhere in his text and forgotten the context? Or was it intentional? Did he have plans for Anna's future that went beyond protective magic?

"What does it say?" whispered Anna.

"I don't remember the details," Ambrosia seemed distracted, "It was more like a riddle than a spell. There was something about ripping out hearts… It mentioned blood and fire."

"Sounds great!" Anna scoffed.

"There's a reason ancient magic is rarely performed these days," Ambrosia inclined her head, "The Shadow Tribunal keeps the original parchment for that ritual protected. It is safe from magic users. Or, rather, it *was* until you demonstrated that vampires and mages are not always separate entities."

"I don't plan on doing any ancient rituals," assured Anna.

"You didn't plan on performing a minor miracle yesterday," Ambrosia replied, "And yet…"

"A ritual where you rip out someone's heart probably requires a bit more intention," reasoned Anna.

"You never know," Ambrosia smiled. Her fangs were hypnotically white.

"Have you given any thought to what you will do next?"

"What do you mean?" Anna frowned.

"You are a subject of prophecy, *destiny driven*. You have the attention of the Shadow Tribunal and the Council of High Fae. You're famous. Doors are opening for you. Now is the time to pursue your ambitions."

A sudden chill gripped Anna's chest. She could imagine how someone else, someone with more ambition, would love to be in her shoes right now. Ambrosia made it sound as though Anna could charge hundreds of dollars for signed autographs. She could stage a revolution or start a cult. But Anna didn't want fame or power. There was a difference between being looked at and being seen. Everyone was looking at her but only Finn, Cassie and Dex made her feel seen. She wanted to be left alone. To live her life with the people she cared about. Her happiness required less attention from strangers, not more.

"You needn't look so alarmed," Ambrosia smiled, "We are not like the Council of High Fae."

"They wanted to *discuss my future* too," Anna pointed out.

"They wanted to dictate your future," Ambrosia corrected.

"But not you?"

"From what I've observed of you thus far," Ambrosia mused, "Your goals are unlikely to conflict with that of the Vampiric Alliance. However, I won't pretend that I'm not curious to hear you articulate your aspirations."

"Right now," Anna shrugged, "My goals include relaxing by the fire and, maybe, having another sausage."

"And in the long term?" Ambrosia studied her face, "What do you wish to achieve?"

"Nothing," Anna answered honestly, "I just want a normal quiet life with the people I love. Sorry if you were hoping for something grander."

"A normal life is not *nothing*," replied Ambrosia, "It is an admirable goal, though I fear it's beyond the Tribunal's ability to provide."

"I'd settle for everyone forgetting about this prophecy stuff," sighed Anna.

"We can make it known that you are not to be bothered about matters relating to the prophecy," Ambrosia offered, "At present, there's a queue forming outside your residence. Many wish to volunteer aid to your noble cause."

"My noble cause?"

"*The broken worlds will come together as one*," quoted Ambrosia with a wink, "Shall I give the order to have them disbanded?"

"That would be great," Anna looked suspiciously into Ambrosia's inscrutable face, "but I'm assuming you want something in return?"

"Friends help each other," she shrugged with an innocent grin, then added pointedly, "And keep each other apprised of *interesting information*."

"You want me to spy for you?" Anna raised her eyebrows, "I can't imagine there's much I can tell you that you don't already know."

Ambrosia chuckled, "Let me speak plainly then. The Underfae community is intrigued by you. If you plan to do any more *unconventional* magic, we would like to hear about it before rumours of it reach our ears. And if you have any issues with the faerie community, be it Underfae or not, we'd like to know about it before you take action."

"What if someone attacks me?"

"Defend yourself, of course," Ambrosia said, "but, please, call me afterwards. If things get politically or physically messy, I can help."

She handed Anna a black business card with raised lettering. Anna put the card in her pocket. She'd left a question unspoken.

What if my issue is with the Shadow Tribunal?

Laughter exploded from the group sitting around the bonfire.

"I believe it's time to rejoin the festivities," Ambrosia stood, offering her hand to Anna, "Shall we?"

***

When Anna, Finn, Cassie and Dex reached the van, the forest was quiet and still.

"Can someone else drive?" Cassie yawned.

"I can," Finn offered, climbing into the driver's seat, "You won't get car sick in the back?"

"I might," Cassie smiled weakly, crawling into the back seat with Dex, "But it's better than falling asleep at the wheel."

"True," Finn buckled his seat belt, "Just, tell me if you need us to pull over."

Finn rested his hand on Anna's knee as they flew along the dark highway. It was a simple gesture yet somehow intimate. It said, *"We're on this journey together."* She'd seen her parents do it a thousand times and never given it much thought.

"I like this," Anna whispered.

"What?" Finn didn't take his eyes from the road but gave Anna's leg a gentle squeeze.

"All of us together," Anna placed her hand on his, "Just a group of friends coming home from a big weekend. No crazy dramas."

"Do you regret coming to the Solstice?" Finn frowned.

"Weirdly, no," Anna replied, "I was having a great time before all the craziness. I'm glad I got to meet your family."

"They're a lot," Finn blushed.

"They're great," Anna assured.

"Are you sure you want me at your family's Christmas lunch?" asked Finn.

"I'm sure," Anna imagined Finn interacting with her family, "I'm more worried about whether any of them will be able to tell something's off with me. Telling them *I died* is not exactly a festive announcement, and I know they're Unseeing but I don't want to lie to them."

"I get it," Finn agreed, "It was hard enough keeping things from you when we'd only just met. Keeping everything from your family must be torture."

"It'll be easier with you there," Anna smiled, fidgeting with Finn's sleeve. "I've never brought a guy home before."

Finn glanced over and grinned.

"Shut up," Anna laughed, blushing.

"I didn't say anything!"

"You were thinking loud."

By the time they arrived at the Grotto, the sun was peaking over the horizon. Dex and Cassie slept in a pile of limbs on the back seat while Anna struggled to keep her eyes open.

"All your stuff's at Rupert's, right?" Finn whispered, "Are you living there now?"

"I guess," Anna didn't know what her plans were, "Just until everything blows over."

"What if it doesn't blow over? That prophecy sounded pretty-"

"Oh, it's fake," blurted Anna.

"What?" Finn blanched, swerving the van.

"Careful!"

"Shit," Finn focused on the road with a furrowed brow, "What do you mean it's fake?"

"I couldn't say anything before, with all those people around but…" Anna explained the false prophecy, and how Rupert had misled the High Fae Council.

"I don't get it," frowned Finn, "Rufus had a solid case without the prophecy."

"Maybe they didn't want to take any chances?" Anna guessed.

"Maybe." Finn was silent for the remainder of their journey to The Grotto.

***

Later that day, when the sun had risen, Anna woke in Finn's bed to the smell of coffee and melted butter.

"Pancakes?" Finn offered, as she entered the kitchen.

"You know it," Anna yawned, "Thanks…Henry."

"*Henry?*" Finn laughed, raising his eyebrows.

"Do you prefer it to *Finn*?" Anna asked.

"I never really thought about it," Finn shrugged, "I always introduce myself as Henry but I like Finn too. Especially when you call me *your Finn*," he winked.

"I'm glad" Anna smiled, adding maple syrup to her pancake.

"What brought this on?" Finn asked.

"Nothing…" Anna shrugged, trying to look casual. She didn't want to repeat the things Gemma had said about him. Not now that her life was finally feeling back on track. Maybe she was wasting Finn's limited time. It might be a selfish fantasy to imagine their love would overcome the barriers of reality. But they could have today. They could have now.

"Good morning!" Cassie stretched as she emerged from her bedroom, "Ooh, pancakes!" Cassie loaded her plate before taking a seat next to Anna, "Can I grab the rest of my stuff from your granddad's after breakfast? I want to do some laundry before I head to Mum's tomorrow."

"Sure," Anna replied, remembering Christmas was only a couple of days away, "Do you have any special traditions?"

"Tomorrow we'll be baking Christmas Eve cookies and drinking *Merry Margaritas*," Cassie smiled, "On Christmas Day, Mum endures my annual rant about how Christmas is a bastardisation of Yule, and then we watch a bunch of soppy Christmas movies."

"Sounds perfect," laughed Anna.

"Religious mythology aside," Cassie added extra syrup to her plate, "we both like the sentiment behind the holiday. It's a nice excuse to spend time together."

Dex emerged from Cassie's study, staring at his phone. He was uncharacteristically quiet as he took a pancake and sat down.

"What about you?" Cassie prodded Dex in the ribs, "Any Christmas plans?"

"I was just texting Arik," Dex murmured, "I guess we'll be spending the day together. Just us. *Bonding*."

"That's great!" exclaimed Anna. She couldn't see any reason why Dex wasn't excited, or at the very least, pleased to be seeing his brother for Christmas.

"We're meeting tomorrow morning," Dex looked pale, "Arik booked us into a luxury hotel. We're getting spa treatments. It'll be great."

"Then why do you look sick?" Cassie frowned with a laugh.

Dex rested his head on the counter, "What if it's horrible and awkward?"

"It probably will be at first," Cassie laughed with a shrug.

"Great."

"But *after that*, it'll be fine," Cassie assured, "and you might even have fun!"

"If it's not, can I come to your Mum's place and have some of those Merry Margaritas you mentioned?"

"Of course," Cassie smiled, "But you have to help make the cookies too."

CHAPTER 34

Merry Christmas

Christmas Eve with Rupert was a strange affair. Anna woke to find the jungle outside her window had transformed into thousands of pine trees covered in thick snow. The gadget-cluttered manor had been decorated in tinsel and fairy lights, and an enormous tree had been erected in the centre of the library. Only a few gifts sat under its branches, but the sight of them cheered Anna all the same. She added a few parcels to the collection before following the allure of sizzling bacon to the kitchen.

"Merry Christmas!" Rupert beamed, handing Anna a mug of spiced eggnog.
"Merry Christmas," replied Anna with a smile.
Tabitha rubbed against Anna's leg, purring.
"This place looks incredible," complimented Anna, "How did you get it to snow outside?"
"The grounds outside the manor are more illusion than nature," winked Rupert, "It's been too long since I've changed things up."
"How long?" Anna squinted, remembering the book she'd found in Cassie's office.
"Many years," Rupert sighed.
"Decades?" Anna prompted, "...Centuries?"
"Centuries?!" Rupert laughed, "How old do you think I am?"
"I don't know," Anna shrugged emphatically, "Cassie has a book with *your symbol* on it and it looked ancient. It was about the Morrigan's Shield, which is what the Council of High Fae called you..."
"Indeed," Rupert put his mug down and cleaned his spectacles, "What I am about to tell you is a great secret. Please do not tell anyone, not even your friends. Do I have your word?"

Anna nodded.

"the Morrigan's Shield is not a singular person," he explained, "It is a title. The previous Morrigan's Shield trained me and one day I shall take on an apprentice to take over from me. Magic is entwined in the training process that makes people forget the old and remember the new. For example, Empress Aiyana remembers *me* from her youth, hundreds of years ago. the Morrigan's Shield of that time was a woman, employed by the Elven Empire to authenticate prophecies. She was also one of Aiyana's tutors."

"That's why she was weird when she saw you?" Anna put the pieces together, "She remembers *you* teaching her. You used to be an authority figure in her life."

"Indeed." Rupert smiled, "It was generations before my time but I have studied the journals of all who came before me."

"Were they all human?"

"Yes."

"How did you get chosen?" Anna asked, "Were you already a wizard or did that happen in training?"

Rupert took a long sip of eggnog and leaned back in his chair. He watched the falling snow outside the window before answering, "Each of us is chosen by Morrigan herself."

"Wha- How?" Anna frowned. "I thought we were cut off from the Faerie Realm."

"*They* are cut off from *us*," Rupert corrected, "But the Morrigan is on our side of the barrier and, when the time is right, she has plans to reopen it and reconnect our realms to be whole once more."

"What about the danger?" Anna frowned.

"Humankind has come a long way since our worlds were separated," Rupert assured, "It's entirely possible we now pose the greater threat. Either way, the divided realms were never going to be a permanent solution."

"How do you know?"

"Because a locked door is still a door," Rupert replied, "It was always going to be a matter of time before someone opened it."

Anna stared at her empty mug, "When you said they are cut off from us... It's blocked both ways, right?"

Rupert gave Anna a grave look.

"*Right?*" Anna stared pointedly.

"There is a way for us to go there," Rupert confirmed, "But there's no way to return."

"How do you know?"

"Your grandmother, Betty, found a way to get to Faeden," he said, rising from his chair and placing his mug in the sink. Mechanical arms began scrubbing it clean.

"Let me show you," Rupert gestured for Anna to follow him.

He led Anna to the wall of portraits, pointing at a black-and-white photo on the far left. She thought it was Liz, at first glance, but upon closer inspection she saw subtle differences. Betty's nose was a bit wider, her eyebrows were thinner and she had a small gap between her front teeth. The label under the photo read: *Gone (Faeden)*.

"I met Betty at university," Rupert smiled at the photo, "We both spent most of our time in the library. It wasn't long until I swapped my engineering texts for mythology and ancient history just so I could bump into her in the stacks and say hello."

"Did she introduce you to magic?"

"She helped me lift my Veil of Unseeing," Rupert nodded, "She opened my mind, and my heart, to endless possibilities."

"Was she a witch?"

"A wizard, of sorts," Rupert answered, "Her mother, your great-grandmother, was the Morrigan's Shield at the time. Betty was furious when the Morrigan chose me as the next apprentice instead of her. She refused to speak to me for quite some time."

"Obviously she got over it," Anna smirked.

"Eventually, yes," Rupert grinned, "She acknowledged I couldn't control the Morrigan's choices any more than she could."

"So, how did she end up in Faeden?"

"Betty's greatest passion was learning about faeries. Their rules, their world. Everything. She hunted down every morsel of information she could find on Faeden. She interviewed the oldest Fae families she could find. Somewhere in her research, she must have found a loophole in the barrier spell."

"So, she abandoned her family just to satisfy her curiosity?" Anna couldn't believe anyone could be that selfish.

The smile faded from Rupert's face, "She didn't mean to leave us permanently," he said, "I came home to find a note saying she'd figured out how to open the door. There were instructions for a ritual. She needed a drop of blood from both her mother and her daughter. We followed the plan but nothing happened. It failed."

"She gambled everything on a hunch?"

"Betty had many admirable qualities," Rupert touched the photo's frame gently, "Patience wasn't one of them."

"How old was Mum?" Anna asked quietly.

"Sixteen," Rupert dropped his hand from the wall, "Diana swore off magic after that day."

"Is that when she asked you to wipe magic from her memory?"

"No, that didn't happen until she was pregnant with your sister," Rupert answered sadly, "Without the Veil, the Fae community often assumed she was a witch and would approach her for magical aid. She believed blocking her memory, making herself *Unseeing*, would ensure she, and her family, would be left in peace."

Anna had never considered that the Veil didn't just stop people from seeing magic, it also protected them from being seen. She wondered what she would have done in her mother's place.

A sound in the corridor distracted Anna from her thoughts. Boggle clanged toward them wearing a bright red hat and coat, announcing cheerfully, "Merry Christmas! Santa is here!"

***

Anna flipped through pages of the leather-bound journal Cassie had left under the tree for her. A message on the front page suggested Anna should use it as a grimoire. She had even added a couple of simple spells with room for Anna to write notes in the margins.

"I must admit," Rupert smiled as he unwrapped the fountain pen Anna had bought him, "I do miss celebrating holidays with family."

"You could always come tomorrow," Anna offered.

"I'm afraid it remains safer for me to stay away," Rupert sighed, tossing wrapping paper to Tabitha who pounced on it with wide-eyed excitement.

"Even now I've put them in danger?" Anna pressed.

"Especially now," Rupert replied gravely, "No one outside our trusted circle can know you and I are related. The temptation to come at us through our family would be impossible to resist."

"Yeah, I get it," Anna pouted, "at least we have today."

Rupert smiled, "That we do."

That night, after consuming her weight in roast turkey, chestnut stuffing and mince pies, Anna went to bed feeling full and content. She woke briefly during the night when the tickle of a pen danced across her hand. It was an indecipherable scribble, presumably from Cassie, who seemed to have drunk a few too many *Merry Margaritas*.

"Love you too, Cas," Anna chuckled as she drifted back to sleep.

***

Though Christmas lunch wasn't due to start until midday, Anna arrived at her parent's house shortly after breakfast. She peeled potatoes in the sink while her father foraged for fresh herbs in the garden. Watching her mother cut slices of seasoned ham, Anna tried not to stare at the misty fog clouding her head. *She asked for this,* Anna reminded herself, *she's happier this way.*

"Have you heard from Granddad Rupert lately?" Anna asked in an airy tone.

"Just the usual gifts in the mail," her mother sighed, "I'm sure he's on a cruise to Antarctica or something."

"Do you miss him?"

"Sometimes," she paused, with a dazed look, "But we were never that close. Why?"

"Just wondering."

"I noticed he hasn't sent you a gift this year," her eyes narrowed, "I thought it was an oversight but…Have *you* heard from him?"

"I-" Anna felt the heat rise in her face. It was one thing to omit information from her mother but it was another to outright lie, "Yeah- yes. He reached out a few weeks ago. We spent the day together yesterday."

"I see," Anna's mother looked away from her, "Is he well?"

"Yes," Anna answered gently.

"That's good," Diana sniffed, "I'm glad."

"He misses you."

"He's always welcome here," she muttered, "He knows that."

"Are you okay?"

"Of course," Anna's mother turned with a plastered-on smile, "Let's get these potatoes in the oven. GORDON, CAN YOU COME IN AND WASH UP, PLEASE?"

A few hours later, a white sedan pulled into the driveway.
"Traffic was a breeze!" Liz beamed, briefly hugging Anna before fiddling with the baby seat.
"Sorry we're so early," Mark said to no one in particular as he helped Grandpa Bert out of the car, "We thought it'd be madness coming back from the airport but the roads were practically empty."

Grandpa Bert leaned heavily on his cane as he emerged from the back seat.
"Bert, Linda!" Diana greeted them warmly, "How was your flight?"
"Long, as always," Linda smiled wearily, "But the hours go by quickly when you've got a good book." she winked at Anna and pushed a heavy pile of gifts into her arms, all of which felt like hardcover novels, "Put those under the tree for me, dear?"
"Sure thing, Gran," Anna smiled, kissing her cheek. Some things never changed.
"At least we got proper leg room this time," Grandpa Bert sighed, "It's torture when you can't move your legs, cramming us all in like sardines. What happened to putting the customer first?"
"They realised it's more profitable to put them last," Mark replied with a commiserating grimace.

The family went inside and nibbled on pre-lunch snacks while Clara waddled around the room, investigating this and that. She was a serious child, staring daggers at anyone bold enough to hold her gaze for too long. When she got tired, she climbed onto Anna's knee and fell asleep on her lap. Anna patted Clara's head softly.
She'd prepared for a full day surrounded by humans. Humans who Anna absolutely would not, *could not*, feed on. She'd gorged on blood before leaving Rupert's manor that morning. But this feeling wasn't a craving for blood. Her yearning went deeper than that. She want to start a family, like Liz had done. But what would that look like for Anna? Surely she was just feeling pangs of jealousy because Liz seemed so happy.

She stared at Clara sleeping peacefully. Her innocent eyes didn't have the Veil clouding over them. Anna wondered if all children could see magic.

After all, no one is born with a closed mind. With a tug of bittersweet longing, Anna finally asked herself the question: *Do I want to be a mother?*

Her gut said yes but, despite being in her thirties, she barely felt like an adult. She still watched cartoons and read comic books. How could she possibly raise a child? Not to mention, what kind of child would she even have? Certainly not a human one. Not the sort her family could babysit. Her child would probably have fangs and reflective eyes. It would eat any fingers that tried to pinch its chubby cheeks. It would be a monster. But, looking at the adorably stern expression on Clara's face...

"Oops, you're not getting clucky are you?" Bert grinned at Anna, "We haven't even met your new beau yet!"

"No!" Anna blushed, "She's just cute, that's all."

"She is!" Liz beamed, stroking her daughter's pink cheek, "What time is Finn arriving?"

"I told him midday," Anna felt suddenly anxious, "Please be cool when he gets here, okay?"

"Why wouldn't we be *cool*?" Grandma Linda laughed with mock-offence, "We're a cool lot. Mark, were we not cool when you first met us?"

"You were very cool," Mark nodded with a conspirational grin, "I was almost intimidated by how cool you were."

"Shut up," Anna sighed, feeling heat rise in her face, "You know what I mean."

"We won't poke and prod," Liz promised, then added with a whisper, "but he is a bit late."

Anna turned to check the clock on the wall. It was ten minutes past twelve. A timer went off in the kitchen.

"That'll be the potatoes," Diana turned.

"I'll get it," Gordon jogged to the kitchen.

"Thanks, love," Diana called after him, sipping her wine, "I don't know how I'd manage without that man."

Anna checked her phone. No messages.

She called Finn. It rang out. *Does he even have his phone?* Anna tried to remember the last time she'd seen him with it. He might have lost it on the Fighting Field. Maybe Bass took it?

"What's up?" Liz whispered, shifting Clara onto her lap.

"It's not like Finn to be late," Anna muttered.

"Maybe he got turned around," Liz shrugged, "All these streets look alike. I'm sure he'll be here any minute."

The more Anna tried to tell herself things were fine, the stronger her sense of foreboding became. She was about to call Rupert when her phone rang.

"That'll be your missing man," Mark grinned, "Give him hell."

Anna forced a smile and then slipped into the bathroom to take the call.

It wasn't Finn calling.

"Anna?" Dex yelled into the phone. Sirens wailed in the background.

"Dex?" Anna called, "Dex can you hear me? What's going on?"

"Get back to Rupert's ASAP!" Dex stammered.

"What's happened?"

"Fire. My place and yours," the phone crackled, "Check the news."

Anna ran back to the living room and turned on the TV, flicking channels until she found one showing the news.

"...urgent update. Brisbane firefighters are still working to extinguish concurrent infernos that have broken out at apartment buildings in Toowong and Fortitude Valley. While it's believed all occupants were able to evacuate in time, there is now concern that neighbouring buildings will catch..."

Aerial shots flicked between the blazing apartment buildings, each engulfed in billowing clouds of black smoke.

"Have you heard from Finn or Cassie?" Anna gasped into the phone.

"No, Cas should be with her mum," Dex whimpered, "I thought Finn was with you?"

"He hasn't shown up yet!" Anna ran outside, looking down the empty street.

"Arik and I will go check the Grotto now. You get somewhere safe."

"I'll meet you there," Anna couldn't breathe.

"No, Anna!" Dex yelled, "Go to Rupert's."

Before she could answer, the call ended. Anna hobbled back inside. The floor seemed to sway under her feet.

"What's going on?" Diana gasped.

All eyes were on Anna. The news flashed more visions of smoke and fire.

"My apartment's on fire," Anna pointed numbly at the TV, "I- I have to go."

"We'll all go," Mark offered.

"No," Anna stammered, "Stay here. Please. I'll let you know if I need anything."

She pulled onto the highway in her hatchback. The sun was out in full force. Balancing the draining lethargy of the scorching rays against her heart-pummelling panic, Anna struggled to focus on the road. A message popped up on her phone.

Dex: *Cassie's not answering. Her Mum said she went back to The Grotto last night.*

She pulled into a rest stop on the side of the road, running to the toilet block. She barely noticed the putrid stench as she used the door of the nearest cubicle to return to Rupert's manor.

"What's going on?" Rupert rushed to meet her, "The portraits all changed so suddenly…"

"My place is on fire," Anna answered in a rush, "So's Dex's… And we can't get hold of Finn or Cassie."

Anna turned back to Rupert's front door, holding her magic key and focusing on Finn's bedroom. A lock appeared on the door but the key wouldn't turn. The smell of burning timber wafted through the keyhole before the lock disintegrated into ash.

"What does that mean?" gasped Anna. She hoped Rupert would contradict the obvious answer.

"There's no longer a door where you're trying to go," said Rupert gravely.

"What now?" Anna grasped the key so firmly she could feel its teeth breaking the skin on her palm.

"I'll go to Diana," answered Rupert, "The family needs protection."

"But-"

"I care for your friends," Rupert was pale, "but they can protect themselves in ways our family cannot. If it were up to me, you would stay here, safe, until the danger has passed."

"I'm not abandoning them!"

"I know," Rupert placed his hands on her shoulders, "Go back to your car. Drive to The Grotto. Carefully. Make sure you're not followed. Keep your phone on you and don't forget to use your pendant if you need it."

Anna didn't have time to argue. She ran back to her car and drove. The journey to The Grotto felt like an eternity. There were too many cars on the road. Police had speed traps around every corner. The clear, blue sky mocked her with its placid beauty while Anna imagined every horrible scene that might await her.

Finally, Anna sped down the long, dirt driveway to Cassie and Finn's house. There was no billowing cloud above the treeline but a smoky grey haze hovered like dry mist. The smell of burnt wood powdered Anna's lungs and made her eyes sting.

She stepped out of the car into a nightmarish scene. The ground was black. The forest was silent. All that remained standing of Finn and Cassie's home was a few charred skeletal beams. Among the debris, where the front door used to be, the metallic frame of Finn's wheelchair sat in a disfigured heap. Steel sheets from the roof covered bits of rubble like a crumpled, metal blanket. The trees surrounding the house were unnaturally close together. Their trunks were blackened, but they hadn't burned completely. *Finn.* Anna recognised his earth magic. He'd stopped the spread of the fire. He'd protected the rest of the forest, and all its inhabitants, at the expense of his own home.

"Calypso?" Anna beckoned desperately with her mind, *"Are you there?"* A distant squeak answered her call. The fruit bat's leathery wings flapped through the haze toward her. It landed on her outstretched arm, shivering despite the heat. Anna hugged him gently.
"Are you okay?" she asked, *"Did you see what happened?"*
The fruit bat nodded and closed its eyes, projecting its memory.

Gliding through the night sky. The house is quiet. No lights are on.
Figures in balaclavas emerge silently from the forest. They surround the house. One smashes a window and throws something small and round through it. BOOM. Fire. Shouting. Cassie and Finn run from the house. Cassie flicks her hands and five of the strangers go flying backwards. Finn grabs two more strangers. He tosses them across the garden. He's yelling. The fire is out of control.
Cassie sprints around the boundary of the house, chanting. The fire and smoke curl inward against an invisible barrier. She falls to her knees but

maintains the spell. Finn places his hands on the ground. The trees come to life. The largest ones form a barricade while the smaller ones spit sharp branches at the masked figures. One is hit in the chest and falls to the ground, crumbling into dust. Another is pulled underground by snaking roots. Finn returns to fighting three figures at once. Cassie drops the protective sphere. An inferno blasts into the air. Cassie draws something on the back of her hand with a shaking finger. Her nose is bleeding. A figure grabs her. Teeth pierce her neck. She gasps. Her skin pales.

She topples to the ground. Finn bounds over, half wolf, and rips the figure in two. He reaches for Cassie. Her body is limp. Her eyes are glassy.

He falls to his knees with an agonised scream. A lightning-fast figure covers his mouth with a damp rag. He struggles. Three more restrain him. His eyes droop. He goes limp. A black van pulls up. The figures load Finn into it and drive away.

Cassie is left behind.

The house burns to rubble.

The fire dies.

All is quiet.

Anna's stomach lurched. She let Calypso fly way before vomiting into the cracked remains of a potplant. She looked again at the pile of rubble. Cassie's body should be on the other side of it. She didn't want to look. Didn't want to see it. *Her.*

Despite every instinct telling Anna to stay put, her feet began walkign around the perimeter of the debris. When she reached the spot where Cassie's had fallen, there was nothing.

"Where is she?" Anna muttered to herself.

"Dex took her," a voice spoke softly to Anna's left.

Anna lunged, pinning the figure to a nearby tree. Arik appeared under her hand, gasping for air.

"What the fuck?!" Anna snarled. Gripping his neck tighter.

"P-please," he rasped, tapping her arm.

Anna dropped Arik into the soot and dust, "Talk."

Arik coughed and rubbed his neck, "I'm so sorry, Anna. Cassie is - "

"Dead." Anna finished with a prickling in her chest.

Arik nodded, "We found her here and decided it would be best to return her to her family. Dex thought you'd come so I elected to wait here while he took my car to -"

"He can't drive," Anna argued.

"It's enchanted to drive itself," Arik replied patiently, "But we couldn't send her alone so-"

"Why didn't you go instead of Dex?"

"I've never met Cassie's mother." Arik spoke softly, "Dex knows her. We agreed-"

"She can't just be gone." Anna's grief spilled over.

"I'm sorry," Arik patted her arm.

"No," Anna choked, "No, she...she..."

"She's going back to her family," Arik assured, "It's the right thing to do."

"But..but..." *She gets car sick if she's not driving.*

CHAPTER 35

Smoke and Mirrors

"Why didn't you come in?" Dex's voice was hollow as Anna pulled away from Mrs Nakamura's house.

"I'm the reason her daughter's dead," Anna answered flatly as she started the ignition, "She doesn't want to see me."

"That's not true," Arik furrowed his brow.

"If it wasn't for me," Anna kept her eyes on the road so neither brother could see the wetness in her eyes, "None of this would be happening."

"That doesn't make it your fault," Arik replied.

Anna was too exhausted to argue. They'd never understand. After all the warnings Rupert had given, she hadn't protected the people she loved from becoming collateral damage in someone's sick game. Whoever sent those masked men hadn't done it just to abduct Finn. They'd wanted Anna's attention. They wanted her under their thumb. They'd killed Cassie to show her they were serious. Or worse, because she'd been in the wrong place at the wrong time. *Why did Cassie go home last night?*

Anna stopped at a public park and used the door to a storage shed to return to Rupert's manor. Arik was enthralled by the manor but Anna barely noticed his reaction. Rupert wasn't back yet. She suspected he wouldn't return until the threat was over. At least she could trust that someone was keeping her family safe.

"What now?" Dex asked.

"We need to get Finn back," Anna muttered.

"Yeah, but...how?"

"Whoever took him *wants* me to find him," Anna thought out loud, "Once they send a location we'll make a plan."

"They think you're a super powerful sorceress," Dex reminded her, "They won't send a location. They'll expect you to find him with magic."

"I can do a locator spell," Arik offered, "I just need something of his."

"They'll probably have him magically hidden until they're ready to be found," Dex replied, "How long can you stay with us?"

"Not much longer, I'm afraid," Arik frowned, "My leave ends at sunset."

"Surely they'll try something else if I don't show up," Anna suggested hopefully, "...right?"

Dex dropped his gaze, "If you don't show they'll think one of two things. Either you're not powerful enough to do whatever spell they want or Finn isn't important enough to lure you out. In both cases..."

"They'll kill him," Anna toppled back against the wall, sliding to the floor and hugging her knees to her chest. She couldn't stop replaying the vision of Cassie's lifeless body toppling to the ground. The tiny gasp she'd made...she hadn't even had time to scream. The possibility of losing Finn too was just too much. She rested her head on her knees and closed her eyes, drifting away from reality while Dex and Arik strategised.

"...No," Dex's voice carried into Anna's mind, "If Bass is behind this, then the whole Elven army is compromised. You can't trust *anyone* else."

"I have to say something," Arik replied, "My commander knows where I've been. She'll be expecting a report on the fires. To lie would be treason."

"So, basically, you can't help at all?" Dex snapped.

"I'm *trying* to help you," Arik replied, "But Henry's life isn't the only one on the line."

"What does that mean?" Anna lifted her head.

"Any more interference from the High Fae in Underfae matters could start a war." Sharp lines cut between Arik's eyebrows, "We've been warned. The Vampiric Alliance is watching."

"Maybe the Alliance can help us?" Anna suggested.

"Or they're behind it," Arik replied pointedly, "to control you."

Anna hadn't described her vision of the attack to Arik and Dex but Cassie's wounds would have made it clear she'd been killed by a vampire. The men who took Finn weren't just random mercenaries. They were vampires. Perhaps the Alliance was behind this.

"It sounds like the war's already started then," Dex shrugged, "What's left to lose?"

"Trust me," frowned Arik, "When it's actually war, you'll know the difference."

"In other words, this is all *our problem*?" Dex spat, "Let the savage vampires and filthy werebeasts squabble amongst themselves, hmm? Keep your pretty, elven hands clean, right?"

"You know that's not how I feel," Arik sighed, rubbing the bridge of his nose.

"You've picked your side," Dex muttered.

"I'm here, aren't I?"

"For how long?"

"This isn't helping!" Anna cried, "Arik's doing the best he can, Dex, just like you!"

"What do you suggest, then?" Dex huffed.

"I was going to say we should ask Elowen for help," Anna muttered, "But if Arik's right, she won't be able to intervene either."

"For *fuck's sake*!" Dex had a manic look in his eye, "I thought you loved Finn! Wouldn't you rather get him back than play this political *fucking game*?"

"And how long do you think Finn will live if there's a war?" Anna retaliated, "He'd volunteer for the frontlines to protect his family. We can do this without making everything worse. We just have to be smart."

"Fine!" Dex threw his hands in the air, "How do we do that?"

"We have a library full of magic books," Anna spoke with more confidence than she felt, "We'll find something. Arik, go home and find out what you can. If you come up with anything…"

She was going to say *call me* but their phones didn't work inside the manor.

"Do you know how to do Cassie's hand message spell?" Anna asked.

"Yes, it's a simple transference spell-"

"Great, send me a message with any information you find, okay?"

"I will," Arik stood, "I promise."

***

Precious hours passed as Anna and Dex scoured the library for any spells that could be useful against an unknown enemy. Anna's mind kept interrupting her focus with images of what might be happening to Finn. Were they torturing him? Was he afraid? What if he was already dead?

Cassie had included the *Handy Transference Spell* in Anna's new grimoire. Anna stared at the handwriting. She'd never get another message from

Cassie again. This grimoire was all that Anna had left of her.

She and Dex practised the spell on each other for as long as they dared. Anna mastered it quickly while Dex struggled to get any results at all. He made up for his lack of magical abilities by eclipsing Anna in the reading department. He could speed-read twenty books before Anna had time to comprehend one table of contents.

"Why do they have to make spells sound so complicated?" Anna groaned, squinting at the tiny handwriting in an ancient grimoire, "And what's all this *Eye of Newt* nonsense?"

"Herbalists used to write in code," Dex answered without looking up, "Otherwise people would copy their recipes and steal their source of income. Eye of Newt means mustard seed."

"Right," Anna cocked her head, "So when it asks for Cat's Foot?"

"Ivy leaf."

"Blood of Hestia?"

"Chamomile."

"Semen of Hermes?"

"Oh, that one's not code, actually."

"Really?" Anna raised her eyebrows.

"No, it's Dill," Dex smirked.

Anna laughed and then felt ill. Cassie was dead. Finn was missing. How could she find anything funny right now? She picked up the next book in her pile, flicking aggressively through the pages. This one was more promising than the last. The spells were current, referencing ways to incorporate modern technology into spellwork. Anna scribbled notes onto scrap paper.

More hours passed. Anna's eyelids grew heavy. She looked up to see Dex asleep on a thick book, drool covering the dusty pages. Had she been asleep too? It felt late. Tabitha purred on her lap. Boggle was nowhere to be seen. Anna scratched her hand. There was a message on it.

We need to talk in person.
~ Arik

Anna relaxed her eyes to see the magic swirling through the air of the manor. She tugged on a nearby tendril of it and wrapped it around her finger, charging her spell. She replied.

Meet me in the guest's chamber where we talked on my last visit.
~ Anna

Anna approached the front door of the manor while holding her key and visualised the room where she'd spent the night pacing. The lock on the door transformed into beautifully embellished gold.

"Did you come directly from Rupert's manor?" Arik whispered in shock, looking through the open door.
Anna nodded.
"You've bypassed Bloody Mary," Arik looked pale, "And the palace security."
"I won't abuse the privilege," Anna promised.
"It's not that," Arik muttered, "I've always been told it's impossible to enter or leave our realm without Bloody Mary."
"Rufus got here through shadows," Anna shrugged.
"He what?" Arik's eyes were wide.
"At the council meeting," Anna explained, "He said he came by Shadow Walking.'
"What did the council say about that?" Arik frowned.
"They mostly seemed impressed," shrugged Anna, "Your mother seemed frustrated."
"She wasn't surprised?"
"Only when he appeared out of nowhere," Anna recalled, "But not when she found out how."
Arik looked out the window, concern contorting his face.

"Why did you need to talk in person?" Anna prompted.
Arik blinked, returning to himself. He glanced around the room and then, deciding it was safe, withdrew a thick envelope from his vest.
"I found this," he said, laying out its contents on the bed, "I have to return it before it's missed."
Anna inspected the items. The largest was a world map covered in strange symbols. Three locations had been circled in red marker. It was accompanied by a crumpled photograph of an ancient-looking spell, and an offcut of paper that said:

He has found a way to free her.

He will use the girl and her lycan prince.

"The spell is, apparently, a ritual for invoking Chaos magic," Arik looked jittery, "But it's written in an indecipherable language..."
Anna looked at the photo. The archaic lettering morphed into English as she focused on each word. The wording was alarmingly familiar.

From thy world, thy must depart.
Claim the mighty lycan's heart.
Fires dance upon the air.
Sacrifice a virgin fair.

Trust thy foe with love most pure,
Pain of loss thy must endure.
Thy mirror's captive set unbound,
The missing damsel must be found.

Seek thee out an ancient beast,
Imbibe night's power with a feast.
Blood to blood, repair the rift.
Almighty power is thy gift.

With a sickening jolt, Anna remembered where she'd seen this ritual before. Hanging on the wall in Rufus Kingsley's office.
"The map shows where ley lines intersect in the Mortal Realm," Arik shuffled the papers around. He hadn't noticed her reaction, "The ones most likely to be used for this ritual have been marked."
"Do you know who left the note?" Anna asked.
"I was fortunate to come across this much information," Arik shrugged apologetically.
"Well, thank you," Anna said, "I realise you've stuck your neck out for us. I'll make sure Dex knows it too."
"I didn't do this for you or Dex," Arik lowered his voice, "With everything that's been going on lately, it seems my mother has become more concerned with maintaining her power than protecting our people."
"You think she'd risk starting a war with the Underfae?"
"If it distracts our people from revolution, then yes," he said darkly.
"Are things that bad here?" Anna frowned. Though she'd only been in Alvara a short while, the people had seemed happy enough. Then again,

she'd only seen what things were like for those living in the palace.

"I'll keep you updated with any intel I'm able to collect," he promised, ignoring her question.

"Just be careful," she warned as they headed for the exit.

Before she could use her key to change the lock, the door opened.

"Good evening, Miss Green," the Empress smiled wickedly. She stepped into the room with two guards following close behind, "It would seem I owe you thanks. You've uncovered a traitor for me."

"I'm no traitor," Arik stepped backward, as the guards approached, "I'm trying to keep our realm safe."

"You've stolen confidential information," Aiyana spoke formally, "Conspired behind my back and allowed an outsider to infiltrate the palace. These are treasonous acts."

"M-Mother?" Arik stammered.

Anna had never seen Arik afraid. Not even when she'd strangled him. The guards looked conflicted. It occurred to Anna that they were probably friends with Arik. They might have trained together. The guards moved forward to apprehend him with grim frowns etched on their faces.

Anna stepped between Arik and the guards, "Stop!"

"Do not presume to give orders, *child*," spat Aiyana.

"Please," Anna begged, "He's *your son*!"

"I don't have the luxury of affording my family special treatment," Aiyana replied, "Nor can I gamble the safety of this realm on the whims of a vampire."

"What does that mean?" Anna eyed the Empress.

Aiyana held up the photo, "You can read the spell, can't you? Tell me what it says or I'll have both of you killed."

Anna stared at the Empress in shock. Aiyana gazed back with cold resolve.

"What makes you think I can read that gibberish?" Anna bluffed.

"If the prophecy is accurate," Aiyana seethed, "You are destined to perform this ritual."

Something moved in the corner of Anna's eye. She risked a glance past the Empress to the mirror on the dressing table. Bloody Mary winked back. Her rasping voice echoed in Anna's mind, *"I will help you,"* she promised, *"If you agree to do as I say."*

"Okay," Anna said to both Bloody Mary and Aiyana.

"Come to the table."

Anna took the photo and walked past Aiyana. She sat at the dressing table, placing it within view of the mirror.

"I need a pen," Anna turned to the room. Arik offered a marker from his pocket, staring incredulously at Anna.

"Let me use your hands." Mary's voice echoed in Anna's head.

Anna looked into the mirror. Where her reflection should have been, Mary grinned back. Anna gave a slight nod.

Her hands moved across the photo, writing words without any input from Anna. When it was done, Anna stood and passed Mary's work to Aiyana.

"*This* is the ritual of Chaos?" Aiyana raised an eyebrow sceptically.

"It is," Anna lied.

Aiyana read the words silently with a mirthless smile.

"You forgot to put in any ritualistic instructions, dear," scoffed the Empress, "You truly are a *novice* at magic. Saying these words will do nothing. Observe…"

In a condescending tone, Aiyana recited the incantation Mary had written.

"Beyond the glass where shadows reign,
I claim the power, I break the chain.
Queen of Chaos, I now decree;
I take your place, fly now, be free."

One second Aiyana was smirking derisively, the next she was gone. The guards looked frantically from the empty place to Anna. One extended his sword to her throat, "What did you do?"

"Nothing!" Anna gasped.

"She did it to herself," Mary appeared between the guards. Despite her elongated fingers and pointed teeth, she had an otherworldly beauty to her. Her previously damp hair had dried into smooth waves of indigo-blue, which she pushed aside to reveal huge turquoise eyes. Her skin now shone like an iridescent pearl, free of algae and muck. She stroked the sword at Anna's throat with an elongated finger. It transformed into a flopping silver-scaled fish. The guard dropped it and jumped backwards.

"I was bound by an agreement with the Elven Empire," Mary explained,

"and, as you witnessed, your Empress has released me. She now holds my place in the void. If you wish to see her, simply call her name three times."
The other guard approached the mirror, "Empress Aiyana," she spoke cautiously, "Empress Aiyana, Empress Aiyana."
The mirror remained blank.
"Oh," added Mary with a wink, "She's not your empress anymore. One cannot be gatekeeper and ruler at the same time. "
The guards looked at one another, neither daring to speak their Empress's name without affording her the proper title.
Arik approached the glass, "Aiyana. Aiyana. Aiyana."

The pointed features of the ex-Empress faded into view. She struggled to move in the inky darkness, kicking and punching at the nothingness that engulfed her. Her skin had turned blue and her hair had become tangled in her sharp crown. Her gown billowed around her, making her resemble an enormous angry jellyfish. Anna moved in front of the mirror, trying to assess whether Aiyana could see them. The trapped elf yelled furiously but no noise passed through the glass.
"She'll get the hang of it," Mary yawned.
"What if she doesn't?" Arik looked concerned.
"You could put her out of her misery, I suppose," Mary shrugged, "There's no time in the void, no aging, and nothing to hurt oneself with, so she won't manage it on her own. But, if you do kill her-" She looked at Arik, "You'll need another to take her place, lest the monsters of Faeden rain down upon you." She giggled.
"You can't bring her back?" The female guard asked.
"I *won't* bring her back," Mary answered in a vaguely threatening tone. She turned her back on the mirror as Aiyana faded from view.

"What happens now?" Anna looked around the room.
"It seems you require a new ruler," grinned Mary.
"Y-you intend to rule the Elven Empire?" The male guard looked terrified.
"A flattering offer, but no," Mary smirked, shifting her giant eyes to Arik. The guards looked at Arik too. He stared back blankly.
"I don't," Arik stammered, "I wouldn't presume to…We should have our people vote."
"And who will take responsibility for your people's well-being until then?" Mary prompted, "Who will ensure a vote occurs at all, instead of a mad rush for power from the lower Kings and Queens of your realm?"

Arik looked at Anna. She knew the entire realm was at stake but couldn't help but feel something had just gone right. Finally, a ruler who didn't hunger for power. Arik's fear of taking the crown only served as proof that he'd do a good job. He cared about his people. More than that, he cared about all people. This could be the first step toward the High Fae and Underfae seeing eye to eye.

But what about Aiyana? She couldn't die in the void but she didn't look comfortable. She was a cunning woman. How long would it be before she found a way to force her freedom? Anna couldn't worry about that right now. Finn was in danger and now Anna had all the information she needed to save him.

"I think you'll make a fine Emperor," Anna bowed to Arik.

The guards glanced at each other and then knelt at Arik's feet, "What are your orders, Your Majesty?"

***

Back at the manor, the rising sun illuminated the snowy forest in gold and magenta. On any other day, Anna would have found it beautiful but the sight gripped Anna's heart with fear. Finn had been gone more than twenty-four hours. At least now Anna knew who'd taken him, and where she'd have to go to get him back.

"Where have you been?!" Dex snapped.

"I left a note," Anna put up her hands defensively.

"Gone to Alvara - back later," Dex read sardonically from a scrap of paper.

"I was in a rush," Anna admitted.

"What if things went pear-shaped?" he demanded, "I wouldn't be able to help you. I can't even leave the manor without *your key*!"

"I- I hadn't thought of that," Anna admitted, feeling guilty.

"What were you even doing?" Dex sighed.

"Arik wanted to meet," Anna answered.

"...And?"

Anna recounted everything that happened from the clues pointing to Rufus to Arik's sudden rise to power. Dex looked like he might faint. Anna ushered him to the closest chair.

"So my mother is...?"

"Trapped in the void between realms," Anna finished, "I think she's meant to be the next Bloody Mary, once she's figured out how things work in there."

"She deserves it," Dex smirked, "but she won't tolerate being caged for long."

"That's a later problem," Anna rubbed her forehead. She tried to ignore the coil of anxiety wrapped tightly around her spine, "Right now, we need to focus on Finn."

"And you think Rufus took him?" Dex asked.

"It makes sense," Anna explained, "He'd hire vampires for his dirty work. They couldn't go into our houses to grab us so they set fires to flush us out. He knows how much I care about you. And he'd know where we all live from our employment records."

"But why do this?" Dex frowned, "He could just ask for your help. What the hell is he thinking?"

"I don't know," Anna sighed, "But right now all that matters is he has Finn and I'm going to get him back."

"*We're* going to get him back," Dex corrected, "Even though it's a trap and we don't know where to go."

"I know where to go," corrected Anna, "The answer was on the map Arik showed me. He said they'd circled all the likely places. One was Silverbark Ridge."

"That's where Finn's pack goes to transform."

"Exactly. It can't be a coincidence."

"Okay," Dex stood, "I've got a pile of spells neither of us can do and you've got a location that has no doors we can use for quick access. What now?"

"Now," Anna headed to the manor's door, "I need to make some phone calls."

"Okay," Dex crossed his arms, "Then what?"

"Then," Anna tried to show more confidence than she felt, "We show Rufus what this *vampiric sorceress* can do."

CHAPTER 36
The Ritual

Finn's head was pounding. Blurred stars faded into view. He couldn't move. His hands were numb. Coarse ropes dug into his skin, binding him in place.

"He's coming to again," someone called, "Should I give him another dose, sir?"

"No," replied a deep, gravelly voice, "It's nearly time. Light the fires."

Heavy footsteps receded. A colony of bats flew overhead. The droning cries of cicadas echoed through the forest. As he tried to reach out with his magic, a stabbing pain burst from the palms of Finn's hands. He winced at the silver nails protruding from his palms. His magic was blocked. He couldn't call the trees to aid him. He couldn't even transform. The beast within him thrashed and snarled. His wolf was afraid.

"It seems our girl is late," said the gravelly voice, "I hope you two haven't had a falling out."

Rufus Kingsley leaned over Finn, blotting out the stars with his cold, black eyes.

"You?" Finn struggled against the ropes.

"Me."

"Why are you doing this?" Finn demanded. Beads of sweat dripped down his neck, "Anna trusts you. Whatever you want from her...you could have just asked."

"Good to know," Rufus replied, picking at his fingernails, "Couldn't take the risk."

The odour of gasoline assaulted Finn's nostrils. Bursts of fire erupted from flamethrowers at the edge of his vision. The guns were aimed at the sky.

Coupled with the summer night, the heat was intense.

"What is all this for?" Finn choked.

"It's a coronation," Rufus smirked.

"What?"

"The Forgotten Deity's crown ring a bell?"

"That prophecy is false!" Finn yelled, "Rupert made it up."

"Actually, I made it up," Rufus replied, "Based on some very real magic."

"What?! Why?"

"I needed someone to perform the Chaos ritual," shrugged Rufus, "Someone who's *departed from this world*, as in *dearly departed*. Anna fits the bill nicely, don't you think?"

"If you needed a vampire," Finn struggled against his ropes, "Why not do it yourself?"

"Rupert refused to teach me magic," Rufus scoffed, "I had to find, or *create*, a vampire who Rupert would take under his wing without question. Imagine my delight when one of the faces from his pathetic portrait wall appeared *right in front of me* while I was looking for a new suit! I could have turned her right then and there, of course, but I couldn't risk Rupert knowing I was involved."

"So you gave her a job and... what?" Finn coughed, "Waited months to turn her?"

Rufus shrugged, "I've waited centuries for this moment, what's a few months if it ensures Rupert doesn't suspect me? Though I admit, I did get a little restless. After all that time watching and waiting, pretending to be various temps, it got old. That damned witch was always so interested in getting to know me. I had to make up a new life story every time. And Anna was so *careful*... it was hard to find a plausible opportunity to get her killed. I'd started planning a home invasion when Mr Duke's birthday plans popped up. I recommended Rock Bottom and then had a matter of hours to bring everything else together."

"You hypnotised that group of men to attack her?!" Finn spat, struggling against the ropes. He didn't care about himself anymore. He'd break every bone in his body if it meant he could tear Rufus apart.

"Of course not!" Rufus raised his hands innocently, "I *paid one of them* to rough her up a bit. He was meant to make it look like a random attack but leave her alive enough for me to turn her. I would have been her saviour. Rupert wouldn't question my involvement but I'd be her sire nonetheless.

Fucking humans. Useless. From what I can tell, the idiot used my money to get drunk with his friends and forgot his assignment completely."

"So you don't know who Anna's sire is?"

"No idea!" Rufus laughed with sickening glee, "If I hadn't made up that prophecy I'd be convinced it was fate!"

Finn's head was pounding. He tried to take a steadying breath but chocked on the petrol fumes. "Why do you need this ritual performed anyway?"

"I don't really," Rufus chuckled, "Just half of it."

Finn clenched his jaw. He was in no mood for riddles.

"When I first learned the spell existed," Rufus continued, lifting the ancient parchment into view, "I assumed I'd need the power of Chaos Magic to free my Marielle. But, as it happens, freeing her is one of the steps! Each step will grant Anna the power to complete the next so I'll be happy if she only gets halfway through before she burns out."

"You expect her to die for you?!" Finn thrashed against the ropes.

"I expect her to die for *you*," Rufus corrected, "but first, you'll die for her...It'll all be very romantic."

"What the hell does that mean?" Finn's bindings felt tighter.

Rufus leaned closer, whispering into Finn's ear, "The ritual calls for a lycan's heart and a virgin sacrifice. I happen to know your death will cover both-"

Cold flooded through Finn's body. How could Rufus know that? Had he been watching from the shadows of their bedrooms? No, he'd never been invited into his or Anna's houses. The Solstice. They'd talked about it there. Rufus must have been there, hiding in the shadows.

"-which means Anna won't need to kill you *and* some poor kid." Rufus smirked, "So, you see, I'm not a complete monster."

"She'll never do it," Finn growled.

"I can be very persuasive," Rufus smiled.

Finn stared at Rufus.

"They never should have stolen her from me," Rufus continued. He didn't seem to be speaking to Finn anymore but rather musing out loud, "She's been imprisoned for hundreds of years and, without my help, she'll be trapped forever. Am I so evil to want her set free?"

"You're murdering people in her name," Finn growled, "I can't believe she'd want that."

"She'd love it." Rufus countered, "We've killed hundreds together. When we met, *she* was a *he*, going by the name Jaynus. He transformed me into a vampire and I led his army. King Slayer, they called me...Now it's just *Kingsley*."

Finn remained silent. His ropes were loosening. Silent pops against his skin suggesting someone was cutting through the thick rope strand by strand. He didn't know who was doing it, or how, but his new plan was to keep Rufus talking long enough to escape.

"Later," Rufus continued nostalgically, "Jaynus grew bored. As immortals tend to do. He transformed himself into *Marielle*. We lived together among mortals. My secret goddess. My love. Then the elves trapped her because they were too weak, *too cowardly*, to fight for themselves. These days, her real identity has been all but forgotten. They treat her like a slave. A joke. You might know her as *Bloody Mary*."

Dozens of tiny feet skittered away from the clearing, as though the name itself caused fear in all living things. Finn had heard the tales surrounding Bloody Mary. Trapped by the Elves long ago for crimes unknown. Forced into eternal servitude as the gatekeeper between Alvara and the Mortal Realm.

"There must be another way to free her," Finn reasoned, hoping Rufus hadn't noticed the slack in his ropes.

"Not one within my control," Rufus replied.

"But-"

"Hush now," Rufus held a finger to Finn's lips, "I think I hear our girl approaching."

The roaring engine of a motorbike, Finn's motorbike, grew steadily louder as it approached. The bike stopped just short of the mercenaries. The rider dismounted and removed their helmet. Finn's heart dropped. It was Anna. She'd come alone.

"Let her through," Rufus instructed.

Anna walked slowly toward Rufus, her hands raised in surrender.

"Alright, here I am," she spoke slowly, "You got me. Now let Finn go."

"If I let him go," Rufus sighed, "You won't be able to perform the ritual."

"What ritual?" Anna raised her eyebrow.

Rufus handed her the parchment. She squinted at the spell. Finn could smell her sweet, floral scent on the breeze. He wished she'd tear up the parchment and run.

"I can't-," stammered Anna, "I won't do this. I'm not killing anyone. Especially not Finn."

"He'll die either way," assured Rufus, "But, if we do it my way, he'll come back as a vampire. You'll be able to spend eternity together. Won't that be nice?"

Anna's scent was stronger now. If he didn't know better, Finn could have sworn she was standing right next to him rather than across the clearing.

"Why are you doing this?" Anna pouted. There was something...*off* about her.

"To reclaim what's mine," Rufus replied.

Finn gasped as invisible fingers entwined with his. An unseen hand jumped to cover his mouth.

"It's me," Anna breathed in his ear, "Get ready to run."

Anna's invisible hands carefully worked on removing the silver nails that pinned Finn's hands to the makeshift altar. Across the clearing, Anna's doppelganger kept Rufus occupied.

"What if I refuse?" Other-Anna prompted.

"I'll kill you both," Rufus answered.

"Then who will do your ritual?"

"I'll find another," Rufus sneered, "You have a sister, don't you?"

Other-Anna furrowed her brow and fell silent. She appeared to be considering her options. Meanwhile, the real Anna had successfully removed the nails from Finn's hands. A blissful tingle radiated from Finn's palms where his skin was already healing. He lowered his arms as slowly as he dared, hoping the scent of his blood wouldn't draw attention.

Rufus started to turn his head.

"What about the others?" Other-Anna asked quickly.

Rufus snapped his attention back to the imposter.

"What others?" he growled.

"It turns out werebeasts don't like it much when you fuck with one of their own," Other-Anna explained. An impish grin spread across her face as the forest erupted with howls. A dozen enormous dingoes emerged from the bush, accompanied by a monstrous crocodile, and a hulking Tasmanian devil.

Finn rolled off the table. The ropes fell away from his body. From the ground, he could see they'd been gnawed apart by tiny teeth. Rat tracks led from the base of the altar into the surrounding bush.

"Run," Anna's voice whispered urgently in his ear.

Her invisible hands pushed him, but he grabbed onto them.

"Not without you," he panted.

The howling continued as the werebeasts circled closer. Finn's wolf snarled within him. He was free and thirsty for blood. Rufus was so close.

"You think my guards didn't bring enough silver bullets for this?" Rufus yelled over the clamour of the growling werebeasts.

"What guards?" Other-Anna retorted, tipping her head mockingly.

Too late, Rufus turned his attention to the perimeter where his mercenaries were positioned. Each stood with an unnatural hunch. Their heads were slumped and their bodies limp, like puppets hung on a wall. Then, all at once, they dropped to the ground.

"Finn, please!" Anna whispered desperately in his ear, "I need you to go, now!"

The fearful tremor in Anna's voice brought Finn back to himself. Despite his desire to rip Rufus to shreds, he allowed Anna to push him toward the forest. He scrambled on his hands and knees through the dirt until he was safely engulfed by his pack. An enormous dingo weaved toward him. She crouched next to him and used her teeth to toss him unceremoniously onto her back. Then she ran.

"Gemma, no!" Finn yelled, "We have to stay and fight! Take me back!"

Gemma didn't stop. The forest was a blur. She didn't slow until the sound of howls had faded. Finn toppled off her into the dirt.

"What are you doing?" he cried, "We can't just run and hide. Take me back!"

The giant dingo blinked at him with yellow eyes. With a sickening crack of bones, she transformed back into her human form. She rolled her eyes and stalked over to a nearby tree, removing a backpack from its branches. She handed Finn a bottle of water before extracting clothes for herself.

"This is your girlfriend's plan," said Gemma flatly, "Do you trust her or not?"

CHAPTER 37

Fool Proof

Anna watched Gemma carry Finn safely out of sight. Other than to whisper warnings to Finn, she hadn't taken a breath or allowed her heart to beat since entering the clearing. She couldn't let Rufus or his vampire mercenaries know she was there. But now Finn's pack was making a ruckus, that wouldn't be a problem.

"How did you- ?" Rufus was visibly shaken as he stared at Anna's doppelganger. His guards lay dead on the grass. Each soldier's heart had been ripped from their chest.

"Magic," Other-Anna shrugged savagely, "Isn't that why I'm here?"

Dex was doing a fantastic job. Rufus was convinced by the glamour spell. Jedda's coven had outdone themselves. Even Roxy's gang of vigilantes, under the same invisibility spell as Anna, had perfectly timed the mercenaries' execution with the first howling of the werebeasts.

Now, only Anna's task remained. *Neutralise the threat.*

"I didn't realise you were such a ruthless killer," Rufus squinted his dark eyes as he regained his composure.

"I'm full of surprises," Dex smirked.

Anna crept toward Rufus's turned back, slowly drawing a wooden stake from her pocket.

"I'm sorry," Rufus lowered to his knees, "I went about this all wrong. I see that now. But I think you'd agree there's no such thing as going too far when it comes to saving the people we love. Let's make a deal. Whatever you want."

Anna froze. Rufus's sudden surrender wasn't part of the plan. But she was so close. The stake was in her hand. One quick move and it would all be over. She just had to *do it*. She'd killed before. So what if he was on his knees? He'd have happily killed her.

"What I want," Dex leaned over him, contorting Anna's face into a cold, pitying stare, "Is for you to die."

Before Anna could pounce, Rufus moved faster than she could fathom. His hands were around Dex's neck. The glamour dropped. Dex was himself again.

"Where is she?" Rufus growled, tightening his grip, then shouting into the clearing, "Show yourself or I'll rip his head off!"

"No!" Dex gasped, "Stick to the plan."

Anna moved silently toward Rufus. Holding her breath, she forced her heart to stop again.

She managed to line up the point of the stake to his back, approximating where his heart would be. Her stomach and shoulder itched where she'd been shot. The wounds suddenly stung. Something moved under her shirt. *Oh, no.*

TING. TING. CRUNCH.

The bullets hit the metal on her belt before dropping into the gravel.

Rufus whipped around and, in an instant, held Anna's neck in a vice like grip matching Dex's. A wash of warm air passed over her skin - the invisibility spell had dropped. Roxy and her vampire gang were now also visible, standing over the dead mercenaries. Rufus squeezed tighter as he took in the scene.

"Well played," he smirked, "For someone who cares so much about her friends, you don't seem to mind putting them in danger when it suits you."

"Let Dex go," Anna rasped, "It's me you want."

"Make me."

"What?"

"You heard me," Rufus raised his eyebrows, "You're Rupert's apprentice. Use your magic."

Anna's plan hadn't been perfect but she'd never considered it could go so wrong. She'd sent bats to get a layout of the area. Then rats to gnaw through Finn's ropes. Jedda's coven, who'd been all too eager to get justice for Cassie, cast the world's best invisibility spell. Anna had even trusted Gemma with Finn's life! How could everything fall apart now? Dex was never meant to be in danger. If he died because of her... She didn't know what she'd do.

Rufus could easily rip Dex's head off before anyone from Roxy's gang could even take a step. Anna had to play for more time. She couldn't do magic while her mind was racing like this. She was too frantic to focus. "I- I can't," Anna breathed.

Rufus loosened his grip on her but didn't let go.

"I'm not a powerful sorceress," she admitted, "The magic I did on the solstice was a total fluke. If you have to kill someone, please...Just kill me and let Dex go."

Rufus stared at her with calculating eyes. Anna was suddenly aware of the silence surrounding them. The werebeasts had agreed to save Finn but, having done that, they must have gone. Roxy and her gang watched helplessly from the treeline. Rufus dropped Dex unceremoniously to the ground. He coughed and spluttered as he tried to pull air through his bruised, swollen neck.

"Go," Rufus barked at him, then directed his order to Roxy's gang, "All of you. Go. Now."

Nobody moved. Roxy caught Anna's eye. Straining against Rufus's grasp, Anna nodded. Roxy approached Dex slowly as Rufus watched her with terrifying stillness. He allowed her to pick Dex off the ground and carry him away. Then, in a blur of colour, everyone disappeared beyond the treeline. Rufus and Anna stood alone in the clearing. He loosened his grasp but continued to hold her in place.

"If you're not Rupert's apprentice," growled Rufus as he ripped the pendant from Anna's neck, "how did you come to have this?"

"I stole it," she lied.

Rufus barked with laughter, "You're a terrible lia-"

CRUNCH.

Anna plunged the stake through Rufus's ribcage. His hand remained wrapped around her neck as he looked down at the spike of wood and smiled.

"I'm thousands of years old," he hissed, "Did you honestly expect a splinter like that to kill me?"

With his free hand, Rufus pulled the stake from his chest and tossed it aside.

"Leave her be, Rufus," Rupert strode into the clearing.

"Speak of the devil," grinned Rufus, gripping Anna's neck tighter, "You're just in time to see your young apprentice lose her head."

"Let her go," Rupert spoke with chilling calm, "This is your last warning."

"I'll make you a deal-"

Before Rufus could finish, Rupert snapped his fingers. Anna and Rufus were blown apart by a sudden gale-force wind. Anna flew backwards, snapping through branches as she grappled for something to grab on to. She smacked into a thick tree with a crippling thump. Explosions and crashes sounded from the clearing, lighting up the sky. As she stood, eager to get back to the action, someone grabbed her arm.

"Wait," Dex whispered. Roxy and her gang hovered nearby.

"Are you okay?" Anna inspected Dex for signs of lasting damage.

"I'm fine," he brushed her away, "But you won't be if you go barging into *that*."

The ground shook. A giant cloud of dust surged from the clearing.

"I can't just sit here!" Anna pushed Dex aside.

"Anna, wait," Roxy's voice pulled a shiver down Anna's spine, making her stop. Suddenly the pieces fell into place. The shots. Jedda. Roxy. But Anna couldn't focus on that now. She had to get back to Rupert, "Don't make me stay here," Anna pleaded. "I want to fight."

"You deserve to," Roxy nodded, "Just make sure he gets what he deserves. Make sure he knows how it feels."

Another tingle ran along Anna's back, "I will."

The earth was cracked and broken. Something that looked like lava bubbled in a puddle near a jagged formation of razor-sharp ice. Broken wood protruded from the ground where no tree had been before. Rupert manipulated a snaking vine covered in thick spikes. Whenever it got close to Rufus, however, the vampire would disappear in a burst of shadow. Rupert scanned the battlefield for any sign of Rufus.

Anna was about to run over to help when her doppelganger ran onto the field instead. *Dex?* Anna's heart shot to her chest. She didn't know how Dex had reactivated the spell without the coven, or why, but she stayed hidden so she wouldn't ruin his plan. Whatever it was.

"Are you okay?" Other-Anna called as she ran into Rupert's arms.

"I'm fine," assured Rupert, "But you shouldn't be here, go back to the forest where it's sa-"

Rupert stared blankly at the Other-Anna. A trickle of blood dripped from his mouth before he crumpled to the ground. Other Anna turned with a malicious grin, raising a blood-stained hand to her mouth and licking her fingers as she transformed back into Rufus.

"NO!" Anna ran from her hiding spot but it was too late. Rupert was gone. Her blood couldn't heal him now.

Rufus stood over them. Triumphant.

Anna couldn't bring herself to move. She held her grandfather's limp body in her arms, weeping onto his still-warm chest. His sightless eyes reflected the stars above.

"I'm sorry it had to go down this way," Rufus flicked dust from the shoulder of his pristine suit, "You'll find it's easier if you just do as I say."

"Fuck you," Anna sobbed.

"I don't know why you're being so resistant," Rufus replied, "Yes, this part will be messy but I'm giving you a convenient excuse to make your boyfriend immortal. How long do you think you'll stay together while he's still aging?"

"Fuck. You." Anna scowled.

"Fair enough." Rufus slowly circled Anna.

Anna rested Rupert's head on her knee. He looked the same and yet, somehow, it wasn't Rupert anymore. Like a cardigan he'd tossed aside, Rupert was elsewhere and this was just a discarded thing he'd left behind. Anna unfocused her vision so she could watch the final dregs of energy float away from her grandfather's body. The soft golden light was nothing compared to the wellspring of energy swirling around her. The magic fight had left the clearing full of power. *Power waiting to be channelled.*

Anna lowered her head back to Rupert's chest. She gripped the tweed of his coat with white knuckles as she focused on drawing the energy into a form she could control. Unlike last time, she wasn't going to channel it through her body. She wouldn't let it burn her again. She wrapped the magic around herself like a cocoon, leaving loose threads to pull on as she needed them.

"Whenever you're ready," Rufus drawled, having seen nothing, "Let's get on with it. Sounds like our sacrifice has decided to return."

Anna could also hear the guttural growls of a large wolf. Rufus smirked as the three-legged beast crossed into the clearing. He wasn't alone. Finn's pack, in beast form, stalked in formation. Dex, Roxy and her gang followed behind.

The smile left Rufus's face when Arik, Colonel Bass and a small army of lycans in their humongous wolf forms emerged side-by-side with Ambrosia and, Anna assumed, the other members of the Shadow Tribunal.

"You think I can't take the lot of you?" Rufus scoffed defiantly. He didn't seem so confident now, "I've defeated armies. I've -"

CLANK.

Manacles of pure light encased Rufus's limbs, neck and torso. He couldn't escape into the shadows now. Anna stood, maintaining her focus on the conjured chains while considering what to do next.

"Make sure he knows how it feels." Roxy's voice echoed.

Anna exposed her fangs, "This is for my grandfather."

She forced herself into Rufus's mind, focusing on his memory of killing Rupert. She entwined her grief into the memory. Adding the pain Rupert would have felt at being stabbed. The shock of releasing Rufus had tricked him. Grim comprehension flicked across Rufus's face. He cried out in agony.

"This is for Cassie," Anna snapped her fingers, forcing him - again - to feel the pain he'd caused. Not only to Cassie but also to Cassie's mother, Dex, Anna, Jedda and everyone who cared for her.

"Please," Rufus begged, "I just wanted my Marielle back."

"She's not yours!" Anna exclaimed, "Mary's free. You did this for *nothing*."

"You're lying!" Rufus rasped, shaking his head uncertainly.

Anna nodded to Arik.

"It's true," he confirmed, "She's been free for several hours."

"N- No," Rufus stammered, "She's mine!"

"And yet..." Anna gestured around the Mary-free clearing before stepping forward and whispering, "Mary is not your property to keep. I am not your pawn to control. You've spent thousands of years using people. Hurting people. Thinking it makes you strong. Let's see how long you last when you're on the receiving end of all that pain."

Anna brought all of Rufus's memories to life, forcing him to feel every moment of fear, agony and helplessness he'd caused. From the bruises on

Dex's throat, to his mother's body tearing open to bring him into the world. "KILL ME!" He screamed on his knees, "MAKE IT STOP!"

Anna looked at Finn and his pack. They snarled, eagerly pawing at the ground.
"He's all yours."

Blood and sinew spattered the charred ground as Anna picked up Rupert's body and walked through the stunned crowd.

CHAPTER 38

What Comes Next

The manor was dark and cold. Anna had never been in Rupert's bedroom before. It was covered in books and half-finished gadgets, just like the rest of the manor. She realised with a sharp pang that those gadgets would never be finished. Rupert would never read another book or scribble another note. A cold mug of tea sat on the dresser, abandoned forever.

She laid Rupert's body on his bed. It wasn't like the movies. He didn't look like he was sleeping. His skin was ashen, turning purple and waxy. His hands were turning blue. His eyes, though closed, seemed to have sunk into his skull. Anna placed Rupert's spectacles on the bedside table. One of the lenses was cracked.

Transferring what was left of her magic cocoon into preserving Rupert's body, Anna wished she could tell her mother what had happened. Or anyone in her family. She didn't want to go through this alone. No one knew Rupert like she did, but her mother had once. How could Anna explain what had happened without breaking Rupert's promise to keep her mother blind to magic? She covered the blood-dampened wound in Rupert's chest with a blanket. It wasn't bleeding anymore.

Tabitha jumped onto the bed and pawed at Rupert's leg.
"Where's papa gone?" The cat asked.
"I don't know," Anna said, stroking Tabitha's ears.
"Will he come back?"
Anna shook her head and blinked back tears.
Tabitha lowered her head with low, sorrowful meows. Anna sunk to the floor and let the flood of grief wash over her. She cried until her throat was dry and her eyes stung.

"He's in a better place now," Mary emerged from the shadows.
Tabitha hissed and ran under the bed.

Anna jumped to her feet, "What do you want?"
Mary tilted her head, apparently confused.
"Are you here to kill me?" Anna prompted, unsure if she even cared at this point.
"I do not intend to harm you, child."
"Then what do you want?"
"To help you." The faerie spoke as though this was obvious.

"Aren't you upset about Rufus?" Anna asked sceptically.
"Why would I be upset? "
"He was your lover... now he's gone."
"He's gone from *this* realm," corrected Mary, "I'll see him again once he's settled into his next self. Hopefully, he will be less tiresome in his next form."
"Do you know where he went?" Anna frowned.
"I can guess," Mary gazed absently at the wall, "As for Rupert...I know."

She glided past Anna to sit on the bed with Rupert's body. She brushed his cheek softly with the back of her long fingers, "I transported his essence to the realm I thought he'd like best."
It hadn't occurred to Anna that Mary had access to more worlds than the Mortal Realm and Alvara.

"How did you know Rupert?" Anna whispered, suspecting she already knew the answer.
"He was my shield."
"You're the Morrigan." Anna breathed.
"I go by many names," Mary confirmed with a placid smile.
Anna felt giddy. She was sitting on a patchwork quilt, next to her dead grandfather, talking to a supremely powerful being. She should have cared more. She should be in awe, or something, but all she could think about was Rupert and what Mary, the Morrigan, had been to him.
"Why would you need a shield?" Anna wondered aloud, "You're so powerful."
"I am bound by the laws of Faeden, even here," Mary explained, "For

example, I cannot lie. I must always keep my word. I cannot accept gifts, only trade."

"So?"

"So," Mary leaned in, "A human cannot take advantage of a faerie they cannot find."

"Rupert, all the Morrigan's Shields, made sure no one knew who you were," Anna concluded.

Mary nodded, "Rufus never knew me as Morrigan. Only Jaynus and then Marielle. My true name must be protected."

"So why tell me?" Anna asked, "Do you want me to be the next Morrigan's Shield?"

Mary nodded, "You will be the last, I think."

"That's... ominous," Anna laughed nervously, "What makes you think I'll accept?"

"We made a deal," Mary inclined her head, "I help you, you do as I say."

"That wasn't-," Anna stammered, "That was just in the moment. I didn't mean- "

"Time limitations were not specified," Mary grinned with sharp teeth, "but, as a human, you are not bound by your word. If you'd prefer I choose another, I shall simply remove myself, and this place, from your memory and..."

"Wait, no!" Anna hadn't given much thought to the name of Rupert's home, *her home*, before now. Morrigan Manor. Rupert hadn't created this place, he'd inherited it. Anna didn't want to lose it. She'd already lost him. More than that, the thought of missing this opportunity made Anna's stomach coil. She'd trained with Rupert. She'd proven herself capable. She could be trusted with the Morrigan's secret. More importantly, she wanted this.

"What do I have to do?" Anna asked.

"Continue on your path," Mary answered, "Complete the ritual."

"The Chaos Ritual?" Anna jumped back, "Are you kidding me?! I'm not ripping out a lycan's heart or killing someone just because they've never had sex- "

"Those are not the requirements," Mary stared at her with bulbous eyes.

"I'm pretty sure they are," Anna scoffed.

"You will understand soon," Mary spoke cryptically and then vanished.

A scroll of ancient parchment remained where she'd sat.

The ritual.

Unable to focus on anything past confusion and grief, she left it on the floor.

***

Anna invited Finn and Dex to stay with her in the manor. She didn't tell them about Mary's visit. Things felt different, strained, between them.

Finn avoided everyone, disappearing into the vast forest surrounding the manor and only returned to shower, eat and sleep. Some nights he didn't come back at all. Anna wondered if he secretly blamed her for Cassie's death. Or was he angry she'd encouraged the pack to kill Rufus?

Either way, he was clearly having second thoughts about their relationship. She couldn't blame him. Anna barely recognised herself anymore. She missed Cassie. She missed Rupert. Her grief had made her a shell of who she used to be but it was more than that. Anna was a murderer now. Not just an inexperienced vampire who'd slipped up a few times but a powerful creature who felt no guilt over ending another's life. She'd planned Rufus's death. She plunged the stake in his chest. Sure, Finn and his pack may have *technically* ended his life, but Anna was the reason he'd begged to die. She'd destroyed him before they got a chance to.

She wasn't ashamed of who she'd become but it was unsettling how quickly she'd changed. She scrawled her first spell into her grimoire, *The Karmic Curse.*

Dex distracted himself from his grief by trying to figure out and fix all the gadgets in the house. Random explosions and electrical fires quickly became commonplace in any room he occupied. One morning, as Dex served his first successful batch of kitchen-prepared omelettes, Finn entered the kitchen with a grim expression. He was in an old wheelchair they'd salvaged from a shed at Finnegan Farm. Parts of it were rusted, and the wheels squeaked, but it was better than the melted remains of his other one.

"How're you doin', man?" Dex smiled, offering Finn a plate.

"Fine," Finn answered flatly, taking the plate.

"Do you want to talk?" Anna suggested gently, "About anything?"

"No, I- " Finn frowned, avoiding eye contact, "I need to think."

He turned back through the doorway. It felt like he was fading away. Like their relationship was drifting out to sea and, no matter how hard she swam, Anna couldn't reach it.

"I love you," Anna whispered as he passed.

He didn't reply. Anna stared after him. The silence felt...final. Her heart sank. They were done. It was just a matter of time before one of them put it into words.

"I found an interesting book in the library," Dex nudged Anna with his hip, "Come and see."

Welcoming the distraction, Anna followed Dex to an old journal sitting open on one of the cluttered desks. Looped handwriting on the first page said it was *Property of Elizabeth Bolt.*

"Your grandmother, right?" Dex prompted, "Betty?"

"I guess," Anna flicked through the pages. Scrawled notes filled the spaces around diagrams of strange creatures and unfamiliar maps.

"The Garden of Faeden," Anna read, *"is the pride of the Seeley Court. Growing in its heart, one can find The Great Tree or Tree of Life. It's fruit is said to hold miraculous power."*

"I was looking for a way to make more keys to the manor," Dex explained, "Rupert didn't organise his notes very well."

"I know it's not ideal," Anna closed the book, "But if you need me to take you anywhere, just let me know."

"Now that you mention it," Dex smiled, "I was thinking you and I might benefit from a nice distraction from ...everything."

"What did you have in mind?"

"Shopping in Paris?"

"I can only open doors I've passed through with the key on me," Anna reminded Dex, "I've never been to Paris."

"Remember the mechanism by the door?" Dex grinned, "The one Rupert used to bring Cassie here? I found a book of codes that can open doors all over the world. I just need you to get us back."

***

Paris, so full of life and beauty, felt almost cruel in its vibrancy. The bustling streets, the scent of fresh croissants, the laughter echoing from cafés, even the awe-inspiring silhouette of the Eiffel Tower. All of it seemed to mock the emptiness Anna carried inside.

Dex, filled with resilient enthusiasm, led her from shop to shop.

"Cassie wouldn't want us to mope around forever," he said, pulling Anna's hand, "She always focused on the positive, so that's what I'm going to do. I'm not dwelling on losing my best friend or my apartment burning down. I'm *celebrating* the opportunity to buy a whole new wardrobe with you."

"That's the spirit," Anna forced a smile, "I guess."

"And you're not going to dwell on everything that's gone wrong," Dex continued, "but celebrate your newfound badassery."

"Sure."

"Just let the retail therapy work its magic."

It took a while for Anna to find anything she wanted to buy but, soon enough, her arms were laden with bags of clothes and books. Most of the purchases, however, weren't for her.

"Buying gifts for Finn won't get him to open up any faster," cautioned Dex as they left a high-end boutique.

"I know," assured Anna, "But he lost everything too. He needs some essentials."

"I don't think you can reasonably argue that a couture suit falls under the category of *essential* for Henry Finnegan," Dex laughed, "When do you imagine he's going to wear it?"

Anna turned away, pretending to admire the Eiffel Tower. She blinked back a tear.

"Funerals," she answered quietly.

CHAPTER 39

A Seat at the Table

Cassie's funeral was held on a beautiful, clear morning. At least two hundred people came out to celebrate Cassie's life and mourn her passing. Dozens spoke over her grave, marked by a tree rather than a slab of stone. A Maori woman wept as she thanked the people for coming. She seemed kind. Jedda never left her side. Anna remembered Cassie's Christmas tradition.

"...Just Mum and I baking cookies and watching soppy Christmas movies..."

Anna wondered if Cassie's mother would continue the tradition alone or ignore all future Christmases. Surely it would be too painful to celebrate them.

Dex stood over Cassie's grave for a long time, blending in with the silent choir of sombre mourners. Anna watched from a distance. She didn't deserve to join the crowd, nor could she bring herself to leave. If it hadn't been for her, Cassie would still be alive. Anna shouldn't get to grieve with the others, but she should see the damage she'd caused. She wiped her face with her damp sleeve.

"Here," Finn's voice was soft. He held out a handful of tissues. Anna took them with a grateful sniff.

"Have you spoken to Cassie's mum yet?" he asked, "She wants to meet you."

"She should hate me," Anna shook her head.

"She doesn't blame you, Anna," Finn frowned, "Cassie came back to The Grotto that night because she had a bad feeling. She knew something was up. She's the reason we came out fighting. She's the reason we even had a chance."

"I'm the reason you guys got attacked," Anna argued.

"That's not fair," he said.

"It's true," Anna shrugged, "You'd be better off if you'd never met me."

"You can't honestly believe that."

"Don't you?" she whispered.

Finn looked up at her with sadness. Anna knew their relationship was over but she couldn't help getting lost in his eyes. They were a lush, green forest she wanted to explore forever. He moved closer to her. She almost dropped onto his lap out of habit. She desperately wanted to wrap her arms around him again. It was a fresh heartbreak to realise she'd have to police her behaviour around him from now on. All the little touches of affection she'd grown used to sharing with Finn were off the table. Assuming she'd get to see him at all.

"I could never regret knowing you, Anna," he answered quietly.

"But this is it, right?" Anna prompted. She knew Finn was too kind to say the words, but she needed the closure of hearing them, "You're done with me. With us?"

Finn furrowed his brow.

"I get it," Anna sniffed, "It's fine. We're done. That's fine."

She couldn't stand looking into his eyes for one second longer. She ran into the crowd, allowing herself to get lost among the sea of tearful faces.

Moving absently, she bumped into someone and turned.

"Anna?" Jedda had Cassie's mother on her arm, "Anna, this is Kiri."

Before Anna could react, Kiri embraced her in a warm hug, "Cassie spoke of you often, and always with love."

Cassie and her mother shared the same broad face and nose. Anna imagined Cassie would have eventually looked like this if she'd been given the chance to grow old.

"I'm sorry, I-" Anna stammered, sobbing like a child into the woman's shoulder, "It's all my fault."

Kiri stepped back and frowned. Anna expected to see anger in her deep brown eyes, but there was none. It seemed Kiri shared her daughter's ability to look directly into a person's soul.

"My daughter blamed herself for your death," Kiri sighed, "And now you blame yourself for hers. Meanwhile, the violent men who did all the killing are forgotten."

She took Anna's hands.

"If you wish to honour my daughter's life," she instructed, "Find a way to bring more joy into this world. More magic. More life. More love."

Before Anna could think of a reply, Kiri kissed her cheek and wandered back to the throng of people surrounding Cassie's grave. Jedda hung back.

"I need to talk to you," she shuffled awkwardly on the spot, "I've been, um, keeping something from you -"

"I know," Anna cut her off.

"You...*know*?" Jedda's eyes were wide.

"Does Roxy know?"

"Yeah," Jedda looked guilty, "But I only told her the night Cas died."

"I thought so," Anna nodded.

"Call me later, okay?" Jedda added stiffly, "We should talk more but...not here. Not now."

"Sure," Anna agreed. Jedda gave her meek smile before jogging back to Kiri's side.

Though surrounded by people, Anna had never felt more alone. She'd lost so many people. Not just to death but to secrets, lies and betrayal. She couldn't fall apart in Finn's arms anymore. She couldn't kiss his freckles or smell his hair. Shards of Anna's broken heart tore at her chest. She'd brought this on herself. Despite what Kiri had said, this *was* her fault. All the blood and death. All the pain and loss. If someone had to die, it should have been Anna. She should be the one in this grave, not Cassie. At least, if she was dead, no one else would suffer because of her.

Anna's chest was tight. She couldn't breathe. People were looking at her. They whispered behind cupped hands. She didn't stick around to listen to what they were saying.

She ran faster than the wind. She had no idea where she was going but it didn't matter. The further she could get from everyone, the better. When she finally stopped, she looked around and gave a hollow laugh. She was standing in the alley outside Rock Bottom. The exact spot where she'd been killed. She slid down the graffitied wall, replaying the final moments of her life on a loop. There was a savage satisfaction in reliving the torture. It couldn't hurt her now though. Not after Roxy had told her not to let her past, or your fear, control her.

"Is this a bad time, ?" A haughty Irish accent spoke above her.

Anna hurled herself at the stranger. She pinned him against the wall, breaking several bricks with a loud crack.

"Well, fuck me!" coughed the vampire with an unfazed grin, "Aren't you feisty!"

The vampire had short, bleached hair, thick eyeliner and a metal eyebrow piercing. His skin was unnaturally smooth but for a long white scar, which cut his face from the edge of his hairline to his chin.

"How many times have I told you not to sneak up on young ladies?" drawled the voice of a woman. Anna turned to see Ambrosia Laurant strolling toward them. She wore a glamorous black satin gown, holding a gothic parasol over her perfectly styled hair.

"Especially," Ambrosia continued, "those capable of destroying you with the flick of their wrist."

"Oomph, here's hoping," the man smirked, winking at Anna's glare.

"What do you want?" Anna glowered.

"The man in your grasp is Jasper Gadsby," answered Ambrosia, heels clicking on the pavement as she approached, "He's a fellow member of the Shadow Tribunal. We've come to invite you to join us."

Anna released her grip on Jasper. He seemed disappointed to have his feet reconnect with the ground.

"Why?" Anna demanded, "Am I on trial? Do I need a lawyer?"

"Considering what happened to your last legal advisor," Ambrosia gave a sly smile, "I doubt you'll find one willing to take you on."

"I'll take her on any time," Jasper's eyes wandered up and down Anna's figure.

"You can both fuck right off," Anna snarled, stalking away from the pair.

"We realise this is dreadful timing," Ambrosia quickened her pace to catch up, "but you are a hard woman to track down."

Anna didn't slow down.

"We wanted to let you grieve," Jasper strode next to Anna, attempting to link arms. She batted him away. He grinned, "but time is of the essence."

"How did you find me?" Anna stopped.

"The funeral," Ambrosia replied, pouting her perfect red lips, "We intended to approach you when it was over but you left rather abruptly."

"So, you've been stalking me?" Anna concluded.

"Yes!" Jasper grinned.

"No!" Ambrosia frowned at Jasper.

"A bit," Jasper winked.

"We've been discretely waiting for an opportune moment," explained Ambrosia diplomatically.

"To drag me before the Shadow Tribunal so I can… what? Promise to be good?" Anna predicted, "Only do magic *when you say so*...?"

"You misunderstand-" Ambrosia began.

"Of course," Anna rolled her eyes.

"We don't want you to *stand before* the tribunal. We want you to be part of it." Ambrosia offered her hand, "We want you to *join us*."

Anna stared.

"We're offering you a seat at the table," Jasper grinned. His scar stretched over his lips.

"Why?" Anna asked blankly.

"Why do you think?" Ambrosia smiled. The world around the stunningly beautiful vampire seemed duller by comparison.

The Helena line of vampires are known for their debilitating beauty.

Anna had reread the vampire textbooks a few times now.

"What if I told you the prophecy was false?" Anna asserted.

Jasper waved his hands dismissively, "Prophecies are nothing but bullshit with good marketing."

"What does that mean?" Anna scoffed. She didn't want to show her intrigue. Jasper was the first person from the magical community who didn't act like the prophecy was some sort of sacred calling.

"Imagine there's a prophecy that says it will rain on Christmas day," Jasper leaned forward as though explaining a devious plot, "But it doesn't...so people say it must mean *next year*, or the one after."

Ambrosia rolled her eyes as though she'd heard this before.

"Say it doesn't rain on Christmas day for a hundred years," Jasper added, "People will broaden their interpretation of the prophecy to say that confetti is a *rain of paper*. They throw a parade. Paper rains down. *Huzzah!* The prophecy has come to pass!"

"So, you don't care about the prophecy," Anna concluded.

"We do," Jasper assured, "Not because it's real but because most people believe it is."

"Having you in the tribunal looks good for us," Ambrosia summarised, "The Underfae have been restless for some time. Non-vampires, particularly werebeasts, have demanded a voice. You could be that voice."

"Or you could have a werebeast on the tribunal," suggested Anna, "And a representative for every other type of Underfae."

"We are not a democracy," Ambrosia tilted her chin upward, "We do not answer to our subjects. We lead them. We protect their freedoms from the constricting rule of the High Fae and they should be grateful."

"But we'd like to avoid an uprising if we can help it," Jasper added.

"So, if I accept," Anna stopped, turning to face Ambrosia and Jasper, "Would I be an equal member or just a publicity token?"

"Officially, you'll be equal to the rest of us," Ambrosia raised an eyebrow and shifted her gaze sideways.

"But, unofficially…?" Anna raised an eyebrow.

"The Shadow Tribunal has had one seat per clan since it formed," Jasper shrugged, "Some members don't want to change things. They'll probably try to squash your ideas. And you."

"It'll be standard hazing," Ambrosia assured, "I faced quite a bit of resistance when my predecessor retired, as did Jasper when he took his seat."

"We all saw what you did to Rufus, though," added Jasper, "You'll be fine."

"You're not mad I killed him?"

"Rufus Kingsley's demise diverted a major headache," said Ambrosia.

Anna almost laughed. If by *headache* Ambrosia meant war between Vampires and High Fae, or an uprising from the werebeasts, then yes. Anna had diverted a headache.

"He's been a pain in our collective asses for a while," added Jasper, "But he was old as hell so none of us knew how to kill him. Kudos on that."

"You're welcome, I guess," Anna felt strange accepting praise for murder.

"So, what do you say?" Jasper asked with a glint in his eye.

Anna looked from Ambrosia's porcelain face to Jasper's scarred grin. If there was no chance the other Underfae would get representation without her, what else could she say? She wanted to make the world better for people like Finn. She wanted everyone to feel safe and protected.

"Fine, I'm in."

CHAPTER 40

The Talk

"Does this mean you won't be working in our little office anymore?" Dex pouted over blood and crumpets in the library while Tabitha rubbed against their legs.

"I'll be in the same building," assured Anna, "Mostly working with Ambrosia"

"I guess *Kingsley & Laurant* will just be *Laurant* now," Dex laughed.

"Who knows," Anna gulped down blood like a shot.

Finn appeared at the edge of the sofa, "Can I talk to, you Anna?"

There was an off-putting tremor in his voice.

"Uh, sure…" Anna followed Finn out of the room, glancing at Dex who shrugged quizzically.

They didn't speak until they'd entered the training room and closed the door. Finn's whole body was tense. His cheeks were flushed red.

"Finn?" Anna asked, "Are you okay?"

"No!" he snapped, "Are you serious?!"

"What?" Anna took a step back.

"*We're over?!*" Finn exclaimed, "Just like that! You didn't just dump me, you decided - *for me* - that *I'm* done with *you!*"

"Aren't you?"

"No!" Finn yelled, "Of course not!"

Anna couldn't believe her ears. She frowned, "But…you haven't spoken to me all week. You've barely even looked at me."

"I told you I needed to *think*," he exclaimed, "I was *thinking*. I needed time to figure some things out."

"If it takes *days* to figure out if you still want to be with me," Anna asserted,

"Then the answer is obviously no."

"I wasn't thinking about that," Finn rubbed his forehead, "Of course, I still want to be with you. I love you."

"Really?" It was a struggle to hide her smile. She'd thought he was done with her and yet here he was, saying he loved her like it was a given.

"I was thinking about losing Cassie and The Grotto," Finn continued, "and...I was mad at you but I didn't know why. I wanted to figure it out before I talked to you.'

"It's because everything would be fine if I- "

"No," Finn insisted, "I don't blame you for what happened."

"But-"

"Please," Finn implored, "Let me finish."

"Okay," Anna took a step forward.

"You think I'm weak."

"What?"

"When you untied me," said Finn, "We could have fought Rufus together but you had Gemma carry me off. I love that you came to save me but I hate that you *always have to save me*. You sent me away like some fragile, helpless thing. Is that how you see me?"

"No!" Anna exclaimed, "Not at all!"

"Then why?"

"Because Rufus needed you for the ritual," Anna thought that was obvious, "Getting you away from him, and me, was the smart move."

"You could have *died*, Anna," Finn's voice was hollow, "I couldn't save Cassie but I'm not useless."

"I don't think you're useless," Anna took another step closer, grabbing Finn's hands, "I saw what happened when you and Cassie were attacked. You were incredible."

"It wasn't enough," Finn scowled, "It's never enough. That's the problem."

"Don't be so hard on yourself," whispered Anna.

"But it's true!" Finn exclaimed, "Do you know how exhausting it is to constantly hold back every negative emotion, to keep my wolf in check, to maintain the peace, all while people treat me like I'm helpless and weak? Then, when I finally get a chance to prove myself... I fail. I don't think I'm weak but maybe I am. Either way, I hate knowing you think of me that way."

"I don't!" Anna exclaimed, "I've never thought of you like that. Don't you

371

remember the solstice?"

"When you saved me?" Finn replied flatly, "And my whole pack."

"I saved Toby *from you* that day," Anna reminded him, "You would have killed him, and probably Dane too... But I'm talking about after that. When you told Dex to take me and run."

"What about it?" Finn looked at her with renewed interest.

"You were hurt. Bleeding," Anna touched his chest, "The last thing I wanted to do was leave you there but you told me to go so I did. Why did you want me to go? Did you think I was weak?"

"No," Finn said, "Bass wanted you, not me, so -"

"Exactly," Anna squeezed his hands, "Getting you out of there was important because the ritual couldn't happen without you. I figured, even if things went wrong, Rufus would have to keep me alive until they could find you, or someone else, to sacrifice. Then you'd have time to rescue me from him."

Finn raised his eyebrows, "Part of your plan was to have *me* save *you*?"

"It was a contingency plan," Anna admitted, "But yes."

Finn smiled. His shoulders had relaxed. He pulled Anna toward his broad chest. It was bliss to be in his arms again. Every building in the world could burn and she'd still have a home in his embrace.

"I admire your strength," whispered Anna, "and I have never, *ever* thought of you as weak or fragile."

"Really?" Finn smiled.

"Really," assured Anna, resting her head on his shirt, "Are we okay now?"

"I mean," Finn wrapped his arms around her, "I don't love how easily you gave up on us."

"I'm sorry," Anna cringed, "Gemma said some things at the solstice... I guess I talked myself into thinking you'll be happier without me."

Finn frowned, "What did she say to you?"

"It doesn't matter," Anna tried to smile, "I don't think she's over you."

Finn leaned back, looking Anna in the eye, "What did she say?"

"That I'll ruin your life," Anna shrugged, "That you'd be happier with someone else."

"Anna," Finn took her hands, "I love *you*. No one else can make me as happy as you do-"

"That you want children."

Finn paused.

Anna instantly wished she could take it back. The words hung in the air between them.

"She shouldn't have told you that," Finn answered stiffly.

"But you do." Anna surmised.

"Do *you* want kids?" Finn asked.

"I don't know," grimaced Anna, "It's more complicated for me...What I want doesn't matter right now. We're talking about you."

"It matters to me," Finn pulled Anna's hand to his chest, "You. Me. Us. It's all the same conversation. When I told Gemma I wanted to be a father, I was venting my frustrations about how becoming a werebeast had ruined my life. I was telling her how I didn't want to spread the curse to my kids. I assumed I would have to try to adopt someday but, being a single man with a low-paying job, I didn't like my chances. I'd given up hope that I'd ever find someone. I thought I'd be alone forever. Things are different now."

"But you still definitely want kids?" Anna concluded.

"It's so early for us to be talking about this," Finn sighed, "but yeah, one day. Do you?"

"I guess?" Anna shrugged.

"Can you do something for me?" Finn said gently, tucking a strand of Anna's hair behind her ear, "Think about whether or not you want to be a mother. With or without me. You need to be *sure.*"

"I will," Anna blinked. Her answer could mean the end of their relationship. Kids aren't something you can compromise on. You either have them or you don't. What would her life look like if she had a child with Finn? Would they need to adopt? Would it be a human child? Would she get to spend a few decades playing Happy Family and then have to watch them age and die while she lived on for centuries?

"When do you want an answer?" Anna asked.

"Whenever you're certain," Finn kissed Anna's cheek, "Like I said, it's way too early to be talking about stuff like this."

Anna leaned into Finn's chest, "You're right, we've got time."

"One more thing..." Finn added in a whisper.

"Anything," Anna smiled, happily breathing him in.

"Let me teach you how to fight," he said, "And next time something happens, we face it together. Deal?"

"Deal," Anna grinned, looking around the training area, "Should we start now?"

Finn took Anna through a few basic defensive moves.
When she'd mastered them, he pretended to attack her in slow motion.
..*Palm Heel Strike, Groin Kick, Hammer Fist Strike, Eye Gouge...*
Anna fought him off over and over until the moves started to feel instinctive.
They sped things up, bit by bit.

The training was more exhausting than Anna had anticipated but it turned out physical activity served as a welcome distraction from grief.

"You know," Dex crunched into an apple from the doorway, "There are better ways for a couple to get sweaty and breathless."

CHAPTER 41

Fire in the Air

It was New Year's Eve. Anna admired the city skyline from the Kingsley & Laurant rooftop garden. Screams of drunken laughter echoed from the streets below as people gathered to watch the fireworks. She turned to Finn, sprawled on a makeshift nest of pillows and blankets.

He dipped a juicy red strawberry into a pot of melted chocolate. Pink juice dribbled down his chin as he bit into it. He scrambled to grab a napkin before the juice stained his shirt.

"Are you trying to seduce me?" Anna laughed.

"That depends," Finn blushed, wiping his face, "Is it working?"

"Maybe," Anna winked, skipping over to join him.

She kissed him lightly, licking strawberry juice from his lips. Finn closed his eyes, lowering his mouth to meet hers.

"This was a great idea," Anna whispered, "The stars are beautiful."

"Just like you," he gave a cheesy grin.

Anna crinkled her face and stuck out her tongue.

Finn laughed, "Ooh, even better!"

She looked into his eyes. They sparkled in the candlelight. He pulled her onto his lap and kissed her cheek. His pupils expanded as his smile shifted into hunger. He kissed her again with urgency. His hands slid to her hips, pulling her into the heat of his body. Anna quivered at the sudden intensity. Sparks of desire danced across her skin. The delicate scent of strawberries lingered in the air, mixed with anticipation and lust.

"Finn?" Anna whispered.

"Mm?"

"Remember when you said you always have to hold back?" She undid the buttons on his shirt, "and had to resist your *animal urges*?"

"Don't wuh- worry about that," Finn's breath caught as Anna caressed his neck with her tongue.

"I'm not worried," Anna continued kissing her way down Finn's chest, "I don't want you to worry about it either."

"How- fuh," Finn gasped as Anna undid the button on his pants, slowly unzipping, "H- how do you mean?"

"I want you to let go," Anna whispered, "Don't hold back."

She slid her hand under the waistband of his underwear. He was already hard. Anna pulled him free of the binding fabric.

"Oh, fuck," Finn whimpered as she engulfed him with her mouth.

It was a tantalising power to make him twitch at her lightest touch.

His fingers traced her spine and tangled in her hair. He shrugged off his shirt. The candlelight accentuated the plains and valleys of his muscular chest.

With a grin, Anna pulled him on top of her. His eyes flashed with the golden amber of his wolf. He kicked off his pants and buried his face in her neck, inhaling her scent.

"Mmm," Anna clawed her fingers down his back.

Finn ripped open her dress. Tiny clicks sounded in all directions as a rain of plastic buttons hit the tiles.

"Is this what you want?" Finn whispered, nipping at her exposed skin.

"Mmmore," she moaned.

A guttural snarl erupted from deep within Finn's chest. He rolled Anna on top of him. Anna leaned back. Unclasping her bra and tossing it aside. Finn pulled her forward, burying his face in her breasts. She wrapped her thighs around him, pulling up so her nipples hung above his licking, nipping mouth. Teasing him. Just out of reach. With a strangled moan, he pulled her closer. Burying his face in her again.

Finn sat up, pushing her hips down his torso until she was pressed against his crotch. She could feel him, hard and pulsating. Only her thin, cotton underwear separated them. He pressed his lips together, lowering Anna onto her back and then pulling the fabric slowly down her legs with excruciating restraint. Her heart pounded. Finn knelt at her feet, slowly stroking his hands along her legs before parting her knees with sudden ferocity. Anna gasped with delight.

He licked his lips, admiring the view between her thighs. She was dripping wet. The cool air clung to her exposed skin. At last, Finn pounced with a hungry snarl. Anna squealed as his touch engulfed her senses.

His tongue.

His fingers.

His teeth.

Anna lost track of which parts of Finn were doing what.

All that mattered was his spine-tingling, leg-trembling touch.

Shimmering ecstasy bubbled within her.

He coaxed her to release.

Every touch caused new ripples of sensation.

Every lick pushed her closer to the edge.

And then...

The stars exploded...

"FUUUUUCK!" Anna couldn't be sure if she'd yelled out loud or in her head but she didn't care. Dizzy euphoria crashed through her like a tsunami. Shuddering spasms rippled through her, lapping back over themselves as they returned to their point of origin before flowing out again.

"Did you just...?" Finn whispered.

Unable to form words, Anna nodded, pulling his face to hers for a hungry kiss.

A wicked grin spread across Finn's lips. He traced his finger from the nape of Anna's neck to her belly button. Anna's breath caught. With renewed intensity, he dove back in.

Tongue...

Fingers...

Teeth...

"Oh my GOD!" Anna moaned. Her fingers ripped through the picnic blanket.

Finn was insatiable. He made her squeal and squirm again...

And again...

It was coming in waves now. Floods of ecstasy washed away her senses, flowing through her with toe-curling pleasure. Ebbing just long enough to make her thirst for more.

Again.

Again!

She melted into a puddle of orgasmic delight.

"That was a good warm up," Finn stood with teasing grin, allowing Anna to catch her breath.

Gentle light danced on his perfect, glistening body. His eyes traced every inch of Anna's blushing skin. Her legs were jelly. She reached for him, desperate to feel his touch on her skin again. He adjusted the strap on his prosthetic and then leaned down, scooping her up as though she weighed nothing.
"Have I worn you out?" he kissed her cheek softly.
"Momentarily," Anna smiled.
He let her feet fall to the ground, holding her waist as he led her in a gentle waltz.
"I thought you didn't dance," Anna chuckled.
"Only when I'm naked," Finn winked.
Anna grinned.

His grip tightened on her waist. Anna leaned into him. The tips of her nipples brushed against his bare chest. He pulled a long, sensual kiss from her lips. Anna pressed against him. He moaned, pushing her against the closed elevator doors. The cold metal sent a thrilling shock through Anna's system. She was ready to melt again.
Anna curled one of her legs around his waist. He released a guttural moan as she rubbed her wet opening along his shaft.
Up and down, pulling him closer.. and closer...until he was inside her.

Finn gasped. He pressed his forehead to hers in a shuddering fever. She wrapped her other leg around him. He held her weight effortlessly, thrusting into her. She moaned at the sensation of feeling Finn inside her, against her, all around her. She bit her lip to steady her breath. She could feel another tidal wave building. But it was Finn's turn.
Finn moaned and grunted as Anna trembled against him. He stepped back from the wall, still holding Anna as he dropped onto their nest of pillows.

Now on top of him, Anna angled her hips to take his full length inside herself. She thrust against him. He gasped and moaned.
She rode him through another orgasm while fireworks exploded overhead.
Bouncing.
Squeezing.
Kissing

Licking.

Finn gasped, "I'm... I'm about to - "

His eyes rolled back in his head. His body shuddered. His breath caught in his throat and a deep, growling grunt erupted from his chest. Anna allowed the final wave of pleasure to consume her before collapsing on his chest in a sweaty heap.

***

Most of the following morning was spent in bed, though neither Anna nor Finn got much sleep. Eventually, however, their growling stomachs forced them to venture downstairs. Anna consumed a full bottle of blood and left Finn to scarf the contents of the fridge while she searched for Dex. She found him reading on a sofa in the library with Tabitha purring on his chest.

"Morning," smirked Dex, "Or is it afternoon now?"

"Who cares?" Anna responded with a dreamy smile, "How was your New Years?"

"Clubbing with Roxy," Dex yawned with a weary grin, "She's hardcore. I need to up my game."

"I'm glad you had fun," Anna chuckled.

"She asked about you," he continued, "Finn should watch out, I think she might have a crush on you."

"Should I be worried?" Finn appeared at Anna's side carrying a large mug of coffee and a bowl of scrambled eggs.

"Well, actually..." Anna bit her lip, "I've been meaning to tell you both something."

Finn's smile faltered.

"It's nothing like that!" Anna laughed, "I just know why I'm on her mind, that's all."

She looked apprehensively from Finn to Dex.

"Well?" Dex raised his brow.

"You can't tell anyone," warned Anna, "Promise?"

"Cross my heart," swore Dex.

"I promise," Finn replied with a furrowed brow.

"She's my sire," Anna confessed, "Accidentally."

"Come again?" Dex blinked.

"Roxy and Jedda had an arrangement," Anna explained, "Roxy would supply Jedda with vampire blood, which Jedda used to add a little *euphoric kick* to her cocktails at Rock Bottom. An added benefit was the healing powers stopping people from getting hurt in the mosh pit or overdosing. And I'm sure it generated great tips."

"Holy shit," Finn huffed, "That is *not* okay! She was drugging people!"

"I mean…" Dex crinkled his nose, "It's not like vampire blood is *harmful*. It heals you and puts you in a good mood… I get it."

"*Seriously?!*"

"Consider this," Dex held up his finger, "Anna wouldn't be here right now if Jedda hadn't slipped her Roxy's blood."

"That doesn't make it okay," Finn looked conflicted, "People deserve to know what they're drinking."

"She's stopped now," Anna hugged Finn's arm.

"What does this mean for you and Roxy?" Dex asked.

"She's taking some time to figure things out," Anna replied, "She said the idea of controlling me, or anyone, makes her feel gross so she's planning to avoid me until she knows how to ensure I have free will. She doesn't want to slip up and tell me to do something instead of asking."

"And no one can know?" Dex prompted.

"Preferably not," replied Anna.

"Because of the *infamous prophecy*?" Dex guessed.

"Among other things," Anna shrugged, "It makes Roxy a target and complicates things with the Shadow Tribunal. I'm meant to be *clan-neutral* but I'm part of the Ferosha bloodline."

"I still can't believe you agreed to join them," Finn scooped scrambled egg into his mouth.

"I can advocate for unrepresented Underfae," rationalised Anna, "It's about time everyone started working together. I'm thinking of accepting the Elven Ambassador role too."

"What?" Dex sat up. Tabitha bolted from his chest with an angry hiss.

"Arik's been supportive and it makes sense, right?" Anna shrugged.

She didn't want them to know how much she wanted this. She'd never been one to care about careers and status. She'd always thought positions of power were for workaholics or egomaniacs. But this was *important*. She could bring people together. Encourage communities to be more open minded and supportive of one another. It was one thing to wish for world peace and another to actually work towards it.

Whether she became a mother or not, she wanted the world to be safe for her family. For everyone's families.

"I guess," Dex slouched back on the sofa.

"Are you sure about all this extra work?" Finn murmured, "It's a lot to take on and I know you prefer the quiet life."

"I think my quiet life is over," Anna sighed wearily, but added, "I want this. I'll need your help though."

"Anything," Finn kissed her forehead.

"Same!" Dex blew several exaggerated kisses through the air, "Whatever you need!"

"Thanks," Anna beamed, "What are you reading?"

Dex held up his book with an impish smile.

"It's called *Power of the Flesh: Sex Magic through the Ages*," he mused, "I picked it out for the illustrations but it's quite an interesting read."

"I'm sure," Finn blushed.

Dex tilted his head, staring at Finn with renewed interest. A wide grin branched across his jawline, "So, Anna sacrificed a virgin after all, eh?"

"Shut up," Finn smiled bashfully at the same time Anna scoffed, "What are you talking about?"

Dex flipped to a page near the beginning of the book and read aloud:

"Sex can be defined as... Blah, blah, blah...In the context of Sex Magic... Yadda, yadda...The magical energy created by orgasm can fuel extremely potent spells. This energy is never more powerful than when one or more participants are experiencing sex for the first time. While many believe the concept of a 'virgin sacrifice' originates in blood magic, practitioners of sex magic argue that one's sexual experiences do not manifest in the blood therefore sacrificing a virgin on an 'altar of lust' is the only magically relevant practice in this area..."

Dex snapped the book shut, "You get the idea. There's one less virgin in the world."

"Come off it," Finn was bright red now.

"I told you it's an interesting read," Dex shrugged.

Anna's heart was racing.

"I need to check on something," she announced, untangling herself from Finn's arms and running from the room.

"Is everything okay?" Finn called after her.

"Yeah, yup," Anna waved dismissively over her shoulder, "Be right back!" She ran to Rupert's room. His body was still cocooned in Anna's magical preservation spell. She groped under the bed until her fingers brushed the rough paper of the ancient scroll. Sitting on the musty grey carpet, she studied the ritual with fresh eyes.

"Mary, Mary, Mary?" Anna gasped.

"You only need to say it once," Mary sprawled on the bed next to Rupert's magically preserved body, running her hand over the cocoon. "Though I'm thinking of changing myself again. This form, and its name, have become tedious. I just can't think of who to be..."

"Does this ritual need to be in order?"

"It's the *Chaos* Ritual," Mary raised an eyebrow, "Why would it be orderly?"

"Sacrificing a *virgin fair*," Anna read in a rush, "and claiming a lycan's heart. That's Finn, isn't it? When we... Under the fireworks last night, those were *fires dancing upon the air*?"

Mary smiled.

"Why is it in riddles?" Anna exclaimed.

"Faeries cannot lie," Mary stated, "but we use words to our advantage. Understanding that things are not always as they appear is important for any faerie spell."

"So, it can be interpreted in different ways?" Anna nodded, "Just like a faerie's word?"

"Exactly," Mary slid from the bed, joining Anna on the floor.

"Does the first line mean death?" Anna reread the line, "Departing this world?"

"Departing *your* world," Mary corrected, "It could mean death... But you lingered in your world after you died."

"But I've *departed my world* by being here though, right?" Anna guessed, "And visiting the Elven Realm?"

"Indeed," Mary looked thoughtfully into space, "It could mean that."

"Or it could mean something else?" Anna questioned, "Something that I haven't done yet?"

"Possibly."

Anna scanned the remaining lines of the ritual.

Trust thy foe with love most pure.
She'd trusted Gemma to take Finn away from Rufus.
Pain of loss thy must endure.
Rupert. Cassie.
Thy mirror's captive set unbound.
Mary.

The missing damsel must be found.
"Who's the missing damsel?" Anna questioned.
"Time has not revealed that yet," Mary shrugged.
"I thought you were going to help me," Anna complained.
"And I shall," Mary picked dirt from her sharp fingernails, "When you're ready."

Mary glanced at the last line of the ritual.
Almighty power is thy gift.
"What's the secret meaning behind that?" Anna asked. She looked up to find Mary had, frustratingly, vanished once again.

CHAPTER 42

Several Months Later

Laurant & Green was an elite, multi-billion dollar company. What the company did to earn its fortune, however, was frustratingly unclear to the general public. Anna strode across the lobby in her designer jumpsuit. Her knee-high combat boots made no noise as she crossed the shining marble floor.

"Any messages, Jackie?" The receptionist jumped at Anna's sudden appearance.

"Miss Green!" Jackie's Unseeing eyes shot from Anna to the computer, "Wallace has all the professional enquiries. Several people sent condolence messages and flowers for your grandfather. I've forwarded those to your office."

"Great, thanks," Anna checked her watch, "Can you let them know I'm heading to the meeting now?"

"Will do," Jackie picked up the phone as Anna breezed past her into the elevator.

In the months since she'd joined the Shadow Tribunal, Anna had yet to attend a meeting where they didn't try to dick her around. Today was no exception. It had been scheduled hours after the details of Rupert's funeral had been announced. She knew better than to think the clash was accidental. The conniving vampires obviously wanted her to miss the meeting. Perhaps they wanted to vote on something that wasn't in the best interests of non-vampires. Maybe they just wanted to shut her out for fun. Either way, she'd begrudgingly left her family mourning over Rupert's grave so she could be here on time.

"Anna!" Wallace Finnegan ran over with his massive binder as she stepped from the elevator, "They changed the location from here to the chambers in Romania."

"Of course they did," Anna rolled her eyes, pulling her key from the chain around her neck.

"Doesn't that only work if you've been there before?" Wallace frowned.

"Ambrosia gave me a tour of all the VA-owned facilities before I hired you," Anna smiled.

Ambrosia had become one of Anna's closest friends. She'd trained Anna on the procedures of the Tribunal and always offered a friendly shoulder for Anna to cry on. In the initial week of Anna's new role, she'd needed that shoulder a lot. Now, she and Ambrosia were equals. Ambrosia handled the PR for the Vampiric Alliance while Anna managed communications.

She'd arranged meetings with werebeast packs around the world, listening to their grievances and suggestions. They didn't ask for much. They were more concerned with being heard than anything else.

The other Underfae were a different story. She'd been overwhelmed with phone calls and emails from hedge witches, ghouls, succubi, and more. All desperate for support.

In the end, she'd set up a streamlined system of contact teams in each capital city. Most Underfae just needed counselling or verbal support. Others, with big ideas or serious problems, were escalated to Anna. She'd work with them to find solutions. Often appealing to the Tribunal for support. Though it was painful to get a majority vote on her side, she was learning how to best appeal to each member. Her latest success had been commissioning a sister app to the BloodBank delivery system for ghouls, where they could sign up to receive organs from medical waste. They needed to consume dead human organs to survive and, until now, had been resorting to grave digging. Not only had the app helped the ghoul community, the Vampiric Alliance now had a new stream of revenue.

Wallace handed Anna a thick manilla folder, "The meeting agenda's stapled on the internal. Background notes are sorted in order of proceedings. Feedback from Henry and Dex are on post-its throughout. Here's a pen."

"Thanks," Anna flicked through the file and then opened the nearest door, stepping into Romanian VA Council Chambers.

The temperature plummeted. The chambers were deep within an ancient castle, lit by candles along the rough, stone walls.

"Right on time," Ambrosia smirked triumphantly. She stood up from a large, U-shaped table in the centre of the room. Six others, including Jasper, turned their attention to Anna. They each sat in matching throne-like chairs, arranged evenly around the outer edge of a U-shaped table. Each had a different animal carved into the back of it, representing their vampiric bloodline clan. A cheap, fold-out chair had been added for Anna. She smiled and shook her head.

"Ms Green," a round, ruddy-faced man gave a stiff smile, "What a relief you were able to attend."

Vlad Raynor represented the Tantalus clan. Anna couldn't help but notice how similar he looked to the stocky boar carved into his throne.

"The pleasure is all mine, I'm sure," Anna replied diplomatically, walking toward her chair. She pulled on the invisible cocoon of magic she'd taught herself to maintain at all times. Flicking her wrist, she turned the fold-out chair into a throne equally ornate to the others with a wolf's head carved into the top, "Shall we begin?"

The council stared.

They hadn't seen her perform magic since her showdown with Rufus.

"Yes...Well. Right," Vlad stammered, "Camilla?"

All heads turned from Anna to a woman with skin as dark as a mine shaft and a snake-like crown of woven braids. She sat below the symbol of a lion. *Narcissa clan.*

"By all means," Camilla spoke softly, inclining her head respectfully in Anna's direction, "Let's proceed."

"First on the agenda," Ambrosia began, "Our PR has taken a hit over this missing children issue. The count is up to five. All were taken from the safety of their bedrooms. Parents were home at the time. No sign of intruders. The victims were all under the age of three."

"This sounds like a problem for the human authorities," Vlad scoffed.

"Yeah, who cares?" Jasper yawned, "If they're breaking into human houses, it's obviously not vampires."

He'd changed his appearance three times since Anna had last seen him. Today, his hair was jet black and his skin caramel brown. His eyes had switch from blue to violet and his cheekbones and nose were sharper. If it hadn't been for the telltale scar crossing his face, Anna wouldn't have recognised him at all.

"We should all care," Ambrosia answered, "The Underfae are being blamed. Everyone wants answers."

"Considering the witches can revoke the magic in our Sunlight Sigils whenever they please," Camilla mused, "it would be wise to take this matter seriously."

"We have a witch of our own now," Vlad shifted his gaze to Anna, "Why should we continue to appease those demanding hags?"

"I have neither the time nor the interest in replacing the thousands of witches *who are kind enough* to provide services to the Underfae," Anna retorted, "Though I have received intelligence from the Elven Empire on this matter. Assuming you care enough to hear it?"

"How wonderful that your role as ambassador has proven beneficial already," Camilla murmured, shifting her eyes to Ambrosia.

When Anna had accepted the role of Elven Ambassador, rumours had flown in both communities that Anna was a spy. She and Arik simply worked too well together. Dex had been welcomed back to Alvara with open arms. Several balls had been held in his honour and, though precious few Underfae attended, both High Fae and Underfae had been invited.

"What information have *our new friends* gathered?" Ambrosia replied pointedly, returning Camilla's stony gaze.

Anna walked to the centre of the room to present her findings.

"A nanny cam recorded the abduction," she reported. Anna held up her phone for the council to watch. Their superior vision negated the need for a projector or larger screen. The infant appeared to speak to an unseen figure in the floor-length mirror of their bedroom. He nodded and then climbed through the glass. He didn't return.

"So it's their fault?" Vlad gave a bellowing laugh as Anna returned to her seat, "The former Elven Empress is collecting children in the void. Our PR problem is solved!"

"Maybe so," Camilla narrowed her eyes, "But Aiyana is smart. She plays a long game. Why would she do this?"

"Isn't it obvious?" Jasper drawled, "If you want to be fired, do a catastrophically bad job. She just wants to be released."

"We've gone from discussing a human problem to an elf one," whined Kamiko. Sitting under the draconic symbol of the Midas Clan. Kamiko was the oldest member of the council but she looked, and often behaved, like a spoilt ten-year-old, "Can we move on to something that matters?"

"If the elves plan to release Aiyana then this is the most important issue on our agenda," Camilla replied, "With no gatekeeper, faeries would regain access to the Mortal Realm."

"Five missing children is nothing compared to what they'd do," Ambrosia agreed, "and we'd be powerless to stop them."

"What's the solution then?" Vlad prompted, "We can't control what the elves do. Not that we haven't tried…"

"We should send our Ambassador to retrieve the children," Kamiko suggested with a sinister grin, "as a gesture of goodwill."

The other council members nodded.

"How do you propose I do that?" Anna frowned.

"You elected to act as peacekeeper," Camilla shuffled her papers as though the matter was settled. "Figure it out."

"Neither Cassius nor Kareem have spoken on this matter yet," announced Ambrosia, somewhat frantically. The group turned to the thrones opposite Anna. On one, a swirling, spectral form filled the space under a jellyfish carving. Leader of the Morpheus clan, Cassius travelled via astral projection, exploring people's dreams and feeding on the energy of their hopes and fears. His body rarely left its resting place. Today was no exception.

"Any thoughts, Cassius?" Ambrosia prompted.

"Perhaps you could locate Bloody Mary," wheezed the swirling air, "She inspires the most delicious nightmares…And, of course, she once held the power Aiyana now wields. She may have advice."

"Good idea," Anna replied, masking her frustration. Despite multiple attempts to conjure the faerie for guidance, Anna hadn't heard from Mary in months.

"Kareem?" Ambrosia raised her eyebrows at a man with steely black eyes and a dark turban. His throne featured a carving of a bear, representing Anna's line, the Ferosha Clan, "Any thoughts?"

"I have faith in Miss Green," he said simply. Anna couldn't detect any sign of sarcasm as he continued, "I'm sure she'll recover the children but, should she fail, I would welcome the return of faeries to our realm."

"We're not about to get into the Faeden debate again, are we?" Jasper rubbed his temples.

"No." Camilla replied forcefully before consulting the agenda, "Moving on. Kamiko, you have a proposal to increase our profits this quarter, correct?"

"Premium membership," Kamiko unravelled a handmade poster with a flourish, "Customers can pay a higher rate for exclusive benefits within the blood or organ delivery apps…"

***

Anna toppled into bed in the early hours of the morning. She wasn't surprised when Finn didn't wake. Extra long work days had become the new normal for her. She watched the blankets rise and fall with Finn's rhythmic breathing, savouring the precious moments of peace.

With only a few hours to get some sleep before the circus of meetings, calls and emails started all over again, Anna let her mind drift.

She imagined a world where she and Finn had a little boy. He had green eyes and copper hair, like his father. He loved to run around in the sun. The three of them would go to the beach and splash around in the waves and then lay in lush grass eating ice cream. Every night, she and Finn would read him a story until he fell asleep.

"Excuse me, Madam?" Boggle roused Anna from her fantasy, "You have an incoming call."

"No work until sunrise!" Anna groaned.

"It's from your sister," replied Boggle.

"What?" Anna sat up and pressed the button that turned Boggle into a handheld device. She hurried out of the bedroom to avoid waking Finn.

"Liz?" Anna whispered into the mouthpiece, "What are you doing up at this hour?"

"Do you have Clara?" Liz sounded frantic.

"Wh- No," Anna's stomach sank. "Why?"

"She's gone!" Liz cried, "I heard her babbling on the baby monitor so I went to check and she's just…she's gone! All the doors are locked and her window hasn't been opened. I don't know what could have happened!"

"I'll be right there," Anna promised, "It's going to be okay. I promise."

Instead of returning to the bedroom to get dressed, Anna ran down the corridor to the wall of family portraits. Her body turned to ice as she read the plaque under Clara's image: *Lost (Faeden)*.

"It is time," Mary appeared, "You're ready."

What did you think?

Thank you for reading When Lambs Grow Fangs!

If you enjoyed this story, **please leave a review on Amazon, Goodreads, and wherever book reviews are found** so other people with your brilliant taste will can find it too.

If you didn't enjoy it, **please also leave a review** letting people know what you didn't like about the story*.
This can help my book find the right audience.

*If you didn't enjoy this book because you found spelling and/or grammatical errors, please do not post them on Amazon as doing so can get the book removed.
Instead, please report any mistakes you find via the form on my website: **RebeccaWade.net**

Thank you!

Acknowledgments

I would like to extend my heartfelt thanks to those who made this book possible.

First and foremost, my deepest gratitude goes to Bridget Sweeney. She read this story when it was in it's messiest form. She gave me supportive feedback and encouraged me to keep going. Your friendship means the world to me.

To my mum, Gillian Thomas, thank you for your incredible attention to detail and willingness to proof read a book that's outside your preferred genre. (Especially the spicy scenes!)

I am also grateful to Amber Braun, a fellow writer, for her invaluable suggestions that helped shape my ideas into a cohesive narrative. Your feedback on pacing and character development, in particular, was invaluable.

Lastly, I want to thank Cameron Ball for being a constant source of inspiration and for pushing me to explore new creative avenues. Your love and support has helped me in ways you'll never know.

To each of you, I am deeply appreciative. This book would not have been possible without you.